I SHOULDN'T FEEL THIS WAY

I SHOULDN'T – VOLUME 1

MINA ALEXIA

Black Rose Writing | Texas

This is a work of fiction. Names, characters, businesses, places, events, and incidents are either the products of the author's imagination or used in a fictitious manner. Any resemblance to actual persons, living or dead, or actual events is purely coincidental.

ISBN: 978-1-68513-284-2
PUBLISHED BY BLACK ROSE WRITING
www.blackrosewriting.com

Printed in the United States of America
Suggested Retail Price (SRP) $26.95

I Shouldn't Feel This Way is printed in Garamond

*As a planet-friendly publisher, Black Rose Writing does its best to eliminate unnecessary waste to reduce paper usage and energy costs, while never compromising the reading experience. As a result, the final word count vs. page count may not meet common expectations.

To my devoted readers,
who were there from the beginning, with love
-M

There is a music appendix at the end of my novel and on my blog for
readers who enjoy novel soundtracks: mina-alexia.com

I SHOULDN'T
FEEL
THIS WAY

PROLOGUE

April 7, 2011
2:00 a.m.

I am a runaway, lost at sea.
I am a broken bird, yearning to fly free.
I am a sinner, unworthy and unholy.
I am a rose, wilting slowly.
I am a raindrop, touching your cheek.
I am a child who plays hide and seek.
I am nothing, and yet I am everything.
I am contradiction and complexities.
I am a face with a hundred entities.
I am love and I am hate.
I am the voice that cannot communicate.
I am a melody, haunting and sad.
I am a soul that has slowly gone mad.
I am death in a living body.
I am a dangerous opium poppy.
I am rage, running through my veins.
I am pain, bound in chains.
I am isolation, imprisoned in my mind.
I am abandoned and left behind.
I am tenderness, soft and kind.

I am trust, naïve and blind.
I am remorse, shattered and frozen.
I am the path I have not chosen.
I am sadness, drowning in an ocean
I am faith, yearning for devotion
I am madness, rebellious and wild.
I am sanity, safely filed.
I am wisdom, cursed and blessed.
I am a name that will burn in your chest.
I am a journey, destination unknown.
I am a heart turned to stone.
I am forever alone...
Forever alone.

One last tear drop smudged her diary before she closed it shut and turned
out the lamp.

CHAPTER ONE

When I tell people how old my parents are, they usually end up laughing, thinking I'm joking or pulling their leg. And when I tell them I'm not, I get the following reaction: "Oh… okay…" and then an awkward silence. Everything feels uncomfortable afterward, like I have to explain how that happened. My mom and dad were young when they had me—sixteen, to be exact. Most people would ask themselves, "What the hell were they thinking having sex at that age? What households were they raised in?" Well, when you're a hormonal teenager and not practicing safe sex, pregnancy can happen no matter your upbringing.

Natalie Rose Miller and Noah Mason Hunter welcomed their first-born child to the world on April 6, 1995: a healthy baby girl who had her father's ocean eyes and a head full of dark brown hair. They named her Aria Sophia Hunter. And that little girl… was me.

For the first four years of my life, I lived with my maternal grandparents. My father came from a wealthy family, and they were against the pregnancy from the moment they found out about it. They offered my grandparents a great deal of money to persuade my mother to get an abortion. But that didn't happen because Grams and Granddad are strict, God-fearing Catholics. Disappointed in their daughter, they wouldn't let her abort me, regardless of the extra figures that were added on those personal checks.

The plan was to give me up for adoption after I was born, but as soon as my grandma held me in her arms, she fell in love. Raised by my grandparents, I rarely ever saw my mom… never saw my dad, either. Natalie was too busy being a teenager instead of taking responsibility and caring for me. Gran always had to remind me she wasn't my "mommy"; I had picked up the habit of thinking she was.

When my father finally turned eighteen, he stepped up to the plate to marry my mother. But she refused his proposal since she was already engaged to somebody else; my drunken, abusive stepdad, Robert Mitchell. Of course, I didn't know all of this. I was too young to even understand how the world works. Rob, Mom, and I ended up moving into a grungy old apartment in New York back in '99. We made the big move from New Hampshire because Mom wanted to pursue her dreams as a designer in the fashion industry. Rob made her all these promises that he never kept, and she wound up working in retail while my stepdad held down a job as a mechanic. His rundown garage was near the rough side of Manhattan.

Life was depressing. I grew up having to take care of my two half-siblings, while Mom and Rob constantly fought over money, his drinking, his failed promises, and his extreme forms of discipline. To be straightforward, I didn't have a good relationship with my parents. My stepdad treated me as if I didn't exist, and when I got noticed by his radar, it was usually because I pissed him off for not doing my chores properly. According to him, I was a "constant fuck-up," and he drilled that into my head on the daily. He was abusive, and I had grown to hate his guts.

I knew nothing of my biological father. All my life, I thought he didn't want me. It wasn't until the beginning of my senior year that I discovered the truth. My life drastically changed after that, and everything I knew about the rules of attraction went out the window.

༺༻

It was a rainy fall evening, and I was curled up in a blanket on the living-room sofa. The radiator was broken—which sucked—but this happened regularly. I was used to it. To keep warm, I had put on two woolen sweaters and a pair of sheepskin Ugg boots. The apartment was freezing, which made it hard to concentrate on my schoolwork. Terry and Tiffany were oddly quiet—probably glued to the television, watching cartoons, I thought. My siblings were fraternal twins, seven years younger than me. I loved them to bits, but they usually got on my nerves when they wanted to.

The math homework that was sitting on my lap wouldn't complete itself. Rubbing my hands together, I picked up my pencil to finish the algebra equations when the phone suddenly rang. I was expecting it to be my Grams because she usually called on Thursday evenings to check up on me. But it wasn't her. An unfamiliar voice that belonged to a man was on the other end of the line. His voice was deep and warm… it did something inside of me when he asked if he could speak with me. When I told him who I was, there was a long pause before he answered, "Aria… I'm your father, Noah."

Standing there with the phone to my ear, I was in shock. Throughout the seventeen years of my life, I believed that my father never loved me and had deliberately abandoned me and my mom. It didn't help that my grandparents always trash-talked him and his family. I was not prepared to have a conversation with him. So, I hung up.

Ten seconds later, the phone rang again. My heart was racing a mile a minute and my hands were shaking.

Finding my courage, I braced myself for confrontation and picked up the phone.

"Stop calling me! I don't want to talk to you! I don't even know you!"

"Aria, wait! Don't hang up, please hear me out, I—"

"No!" I wiped my angry tears and looked out the window. "You waited all this time to realize I existed? You're seventeen years too late!"

"I just—"

But I didn't want to hear his excuses. I told him off before disconnecting again. How was this happening? Why was this happening? What did he want from me? The only information my mother had ever given about Noah was that he was her high school sweetheart, knocked her up at sixteen, and avoided taking responsibility like he should have done. I was a product of their teenage impulsivity… another statistic.

Feeling upset, I couldn't study anymore. I couldn't eat. I couldn't do anything. I needed Mom to get home so that I could put phase one of "Operation Truth Serum" in action. She had all the answers to my questions, and I deserved honesty. Why was Noah Hunter suddenly looking me up out of the blue? I couldn't figure it out. I had to wait for Mom.

⊰⊱

Time moves slowly when you're expecting someone to arrive. I kept staring up at the ugly bird clock Rob had got my mother about ten Christmases earlier. He never bought her anything fancy—couldn't afford it. I didn't care about materialistic things, but I always noticed the look of disappointment on Mom's face every time she opened her Christmas gifts. Holidays were depressing to me; it was only a reminder of everything that was missing in my life.

Sitting at our dining table, I attempted to finish my homework when the front door unlocked. It was nearly seven-thirty, which meant that Rob wouldn't be home for another two hours. My nerves were getting the best of me, but I tried to remain calm as my mother walked in. She was only an inch shorter than me, thin framed, and her eyes were blue, fading to alabaster gray. Unlike my long, dark locks, her hair was short and wavy, and she had dyed it ashy blonde. The roots needed some retouching. Her skin was pale, but that was to be expected during the winter in New York. Her best feature was her face. Regardless of the wrinkles that were creasing her forehead, she looked beautiful. My mother didn't need makeup to turn heads. I really couldn't understand what she saw in my stepdad. He wasn't the most attractive-looking man—overweight because of all that beer he drank every day, and he had lost a lot of his hair (which explained the big bald spot). His eyes were brown, his face was clean shaven, and he had a raspy voice when he spoke. Rob had a gambling addiction. He was also an alcoholic in denial.

"Hey, sweetheart, can you help me with these grocery bags?"

I said nothing and rose to my feet, grabbing a brown paper bag before following my mom into our claustrophobic kitchen.

"I'm making fettuccine Alfredo tonight. How does that sound?" She was chipper, but I certainly wasn't.

"Yeah, that's fine." I didn't want to beat around the bush. "Mom, I need to talk to you."

"What's up?" She started putting groceries away in the fridge.

"It's about Noah."

"You know I don't like to discuss your father."

Might as well get straight to the point, I thought.

"He called earlier."

The eggs suddenly dropped and cracked around my mother's feet.

"Shoot! I didn't mean to do that!" She looked at me with a worried expression. "Could you pass me a rag?"

An awkward tension was creeping up on us, and it made me uneasy.

"I want to know exactly what happened between you two," I said, crouching to the floor to gather broken eggshells.

"Aria, I told you, we were a couple of crazy teens in love. I got pregnant with you, and he ran away from his responsibilities." She wiped the laminate floor, cleaning the egg yolk before standing.

"You didn't tell me why."

"*Why?*" Mom repeated. "How should I know? Probably because of his psychotic family."

"How come you never talk about them?"

"Because it's a painful part of my past, and you were way too young to sit down and have a discussion about it."

"I'm not 'way too young' anymore. I'm seventeen and mature enough to know the truth."

"What did he want? How did he get this number?"

"I don't know—I was too angry to let him speak. I pretty much told him to go to hell."

"Good. I would've done the same." She rinsed the towel in the sink and washed her hands.

"Obviously, he wanted to get in touch with me." I folded my arms in my chest and leaned against the counter.

"I think it's time to get that landline changed. I'll speak with Rob about it tonight."

"Why do I feel like there's so much more you're not telling me?" I insistently asked.

"I've told you everything you need to know, sweetheart." Mom turned off the tap and met my gaze.

"Then why do you want to change our home number?"

I wasn't sure why I was so bothered by that.

"So that he won't call and harass you further."

"He wasn't harassing me, I just…"

Okay, I wasn't defending the guy, but it felt like I was—and that was seriously screwing with my head.

"Aria, I'm just trying to protect you."

"From who?" I shouted. "From what?"

"From *him*!"

"What did he do, Mom?"

"What did he *not* do?" she scoffed. "The last thing I want is to have Noah show up out of nowhere, looking like the knight in shining armor who's come to save the day when in reality, that image of him is an illusion. There are no happy endings in the Hunter family. Mark my words."

"First, I'm not a damsel in distress, so please stop projecting your personal feelings toward him on me. You're not related to the guy. *I* am. I have his last name—not to mention half of his genes!"

"We moved to New York for a reason. A fresh start, new beginnings."

Yeah, and look how great that turned out.

"Stop treating me like a little kid and just tell me what happened between you two! I deserve to know!"

My mother stopped putting the groceries away in the pantry and looked at me.

"You want to know the truth?"

I stayed silent and waited.

"Fine. Here it is…" She took a deep breath and iced her tone. "Olivia Hunter is a conniving, manipulative *bitch* who constantly interfered in my relationship with Noah. She gets off on destroying lives, and she's responsible for ruining mine. Your father attempted to get shared custody of you when you were younger, but he always failed the court-ordered drug tests."

I couldn't believe it. It stung to hear those last few words. "How long ago was this?"

"It doesn't matter," Mom answered.

"It does to me!"

She sighed and ran her fingers through her hair. "You were five years old."

"You could have told me the truth!"

"What kind of mother would sit down with her toddler and tell them that their daddy can't be in their life because he has a cocaine dependency? It wasn't like a month-long custody battle, Aria. He had a terrible addiction for years! God only knows if he still does."

"It would have made a world of a difference!" I yelled. "Because at least I would've known he tried! At least I wouldn't have grown up believing he never loved me and didn't want me!" Tears streaked down my face as I stormed out of the kitchen.

"Sweetheart, come back!" Mom shouted, but I was too upset to continue the conversation.

"Aria!"

Shutting the door behind me, I locked myself in my room and tried to calm down. My mind was reeling. This was too much information at once. Impulsively, I marched out the door, picked up the phone in the living room, and tried to retrace the call. I needed to hear Noah's side of the story. I was tired of being lied to.

Adding to my unfortunate luck in life, the number was blocked, so I resorted to different resources and immediately hopped online. My sole intention was to hunt him down. But my efforts were fruitless. He didn't have a Facebook account or Instagram. Nothing.

"Aria," said Mom, stroking my hair. "I'm sorry I didn't tell you. I was just trying to protect you. Please believe that. I'm your mother, and I love you."

Rising from my chair, I noticed tears in her eyes; it pained me to see her sadness. I ignored my anger and gave her a hug.

"Your father never abandoned you, Mom. You never grew up believing he doesn't love you. That's why it hurts so much—because he hasn't been there for me." I quietly sobbed on her shoulder.

"I know, darling, I know. I'm so sorry." She rubbed my back and kissed the side of my head, comforting me through the hurt.

☙❧

As the days passed on, I had hoped and prayed that Noah would contact me again. But there were no more phone calls. I knew nothing about him other than the few details my mom had shared with me. I didn't know what his profession was, where he was living, and whether he was still battling an addiction. All I had was a long list of questions that needed answers.

It wasn't until a week later that my mother got served with legal documents from an attorney. Noah was taking her to court to get custody of me. By the time we sat down at dinner the following evening, the subject of my father had become a trending Twitter hashtag: #DeadbeatDad.

"Why the hell is he trying to get custody now, after all these years?" asked Rob, slicing a piece of steak.

"It's pointless if you ask me," Mom replied. "Aria will be eighteen in April. By then she'll be a legal adult. He's wasting his time." She paused and took a sip of soda. "Although, I'm not surprised. He's just trying to prove a point. That's why he's taking this to trial."

"Well, it wouldn't be so bad having the kid dumped off at his place for a year," my stepdad grumbled with a mouthful of meat.

"That's not funny." She smacked his arm and glanced at me. "He was only joking, sweetheart."

Mom tried to reassure me with what seemed like a comforting smile. But I knew better. Rob didn't give a crap about me.

"Chances are," Mom continued, "the judge will rule in our favor because of Noah's history with drug abuse, so I'm not worried." She grabbed the tongs and served some salad onto Terry's plate.

I made no commentary and listened. The whole situation had me confused. All I knew was that my thoughts and feelings were important for ruling a decision in the courtroom, and I honestly did not know what to expect.

CHAPTER TWO
ARIA

It was a gloomy Monday afternoon on November 5, 2012, when I stepped inside New York City Family Court and came face to face with my father. At first, I didn't recognize him, but I assumed he was the man with dark curly hair dressed in a blue suit and tie. He was sitting next to his younger looking lawyer. They both stood up and faced us when we walked inside. My father hardly gave me a second glance, while his lawyer just stared at me. Clad in a dark gray suit, he had short brown hair that looked freshly cut and a masculine jaw, with the most intense blue eyes I had ever seen. There was a flawless symmetry in his face, and he was quite tall, approximately six foot two. For a man of the law, he was extremely handsome and could have passed for a model. I felt myself blushing when his eyes followed me to my seat.

Why won't my father look at me? I wondered.

From what I observed, he appeared to have not aged so well compared to my mother and had a bit of a paunch.

"Aria, I'm so sorry," the lawyer said, with tears in his eyes.

Why is he *apologizing? Is he a close friend of my dad?*

I couldn't make sense of it.

"Noah, sit down," the other man said. "Remember what I advised earlier? You'll get to talk to your daughter in due time. I promise."

Oh. My. God.

The man with the curly hair and potbelly wasn't my father; he was the lawyer representing Noah—the youthful man with ocean eyes. How did

I not connect the dots? I had never seen a photo of my dad before. Mom had kept no pictures of him, so I had no idea what he looked like. Those eyes should've been a dead giveaway. How could I have missed such a crucial detail? If I made a comparison between my parents, Mom definitely looked a lot older. I guess the hard times in life had aged her.

My estranged father kept glancing at me while I blushed like an idiot. I couldn't hold his gaze longer than two seconds. He looked way too young to be in his thirties.

The court proceeding was long and tiresome, as both lawyers negotiated back and forth, defending their client. When I finally took the stand, the judge asked me to express what I wanted. Personally, I wanted to tell her I didn't feel safe at home, that my stepdad was always drunk and had a history of hitting me. But my mother had made me swear not to say anything, which is why I kept my mouth shut.

These past few weeks had given me an opportunity to think about what I wanted with my father. I was prepared to tell the judge that I didn't want to see him or live with him. But everything changed when I saw the way Noah stared at me. There was so much pain in his eyes… regret. It was as if he knew me, but I had no clue who he was.

To my astonishment, I had a complete change of heart when I finally spoke up. Authority figures made me nervous. Being around strangers gave me anxiety because of my childhood traumas. But I told the judge I always wanted to meet my dad and get to know him. I also expressed that I preferred both my parents to share custody of me.

And so, they ruled it: my father (who I had never met before) had finally got joint custody of his long-lost daughter. Noah Hunter was going to be in my life. A shooting star had fallen from the sky and landed in front of me as a man. He was handsome. He was too flawless to be real. He made me feel something that I shouldn't feel.

೮೪೫೦

We adjourned court, and I followed my mom out of the courtroom, stopping when I felt a firm, warm hand on my shoulder.

"Aria." His voice was deep and husky, and his touch made me shiver.

I slowly turned around and looked into my father's eyes. The intensity of his stare was intimidating, but he softened his expression, flashed a wistful smile, and pulled me in his arms. His cologne was intoxicating, and his body was so warm. I could tell he had a fit physique hidden underneath his expensive suit.

My heart rate slowed down as I held my breath and felt my eyes well up with tears. Why was this happening to me? Why was I getting so emotional? Maybe because all my life I had felt so unloved and unwanted, thrown away like a piece of trash. And now here I was, finally reunited with the man who had made me. All I could feel in that moment was heartbreak… because I *knew* I could never love him like a daughter. It was a crushing reality, but one I had to accept.

He was a walking Adonis in human form, as if a Greek god had created me. I knew I would worship my creator forever when he enveloped me in his arms. It was undeniable. No matter how angry and hurt I was underneath, the faded trace of Noah Hunter's name was scarred on my heart ever since I was old enough to learn who he was. He held me for the longest while in his warm embrace. It was right there in that still-frame second, I felt my heart set ablaze, resurrecting my love for him like a phoenix from the flames. I had never really hated this man, even though I didn't know who he was.

"I'm so sorry I've missed out on so many years," he sincerely expressed. I looked into his eyes and assumed he was hiding his vulnerability; his eyes betrayed him. I wanted to respond, but couldn't speak.

"We have to get going," Mom bitterly stated.

Noah slowly released me and held my hands while he scanned my figure from head to toe. My face flushed with heat as I looked down.

"God, you're so beautiful. You're *beautiful*, Aria." His words echoed in my ears like a soul-riveting lyric. I'd always known that I was decent looking, but I don't think I ever felt beautiful until he said it to me. Noah reached for the side of my face and stroked my cheek. It almost made me want to cry again. Rob never showed me affection this way, not even my mom.

"Let me take her out to dinner, Natalie."

"You can take her out on the weekend." Mom grabbed my wrist and pulled me toward her like a protective mother goose.

She was extremely uncomfortable being around my father—probably because he was sex on legs. I hadn't the slightest clue how she could have rejected his marriage proposal. My stepdad was a balding, fat slob, while Noah... *my* father (just saying those words in my head made me feel a sense of pride)—he was perfection. If he wasn't a god, then a demigod for sure. I couldn't believe I was in the same gene pool as this man.

"Why don't you ask Aria before you decide for her?" He sounded angry, but I could tell he was trying to control it.

Perhaps Noah was a temperamental guy. He gave off this intimidating vibe. Maybe because I thought he was beautiful beyond comprehension. I naturally shied away when his eyes cascaded over me. He was the quintessential masculine archetype—buff bod and Alpha personality. I was curious about his testosterone levels and whether that affected his mood. Then I felt totally weird for even having that thought.

"I'd like to go." The words slipped out of my mouth before I could contemplate a response, as if my body and soul already knew where they belonged: in Noah Hunter's presence. Right by his side. My newfound loyalty to him shocked me. This man could have spared me years' worth of loneliness and heartache had he only attempted to get clean and fight for me all the way. I made a promise to myself to address these things with him at some point.

"Aria, your dad's expecting us back for dinner." Mom glared at me.

"He's not her dad, *I* am," Noah assertively replied.

My heart fluttered and my stomach tightened when he stood behind me, resting his hands on my shoulders. The heat radiating from his body was intense, sending shivers down my spine. His protectiveness was overwhelming. I wasn't used to it. Rob used to blame me for getting bullied at school. He never made me feel safe. He never defended me.

"Robert's more of a father to her than *you* could ever hope to be. Where were you these past seventeen years?"

"You moved away!"

"You could easily have found us!"

I listened to my parents argue back and forth before I said, "Mom, please, we've had a long and stressful afternoon. Let's not fight. I just want to catch up and ask Noah all those questions you couldn't answer."

She gave me a worried look and then scowled distastefully at her ex.

"Don't dictate to her, Nat."

"Like your bitch of a mother dictated to you?" she ridiculed. "Don't worry, I won't."

Noah's voice had an arctic undertone as he said, "No need

for low blows." He dropped his hands from my shoulders. I felt depressed from the lack of touch.

"And one more thing," Mom added. "I'm not *Nat,* or *Natty* to you anymore."

"Got it."

Neither of them said a word until my mother broke the silence.

"Look, just have her home by nine o'clock at the latest—and I mean it."

I was so happy, but nervous as hell at the same time. You know that exhilarating feeling you get when you're near your biggest crush? It feels amazing and agonizing all at once… That's how I felt.

"Back by nine, got it."

⊱✦⊰

We were standing on the street in front of the courthouse while Noah signaled a cab to pull over. He opened the back door and let me in first.

"After you," he offered, beaming like a gentleman.

I got inside and he moved in next to me, slamming the door shut.

"Take us to Paradisa restaurant on West 57th."

The cab driver nodded and switched on his left turn signal before easing into traffic. I strapped on my seat belt and silently prayed that Noah wouldn't hear my heart hammering in my chest. I was so nervous.

Releasing a heavy sigh, he leaned back in his seat before he turned his head in my direction.

Oh God. Why is he staring at me?

It was a little unnerving. I felt insecure about my appearance.

"You're more beautiful than I imagined." He brushed a dark strand of my hair behind my ear, and I shivered in reaction. "Look at me." His tone was gentle yet pleading.

I slowly turned my head and met his gaze. Those penetrating eyes were killing me; they were so damn blue. He looked tanned—which surprised me, considering it was almost winter.

"Wow… you really have my eyes." Noah smiled warmly.

My irises were a mix of aqua and blue. Mom always said that I took after my Grams. Her eyes were a blend of topaz and cerulean.

"Your eyes are lighter," I mumbled.

"But yours are alluring."

Alluring. No one had ever complimented me like that before. Growing up, I'd always felt like a tomboy. But that changed once I hit puberty. I wanted to paint my nails, style my hair, wear makeup, and dress up in girly things. By fifteen, I was attracting more attention from boys at school. If there was one thing I prided myself on, it was my body. I took care of it, being athletic. The shelf in my bedroom displayed various medals and trophies I had won during dance competitions. I had some ballet training in my early years, but I loved hip hop, contemporary, swing, Afrobeat, and Latin dances. I recently took an interest in kizomba after watching some YouTube videos.

Sitting in that cab next to—my *dad* made me feel inferior to his beauty. I know that men aren't typically described as "beautiful," but he truly was. He was too handsome for words. I guess I could describe him as an immortal being that never aged and remained eternally youthful. He had a five o'clock shadow, and his attractive eyebrows were light brown and evenly arched. I tried not to stare too long as my eyes wandered down to his hands; they radiated strength and were clean, unlike Rob's calloused hands and dirty fingernails.

"You're married?" I asked, noticing the platinum band on his ring finger.

"Yes, I got married two years ago. My wife's name is Vanessa. I'd love for you to meet her when you visit us in California."

That explained the tan. I was silent and suddenly uncomfortable.

"Forgive me," he said. "I meant *if* you decide to visit. I would never force you to do anything you're not ready for, Aria. You have my word on that."

Why did I feel like crying? Of course, he'd be married. Who wouldn't want to marry this man? He was unbelievably attractive.

"Do I have any other brothers and sisters?"

"Unfortunately, no, but we're trying. Hopefully soon." Noah smiled.

The idea of having more siblings made me sick to my stomach. Secretly, I wanted no more brothers or sisters. But my subconscious was hiding a much darker secret that came to the surface… I didn't want Noah making babies with anyone. Period. That was just my shadow self speaking. We all have one. Don't come for me.

"I know you must feel overwhelmed, but I promise not to rush things. I just want to spend the evening catching up at your pace."

I said nothing as I fixated on my hands and fidgeted with the zipper of my handbag.

"Do you like Gucci, Prada?" he asked.

"Um… I guess?" I nervously laughed. Even though I owned nothing from those famous designer brands, I was sure as hell familiar with the names. Designer "anything" never really appealed to me. But maybe this was just my way of coping with poverty.

"Great. I'll take you out shopping on Saturday, and we can buy you a new handbag." His lips curved into a half smile, and I melted. I didn't care about the handbag. I just wanted to spend time with Noah. We could have gone hiking in the snow, and I would have been happy. Material things are just… material. Nothing could replace love, and it couldn't be bought.

Forcing my brain to accept this recent shift in my reality seemed impossible. Noah wanted to take me out and spoil me. I couldn't tell if this was a nightmare or a dream. It felt like a nightmare because I understood I wasn't supposed to feel this way about my father. Yet I did. And it was a dream come true because he appeared to possess one of the greatest qualities I had always wanted in a father: generously giving without expecting anything in return. That's how a father was supposed to love his daughter—nurture her with unconditional love and support, financially and emotionally. It was an investment… an investment my stepdad didn't find valuable. He hated me, and I felt his contempt every day.

CHAPTER THREE
ARIA

Noah politely pulled out my chair as I sat down, scanning my surroundings in curiosity. The restaurant he had taken me to was upscale and modern. I was thankful that I'd worn a conservative black dress to court. The female patrons were wearing fashionable cocktail dresses. It was semiformal. I loved wearing heels, and I rarely left the house without a pair of pumps or boots—unless I was jogging or going to the gym, then the sneakers would go on. But on that day, I had sensibly matched my ensemble with black tights and round-toed ankle boots.

Soft music played in the background, something by Michael Bublé. I could smell a variety of delicious aromas permeating the air from the chef's kitchen, teasing my appetite.

I feel out of place, I thought. Like I always felt in life… an alien energy on a foreign planet.

Noah was studying me. I felt too shy to say anything, so I focused on the dancing flame of the tea-light candle in the center of our table. This didn't help, though; I could *still* feel his eyes on me. When our server came by, he broke the ice by handing us menus.

"Have you decided on a particular wine, sir?"

Noah seemed to know exactly what he wanted, since he didn't even glance at the menu.

Was he here before, with a date? I pondered.

He ordered a French red wine and let me drink a glass. Mom didn't like the idea of me going to parties and drinking, even though her husband was a damn alcoholic.

"So… tell me about yourself, Aria."

I watched him sip his drink while he gave me his undivided attention.

My face was heating. That stare was just doing things to me. How could anyone focus on a coherent thought while being near this man? His attractive face was my kryptonite. Everything about his appearance seemed to be a vision of perfection I had created before incarnating here… and I was part of that perfection. How?

"Um… well, I'm in my senior year of high school."

"That's great! How are your studies going?" His blue eyes pierced through my defenses. I felt so exposed and didn't like this feeling.

"It's going well," I replied. "I don't have any problems in the world of academia, if that's what you're wondering, Noah."

He gave me a pained expression, as if I had injured him. "You know you can call me Dad, right?"

I nodded slowly. "I just… I don't feel comfortable calling you that—*yet.* You haven't been in my life. You're like a stranger to me." I took another sip of wine and felt guilty, not wanting to hurt his feelings. "I'm sorry."

"It's okay. My bad. I understand how awkward you feel, and you're right. If you're more comfortable calling me by my name, go right ahead."

"I like your name."

Well, that was a lie, because I loved it.

"I was the one who named you. Did you know that?"

I shook my head, captivated by his smile. This was news to me.

"During the first month of your mother's pregnancy, we kept bouncing names back and forth. She wanted to name you Delilah, if you were a girl, and David, if you were a boy."

I certainly don't feel like a Delilah. I laughed in my head.

"She had this long list—but I knew right away what I wanted to call you. Your name came to me in a dream one night. I was walking on a beach, alone. The sun was setting, and the sky was this beautiful coral color. As I approached the shore, the waves kept crashing in and soaking my feet.

"When I looked down, it was as if someone had taken a stick and traced your name in big bold letters in the sand. I rarely remember my dreams, but when I woke up, I remembered every detail and realized it must have held some significance. I told your mother she was going to give birth to a beautiful baby girl. This was way before we actually discovered your gender."

Unbelievable.

"Natalie wasn't too fond of my name choice for you, but changed her mind once you were born."

Thank God.

"When's your birthday?" I asked.

"August second."

"So that means… you're a Leo."

"Yes, I am."

(Not that I believed in horoscopes, but I strongly identified with the character traits of my zodiac sign.)

"I'm thirty-three now. I'm getting old." He chuckled, and I couldn't help but smile because I loved the way he laughed.

He was far from old. Noah could've passed for a twenty-four- to twenty-seven-year-old guy.

"I was very young when I got your mother pregnant."

"You're still young." I blushed, feeling embarrassed that he had this effect on me.

Our server came by the table again to take our orders. He distracted Noah long enough for the crimson color to fade from my cheeks.

For appetizers, Noah ordered some oysters, and then skimmed down the menu before deciding on the main course.

"I'll have the butter-poached Nova Scotia lobster."

"Excellent choice, sir."

"What would you like to eat, sweetheart?"

I couldn't think. My brain found it hard to accept how he called me "sweetheart."

"Um…" I hated how nervous I sounded, desperately scanning the entrees section of the menu. Everything sounded so fancy, and I had never tasted these dishes before.

"Do you like pasta? Fish? Steak?" He was clearly trying to help me out.

I bet I look so stupid.

"I'll have the primavera," I replied, deciding on a pasta dish and praying I'd pronounced it correctly. It was fettuccini mixed with portobello mushrooms, broccoli, black olives, and sundried tomatoes in a basil pesto cream sauce. It sounded appetizing enough to eat.

"That is one of the best pastas on our menu. I'll return shortly with your appetizers." Our friendly server flashed a smile and collected our menus.

I could feel Noah's eyes on me again, triggering my anxiety as I rubbed my arm out of habit. I was ridiculously tense.

"Are you cold?"

"What? Oh—no. I'm fine." I ceased my little tick and took a sip of wine, praying the alcohol would make me less jittery.

Suck it up and get on with the questions, a voice echoed through a cavern in my mind. There was a reason I came to dinner with him. I had to stay focused.

"So," I began, "why did it take you this long to acknowledge my existence?"

I anxiously watched him as he gazed back at me, searching my eyes for the longest while.

"I can't forgive myself for not being involved in your life. I was young, and when I finally got away from my family, I tried to make things right with your mom. But she wanted nothing to do with me. To say that I was angry is an understatement. I got careless and things only worsened in my college years.

"I developed a bad drug addiction, and it hindered me from getting shared custody and visitation rights. I took it hard and started hanging around the wrong crowd. Before I knew it, I was snorting coke so many times a day that I lost count. I'm ashamed of that part of my past, but it's the truth, and I would never lie to you, Aria."

I couldn't believe it. This flawless man sitting before me was a junkie at one point. I should have been angry, but I wasn't. I felt proud of him for overcoming his addiction.

"I needed to get my shit together." He paused and frowned. "Sorry, I shouldn't curse around you. It's a bad habit."

"I don't mind. I'm used to it. Rob cusses me out twenty-four/seven."

He looked outraged by that slip-up of information.

"That son of a…"

Bitch? Yeah, he was.

"He shouldn't speak to you like that. I'll have a word with your mother about it."

Our server finally came and placed a plate full of oysters in the center of the table. He refilled our glasses with some more wine and said, "Enjoy."

"Thank you," Noah pleasantly replied. But as soon as we were alone again, he appeared unhappy. Shutting his eyes, he exhaled deeply before staring at me.

"Aria, I'm not proud of myself for abandoning you. Truth be told, I abandoned myself. I needed to get my life back on track before I could repair our relationship."

"I understand that." I was shocked at my inability to feel angry at him.

"On a lighter note, I kicked my addiction, graduated from law school, and secured a prominent position at a firm. I met my wife shortly after on the job. She was filling in for my assistant for some months—that's how we met."

I wonder how many times he bent her over on his desk and banged her brains out before he popped the question. *Ugh*, I didn't want to think about it.

"There's always been this emptiness in my life, no matter how much I achieved. Nothing filled that void for me. I knew I needed to get in touch with you, and I know you may find this hard to believe, but I love you… very much." He pulled out his wallet and opened it in front of me. "I've had this picture of you forever."

My throat swelled as my eyes filled with tears. I tried to blink them away as fast as I could.

"You were only six months old here." He sighed. "Please forgive me. I didn't know what it meant to be a father when I got your mother pregnant. The whole pregnancy had freaked me out, which is why I didn't get involved. I was a coward and easily influenced by my mother—much to my shame. She had projected her own fears onto me. I was too young to realize it." Noah slid his hand across the table and reached for mine. A spark of electricity jolted through my body upon contact, and I couldn't help but wonder if he felt it, too.

I didn't know what to make of his explanations. He sounded genuine. I just didn't know what to say.

"I want you to spend some time with me and get to know me better. I want to earn your trust and be the father you always deserved. Come to California with me for the rest of the year, Aria. I promise you won't need for anything. Just give me a chance to make it up to you."

How could I say no to those eyes? He was undeniably charming by nature. There was a huge part of me that wanted to escape my shithole of a life and run away from Rob and my annoying siblings, my overbearing mother included. She never protected me from my psycho stepdad.

What would Noah do if he knew the truth? I wondered.

"I can get you enrolled in the best school in the state, and the weather's warm all year round. I know it's going to be impossible if I ask your mom, but if it's something you'd like, I'm sure you could convince her."

And there it was: the decision that would change my outlook on love and sex forever.

"Okay," I responded. "I'll come. I think a change of scenery would be good for me."

"Really?" His face lit up. "I can't tell you how happy that makes me."

My heart skipped a beat.

"Try one of these." He smiled, pointing at our plate of appetizers.

It was my first-time eating oysters, and much to my surprise, they were actually tasty.

⊰⊱

The rest of our dinner conversation was pleasant, and the food was delicious. I had more questions for him, but at that moment, they didn't matter anymore. I just wanted to hear about everything he was interested in—places he had traveled to, people he had met. It turned out that Noah was athletic as well and had a strict gym regimen working out six days a week. He listened to all the musical genres I was into, which was awesome, and he even admitted he had a tattoo. He wouldn't tell me of what, or where it was located. That remained a mystery.

We spent two hours chatting away, laughing and enjoying each other's company while indulging in our meals. I discovered so much about him. It made me crush on him even more. I was scared because my moral compass had gone haywire, spinning in all directions, unable to guide me between right and wrong. But I did my best to stay calm.

For dessert, Noah ordered a delicious New York cheesecake, which we shared between us. His perfect table manners impressed me. My stepdad was the worst person to have dinner with. He broke just about every rule of proper dining etiquette. I guess that explained why Mom didn't like to eat out with him.

Time seemed to go way too fast, and before I knew it, our dessert plates were cleared.

"I should get you home soon before your mother flips out." Noah glanced at his watch.

"Yeah, I'm all set."

He paid the bill, tipping our server generously, which only made me conclude he was wealthy. He shrugged on his long black trench coat and helped me get into my white pea jacket.

We left the restaurant, stepping onto the sidewalk. The sun had finally set. I was a little surprised when Noah took my hand in his. I think he noticed me flinch a bit.

"It's dark and we're downtown. I don't want to let you out of my sight."

Oh, believe me, I don't want you to let me out of your sight either, I said to myself. We got in another cab and were headed back to my place. I didn't realize how exhausted I was until the car started moving.

"Are you sleepy, baby?"

Now *that* was a term of endearment I wasn't used to. This was unfamiliar territory for me, but it made me smile.

"I didn't sleep well last night," I said. "Granddad used to drive me around the neighborhood in his Cadillac whenever I had trouble sleeping. He said I'd go out like a light within five minutes of cruising the block. I get sleepy in moving vehicles from time to time."

"I bet it's because of today, isn't it?"

I nodded, feeling shy suddenly.

Noah shifted closer, his intoxicating scent infusing all around us. He wrapped an arm around my shoulder and said, "You can rest on my chest. I'll wake you up when we arrive at your place."

I didn't know how to receive his affections, but there was a part of me that so badly needed it. His eyes were warm and engaging. I gently settled my body against him, resting my head on his chest. His cologne… I needed to figure out what he had on so that I could buy a replica. Or maybe I could ask him to give me one of his shirts and secretly spray his cologne all over it. But how would I manage that? It wasn't like he was going to take me back to his hotel. However, I had the rest of the week…

"Thank you," I murmured.

"No, thank *you.* Thank you for allowing me back in your life, princess."

Princess? I always felt the slightest twinge of jealousy whenever I saw my girlfriends with their loving fathers. Hearing Noah speak so sweetly to me made me feel warm and fuzzy inside, like he was melting my iced-up barriers and knocking down my titanium walls with little effort. This scared me—big time.

ഐരാ

The drive home took about twenty minutes. I felt uncomfortable when Noah insisted on walking me to my apartment door. The place my family lived in wasn't exactly the best or the cleanest building in the city.

"I can't believe you live here," he said.

On the verge of tears, I felt embarrassed while we took the elevator up to my floor. This wasn't the life I wanted for myself. I never asked to live in this crappy dwelling. Evidently, he wasn't hiding his distaste at the abomination that was my current place of residence.

Noah noticed my reaction and frowned. "Aria, I'm sorry. I didn't mean to offend you. I just thought your mother's husband would have done a better job at providing for you guys."

"It's fine."

No, it wasn't. My pride was crushed.

"I know what you meant," I added. "I don't exactly enjoy living here either, but it's close to his job, and that saves money on gas—at least that's the excuse he gives us." This conversation was stirring up so much anger inside of me. I had to force it all down, deep into my emotional well, where my pristine water turned black and murky.

Noah's mysterious eyes were studying me once again, worried he had hurt me, but I refused to reveal my vulnerability. It would have felt too awkward. We were standing only inches away from each other, and the air seemed to shift between us as we waited in silence.

The elevator stopped with a ding when it reached the eighth floor. I was first to walk out, and he followed, catching up beside me. It was a short stroll down the hallway, covered in puke-green carpeting, before we reached my apartment door. Fishing through my handbag, I pulled out my keys. My heart was beating like a drum. I'd never felt like this before, even when I'd get noticed by cute guys at school. Meeting Noah had forever ruined me. No one else could compare to his perfection. How could they? He was clearly the most attractive man alive. I didn't care that I was biased.

"Well, this is me." I glanced at him, half smiling.

"You have my number, Aria. You can call me anytime—I mean it. If you're ever in an emergency or you need to see me, I'll be on the next available flight." He lovingly cupped my face, pressing his lips to my forehead. I felt light-headed when he pulled back.

"Thank you."

"Don't thank me. It's my duty as your father."

Something was pulling me toward him like a magnet. It was hard to resist that attraction. Leaning in to kiss his cheek, my lips caught the corner of his mouth, barely brushing the edge.

Oh my God. Why did I do that?

Panicking, I pulled back an inch, afraid to meet his eyes. He didn't move.

Why was his breathing so erotic?

Maybe it was all in my head… most likely.

Noah slid his arms around my waist and hugged me. It lasted longer this time, and I enjoyed every second. Bluebirds were singing, butterflies were fluttering around us, and the sun was beaming down, bathing us in warmth. Regardless of how animatedly Disney that sounded, I had escaped this hellish apartment to a place of paradise, if only for a moment in my mind.

"I love you, sweet angel."

My heart swelled as my arms found their way around his neck. Our energy exchange was so comforting. I stole a moment to breathe him in so that his cologne would linger before my stepdad's cigarette smoke would assault my sense of smell.

"I don't want to let you go," said Noah.

Please don't.

"But I have to." He reluctantly released me, and my heart sank. I didn't want to say goodbye.

Gone were the birds, the butterflies, and the radiant sunshine. I was left with a hole in my chest, isolated in darkness.

"Goodnight, Noah." I tried to cheer up.

"Goodnight, beautiful." He smiled gently and backed away from the door, watching me slip inside.

I rarely experienced happiness, but that night was one of the best nights of my life.

೦೮೮

Rob glared at me with hateful eyes as I walked in. He was sitting at the kitchen table with my mom, smoking a cigarette, with a beer in hand. "Took you long enough!" he bellowed.

"There was traffic," I lied, quickly walking past them and escaping to my room. I locked my door before he could follow me. The man always smelled of booze. I hated him.

"Aria… Aria!" Mom called after me, but I didn't want to talk to her. I didn't want either of them to ruin my evening.

Switching on my iPod, I scrolled down the playlist and played "Curse The Night" by The Raveonettes, full blast before I slumped down on my bed and replayed the way Noah hugged me. It was a heavenly visual while the track looped on repeat.

CHAPTER FOUR
AWAKENING

Noah Hunter was staying in the Prestige Suite at the Stone & Sapphire Hotel. Stepping out of the shower, he wrapped a white towel around his V-shaped waist before drying off his chest and arms. A cloud of steam thickened the air as he stepped toward the bathroom mirror, wiping it with his hand. He was in the best shape of his life, having worked long and hard to chisel his body to perfection. His broad shoulders were strongly sculpted through years of dedication to fitness. A spiral of veins had spread around his biceps like vines beneath his skin. His chest was flat and smooth with little traces of hair. A black phoenix had spread its flaming wings around his left pectoral, as if it had dug its sharp talons into his skin, mutilating his heart. Aria's name was inked in red capital letters on the bird's breast. He had got that tattoo when he was in college, and it held a significant meaning for him. A smile touched his lips when he lightly brushed his fingers over it.

Leaving the bathroom, he changed into a pair of black boxer briefs and pajama bottoms before tossing his buff body on the king-size mattress.

"Feels good to lie down." Noah stretched and folded his hands behind his head.

He fixated on the ceiling and flashed back to the past six hours. Aria had grown up to be such a beautiful young lady. He wasn't able to keep his eyes off her during dinner, and he was proud of his daughter for being so strong, compassionate, and forgiving. Noah thanked his lucky stars that she hadn't got mixed up with drugs and alcohol like he had. It tormented him to even recall those times.

Aria was slender, with full, sensuous lips, and big blue eyes. He adored her raven tresses that flowed down the side of her shoulder, reaching past her breasts. Her hair color was unique: it changed into a chestnut hue in the sunlight. She had her mother's beautiful hands, a small nose, and a well-endowed chest that didn't take away from her next attractive asset: her curvaceous bottom. She was quite tall, standing at five foot seven, Noah thought; his wife was two inches shorter (when she wasn't wearing six-inch heels). Noah and Natalie had created a gorgeous daughter together.

Smiling to himself, he felt blessed to have her back. They had a lot of catching up to do, and there was so much he wanted to show her. Noah was confident that he could contribute in positive ways to her life. His only regret was that he hadn't been there sooner. But all of that was going to change. The hardest part was over. Entertaining all the places he would take her when she would visit, he finally drifted off to sleep.

ଔଏଔଓ

The sound of feral moaning and labored breaths filled the room as a blonde-haired woman straddled Noah, moving back and forth, quickening her pace.

"Fuck!" He growled. "That feels so good…"

She kissed him hard and whispered dirty talk in his ear.

"Shit, Vanessa!" He grabbed her hips and flipped her on her back, pressing himself against her.

"Give it to me." She rubbed her silicone breasts, then grabbed a fistful of his cheeks down below, pulling him forward until he was buried inside of her.

Noah hid his face in the crook of her neck, breathing loudly while he surrendered to pleasure. Something strange started happening amidst their steamy lovemaking.

"You're getting tighter." He groaned. "How the hell are you doing that?" Thrusting faster, Vanessa's inner walls contracted around his shaft while she dragged her fingernails down his back and moaned.

"*Oh, fuck…* Nessa… I'm…"

A pressure was building inside of him. Lifting his head, he looked at his wife, but what he saw left him horrified, because it wasn't Vanessa's brown eyes staring back at him… they had transformed to aqua blue. Dark, long hair had sprawled out on the pillow around her face, and those double-D breasts had shrunk and transformed into natural spheres.

"Aria…" Noah exploded inside of her as soon as he said her name.

His eyes snapped wide open as he gasped for air and looked down at his boxers; achingly constricted, he had broken into a sweat. There was no explanation why his daughter had made such a graphic debut in his triple-X dream. But it had become a nightmare; it shook him. Subconsciously, his mind had delivered a subliminal message that held a disturbing significance.

Desperate for release, Noah tugged down his boxers and pulled out his generous length. He quickly relieved himself and tried to focus on the image of his naked wife riding him. But every time he looked up, Aria's angelic face would flicker before his eyes. The minutes passed, and he was still speedily stroking with a sore arm. Relief came rushing in when Noah groaned and shot a big load into some tissues, letting his arm relax.

What the fuck just happened? He asked himself, getting out of bed to clean up.

Those graphic images made little sense to him. He had not conjured his daughter on purpose. Why the switch? He kept questioning, disturbed by the phantom in his mind.

After washing up, Noah settled back in bed and tried to relax. Ever since his younger years, he had a hyperactive sex drive. Getting clean from his cocaine addiction had helped him master sexual discipline. He loved intimacy and had a healthy sex life with Vanessa. Dominance naturally exuded from him, especially in the intimate domain of his bedroom. Noah's high body count of past lovers was a source of shame that he had still yet to reconcile. He knew he was ready to settle down once he had conquered his lustful impulses around beautiful women who were looking for casual hookups. As an experienced lover, nothing had ever disturbed him more than his recent nightmare starring Aria... his own daughter.

With a weighted breath, he reached over to the bottle of water resting on his nightstand and took a few gulps. Quenching his thirst, he rested his head on his pillow and closed his eyes.

It was just a nightmare. Chill the fuck out.

Noah tried to convince himself that Aria's cameo appearance was an accident, concluding it was all because he had been thinking of her before bed.

I'm not attracted to her. I can't be.

It couldn't have been further from the truth.

CHAPTER FIVE
ARIA

I couldn't wait for Friday to come. Noah had been taking care of some business while he was still in New York, so I was fortunate enough to spend some time with him before he flew back to LA. I didn't know how I was going to survive the week. It had only been two days since we last saw each other, and I was too nervous to reach out and be the one to call him first. At school, it was hard to pay attention because my mind was so occupied with him. And when I was at home, I would lie in bed and listen to music all night while trying not to think about him. Yeah, that typically failed. Every part of me was so consumed with him. I couldn't understand how this had happened after just one initial meeting, as if he had sparked a fire within me that could not be put out.

It was a Wednesday evening, and I was sitting at the dinner table with my family when my cellphone vibrated. Setting my fork down, I pulled out my phone, thinking it was probably a text from my best friend, Allyson. But when I read the text, I desperately wanted to excuse myself from the table.

Hey beautiful, how are you doing tonight? I miss you.

It was from Noah. I shoved my iPhone back in my pocket and looked at Mom. "May I be excused, please? I'm not hungry anymore."

"Your mother slaved away in the kitchen all evening," Rob grumbled. "You're gonna sit your ass down and finish your food." He scowled at me with his beady brown eyes, burping disgustingly loud.

"Robert, you promised you'd stop cursing so much."

"She's being disrespectful, Natalie. She should know not to waste food! I work damn hard to put bread on this table."

You work damn hard to gamble it all away.

I rolled my eyes and stuffed my mouth with the remaining veggies and mashed potatoes, all in four hasty bites.

"Done—thanks for dinner, Mom." Gathering my plate and utensils, I speed-walked to the kitchen to place them in the sink. While running to my bedroom, I ignored Rob's relentless complaints. He always had a problem with me. It was getting old.

Collapsing in bed, I turned on my iPod and rolled over on my stomach, swinging my legs back and forth as I texted Noah.

Hey, I'm ok. How r u?

My heart fluttered when he responded.

Just okay? What can I do to make you feel AMAZING? And I'm doing fantastic since the world's most beautiful daughter texted me back :)

Even through texts, he made me blush. I wanted to tell him that Rob and Mom were annoying me and getting on my case a lot, but decided against it. He already gave the vibe that he was very protective of me. I didn't want to cause trouble for Mom, especially if I was going to convince her to let me live with Noah. So, I lied instead and wrote:

I got into a dumb fight @ school with some friends. They're not talking to me now.

He quickly responded:

Whose ass do I need to kick?

I couldn't help but giggle and texted:

It's just 2 of my gfs… and u can't kick their asses :P

My phone received another incoming message:
I'm here for you if you need advice or need to vent.

Taking a deep breath, I felt a little guilty for lying to him as I wrote,

Thanks. I'll be ok though.

Ten seconds later:

I love you, angel.

Reading his words over, I felt a surge of happiness before I texted him back with a line of X's and O's.

Our conversation ended, and Mom eventually entered my room (without knocking, as usual).

"You left the table so abruptly, but you still have dishes to wash. Come on, get up," she nagged.

Loud and clear. Here comes Cinder-Aria.

It seriously sucked being a house slave.

⋙⋘

Stepping out of the doors of my high school, I walked beside my best friends, Jade and Ally. It was a Thursday afternoon, and we were heading out to lunch. I went to a public school, which meant that uniforms weren't mandatory, and the quality of my education was poor.

"You are so lucky, Aria. If I were you, I'd be guilt-tripping my dad until he handed over the credit cards."

I laughed. "I'm still getting to know him, Jade."

"Hey, I'm just saying he's got a lot of making up to do."

We strolled off the school premises and stopped on the sidewalk, waiting for Ally to light a cigarette. I didn't smoke, and neither did Jade.

"So, the usual place, ladies?" asked Ally.

I looked at her and nodded. I still wasn't used to her pixie cut or the green streaks in her blonde hair. Ever since we were little, Ally always had long locks, like Goldilocks. Now she was rocking a punk hairdo and piercings, but it didn't take away from her beauty. Jade was mixed race. Her mother was of Cuban descent and her father was half Puerto Rican and African American. She looked gorgeously exotic. I was envious of her dark skin and hazel eyes. Sometimes I didn't want to be me anymore. If I could have body switched with anyone for a day, I would have chosen Jade in a heartbeat. I didn't think it was fair to inhabit her avatar as a "walk-in" soul permanently. Her personality was amazing.

The three of us refused to eat the oily fried crap that was offered at our cafeteria, which explained why we usually went to Subway for lunch. I was chatting between my friends when we heard loud music blasting down the street. Pretty sure it was "Sweet Disposition" by The Temper Trap.

Jade stopped and turned around. "Damn, that's a sexy whip—probably some rich kid driving Daddy's wheels."

I looked in her direction and saw a black Mercedes-Benz pull up to the curb next to us. I couldn't see who was inside. The mysterious driver turned down the music, and we watched in curiosity as the tinted passenger window slowly slid down. My jaw dropped when I saw who was sitting in the driver's seat.

"Noah…"

My girlfriends glanced at me before leaning downward to get a better look at the handsome man.

"*You're* Aria's dad?" Ally asked, stomping out her cigarette.

"Yes, I am." He put the car in park, stepped out, and walked around the vehicle, standing on the sidewalk with us. I watched him extend his right hand and properly present himself to my friends. "Noah Hunter"—he smiled—"Pleased to meet you."

I was in such a state of shock that I couldn't find my voice to introduce them. But Jade and Ally were more than capable of doing that themselves. The girls clearly had hearts in their eyes, swooning over him. I needed to snap out of it.

"What are you doing here?" I asked, adjusting my schoolbag over my shoulder.

"Well, after what you told me last night, I thought I'd take you out for lunch and cheer you up. But I guess you already worked things out with your friends?"

Ally arched a pierced eyebrow at me, looking confused.

"Uh… yeah, we did," I replied, sensing an air of awkwardness.

"We did?" Jade smirked. She was giving me a hard time on purpose.

"We were just going to Subway, Mr. Hunter," said Ally. "But I think Aria's getting sick of that routine."

"Then I guess I came at the right time. Let me take you out for lunch. You girls can come along too, if you like."

Allyson leaped at the opportunity. "We'd love t—"

"You should spend time with your daughter," Jade cut in. "But thanks."

He smiled at me. I still found it hard to say yes, so Jade gently nudged me forward. "She's all yours, Mr. Hunter! We'll see you back in history class, Aria."

"Nice meeting you girls," Noah said.

He opened my passenger door as I waved goodbye to my friends. The car engine roared back to life when he got in next to me. It was my first time sitting in a luxury vehicle. I felt so out of place. We pulled onto the street when my cellphone vibrated. It was a text from Ally:

Um wth!? You didn't tell us your dad is a hottie! He's an absolute DILF!

My face flushed in heat. Not bothering to text her back, I was embarrassed and worried that Noah saw the message.

"Everything okay?"

"Mm hm." Buckling my seat belt, I folded my hands in my lap. The car smelled brand new.

"I'm sorry for dropping by unannounced."

"It's all right. I don't mind, really."

Of course, I didn't mind. He looked sexy as the day I'd met him. His energy just *oozed* sex. It frustrated me more than anything.

"Technically, your mom doesn't know…" Noah sounded uneasy.

It took me long enough to clue in. God, I was such a ditz sometimes.

"Oh, don't worry about her—I won't say anything," I reassured him.

"Thanks, beautiful." He switched gears and turned down a major intersection.

I was determined to stare out the window throughout the entire car ride because it was too tempting to gaze at him. His profile was so attractive. I hadn't seen him in casual attire yet—but I was sure he looked amazing in anything—birthday suit included.

Noah was wearing a scarf, trench coat, tailored trousers, and smart leather shoes—all in black. I had on a pair of baby blue skinny jeans, a white shirt, and a green cardigan underneath my black leather jacket. I was also sporting some black wedge ankle boots. Jade had said I looked hot when she saw me in the morning. I wore my hair down that day, and I had *a lot* of hair. It took me forever to manage and maintain it. Chopping it off was out of the question, so I made sure I got up an hour earlier in the morning to shower, blow dry, and straighten my locks. Rob used to give me boyish haircuts as a child, which I absolutely hated—*especially* mushroom cuts. Fuck that. And fuck him (not literally—*ew*). Never again. What a traumatizing attack on my femininity—that's how I felt about it.

Glancing at the stereo, I read the name of the song that was scrolling by the screen: Mr. FijiWiji - Submerged (feat. CoMa). The track was a mix between ambient and chillstep. The lyrics were simple but spoke to me.

Why is this happening? I questioned. Reality felt so bittersweet.

My stepdad had never surprised me and taken me out for lunch. Noah barely even knew me, and he was already showing a genuine interest in who I was. Was he somebody that I could grow to trust? Did I already trust him? My heart and mind didn't seem in conflict anymore, which was odd because for as long as I could remember, I had believed I hated him. But sitting in his car, all I could feel was happiness... and then confusion and shame. I was attracted to him. It was wrong.

But maybe it'll go away. It has to, I told myself.

⊰⊱

Noah took me to a nice little Italian bistro that wasn't too far away. We shared a stone-baked veggie pizza and had great conversation. He had a wicked sense of humor.

"I love your laugh, Aria, especially your smile."

"Well, then I guess that means you need to work extra hard to keep me laughing and smiling."

Am I flirting with him? Seriously?

"It doesn't seem too hard of a task," he said.

Fuck. His eyes were seductive as hell.

I watched him reach for the slim crystal vase that sat in the middle of our table. He took out the single white rose and snapped part of the stem off before he carefully tucked the flower behind my ear. I awkwardly snickered. Often, I laughed as a defense mechanism whenever I was nervous.

"See, what did I say? Piece of cake." His voice, his dimpled smile, his eyes—everything about him was so heartbreakingly beautiful. Noah was devastatingly handsome and charming to a fault. He probably knew this since he appeared confident. But it was so sexy.

"What time do you need to be back at school?"

"I still have an hour to kill."

"Do you want to go for a walk through Central Park?"

Smiling, I nodded as he got our server to bring us the bill.

⊱⊰

It was sunny for once. The week before had brought nothing but November rain. I was glad to see the weather was more than agreeable on this day, as if Noah had brought the sunshine with him: a forecast catalyst.

He walked beside me at a leisurely pace as we made our way down a concrete path covered in leaves, crunching beneath our shoes. The trees were almost barren, but I could still see some bouquets of red and yellow hanging from the branches. A crowd was huddled around the fountain, listening to a female street performer singing "Autumn Leaves." The song was originally by Nat King Cole. I liked her version, though. The violin and cello accompaniment made the melody sound so romantic.

"Wear this—there's a chill in the air." Noah unraveled his black scarf from his neck and wrapped it around mine. "I don't want you getting sick."

"Thanks."

"Don't mention it."

His kind gesture made me feel warm inside. I instantly shifted into a heavenly state when I smelled his cologne on his scarf; he had no idea what this did to me. I secretly hoped he would let me keep it.

After a long silence, I struck up a conversation. "I bet you miss the warm weather."

"I do, but it's not so bad over here. Some states are getting hit with a snowstorm already."

My boots clicked against the pavement as we walked side by side, watching joggers and cyclists pass us now and then.

"Do you play any sports, Aria?"

"I was flexible as a kid. Mom put me in ballet and gymnastics throughout middle school, and then I stopped because we couldn't afford the classes anymore. I love basketball and I'm good at it. I also love to dance."

"I can put you in any extracurricular activity you like when you come live with me."

I didn't know how to respond to that.

"Rob had a lot of money when Mom married him," I said. "I remember them fighting about how he gambled away over a hundred grand when I was little. They still argue about it."

Noah was quiet. I could sense that something had put him off.

"Aria, I need to tell you something." He looked at me and frowned.

I stopped walking and faced him.

"That night when I came up with you to your apartment, it shocked me you were living there because my family—well, my mother—she wrote your mom a two-hundred-thousand-dollar check so that she would not come after me for child support. This happened after you were born. There was a secret contract between them—and believe me when I say I had no clue about this until I was in my last year of law school. I guess it explained why she didn't want to marry me all those years ago." He exhaled. "So when you showed me where you lived, I expected it to be a better place. I thought your mom would be sensible enough to invest in a house, or at least a condo in a safe neighborhood."

"Oh."

It was all I could say. Averting my gaze, I tried not to focus on the anger that was bubbling up inside of me. Now it all made sense. That money didn't belong to Rob; it was my mother's (well, technically; it belonged to my grandmother). Mom foolishly gave the money to my stepdad, and he lost it all in a poker tournament at a casino years ago. All two hundred thousand dollars went down the drain. No wonder she went ballistic that night.

"You didn't know this, did you?" Noah said.

I shook my head and heard him curse under his breath. "It's okay, Noah. At least now I know the truth. I wish Mom never married that asshole."

He tilted his head to the side and gave me an inquisitive look.

"Sorry, I curse too," I muttered with a guilty smile.

"Come here." He chuckled, drawing me into his arms. I breathed out softly and let him hug me, taking comfort in his warmth.

"He doesn't hurt you, does he?" Noah pulled back and held my face, his hands covered in black leather gloves.

"What are you implying when you say 'hurt'?"

I watched his expression turn from worry to terror. "Jeezuz, Aria, why didn't you tell me before I dropped you off at your place?" He looked genuinely upset, bordering on rage, though I couldn't understand why. "I'm gonna kill that motherfucker for touching you!"

"Wait, what? No, it's not like that. Calm down."

"Just give it to me straight. Does that piece of shit abuse you?" His eyes were intimidating me. The ocean blue in his irises had completely frosted over, paralyzing me.

"He… he's hit me a few times. But that's it."

"I swear to God I'm gonna kill him—and don't worry about the jail time. I'm a lawyer, which means I'm skilled at bending the truth." He started pacing in frustration.

I was seeing a different side of Noah. It was intense, somewhat scary, and made me feel so unbelievably loved at the same time.

"Why didn't you mention this in court?" he asked. "I could have got full custody of you!"

His angry outburst startled me. I tried to control my trembling lip, fighting my hardest to hold back my hurt. "Like I said, he's only hit me a few times." It wasn't just a few times. I had honestly lost count. "Mom keeps him under control."

"*Under control?* Is he a rabid animal living with you guys? Aria, you're my daughter. No one has the right to lay a hand on you! Do you understand? Do you understand how this makes me feel as your father?"

Pedestrians passed us by, staring at us. I was quivering. Not because I was cold, but because I had upset him. Being around men made me anxious, especially attractive men.

"I already feel like the world's biggest failure for not being there for you," he continued. "This certainly tops it. I let my family dictate my life to me, and as a result, you had to grow up getting beaten every day. This is all my fault."

"He doesn't hit me every day!"

How could I get through to him? He was visibly upset. I had to suck it up and tell him how I felt.

"What did you expect me to say at the court hearing? I didn't know a single thing about you. For all I knew, you could've been worse than Rob. No matter what mistakes my mom made, I'd never throw her under the bus. I asked the judge to grant you shared custody, which is pretty pointless, considering I'll be eighteen in less than six months and none of this will matter!

"And you know what? In some ways, I can't wait, because my life won't be controlled by *you*, Mom, or my crummy stepdad. I can choose my own goddamn path!" I furiously shouted, walking away from him.

"Aria… Aria, hold on!" Noah caught up to me. "Will you just stop for a second?"

I didn't want to stop. I wanted to keep going. I wanted to cry, but I steeled myself and halted, refusing to face him.

"Look at me, please." His voice was gentle and persuasive. No matter how much my brain screamed, *no!* I ignored the command and met his gaze.

"I'm sorry I yelled at you," he sighed. "Sometimes I lose my temper easily. It used to be worse, and I've learned to control it better, but I don't always succeed."

Shifting my weight to my right leg, I folded my arms in my chest and stayed quiet.

"I know my efforts to get custody of you now seem pointless, but this wasn't something recent. I've been trying to get visitation rights for years. We both know why that never worked in my favor. But I changed. Taking this to trial was important to me. *You* are important to me. Can't you see that?"

Was this really about me? Or was it about proving a point to my mother?

"You might not understand it," Noah continued, "but I feel protective of you, and I want you to be in a safe and loving environment. That bastard shouldn't raise his hand on you or any of his kids."

"I understand that. I just don't want trouble for Mom, which is why—"

"Let me finish what I have to say. Trust me, I realize where you're coming from." He looked at me, waiting for a silent confirmation as I nodded. "I understand your feelings of loyalty toward your mother. But now I know more than ever that you belong with me. There's no way in hell I'm gonna be able to sleep at night knowing you're living under the same roof as a violent maniac who feels he has the right to hit you."

You belong with me… Those were the only words that registered in my mind, and I repeated them to myself, as if it were a holy mantra.

"Have you spoken to your mother yet about moving in with me and Vanessa?"

I shook my head. "Not yet."

"Please talk to her about it before the weekend."

"Okay."

He hugged me again, murmuring, "I love you, and I know it's hard for you to believe that, but I'll prove it in time. I want to be here for you."

Tears filled my eyes.

"I should probably drive you back now. I don't want you to be late." Noah softened his gaze. "Please don't pout like that."

I hadn't even realized I was pouting. "Sorry," I mumbled. "I just wish I could spend the day with you."

He paused. "Do you have any tests today?"

"No."

"Exams, pop quizzes?"

"No, we're supposed to be watching some boring film about early American settlers."

"Do you want to play hooky and hang out with me? I can sign you out of school and notify the office, tell them you're not feeling well."

For real? I couldn't believe it.

"Did you let them know I have guardianship over you now?"

"Yeah, I filled out the forms yesterday."

"Excellent." He beamed. "So, what do you say?"

"Um… hell yes! But what about my mom?"

"Leave that to me. I'll call her."

"You're the best!"

I hadn't expected him to be this cool. It was hard to contain my happiness as I wrapped my arms around Noah's neck and kissed his cheek. His laughter made my soul smile. I realized right then that my emotions would always end up in a puddled mess around him. He was the sun to my moon.

CHAPTER SIX
NOAH

I was waiting for my daughter in the school parking lot, hoping she would take her time, just in case my phone call took longer than expected. I had signed her out of school and had told her I would wait for her in the car while she picked up some textbooks from her locker. Now that I had the opportunity, I scrolled down to Natalie's name on my contact list and called her. After three rings, she picked up.

"Hi, Natalie, it's—"

"What do you want, Noah?" She didn't sound too happy to hear from me, as expected.

"Aria wasn't feeling well, so she called me. I showed up at her school and signed her out of her last two classes."

"Put her on the phone. I want to talk to her."

"I'm waiting for her in the car. She's at her locker picking up some things."

"Then bring her home."

"She said she wants to spend some time with me. I'm gonna look after her for the rest of the afternoon. I'll drop her off in the evening."

"If she's sick, then she should be in bed."

"Listen, Natty, it's kind of obvious she wants to see her dad."

"So you help her skip school?" she sounded so condescending.

"No, I'm being here for her."

"Bring her home, Noah. I'm not gonna ask you again."

"Well, frankly, Natalie, you're not asking at all. You're *demanding*. And I'm not gonna bring her home when that bastard has a twitching hand around her."

"What do you mean? What did she say to you?"

"I don't know everything, because clearly, she's protecting you. I know enough to conclude that your fucking husband physically and verbally abuses our daughter. How can you go to sleep at night allowing this to happen? Do you even have a conscience?"

"You don't know what you're talking about…"

"You listen to me, and you listen well," I said, growing angrier. "Because if you don't, I'm gonna make your miserable life much worse than it already is, and I'll *especially* target that asshole. I have the power to do it, I have the money to do it, and I'm directly telling you that you don't want to push me, Natalie. Am I making myself clear?"

"Are you threatening me?" She seemed outraged.

"It's not a threat. It's a warning."

"You want full custody of her, don't you?"

"I wouldn't dream of taking her away from you."

Not like the way you took her away from me and poisoned her mind.

"No one took her from you, Noah."

"I tried to get shared custody. I tried to reason with you many times and—"

"Would you have honestly negotiated visitation rights with me if the tables had turned and *I* was the one battling a drug addiction? No! You would have kept our daughter far, far away from me!"

Shutting my eyes, I tried to calm down. I knew she was right. I had been in no condition to be a responsible father while addicted to cocaine.

"I got clean, Natalie. You went back on your promise."

"I never promised you anything. I had to protect our daughter. You always chose the drugs before her!"

Clenching my fist, I was seconds away from blowing up. But I modulated my voice and said, "I want Aria to live with me for a year."

"Absolutely not!"

"You owe me this."

"I don't owe you a thing!"

"She's already said yes to me."

"Well, I'm her mother, and I say no!"

Fuck it.

"Quit being a bitter bitch. You just can't stand the fact that you refused my proposal all those years ago."

"Get over yourself," she said derisively.

"Instead, you ran away with that loser, cashed in my family's bribe money, only to have it all blown away overnight. You can't fathom how disappointing your life turned out—admit it."

"Shut up!"

"Let me tell you this, so it's crystal clear for you: if you don't allow Aria to come to LA with me, you can kiss your life goodbye. I'll have Child Protective Services at your door so fast that you won't even know what hit you. Your kids will become government property and placed in the system. What system is that? Foster care, sweetheart. And last, your pathetic excuse for a husband will be behind bars. Maybe I'll have you thrown in there with him as well, since you've been a neglectful mother."

"You're bluffing. There's nothing you can do. Aria would never testify against me—and I'm not neglectful!"

"She wouldn't need to. Don't tempt me, Natalie, because I swear on her life that I'd do it. And you would eternally regret it."

There was a long pause.

"You bastard, damn you!" she snapped. "Fine! She's yours!"

"And one other thing… If you mention this little convo of ours to her, you'll be sorry."

"I won't mention a damn thing! Happy? Are we done now?"

My daughter was approaching from the distance, which meant I had to wrap up the conversation. "You have a good day, Nat." I smiled slyly.

"Go to hell, Noah." She hung up.

That went well, I sardonically said to myself as Aria entered the car and strapped on her seat belt.

"Did you call my mom?"

"Yeah, I just got off the phone with her. She's fine with you hangin' out with me. I told her I'd bring you home in the evening."

"Oh, okay, that's good."

"Yeah, so tell me, beautiful, what do you feel like doing, since we're bordering on rebellion today?"

"Um…"

The seconds passed and she still couldn't decide on a destination—clear sign of unresolved trauma.

"I know where to take you." I drove out of the school parking lot. "We're going shopping."

"What? Are you sure?"

"I offered."

"I just… I feel bad."

"Why?" I frowned. "I'm your father. Let me spend money on you. It's my duty."

"It's just…"

"Aria, please. Let me do this for you. There's no need to feel guilty."

She paused for the longest while before she smiled and said, "Okay."

It was the fastest way to cheer a woman up: shower her with gifts.

CHAPTER SEVEN
ARIA

Being spoiled was not something I was used to; it felt… almost unnatural, as if I were playing a part that just didn't align with who I was and the upbringing I'd had. Noah spent eleven grand on a new wardrobe for me: clothes, shoes, accessories, makeup… pretty much everything and anything I wanted. Grams and Granddad would always send me $200 on my birthday, but this was just overboard. We went to several high-end designer boutiques and Noah watched me try on outfits and shoes. I was reluctant at first, but he kept insisting I surrender and enjoy the experience. All it took was for him to flash his credit card, and the salespeople at the store would give us VIP treatment.

"What's the point of being wealthy if you don't spend it on the ones you love?"

I would never forget those words. As a child, whenever I went shopping with Mom and Rob, my stepdad would constantly make a scene afterwards about how my mom had spent too much on clothes, and that my outfits were "inappropriate" for my age. Apparently, a pair of jeans with some glitter was "slutty" on a fourteen-year-old—Rob's words, not mine. I'd often cry on the drive home because of his abusive shouting matches with Mom. He would say the most hurtful things right in front of me, as if I wasn't even there. My stepdad was constantly a critical, mean prick. I couldn't tell Noah about these memories. I felt ashamed, and it hurt to remember.

After an hour of shopping from place to place, we stopped at a clothing store called Chloé on Madison Avenue. I browsed their clothing line and was helped into a dressing room to see if the sizes were okay. Everything seemed to fit just fine, and I had one last item to try on.

Changing into a strapless dress, I loved how the white satin hugged my body in all the right places, with the hem resting above my knees. But I couldn't help but feel self-conscious when I examined my full figure from every angle.

"I'm missing the summer already," the saleslady talked in the background. "Don't you hate this weather?"

"I live in California," Noah replied.

"You and your wife are so lucky."

He choked on his champagne, clearing his throat as he answered, "She's not my wife."

It shocked me so much that I accidentally dropped my bra.

"Oh, I'm sorry. I just assumed because of your wedding band."

Now she probably thinks he's a cheating bastard, taking "the other woman" out on a shopping spree.

"That's my daughter in there."

"Wow! You are a young father. I never would have guessed!"

This was embarrassing.

He laughed off the awkwardness as I stepped out of the dressing room.

"Do you like it?" I nervously met his eyes, interrupting their conversation.

Sat in an armchair, Noah held a glass of champagne and let his eyes roam down my body.

I frowned when he said nothing. "Is that a no?"

His mouth was hanging open, but I didn't know how to interpret that.

"You look… divine."

A flattered smile spread across my face as I felt a rush of relief.

"What about the back?" I asked, pivoting a 180.

"Stunning."

"Those shoes look amazing with that dress," the saleslady added. "You look gorgeous!"

"Thank you."

"I can take whatever you're keeping to the register."

"That would be great, thanks." I handed over four expensive cocktail dresses, three pairs of open-toe heels, some jeans, as well as a few cardigans and vest tops (for casual wear). The store had an amazing selection of clothing that catered to almost every occasion.

"I'll be right out," I said to Noah.

"Take your time, sweetheart."

In the dressing room, I reached back for my zipper and tried to pull it down. Zipping it up had been a lot easier. Timidly, I opened the door and looked for the blonde saleswoman, but she was nowhere in sight.

"Is something wrong?" Noah set the champagne glass on a table and leaned forward.

"Um… it's my dress. I can't reach for the zipper. Can you help me out?"

"Of course." He stood up and stepped inside my fitting room, slightly shutting the door, but not all the way. I assumed he planned to leave quickly.

We were both facing the mirror now, and I couldn't help but feel this indescribable energy when he stood behind me. I could feel his warmth radiating off his body, penetrating my aura field, infecting me with a passionate fever. Never had I felt this way before. I didn't know how to handle it.

"Okay," Noah murmured. "This shouldn't be too hard."

He gathered my hair and brushed it down the side of my neck, causing goose bumps to form down my arms. Gently tugging the zipper, he pulled it down while I focused on our reflection in the mirror. Even though I had heels on, Noah stood much taller than me. I shivered when he placed a hand on my waist.

Why is this happening? Why am I reacting this way? Embarrassed and somewhat naked, I hugged my body so that the dress wouldn't fall.

"Thank you," I muttered, as we locked eyes in the reflective glass.

"Anything for you, beautiful." Noah touched my shoulders and kissed the side of my head.

The contact scorched my skin, triggering a sweltering heat to spread between my thighs. His gaze was seductive—but maybe I was fucked up for perceiving him that way. The whole dressing-room experience felt erotic. What was wrong with me?

"I'll wait for you outside." He left, and I finally let my dress drop to the floor.

My face was flushed. I was… aroused. All my friends had active sex lives. I was always the outcast in some form or another.

Being turned on by an innocent kiss had me deeply concerned. This attraction was wrong. But I couldn't ignore it.

☙❧

Later that afternoon, we had ventured to so many places that we both got tired as we approached Noah's car in the parking lot. He placed my shopping bags in the trunk, filling the back seats before he opened my passenger door like a gentleman.

"Is this your whip?" I asked.

"No, it's a rental. I drive an Audi convertible, the R10 model."

I had no clue what kind of car that was, but I knew it was expensive.

"You'll see it when you come to Cali with me," he continued. "I might even let you drive it. Do you have your license?"

"Yes."

"Great! Then you'll have fun driving my cars." He flashed a charismatic smile and started the engine.

I honestly didn't care about his "fancy toys." I just wanted to be near him. It was like a high. This man made me feel so happy. The entire afternoon felt like a dream come true, straight out of a movie. My reality did not feel real. In fact, I had trouble trusting it, which got me paranoid.

"So, where to, angel?"

"What are our options?"

"Well, I could take you to the theater—we could visit a museum or an art gallery, or we could go back to my hotel, order in, and have a laid-back evening. Which do you prefer? Feel free to add to that list of options."

A laid-back evening. I wanted to spend some quality time, just the two of us.

"I like your last option." I stole a glance at him from the corner of my eye, noticing the way his mouth slanted into the sexiest smile. Maybe this was a bad idea, or maybe I was the bad influence.

ⱷ

I've had to grow up pretty fast throughout my childhood… mostly because it was a hostile war zone. I knew if I disobeyed or acted out, I'd get a "good beating" from my parents, followed by humiliating verbal abuse. They used to chase me around the apartment and hit me… my mother did this a lot whenever Rob wasn't home. He scared me. As a kid, you feel so powerless. Your parents are your world, your heroes; viewing them as the villains of your life is fucking terrifying when you're so defenseless and at the mercy of someone who is responsible for your survival. I remember Mom's nervous breakdowns more than anything. No child wants to see their caregiver slap and hit herself because of unresolved trauma. Whenever she would reach her limit, she would scream, cry, and slap herself. She even went as far as slamming a pot on her head in the kitchen during a fight with Rob.

Many times, he struck me often on the head and across the face. It was demeaning to experience; it decimated my self-esteem as a child.

"Eat shit, you dumb bitch!" Rob would constantly say.

I constantly felt like "a bad kid" because it was too horrifying to see past that illusion and recognize that my parents were the "evil" ones who were abusing me. I couldn't project that reality, so instead, I had internalized the blame until I was mature enough to realize just how fucked up they both were and how desperately I needed to escape my cage of trauma. To get to this point of realization, I read a lot of self-help books. I was a disobedient teenager every once in a while, but my rule-breaking vendettas had always been calculated (with the purpose of getting away with things undetected).

My mother blamed me when Terry cut himself on broken glass in the kitchen. I had been doing the dishes and dropped a glass cup by accident. My brother came rushing in because Tiff was chasing him, and he stepped on the glass, bleeding and screaming in pain. Mom had lost her shit and panicked. A neighbor drove us to the hospital. Terry needed stitches. I was only eleven, and I had begged Mom not to tell Rob that I had caused the accident. But she seemed to resent me for what happened and told him anyway when he came home. As expected, he blew up at me, verbally and physically abused me until I was in tears, begging for forgiveness. It was hard to recall these times in my childhood. It made me angry at my mother. Her passive aggressive side was so hurtful. She should have been keeping a better eye on her son, not blaming *me* for the accident and gloating in satisfaction when Rob "disciplined me."

Last year I tried cigarettes for the first time and had nearly coughed up a lung. The silver lining? It wasn't for me. And that summer, I'd got smashed at Ally's birthday party. I was lucky it was a sleepover. Had I gone home with nothing to show but slurred speech and loss of motor skills, Mom and Rob would've killed me.

Many grown-ups these days think my generation of teenagers are dumb, technologically dependent zombies who have no clue how the world works. But we're actually smart. Well, some of us are. I couldn't speak for some jocks at my school. I was an introverted intellectual. I don't know if I became this way because of trauma, or if it was natural to my identity. Maybe I was a nerd in the closet. Yeah, that made more sense. I tried to blend in with the popular crowd, but I never talked about anything remotely philosophical or thought-provoking with my friends. I felt like a loner deep down… a misfit in my home environment and at school. Sometimes it got exhausting having to wear a mask all the time and hide my pain, but this was how I survived.

Prior to Noah pulling a reappearing act, my plan had been to graduate and move far away. As cliché as it sounds, Paris would've been nice, or

Italy. I liked to dream big. Mom did her best to instill good morals and values in me. She was always good at giving me advice, but she was terrible at taking her own. These were things I was thinking about during the car ride to Noah's hotel. He wasn't talking much—just had the stereo playing at a comfortable volume while we drove through traffic.

"Any idea what you want for dinner?"

You... and dessert.

"I'm not sure."

"Are you always this indecisive?"

Ouch.

"Um…"

"Pizza again?"

He looked over at me. I let my smile say it all.

ౠ

Walking into Noah's hotel suite, I could hardly believe my eyes. It was bigger than my family's apartment. The floor-to-ceiling windows offered a 360-degree view of Manhattan. Luxuriously furnished in shades of cream and espresso, I noticed a minibar in the corner and a massive gathering room. The bedroom was spacious, oozing luxury. I couldn't understand how one person could need for so much space. Maybe he was claustrophobic.

"Wow…"

"You like it?"

"It's amazing…" I stepped out of his bedroom and took off my jacket and cardigan.

"Wait until you see our home. This is nothing compared to where your daddy's living."

Daddy?—that made me cringe. But I smiled when he said *our home.*

"I'm gonna order us that pizza. What toppings do you want?"

"Whatever you're having."

"Come on, I asked you first."

"Green peppers, mushrooms, and diced tomatoes."

"Same as before. I'll remember that next time."

Pizza twice in a row. That never happened in my household. I loved a good veggie pizza, as long as the toppings were diced. There was something about chunky vegetable toppings that really interfered with the taste and texture. If someone gave me a slice with the same toppings that were sprinkled in chunks, I wouldn't be able to eat it. I'm weird, I know.

The sun was setting in the horizon, shifting the sky to a glowing magenta melting into orange. Fading flecks of sunrays glittered on the polished windowpanes of the skyscrapers. I was so absorbed in the architecture that I didn't hear Noah calling my name.

"Aria?" He gently placed his hand on my shoulder.

"Sorry—zoned out." I turned around.

He studied my face and then looked out the window. "It's an impeccable view."

"I wish I had my camera. I love photography," I said, seating myself on the cream-colored sofa.

"Have you taken any classes?" Noah sat beside me and gave me his undivided attention.

"No, but ever since I won a competition last year, I took a keen interest in it. I've been taking photos of almost everything ever since."

"Tell me about this competition."

"It's kind of stupid." I sniggered. "You'll laugh."

"No, tell me." He shifted closer, his eyes lighting up with interest.

"My art teacher, Ms. Clare, was giving away a fancy art set last year. But it wasn't just a charitable giveaway, you had to earn it. So, she challenged everyone in the class to take a photograph of anything that was nature themed. We could enhance the photo in digital software, just as long as we stuck to that rule—you know, trees, flowers, wild animals."

Noah nodded and continued listening.

"She gave us three weeks to produce our winning photo, and throughout those weeks, I was taking pictures of anything I found interesting. This was around the beginning of fall, when all the leaves were changing color. Most of the photos I took were from unusual angles." I paused briefly, wondering if I still held his interest. "Anyway, one time I was walking through Central Park, and it was sunny out, but it started raining out of nowhere. The sky had split in half with two different weather forecasts. It was… incredible. I thought the climate in the city had gone bipolar or something…"

He chuckled a bit.

"But it created this amazing effect because, as the sun was shining, there was a light drizzle of rainfall… like diamonds were pouring from the sky. I noticed a young couple sitting on a bench between two trees, and the leaves were this brilliant crimson color. The man and woman were getting soaked in the rain, but they didn't seem to care.

"So I pulled out my camera and took a photo. The shot was so beautiful. The woman had short platinum hair that was almost glowing in the sunlight while the rain just shimmered over her. I didn't edit or enhance the picture. The only thing I Photoshopped in was a personal quote: 'Every drop of rain that you can't catch, that's how much I miss you.'

"When I won the competition, I felt like I didn't win it fairly. Love, and specifically that couple, had inspired my photograph. It wasn't so much about nature or landscape. I was just lucky to be at the right place at the right time. Mother Nature conveniently showed her magnificence at that moment. I think it was the way he was kissing her that had captivated me the most. It was so tender and passionate."

I wasn't sure why I felt nervous telling Noah all that—maybe because it was personal to me.

"You have a poetic soul, Aria." He smiled and caressed my cheek. "I'd love to see that photo."

"Nah, I'm just a die-hard romantic who's in denial. Ms. Clare framed my picture. It's on display in her art room."

"Why in denial? Who's broken your heart?" he asked, looking concerned.

I couldn't tell him about Trevor—too painful.

"No one important, I mean—growing up, Mom and Rob's relationship gave me the impression that love doesn't exist. And if it's anything similar to what they have, then I don't want it at all. I feel like true love is an illusion that only exists in fairy tales and Hollywood films."

"Are you dating anyone?"

"No."

"Well, I don't believe for a second that you really feel true love is nonexistent, and I also refuse to believe you're not dating a guy. Look at you—you're gorgeous."

I hated blushing constantly around him.

"Not that I have a problem with you seeing boys—" He broke off. "Actually, I think I prefer you staying single for at least another ten years. It'll make my job a lot easier, and I won't have to knock any teeth out."

We both laughed. I stared at him with admiration, wondering if he knew how I felt.

"I can't imagine you going psychotic on a potential date I bring home."

"Trust me, you don't want to find out. I can be a real dick sometimes. You're too young to date, anyway."

This seemed like a great opportunity to test the waters.

"Well, what if I go to that private school you plan to get me enrolled in, and I meet this hot, charismatic guy who is captain of the swim team?"

He shot me a quizzical look.

"And say he's also captain of the debate team, so that makes him athletic, intelligent, and extremely good-looking. Tall, brown hair, seductive blue eyes…"

Oh Lord. I just described Noah.

"Not to mention a muscular build, kissable lips, with a really big—"

"Okay, let's skip the detailed description." He chuckled uneasily. "But go on."

"Heart." I giggled. "Would you let me date him if I brought him home for you to meet? What if he passed the douchebag test with flying colors?"

"Sweetheart, first off, no guy you bring home is ever gonna pass the douchebag test with flying colors. Every man has borderline asshole tendencies, including me. The guy could be on his best behavior and address me as 'sir' all he wants—it's all a façade, because of one blatantly obvious fact."

"Are you saying he wouldn't be genuine?"

"No, he wouldn't."

"And why not? What if he was in love with me?"

"Boys your age are too stupid and horny to understand what love is. They're all conquered by their—libido. Forgive my bluntness, but I speak the truth. The only evidence gathered from all the BS conversations he would have with me is the fact that he's strictly motivated to get in your pants. And there is no way in hell I'm gonna allow that to happen.

"I don't want to see you shed a single tear over some bastard who will break your heart. I'd make any man cry tears of blood if he ever hurt you, but I'd also risk jail time because I don't think I would let him live."

His territorial attitude was disturbingly sexy.

"With that being said," he added, "please be a little sympathetic toward your dad, and try to see things from my point of view. You mentioned I'm still young. Well, I'm admitting that I'm too young to serve a life sentence. I would hate to exchange my Armani suits for orange jumpsuits for the rest of my life." He looked at me with all seriousness, then relaxed his expression and laughed.

"You're so protective of me."

Noah grabbed my hand and gave it a soft kiss while keeping his gaze hot and seductive. Okay, I'll be honest, he probably wasn't being seductive on purpose. It was my sick mind interpreting those stares in immoral ways.

"You're young, Aria. I know that if I say no to boys, you'll date some jerk behind my back. And if you get your heart shattered, you'd keep it from me because you'd know you weren't supposed to date. I wouldn't be able to comfort you and love you back to happy health. I'd rather practice democratic parenting instead of being a dictator. You can date, but I want to meet him first—and no staying out past eleven. If you're gonna have sex, use protection. I can't imagine you as a teen mom."

"Noah…"

This was getting awkward. Fast.

"You're just a teenager. I wish you wouldn't even think about boys that way."

"Noah…"

"I'm gonna buy you a comprehensive book on STDs, with pictures, so you'll know what the consequences of unprotected sex can look like, and—"

"Dad, I'm a virgin!"

He stopped talking after I blurted that out. I couldn't tell if he was more shocked that I'd called him "Dad" or that I'd confessed to being a virgin… which was a lie. I couldn't tell him the truth. I considered all those intimate moments with Trevor null and void because of the way he left me. This was how I coped with the pain of rejection and abandonment: crowning myself as a virgin all over again to ease my shame and to get that lying, cheating bastard out of my system. He didn't deserve my cup of love. But I was afraid to tell Noah what had happened. I guess we all hide from the truth when we feel a deep sense of shame. Rob had shamed me enough when he had walked in on Trevor and me having sex once. He called me a filthy whore, humiliated me, and threw my ex out of the apartment, followed by an explosive fight with my mother when she came home. She didn't defend me. She rarely ever did, which was ironic considering how I was conceived. I just chalked it up to her being afraid of Rob. He was a terrifying rage monster whenever he was drunk and triggered… punching holes in the walls, breaking things, shouting profanity and low blows at anyone who was the target of his wrath. I rarely found my voice to defend myself. My parents had stolen it from me through the abuse I'd suffered.

"Uh, well…" Noah finally spoke. "That's great. That makes me feel…"

Awkward pause.

"Really—happy because…"

God, he looked so uncomfortable. Why didn't I keep my mouth shut? I hated lying. Maybe that's why I always froze up. I had the key to freedom, but I was too afraid to use it and release myself from my own captivity: a web of lies I'd crafted to protect my ego.

"I can't believe I corrupted your mind with all that sex talk," he finally said. "I am *so* sorry." He ran his fingers through his hair and rubbed the back of his neck before he regarded me. "Wait… Please tell me Natalie had that talk with you about the birds and the bees."

"Noah, I know everything about 'the birds and the bees.' I just haven't done…" I lowered my voice. "*It* yet. I thought that might be a good thing for you to know."

"It is. Hey…" he softened his tone. "Look at me, angel."

My hands were fidgety, and I knew why.

Tell the truth! My conscience screamed.

I couldn't. It was painful, and I feared being judged. My ex was the only guy I was intimate with. I fell head over heels for him last year. I genuinely thought we would get married and leave New York together. He'd talked about it with me plenty of times, only to ditch me in the end and break all his promises. Trevor had other plans after he graduated and dumped me for someone else at college. I was shattered. It made me close up inside and develop a mistrust around men and opening my heart. He ghosted me for weeks and then broke up with me through a two-minute phone call, claiming we were going "in different directions." There was a third party involved. He had lied to me.

Maybe he wanted to spare me from more heartbreak, but the awful truth has a way of coming out. Finding his secret Facebook account and his Tumblr blog where he discussed how much fun he was having on "casual dates" broke me… not to mention the shade he threw my way in his disgusting posts. He had emotionally abused me in our relationship, but I always protected him. I didn't retaliate when I discovered his secret socials that day. Instead, I cried my heart out, staring at the computer screen, rejected, betrayed, and abandoned with swords in my chest—ten of them. I had broken down in tears to where I couldn't breathe. A close friend of mine had been the one to link me to Trevor's accounts. I didn't even go digging. It was as if the truth *had* to come to light, regardless of how ugly and hurtful it was. The truth sets you free, and it gives you an opportunity to change your life for the better. I wasn't perfect in our relationship, but I wasn't sleeping around and cheating. We had a rollercoaster romance. At least I could take accountability for my mistakes and not run like a coward, giving no closure. I guess I was nothing but a burden for Trevor because of my "daddy issues." I felt used and discarded. I didn't want to open up about this to Noah; I'd only start crying.

"Are you all right?" he asked, coaxing my chin in his direction.

Get it together, Aria!

I didn't want him to see me in tears.

His eye color had changed in the dim lighting, as if the sun was setting inside a deep blue ocean. It was hard to look at him—my heart couldn't take it; the nonstop skipping was driving me crazy.

Why does he have this effect on me?

"It makes me so happy and proud to know that you love and respect yourself enough to understand that your body is a sacred temple. Every young woman is like a goddess. In your case, you can't just let any guy enter your temple doors."

I figured that out a little too late.

"You should allow entry only to one man who is worthy of worshiping you—someone who can love your naked soul before he can love your naked body. And yes, I just paraphrased Charlie Chaplin's letter to his daughter."

"There's always such a double standard. How come guys can have sex with multiple women and it's deemed as okay, but if a woman wants to be promiscuous, she gets slut shamed?"

He blinked, looking confused. "Are you saying you want multiple lovers?"

"I wouldn't mind having two men in love with me," I teased.

"Just two? You sure you don't want to triple that?" Noah laughed.

"One for each day of the week."

"I should have kept my mouth shut." He sighed, smiling at me. "And for the record, you wouldn't be limited to just that number, believe me. You are drop dead gorgeous and your energy is contagious."

My face heated again.

"Sweetheart, true intimacy isn't like porn. Threesomes are not that glorious as they make it out to be."

"I don't watch porn," I said, digging myself into a hole. "I was only kidding! Besides, I just meant that the inequalities between men and women are unfair."

"I agree with you. I think every woman should have agency over her body and sexuality without being judged for it. But I want you to be loved by your life partner, not sexually objectified for personal gratification. You're too precious to be used, abused, and discarded. Sex and emotions go hand in hand, Aria. That's how I feel about it, and I won't change my mind."

Had he ever separated the two in his life? I was curious to know, but didn't want to be intrusive. Plus, things were already awkward with the sex talk.

"I'm so proud of you," said Noah.

I wasn't.

"Regardless of my absence, you've become a strong young woman who doesn't feel the need to trade her virtue for attention."

I hadn't surrendered my V-card for that reason; I had given it away out of love. I wanted to give and receive love.

"Whether you desired love or wanted to fit in," he continued, "you stood firm behind your beliefs. Being a virgin is something you should pride yourself on. Sexual energy is sacred."

The lump in my throat grew bigger. I should have just been honest with him. But it was harder to reveal the truth, knowing his stance now. I didn't want Noah to think less of me. Sometimes women surrender their virginity to the wrong one because of inner wounds. Sometimes, on your journey to love, you fall for illusions and pay the price. It doesn't mean you're any less worthy of love or a worthless human being. At least that's what I had learned about my personal healing post-breakup.

"As your father, my advice is to never, *ever*..."—he paused dramatically—"have sex."

Comic relief. I needed that, as we both laughed.

"I'm kidding, angel. I know you don't want to die an old maid, and I guarantee that won't ever happen anyway, because you're a knockout."

Is he serious?

"But since I'm your dad, I'm sure your mother would agree with me on this when I say… wait until you're married. I know it sounds unrealistic, and I don't think you were raised by bible-thumping parents…"

I wasn't.

"… But I was raised with a Christian upbringing. Although, to be honest, I'm somewhere between atheist and agnostic. This sounds contradicting, but I'm grateful your mother moved away from your grandparents. They were unbelievably fanatic."

There was bad blood between my families. Grams wasn't so bad, but Noah had a point. My grandparents were devout Catholics to where it made you want to denounce your faith. I guess that's why we visited them only two days a year, during Thanksgiving. Rob always complained about it. They had never approved of my mother marrying him.

"Teens go overboard with rebelling against strict parents who have kept them in social confinement." Noah sighed. "Life feels like a prison. But inevitably, they break free."

"*Shawshank Redemption* much?" I laughed, and he joined me.

"Hey, that's a good movie!"

"Agreed."

"But stay on topic. Don't distract me."

Our conversation flowed so naturally. Nothing felt forced. We covered some serious topics, and he had this amazing ability to take the heaviness and discomfort out from our discussions by adding humor and feeding off my sarcasm. Anytime I got sarcastic with my mom or stepdad, they bitched at me and couldn't understand that I was only trying to lighten the conversation.

"So, anyway…" Noah continued.

I watched him intently, not wanting him to stop talking.

"My point is…" He cursed and then apologized for cussing out loud. Now was the time to speak up and help him out.

"Your point is, you're proud of who I am today. Many unfortunate things have happened, but it could have been worse—a lot worse. Throughout my turbulent times, I rose above it, and you're happy I did."

He smiled warmly and pulled me to his chest, enveloping me in his arms.

"That's exactly my point. See, that's another reason I love you. You're on the same brain wave as me."

I couldn't hide my smile, or that I was bordering on becoming addicted to him, especially that cologne.

"You're so strong, Aria. That day when I watched you enter the courtroom, all I could see was your inner strength. I know it sounds crazy, but I felt it in my gut, and my instincts are never wrong."

His words touched me. I had known Noah for only a short while, and he was already beginning to have a tremendous impact on me. Was this because of the blood bond forged between us? Like a genetic occurrence at conception? I couldn't figure it out. All I knew was that I felt a cosmic connection with him. Being his biological daughter crushed me. I knew he would never look at me the way I wanted.

A knock at the door made me slip out of my melancholy mood.

"Pizza's here. I'll be right back, sweetheart." Noah took out some cash from his wallet and stood up.

I still couldn't get over how incredibly fashionable this man was. Everything about him exuded youth and vitality. Prior to going to court, I had been prepared to confront him and unleash all my pent up anger and resentment. But something had changed when I saw him face to face for the first time. It wasn't like my anger had vanished—it was just sleeping, like an inactive volcano. I wasn't sure what it would take to make me explode in molten lava and become the force of nature I truly was. My darkest emotions were so suppressed. I think I had been reserving all my hatred for my father because of how abandoned I'd felt. Every beating that Rob gave me, every time anything went wrong in my life, I had blamed my father. I was just waiting for the day when I could look him up, show up at his door, blast him, and make him rue the day he left me behind. But my life had taken an unexpected turn.

Noah had come and found me, tipping the scales between love and hate. The only thing that made my scale complicated was that I felt a certain love that I shouldn't have been feeling. I think it was safe to say I had the biggest crush on him. But if I could describe a visual, then picture this:

On the left side of the scale was "love you like a lover," and on the right side was "love you like a daughter." Which side do you think tipped the scale? The right side was weightless because everything I was feeling tipped toward the left. I couldn't even understand why. It was physically and mentally frustrating.

"Do you want to eat on the sofa?" Noah asked.

I looked up at him and broke my train of thought. "Sure. Let me help you with the plates."

 CƷ୫Ͻ

The pizza was delicious. I discovered Noah loved Tabasco sauce on his pie like I did. Was that a coincidence, or a particular food preference caused by genetic influence? I knew that a woman's diet during the prenatal period contributes to a child's eating habits. It was just a coincidence that we both liked the same thing. I needed to stop over-analyzing.

Noah's laid-back personality made it easy to relax around him, which I appreciated. We sat and ate while he told me more about his trips around the world.

"You're so lucky," I said. "I've always wanted to travel. I've been stuck here, and I can't wait to leave."

"You'll be well traveled spending time with me, I promise you that."

All this smiling was going to give me premature wrinkles. Not cool, I thought.

"I've already figured out you appreciate art," he continued, "so I think Italy would be the first place I'd take you. They have beautiful galleries in Florence, and the country itself is immersed in artistic history. Is that what you want to major in, the arts?"

I wasn't sure if I should honestly tell him what I always wanted to be growing up, but I ended up sharing.

"When I was seven, I knew I wanted to be an actor. By ten, I wanted to be a singer. I can carry notes without going off pitch—sometimes… But that dream was short-lived." I let out a little laugh as he looked at me with intrigue.

"At thirteen, I wanted to be a model, but Rob was so controlling with how I dressed. That dream died off quickly." I paused. "And now… here I am at seventeen, still secretly desiring a modeling career. I just felt so unseen in life. Maybe that's why it's appealing to me. I don't think I'd enjoy the pressure that comes with the modeling industry. I'll probably pursue a different passion by next year. Mom never enrolled me in any modeling agencies, so I have zero experience, and Rob looks down on me for even considering it. He says that models are 'drugged up, anorexic sluts that screw every ugly fuck in the business to get ahead,' and—" I suddenly stopped when Noah choked on his drink.

"Are you all right?"

He coughed a few times, pounding his chest. "Yeah… [*cough*]… I'm fine. It just went down the wrong way."

He didn't cuss me out the way my stepdad usually did, which surprised me. Maybe he was trying to leave a good impression.

"I'm sorry, I was just quoting Rob. For the record, I don't agree with what he said about models in the industry. I don't judge anyone who struggles with addiction. How can I? I haven't experienced their life journey. There's always trauma attached to vices."

"You're wise beyond your years and you have incredible empathy. I love that about you. I'm blown away." Noah stroked my hand and kissed it, making my heart smile.

"Thank you… anyway, I buried my head in academics and art. I suck at math and science. I think my best shot is majoring in English Lit and teaching, but I really don't have the patience for that. Who wants to finish school only to go *back* to school for the rest of their lives? I'm clearly in the identity moratorium phase, or to put it simply, I'm stuck at the stage of 'identity versus confusion.'"

He grinned. "Erik Erikson's stage theory… I remember taking a psych course—not familiar with the *moratorium* phase thing, though. I think you should become a psychology major."

A psych major? Someone needed to psychoanalyze *me*. Freud would've loved to have had me on his couch. I had no idea what the heck I wanted to be when I was all "grown up."

"I just feel lost."

"I understand what you're saying, but you're so well spoken, Aria. You have advanced intellect for someone your age."

"English, art, and social sciences are my strongest subjects. Don't ask about my grades in calculus and physics because it's embarrassing."

"I can get you the best tutor when you come live with me. Your marks will significantly improve. Although I support the academic route in life, I want to fully support you as well in pursuing your dream. It's not too late. And…" He took a deep breath. "That idiot stepdad of yours doesn't know what he's talking about. Every industry can be risky, but it's important to have an excellent group of people around you to keep you grounded. I promise that I'll never leave your side. Never again."

I felt overjoyed in that moment, I could hardly contain it. Someone was finally on my team, rooting for me. I wasn't used to this, but I was so fucking grateful.

"I still want you to get into a good college," Noah added. "But I want you investing all your energy towards your dream; it's the only way it can manifest into your reality. I have connections with very important people. I can find you a great agency, and you can do some modeling on the side while you're studying. How does that sound?"

"Do you really mean that?"

"Aria, you are beyond beautiful. Personally, if I had it my way, I'd lock you up and keep your beauty hidden from the world forever. But that's selfish and unfair. If this makes you happy, then I'll do whatever I can to stand behind you and help you achieve your dreams."

How was he so perfect? It seemed too good to be true.

"Aw, baby, don't cry. Come here."

I hated being so sensitive. I just felt things too deeply, and that seemed to be my curse. My ex and his family shamed me for it—said I'm "too sensitive." For once in my life, I felt like an angel had fallen from Heaven to come to my rescue.

"I mean it," Noah whispered. "I'm not going anywhere." He wrapped his powerful arms around me and kissed my head.

My heart was racing, afraid he would hear it. His body felt so familiar, as if it belonged to me. I don't know why I felt this way. Perhaps because I was feeling territorial about him. Maybe it was the beginning stages of chronic possessiveness—more agonizing than anything. How would Erikson label that? Stage 5.5: neuroticism vs. total cray-cray? Yeah… No. I had no logical explanations, and I didn't want to keep questioning myself, because when he held me in his arms, the storm in my chest suddenly calmed and faded away.

"I love you, Aria."

Please mean it forever.

He held my face, staring at me with an intensity that made me feverish. Noah set fire to my frozen soul. My hands were freezing, but his were brilliantly warm.

Eyes of ice, touch of fire. I made a mental note to write that in my diary when I got home.

I had been so deprived of love, and it seemed to come with an expiration date—which terrified me. I had a mother who cared for me and loved me in her own way, yet I'd never felt my emotional needs were met as a child… it was just trauma after trauma in a hostile home environment. Was I too needy? Or was I truly in love with this handsome man who made me melt whenever he looked at me? He made my heart flutter with his soft-spoken words, and I felt a pull at the pit of my stomach whenever he was close to me. Noah made me feel so many conflicting emotions that society would deem wrong and immoral. Was I hell spawn for feeling this way? I wondered what he would think if he knew half the things that went through my mind when I looked at him.

"Let's lighten up the evening with a little music, huh?" He smiled and got to his feet.

"I'll clean up."

"No, leave the plates and pizza boxes."

I watched him with curiosity as he turned on the stereo and shuffled through some tracks. Frank Sinatra's jazzy voice suddenly echoed around me: "Fly Me to the Moon." My mother was a huge fan and always listened to his albums. I laughed when Noah swayed with the music.

"Dance with me."

"Oh my gosh, no!" I covered my blushing cheeks and peered up at him when he stepped in front of me.

"Come on," he encouraged, holding out his hands. "You said you can dance—now show me."

"Yeah, but—"

Before I could make an excuse, he pulled me up in his arms, which left me kind of breathless.

"I'll lead, you follow."

I couldn't stop giggling. Noah looked unbelievably adorable. He guided my left hand onto his shoulder and slipped my right hand into his. I trembled when his fingertips traveled down the curve of my spine. We kept dodging furniture as he led me around the room until we finally planted our feet next to the window. The sun had set, and the city looked so alive in the darkness. We slow-danced in rhythm with the music while Sinatra sang his lyrics in that smooth, vocal jazz. I laughed when Noah twirled me around like a ballerina. His moves were impressive. How was he so flawless?

I breathed out slowly when he pulled me in closer, shifting the energy between us as we slowly swayed side to side.

"You didn't step on my feet," he murmured.

"Were you expecting me to?"

"Maybe." Noah chuckled. "I pulled some slick dance moves on you before I brought it down a couple levels. Did you take ballroom dancing or something?"

I smiled and shook my head. "Not exactly."

"I catch a few episodes of *Dancing with the Stars* now and then," he said. "Those dancers are real pros—amazing choreography."

"Yeah, that show is entertaining and funny at times."

"You mentioned being experienced in Latin dance," Noah said. "Which dances, exactly?"

"Kizomba and bachata."

"Bachata? Wow, that's a sensual dance. Who taught you?"

"Jade's mom is a dance instructor and has a private studio in her basement. The first time I went over to Jade's place, she gave me a full tour, and when we went downstairs, her mom was teaching a class. They were all beginners and mostly people my age.

"There was this cute guy whose partner hadn't shown up, so Mrs. Riviera asked me if I could volunteer for a couple minutes and dance with him… and I did. Apparently, I really impressed her since I learned the steps very quickly. She said I was a natural and encouraged me to participate in her classes. When I told her I couldn't afford it, she offered to mentor me for free. I was reluctant at first, but eventually accepted. This was last year."

"You never cease to amaze me."

I was flattered by his compliment.

"I believe anyone can dance," I said. "It just takes practice and dedication."

"I disagree," said Noah. "Dancing is an art form. Not everyone is blessed with that talent, nor can they emulate the passionate expression of dance. It's the same with singing and acting. Sure, you can learn, but it doesn't mean you master it." He gently brushed his hand down my lower back, and I shivered.

"Are you cold? I can turn up the heat."

"No, I'm fine."

Damn it, he noticed. Before I could say anything else, he spun me around and dipped me.

"… I wasn't expecting that." "I clutched his shoulder.

"Don't worry. I won't let you fall." He grinned. "You have the cutest laugh."

"I love yours." I confessed.

Our eyes locked while he held me in that position.

"You're too sweet."

Maybe I should tone it down, I thought.

He guided me back to my feet and kissed my forehead. The song had ended.

"Let's put the pizza away and watch a movie or something," he suggested.

"Sure, I'm down." I smiled and followed him.

This man is a god. It probably wasn't good that I was idolizing him. You can lose yourself. And I didn't want that to happen.

CHAPTER EIGHT
ARIA

Ho. Ly. Crap. My jaw dropped when I saw Noah unbuttoning his shirt in front of me. I needed a bucket for my drool. Okay, I was exaggerating a bit there, but his body was so… *yum.* He walked past me while unfastening the last button, making me swoon. This man had a serious six-pack. I noticed a hint of ink on his chest, but his shirt was covering it.

"I'm just gonna change out of this shirt," he hollered from the bedroom. "Pick a movie. I've got Netflix!"

It was hard to focus on finding a film when all I could think about was his partially naked body.

After a short while, Noah returned, dressed in a black undershirt and faded blue jeans that hung loosely below his waist—minus a belt. He had the most amazing physique I had ever seen—toned arms, sculpted shoulders… I was jealous of his golden skin. The tank top he had on showed off his midsection like an inverted triangle. I could see the dented grooves of his abdominal muscles through his shirt. It was the first time I'd seen him dressed so casually. He looked like someone I could have met at a bar or at college; someone I would've been attracted to. Had I met him that way, I definitely would've shown signs of interest. But unfortunately, we weren't under those circumstances. Noah was my dad. He was attractive, successful, and smolderingly sweet. But he was my father. It was difficult to ignore the flashing signs around him that read "Unavailable. Keep away."

A part of me wanted to give in to reasonable doubt and suggest we get a paternity test done. (You know… just to be sure I was really his.) Was I implying that my mother was a slut? No, of course not. Although, I would have gladly forgiven her if I didn't end up being Noah's biological daughter. Then I could have my happily ever after.

A girl can dream. I sighed.

"Did you pick a film, angel?"

I closed my eyes and secretly enjoyed the scent of his cologne. It took me to places in my head that I could not describe.

That's it. I'm just gonna ask him. And I planned to make it sound as innocent as possible. No ulterior motive.

"What kind of cologne do you have on?"

Well, that was straight to the point, wasn't it? Great job on subtlety, Aria! I silently scolded myself.

"Why?" He turned in my direction. "Is it too strong?"

"What?" I screwed up my face. "No! I love the scent!"

Yeah… That sounded way too enthusiastic.

"That's a relief. It's *Eternity* by Calvin Klein. Are you sure it's not giving you a headache?"

"Why would you think that?"

"Vanessa is sensitive to cologne and perfume fragrances. She gets headaches if I wear certain brands, so I thought maybe you're the same."

You smell like Heaven. And apparently my idea of Heaven smelled like a manufactured cologne. I could've pitched a great idea for the next CK ad campaign.

Sitting on the sofa, Noah grabbed the TV remote and played the film I had randomly chosen.

"*The Dark Knight Rises.* Haven't seen that one yet," he said. "Nice choice—I'm a fan of the films. By the way, before I forget, do you want any popcorn or anything?"

"No, I'm still stuffed from dinner." I sat next to him.

"Okay, just making sure."

There was a bit of a gap between us. I secretly prayed he would pull me in and cuddle me. Resorting to more subtle methods, I rubbed my arms and hoped he'd notice.

"Are you cold?" Noah asked. "Come here."

I scooted in closer as he lifted his right arm and rested it along the top edge of the sofa. My heart rate was speeding up by the second. I was nervous. Being around him made me feel like I was on a never-ending roller coaster. You know that feeling you get when you're on a scary thrill ride? You reach the top and you're waiting, anticipating the free fall where you either (a) scream your lungs out, (b) close your eyes and breathe it out to the verge of hyperventilation, or (c) just look down and stay silent because you go into shock. Well, for me it was all the above—that's how he made me feel. But at that moment, I was totally doing option (a) in my head.

"Aria, your arms are cold."

"I'll warm up soon."

His body was like a heating pad as he rubbed my arm, causing goose bumps to rise on my skin.

"Did you see the previous films?" Noah's voice was deep and relaxed.

I bit my lip to calm myself. Forcing a quick recovery from my whirlwind of emotions seemed near impossible. My senses were overpowering me all at once—sight, smell, hearing, touch. I didn't know which one was more amplified.

"Yeah, I saw them," I replied. "They were good. I love Morgan Freeman, Liam Neeson, and Christian Bale."

"Great actors. Who's your favorite?"

"I don't really have a favorite—I mean, they're all talented. It takes some serious dissociating to switch personalities on the spot. But if I had to give you some off the top of my head... Natalie Portman, Keanu Reeves, Luke Evans, and Russell Crowe. I have a *long list*, to be honest. I'm a huge movie buff. I just love and appreciate the arts so much."

"Well, that's unusual. I was expecting you to mention someone like DiCaprio or Brad Pitt."

Total eye candy.

"I don't know how they do it," I said. "Getting over the stage fright. I have a hard time answering questions in class when I'm called on. I totally bombed drama class because of my anxiety. It was hard to focus on my lines when I felt like everyone was judging and ridiculing me."

"That's only because of your hostile environment at home. I'm sorry, Aria." He looked at me with a deep sense of sadness. "Damaged inner critic. I'm gonna help you fix that."

"I'm not trying to make you feel guilty. It just sucks dealing with general anxiety. I'm often nervous around new people and I don't trust easily."

"You'll heal. I promise." He squeezed my hand.

I tried to focus on the action sequence that was taking place on the TV screen. But it was a pointless effort. My mind was on other things.

Building my bravery, I shifted closer and pressed my ear against Noah's chest, listening to the slow drumming rhythm, echoing louder in my ear, making my blood rush in my veins. I was in a blissful state of trance. Noah's body had magical properties, and I was falling under a spell that I couldn't seem to break. Was this a curse? Was I an abomination to humanity? Had God punished me for being born out of wedlock to parents who were almost kids themselves when they procreated? Was God even on my side in this, or was I giving in to lustful temptations? Temptations that Lucifer was whispering in my ear. Where do you even draw the line between good and evil in this situation? Had I gone so far off the spectrum of purity that I was corrupting my innocence without even realizing it, without understanding that my desire for my father was strictly sinful and nothing more?

No, I didn't want to believe that. I didn't want to justify these feelings with explanations that would place a huge red stop sign in front of me. I didn't want to see it. I wanted to ignore it and pretend the stop sign didn't even exist, because those feelings, the way he affected me, made me feel more alive than ever. To take away those emotions and label them as wrong would be too heartbreaking—emotional suicide.

This moment here with him was incredible. We weren't just cuddling. The physical contact was deeper and more meaningful than that. We were exchanging energy with each other to harmonize a shared frequency. Our bodies were transferring heat: input, output, circulating as one. I felt like I was one with him.

"Wow, is that strawberry vanilla?" Noah leaned forward and sniffed my hair.

"Yeah, it's the shampoo I use."

"I love your hair. It's so thick and shiny. You could always be a hair model on those Pantene Pro V commercials. Ever thought about that? Don't even think about doing Herbalene."

"Why not?"

"Because shampooing your hair is nowhere near an *orgasmic* experience."

Unless he *was shampooing mine…*

I laughed. The thought of washing and rinsing Noah's hair with any kind of shampoo got me somewhat hot and bothered.

"I prefer the runway," I said.

"Okay, princess, it's your dream." He chuckled lightly and kissed my head.

Half an hour passed, and I finally mustered up the courage to snuggle closer to him and rest my hand on his chest. It scared me shitless making the attempt, but he didn't flinch or reject my hand. Noah sat with his feet propped on the coffee table. He seemed too distracted by the movie to even notice whatever advances I'd make. There were so many things going through my mind. I couldn't focus on the film. Regardless, I stared at the screen and pretended to pay attention.

Everything was going in one ear and out the other, as if I had programmed some kind of filter in my head that would register only his words. Tuning out the audio, I labeled it as insignificant. Noah's voice and heartbeat were the only sounds I wanted to hear.

My chest suddenly felt heavy, and I wasn't sure why. His affection left me craving more.

What do you want? Say it, my subconscious whispered. No, I couldn't. Not out loud, and not within the quiet confines of my mind.

"That scene was awesome!"

Noah's excited outburst startled me.

"Aw, I'm sorry, angel. I didn't mean to scare you." He squeezed me in his arms and kissed my head again, moving a lazy hand up and down my arm. His fingertips lightly brushed against my skin, and the scent of his inebriating cologne teased my senses. *Fingertips, cologne, fingertips, skin, heat, skin, heat, skin, SEX.*

My head was spinning. All thoughts came to a screeching halt the second my subconscious mind finally revealed what I was hiding; it was in a drawer labeled "DO NOT READ." Fearlessly, I opened the folder and stumbled upon a horrifying truth: I wanted him, and I wanted him to want me.

It became crystal clear that I could never love Noah like a daughter. I had already proven that with my hypothetical scale. It was only a matter of time before I flat-out admitted it to myself. There were only two potential outcomes to this tragic tale of love that I was unexpectedly sucked into: I would win his heart, body, and soul, or I would repulse him and he would leave me forever. Abandonment had always been my biggest fear, but this was a risk I was willing to take because there was no way I could ever be happy being only a daughter to him. Eternal estrangement would be an acceptable fate if there was no happy ending for me. Call me selfish—I didn't care. I had a right to be selfish for once in my life. Gathering strength, I convinced myself that I had an ego tall enough to push me to make my next move.

Slowly, I leaned sideways and slumped my shoulder down his chest, past his stomach, until I was resting my head in his lap. I was nervous, but bold enough to follow through.

"Are you tired, sweetheart?"

Crap.

"No, I just wanted to get more comfortable," I replied, curling up in a ball.

Noah reached for the throw blanket resting over the sofa and covered my body with it. "There, that's better," he said.

I took a minute to calm down, since I was on the verge of having a heart attack. My arm slowly slid under the side of my head when he placed his feet on the ground. I guess he thought the elevated angle was hurting my neck. I didn't mind, though.

Minutes later, I felt Noah's fingers gliding through my hair, gently playing with my long, dark locks. The sensation aroused me as I closed my eyes. A forbidden fantasy unfolded in my mind: his hand lingering down my arm, over the curve of my hip, resting it right on my... *oh God.* I had to stop these thoughts. All I could think about was him rubbing me in extremely inappropriate places. But my fantasy refused to evaporate. I imagined an aggressive version of Noah telling me to turn and lie on my back. I'd obey and stare up at him. His eyes would be wild with lust, and he would gaze at my body as if he had complete ownership over it. Then he would unbutton my jeans and slide his hands down my panties, feeling a tight and sodden—

"That was badass!" Noah yelled. "Did you see that?"

And *poof* went the fantasy.

"Oh, yeah—wow." I faked my astonishment. My steamy little dream bubble popped and disappeared forever into an unknown abyss, never to be retrieved again. If I was cold before, I was heating up now. My decision was resolute. Abandoning my devious thoughts, I turned my focus to the TV and tried to pay attention. It would have sucked if he asked me about the film afterwards and all I would have been able to say was "My favorite part? Um... all of it?"

Lame, Aria. Very lame.

CHAPTER NINE
SLOW SEDUCTION

Noah always enjoyed movie nights. He was halfway into the movie when he noticed his daughter had gone quiet. Leaning forward, he carefully peered down at her angelic face, smiling at her beautiful features. She had fallen asleep. Reaching for the TV remote, he switched off the television and gently scooped her in his arms to carry her to bed. Before he could stand, he noticed Aria staring up at him with her sleepy blue eyes. Her gaze, he thought; that's all it took to get him in his feelings. He was nervous and couldn't understand why.

"Hey, angel," he said in a soothing voice. "Close your eyes."

"What time is it?" she mumbled.

"A little past ten."

"I should call Mom."

"Don't worry about her. I'll send her a text."

"I don't want to go home. I want to stay here with you." She was vulnerable in her sleepy state, confessing truths like an honest drunk. The only person who had intoxicated her was Noah. He smiled warmly and held her, easing back against the sofa.

Curling up in his lap, Aria snaked her arms over his shoulders and rested her head in the crook of his neck.

Noah froze. He didn't know what to do. He had planned on taking her to bed so she could lie down comfortably, but he didn't want to get up. Deep down, he enjoyed holding her.

Ignoring his need for contact, he chose her comfort over his own and carried her to bed. The bedroom was large and luxurious. Noah laid her down on the mattress and turned on the bedside lamp. He stood for a moment and stared at her, admiring her youthful beauty as she slept. Her dark, silky hair was sprawled out over a gold pillow. A cluster of cushions rested against the mahogany headboard. Aria's small frame looked even tinier in that bed.

Turning to leave, Noah paused when she muttered, "Don't go. Please don't leave me."

He looked back at his frightened daughter and studied her worried face. She looked so defenseless.

Why is she afraid? He wondered.

How many times had she woken up from a bad dream in the dark without him being there to comfort her? Noah asked himself. His absence in her life truly hurt him.

Her eyes betrayed an inner fear, and he realized right then that she needed him. Abandonment was the last thing he wanted her to feel again as he sauntered back to bed and sat on the edge of the mattress.

"I'm here, beautiful." Noah offered a comforting smile, brushing the hair out of her face. "I think all that shopping tired you out, huh?"

She stared at him with eyes half open as she nodded and pulled his arm to make him lie down. Noah Hunter wasn't a man who would submit to anyone, including his wife. There were many occasions when Vanessa demanded his time and affection, but giving it had to be on *his* terms and at *his* convenience. He was an alpha male, and there was never a time in his life where he relinquished control over himself to a woman.

At that moment, however, he realized Aria had the power to strengthen or destroy him. He would go to the ends of the earth to make her happy, even if she would ruin him along the way. What if his love wasn't enough? What if she wouldn't be satisfied with all that he would lay at her feet? What if she secretly desired revenge and would never love him? There were so many "what ifs." It made him crazy. Noah wasn't used to that kind of vulnerability. He was a man of control, yet with his daughter, he couldn't control her thoughts and feelings. *She* controlled *him*. This realization settled in his mind as he lay next to her.

"Thank you," Aria whispered, moving his arm and curling into his chest.

Noah turned on his side and looked at her. She was like a beautiful blue-eyed kitten. He had to smile. She melted him.

"Are you okay?"

"Mhm," Aria replied, shutting her eyes.

She captivated him, even in her peaceful state. His fascination with her had stunned him. He did not know how he could have contributed to creating such a beautiful human being. She was a part of him, and it filled him with pride.

Caressing her face, Noah brushed her hair back in a soothing motion. She was his precious gift. He had been too young for fatherhood when she was born, but now he thanked whatever powers above for bringing her back to him. He knew he could never let her go. Aria could make him fall to his knees and beg if that's what it took to get her to stay. He realized his daughter would be the only woman in his life who would make him feel so desperate. The only one who could raise him up, or obliterate his pride, and crush him. It scared him to death.

He lay there with her for the longest while before remembering to contact her mother. Quietly, he slipped out of bed and left the bedroom; his footsteps fell silently behind him as he made his way to the living room. Grabbing his cellphone, Noah scrolled down to Natalie's number, and hesitated.

Hopefully she won't bite my head off. He sighed and hit the dial button. Expecting his ex to pick up, it surprised him when a man's voice answered the phone.

"Hello?"

Noah was silent. He glanced at the number on the screen and realized he had dialed Natalie's landline by mistake. Cursing under his breath, he turned toward the windows and braced himself.

"*Hellooo?*" That same voice shouted into the phone, sounding more agitated.

He knew exactly to whom he was speaking with on the other end. He just didn't want Aria to be present when he had this conversation with him.

"Is this Robert?"

"Yeah, who's calling?"

"Put Natalie on the phone," Noah demanded, failing to keep his voice down.

"Why? Who the hell are you and what do you want with my wife?"

Closing his eyes, he paced around the living room and quietly counted to ten, praying he wouldn't lose his temper. It was tempting to give the guy an earful, including a mouthful of broken teeth (once he got the satisfaction of actually punching him in the face).

"Listen, you ignorant fuck," he threatened. "Let me talk to Natalie right now, and I'll reconsider putting you in the hospital when I see your pathetic face."

"Who the fuck do you think you are calling at this hour and making threats? You piece of shit!"

Noah thrust his fingers through his hair in frustration. He could hear Natalie in the background, struggling to take the phone out of her husband's hand. He knew he could hang up and call her cellphone, but he was too prideful to back down from that coward.

"Noah?" Natalie spoke into the phone.

"Took you long enough." He was dying to smoke a cigarette, even though he had promised Vanessa he would quit.

"When are you bringing Aria home? You said after dinner. Do know what time it is now? It's late!"

"Calm down, Natty. She's with me, not some hormonal teenaged boy who's gonna get her drunk and take advantage of her."

"Sounds like a similar experience I'd encountered at sixteen."

"What the hell are you implying? I didn't date rape you. You were a shameless nympho!"

"How dare you talk to me that way!" Natalie cried out while her husband shouted profanities at him.

"Get that asshole on a leash—and don't forget the muzzle." Noah rested his palm against the wall and looked out the window. He couldn't ignore that nagging urge to smoke. It was how he normally dealt with stress.

"Bring her home, Noah. *Now.*"

"She fell asleep. We're at my hotel, and I don't want to wake her."

"Aria has school tomorrow—all her things are at home."

"She brought her book bag with her before we left her school, and I took her shopping, so she can get dressed from here. I'll drive her in the morning."

"Why are you being so difficult?" Natalie yelled. "You've won already! Let me spend time with my daughter before you take her from me by force!"

"No. *You* are the one who's being difficult. And for the past seventeen years, you've been unfair to me *and* to Aria!" His hand trembled with the rage metamorphosing within him.

"Stop blaming me for your failures, Noah! You're not the victim in all this—our daughter is!"

He took a moment to cool his temper before he smashed something. The last thing he wanted was to injure his fist and terrorize Aria. Noah loved his daughter, but there was a lot of animosity between him and his ex. The split had not been amicable.

"She's staying over tonight," he declared. "End of discussion, Nat. You can have her tomorrow. I swear on her life, if I see so much as a scratch on her, I will put your husband in a coma, and chances are he won't ever wake up."

"Save your threats."

He was about to retort with heavier ammunition when he heard the dial tone. She had hung up. It was clear who had won this battle. If Aria hadn't been around, he would have destroyed everything that came in his line of sight like he used to do. Noah was raging inside and had no way of relieving himself of that feeling. Surrendering to temptation, he grabbed his pack of smokes from his trench coat and stepped outside onto the balcony, not bothering to put on a jacket. He stood in the cool night air and opened the ten deck. He had written an inscription inside of the box with a black pen:

I have officially quit smoking.
This is my last full deck, and also a reminder to never touch a cancer stick again.
01-01-2012 — 12AM
N.M.H.

He had remained nicotine free for the past eleven months, and all that hard work and commitment was about to be thrown away in ten quick seconds.

Just light up and take a drag already.

"Noah?"

Panicking, he shoved the cigarettes in his front pocket and turned around. Aria was leaning against the door frame.

"Hey, why did you wake up?" He suddenly felt like an adolescent boy who had got caught doing something he shouldn't have been doing.

"I thought I heard voices."

Noah silently cursed himself. He knew he had most likely disrupted her sleep. Leaning against the railing, he folded his arms in his chest.

"What are you doing out here?"

"I was looking at the view."

"Oh." She stepped on the cold concrete and walked toward him, rubbing her arms.

"You should get inside. It's freezing out here." He watched her face and wondered if she would notice the outlined box he had stealthily stashed away in his pocket.

"I missed you," Aria wrapped her arms around his waist.

Noah hadn't expected her to be this affectionate so soon, but he didn't mind. He held her closely, shielding her from the frost of the night. The wind danced through her hair, whipping it around her face. He tightened his arms around her to keep her warm.

"Sweetheart, you're shivering," Noah murmured in her ear.

"I'm surprised you're not."

"I'm a man."

"Exactly. You're a man, not a bear."

He chuckled at her comment and led her back inside, shutting the sliding screen door behind them. When he turned around, Aria gasped. She was standing by the coffee table with her phone in her hand.

"What's wrong?"

"It's almost midnight. Mom and Rob are gonna flip!"

Walking toward her, he calmly looked into her eyes and said, "Relax. I called your mom and told her you were tired. You're staying the night with me. She's cool with it."

"That's strange…" Aria arched a brow.

"How so?"

"Because that's so not typical Mom behavior."

"Well, maybe you should just trust in your father's charismatic ways with women." He flashed a sly grin.

More like threatening *ways,* Noah thought. He was not to be trifled with. Nobody wanted to be on Noah Hunter's bad side. He took retributive justice to another level.

"You can sleep on the bed," he said. "I'll crash out here on the sofa."

Aria frowned. "Can you please lie down with me for a bit until I fall asleep?"

He seemed to hesitate, but eventually agreed.

Heading back to the bedroom, he teased her and said, "By the way, you snore really loud in your sleep."

"I do not!" She looked mortified.

"Do too…" He laughed, gently nudging himself against her arm.

"Do not!"

"How do you know? Do you listen to yourself when you sleep? You were snoring so loud, I had to shut off the movie because I couldn't concentrate."

Her laughter suddenly faded. She had taken the joke too seriously. Noah could see it all over her sullen face, as if he had sucked all the life out of her eyes.

Shit, maybe it's too soon to joke with her like this. He wanted to make it right, and fast.

"Aria, I was just kidding."

Her expression remained frozen, and then she tackled him so hard he collapsed onto the bed.

"You are *so* mean! Don't joke around with me like that!"

"I'm sorry, it was too tempting." His laughter didn't end as she mounted him and playfully slapped his chest.

"Quit laughing at me!" She giggled when he grabbed her waist and rolled on top of her, pinning her wrists above her head like a lion, challenging his disobedient lioness. He loved expressing his dominance. It made him feel powerful.

Aria stared up at him, lost in the intensity of his eyes. Noah didn't know who was drowning first. Aria's eyes were mesmerizing, yet bewitching. She could beguile any man with just a glance, and she didn't even know it. But Noah did.

"Do you surrender?" He smiled wickedly and tightened his grip.

"Never!" She laughed.

Leaning into her ear, he laced his voice with seduction and murmured, "I was joking. No need to get violent."

"Maybe I like violent."

"Maybe it's time to get changed and go to sleep. Tomorrow is a school day, Missy."

"*Maybe* you should get off me first." She smirked.

"Good point." Noah released her wrists and hoisted his weight off her.

CHAPTER TEN
NOAH

Rummaging through my closet, I finally found a shirt for Aria to wear, knowing it would be too big on her. It's not like I owned anything for a small frame. Her chest was well endowed, but she was tiny, standing next to a bulky guy like me.

"I can give you a pair of my shorts and a T-shirt, since we didn't exactly buy you nighttime attire."

"Yeah, that's fine."

With luck, I found my Harvard shirt and a pair of navy blue shorts, tossing them over to her. It had a pull string, so she could tighten it around her skinny waist. "You'll probably disappear in my clothing, but at least you'll sleep comfortably."

"Thanks." She inspected the clothes and looked at me. "You went to Harvard?"

"Yeah, it's where I graduated from law school."

"That's awesome."

"You could go to Harvard too, you know. Have you thought about applying there?"

"My grades are good, but I doubt I'd get in."

"Why not?"

She shrugged. "I'm still kind of lost. I have no idea what program I want to get in to."

"I can help you. We'll figure it out together. On the upside, you won't have to worry about tuition or any other financial challenges. I've got you covered."

I loved her smile. It was adorably beautiful. For someone who carried a world of sadness inside, her smile seemed to show otherwise, like the sun shining light in the dark.

Grabbing a pair of slacks, I stepped into the bathroom to change and brush my teeth. Today had been interesting. I still wanted to beat that son of a bitch before I left the city. It felt like top priority on my bucket list. I couldn't wait for the moment to deliver my fist to his mouth. But I had to be patient for the time being. Besides, how could I stay angry when Aria was around? She influenced my emotions like no other and appeared to be the magical cure for my nicotine cravings. I'd been so close to lighting up tonight. In some ways, I was glad she interrupted my brief love affair with cigarettes.

Staring at my reflection in the mirror, I didn't want to walk out of the bathroom while she was indecent. As a man, I took care of myself; skin, body, and overall appearance. Fitness was important to me; it went hand in hand with mental health. Peering closer to the mirror, I noticed a couple of thin, stretched lines fading near the corner of my eyes. The thought of aging disturbed me. Dorian Gray Syndrome perhaps? Blinking, I realized my paranoia was getting the best of me.

It's all in my mind.

Sighing heavily, I opened the medicine cabinet and grabbed the tube of toothpaste. I knew I looked young for my age, but getting older gave me anxiety. Aging was something I dreaded. Believe it or not, there *are* men out there who don't like getting old just as much as women don't. We live in a superficial society, surrounded by superficial people. If you go to a job interview with all the right credentials but look like an unattractive slob, they're going to discriminate against you and hire the guy who's got only some of the expected qualifications because he looks like a million bucks and has charisma. It doesn't matter if you're a man or a woman. If you're intelligent and you look good, chances are you'll go further in life compared to the average Joe and plain Jane. That's just how society is. Don't crucify me for it. I didn't write the rules.

Grabbing the dental floss, I cleaned my teeth before stepping out of the bathroom. I was caught off guard when I saw Aria, standing a few feet away from me. She had changed into my clothes... *one* item only.

"Um, your shorts are way too big and there's no pull string."

Strange, I thought there had been.

Struggling to respond, I seemed to have lost my voice. It was hard not to stare at her legs, but I didn't want to make her uncomfortable, so I forced my gaze up toward her face.

"Don't worry about it," I said. "You're getting under the covers, anyway." I walked past her, trying not to look back. My T-shirt was oversized for her, but it wasn't long enough to cover her knees. If she'd raised her arms, I would have seen her undergarments.

O-kay... not going there.

"Do you have any mouthwash?"

"Yeah, it's in the cabinet underneath the sink."

I felt relieved when she disappeared into the bathroom. But it didn't take long for her to return. Like a caring father, I had already pulled back the covers so she could get under them and let me tuck her in.

"You must be exhausted," I said. "Come get in bed."

Now it was safe to lie down beside her, though I didn't get under the blanket. I propped a pillow behind me and reclined into it. Adding to my annoyance, I kept shifting around until I got comfortable. When I twisted my body toward her, I noticed she had pulled the covers down a bit, resting on her waist.

Thank God.

All right, I admit it—legs were my weakness. I loved every part of a woman's body, but there was something about a nice pair of toned legs that made me so...

"Noah?"

I tuned out my thoughts and looked at her. "Yes, sweetheart?"

"Thank you for today. You know—for everything."

It amazed me how she appreciated everything I did for her, even the little things, probably because she had been so deprived of materialistic luxuries growing up. In some ways, I could never forgive my mother for playing God with my life. But I knew I couldn't place all the blame on her, or on Natalie.

"Aria, I love spoiling you. Don't think for a second that today was your last. You have many more shopping sprees to come."

Her eyes lit up as she smiled and moved in closer, hugging my body. The smell of her strawberry vanilla shampoo enticed my senses. Gliding my fingers through her glossy hair, I kissed her on the head.

"Close your eyes, angel. You need your sleep."

"You feel so warm." She purred, resting on my chest. "Can you tell me a story?"

"Aren't you a little too old for that?" I chuckled. Her laughter made me melt, especially when she looked up at me with those baby blues.

"You said you want to make up for lost time. Well, here's your chance. I want to hear my first bedtime story."

"Aria, I'm horrible at storytelling."

A child was more capable, honestly.

"You're gonna need practice if you and Vanessa are planning to have kids."

That was true. Damn it.

"What do you think storybooks are for?"

"Oh, come on, please... Daddy?"

Daddy? Wow, that felt strange to hear. She was breaking down my tough-guy exterior, and I couldn't say no. Breathing out, I thought for a moment.

Okay, what the hell, how bad could it be? Hopefully, my story would bore her to sleep.

I cuddled her as she snuggled up closer. "Once upon a time in a faraway land..."

How original.

"... a beautiful princess was born into the world. Her name was Aria."

Her cute laughter made me smile again, and it was distracting me from continuing, but I went on. "She was the most gorgeous little child, and it was a privilege for anyone who was lucky enough to look upon her angelic face." I played with her hair while improvising my narration. "The king was the youngest to rule the land. It devastated him when his princess was taken during the night, never to be seen again. He swore he would never rest until he found his daughter. And so, he searched far and wide, gathering his knights and forming a deadly army, invading every village to find his long-lost princess. He became notoriously known as Mad King Noah."

I babbled for over ten minutes, trying to piece together a make-believe story that was inspired by real-life events. And slowly but surely, she fell fast asleep. Kissing her head, I softly whispered in her hair, "After many battles fought and so much bloodshed, he finally found her. King Noah swore he would never let Princess Aria out of his sight again, because she was the only reason he lived. He existed for her. Without her, his life was meaningless."

Gently, I lay her head down on the cushion and got out of bed. Before leaving the room, I switched off the lamp and grabbed an extra pillow. Tomorrow would be a busy day for me, and I wasn't looking forward to it, especially since I knew I wouldn't be seeing my daughter in the evening.

₧₧

The room was unbearably hot, which made it hard to sleep. Pulling off my tank top, I threw it on the coffee table to let my skin breathe. I was resting on the sofa, and it took a while to find my comfy spot, but I eventually slept on my back, folding my hands behind my head. There were so many things going through my mind that sleep could not come sooner. I had this big case I was working on, and it was stressing me because it was going to litigation. Being a corporate lawyer had its pros and cons. I had never lost a client. Noah Hunter didn't lose. That word did not exist in my vocabulary.

I was worried about my wife, too. Vanessa was becoming addicted to cosmetic surgery. The year before, she had got two breast implant replacements, liposuction on her stomach and thighs, lip fillers, face fillers, a nose job, a BBL, and a brow lift. I'd had a huge fight with her about her addiction to collagen lip injections and Botox before coming to New York. I told her I didn't want to kiss fish lips for the rest of my life. The trout pout was extremely unattractive (but that's just *my* opinion). We argued back and forth about how she hated her lips, blah, blah… Long story short, I threatened to divorce her if she went through with it again (which I wouldn't really do, but I wanted to knock some sense into her). I felt like an asshole when she'd started crying. She said she always felt insecure about her appearance and just wanted to look perfect. Her definition of perfection differed from mine.

What the hell is wrong with women? I mean, they blame us guys for promoting all these painful beauty practices when they're the ones who insist on going under the knife. We're more than happy with their natural beauty—at least that's how I look at it. I preferred real over fake any day. I never forced my wife to change, nor did I ever suggest she get a pair of silicone tits. In fact, one reason I popped the question to Vanessa in the first place was because, out of all the women I was acquainted with, she was the most down-to-earth, genuine person.

Six months into our marriage, she started hanging out with all the wives of my partners at the firm, and I guess those middle-aged plastic Barbies distorted her outlook on beauty. The glamor of living a Hollywood life had rubbed off on her, and now I was living with a castmate from *Real Housewives of Beverly Hills* instead of the woman I'd married.

I tried not to upset myself with these thoughts as I grabbed my cellphone to set an alarm. When I looked up, Aria was standing right above me. My eyes had adjusted to the darkness, and I could see the terrified expression on her face.

"Hey, is everything okay?"

"I had a nightmare." She seemed to tremble.

Instinctively, I sat up, took her hand, and pulled her toward me. She curled up in my lap and started crying.

"Sweetheart, talk to me." I tried to console her as best I could while she covered her face with her hands.

"I'm sorry," she said.

"Don't hide your face. It's okay to cry." I gently removed her hands and wiped her tears away.

"I dreamed you were gone. You weren't there when I woke up. I tried to call your phone, but it was disconnected, and all your things were missing." She sounded like she was having a panic attack. It broke my heart to realize the extent of her fear.

"Aria, I haven't left. I promised you I would never leave. It was just a nightmare, angel. You don't have to be afraid. Look at me—look into my eyes."

She tilted her head up and met my gaze. "Do you love me?"

"More than I love anyone else."

"You promise?"

"I promise."

"Then prove it."

"I…"

She suddenly shifted her weight and mounted me. The gray Harvard shirt slid off her body within a blink of an eye. I watched in shock as she tossed it behind her.

Fuck… a red pushup bra.

"Aria, what are you—"

I couldn't finish my sentence because my hands had suddenly landed on her breasts, and I swear this didn't happen by my own free will. She *grabbed* my wrists and placed them there.

"I know you want me."

"Stop this! You're my daughter!" I pulled my hands away, but it was no use. Wrapping her arms around my shoulders, she moved her body closer, locking me in place.

"You don't love me?" There was a palpable pain in her eyes, and it made me feel so helpless because I wanted nothing more than to take that agony away. But how? What was she asking of me?

"I do, more than my life." My heart was beating so fast, it reminded me of my near-death experience when I almost overdosed ten years earlier.

"Then show me."

Desperately, I tried to shackle myself to a wall in my mind, but she was sitting right in front of me, almost naked. The animal within wanted to break free and ravage her. Her hands kept brushing up and down my chest before she leaned in and kissed my neck.

Instant arousal. I had a raging hard-on pressing against her panties—and believe me when I say that I wanted my blood to rush anywhere but *there*.

"*Mmm… Noah…*"

Good God, I needed to pause this transgressive scenario.

"Aria, stop! I said, *stop!*" I lost control of my temper as I roughly grabbed her shoulders and shoved her away. I meant to use a stern tone, borrowing a disciplinary tactic straight from the authoritarian parenting guide, but I wound up sounding like a raging, crazed maniac in dire need of anger management. And to make matters worse, I didn't quite know my strength, because I made her recoil from me. She rubbed the area where my hands were, with tears in her eyes. I felt like absolute shit.

"I… I'm sorry," I said. "I didn't mean to yell or hurt you."

"No, it's my mistake—of course you wouldn't want me." She got up and ran into the bedroom.

Before I could catch up to her, my daughter stormed back out with her jeans on, sliding her arms in the sleeves of her shirt. This was a moment of horror for me. Standing still, I watched her switch on the light and pull her coat out of the closet. All my fears and anxieties were coming to life. This was bad. Real bad. She was going to leave me.

"Where are you going?" I panicked, rushing toward her, and grabbing her wrist.

"I'm leaving. I can't stay here another minute."

"It's the middle of the night. I can't let you walk the streets at this hour!" I desperately tried to control my temper.

"Let go of me!" She yanked her arm away.

How is this happening? How? I had cried only twice in my life: once when I was little and my dog died, and the second time was when I had got so high and drunk that I wanted to kill myself because of the guilt I felt about abandoning my daughter. This was going to be the third time I would allow myself to lose it. She was leaving me.

"Aria—Aria, listen to me." I tried to reason with her, feeling embarrassed for breaking down.

"No. I'm done."

Stepping in front of the entrance door, I blocked her escape. She wouldn't look at me, but I could see the tears in her eyes.

"Move, Noah!"

"Look at me!" My voice was strained with emotion as I masked my hurt with anger.

Meeting my gaze, her mascara and eyeliner had run down her cheeks, and it shattered my heart a thousand times over. Painfully constricted in my boxer briefs, my adrenaline had spiked in overdrive as I tried to pull myself together. What a fucked-up combination.

"Take off your jacket," I demanded.

"No."

"Take it off."

"No! Why are you such a controlling asshole?"

"Why are you so fucking stubborn? Take it off!" I closed the gap between us, unzipped her coat, and pulled it off her body by force, watching it fall to the ground.

I didn't know what the hell was happening, but I could sense my self-control abandoning me. The beast within was breaking the shackles off the wall, and I was worried because soon there would be nothing left to hold me back from her.

"You're a fucking prick."

"Anything else?"

"Bastard."

"Wanna to add that?"

"Son of a bitch!"

"You done?"

"I hate you!"

Clenching my jaw, I searched her eyes. Her anger was a front. She was scared of me. I could see it and feel it. Good.

"You don't care about me! You just wanted to prove something to my mother, and you achieved it! Congratulations! Now you can fuck off back to California to your perfect life!" Aria was furious, but her anger didn't repel me. I was amused in a way. We had identical temperament. It felt like an instinct to pull her into my arms and convince her of how much I needed her. But I resisted.

"You don't love me!" she cried. "You never have! You only came back out of guilt—to ease your own conscience! If you ever gave a fuck, you would've taken me from this shit hole a long time ago!"

"That's enough."

"No! I'm far from done."

"I said, *enough!*" I yelled so loud, she jumped.

So much for staying calm.

Glaring at her, I controlled the anger in my voice and said, "You don't know half of what I feel for you. I don't think you ever will."

"Maybe you should fucking open up for once! Is it that hard?"

"I've been trying! Don't dismiss my efforts, Aria."

She scowled at me as I stared her down, causing her to retract. This was the most fucked up feeling I'd ever felt in my life: anger, pain, and arousal.

It was happening. My right wrist went free as the metal shackles fell to the ground. Now there was only the left side binding me, keeping me chained to the wall. I could feel my demon getting wilder, struggling to free itself from the prison in my mind.

"I hate you! I hate you, Noah!" She took another step back, and I matched her steps.

"The line between love and hate is very thin." With my chest exposed, I let her stab dagger after dagger deep into my heart because I was her father. I could survive it. But I still refused to cry in front of her.

"I want to go home. Take me home!" She stood her ground, refusing to give in.

Closing my eyes, I clenched my jaw and focused my strength, as the gatekeeper that protected my thoughts finally walked away from the door with the sign that read: DO NOT ENTER. He was aware of what was waiting for me on the other side, and he knew there was no point in protecting it anymore because I had gained a full knowledge of what was behind it.

Like an outsider, I watched myself breaking free, rubbing my wrists before walking through the forbidden threshold. There was nothing and no one left to restrain my demon now. Entering the blackest void, I was stunned by a blast of white light that nearly blinded me. My vision was blurred, but I regained focus and noticed a tall tree that had rooted itself on top of a clear, calm lake. The sky was champagne gold, splashed onto a pink canvas without a cloud in sight. From the distance, I noticed a few air bubbles, as a head emerged from the water… and then shoulders, arms… A feminine figure was walking out of the lake.

There she was, just as I knew she would be. I was staring right at angel eyes. She was wearing a white dress that was soaked, outlining her hourglass figure. The shape of her breasts and slender thighs were visible underneath the wet fabric. Aria stepped toward me, holding a golden apple in her right hand; it shimmered and sparkled magnificently in her palm. She smiled and waited for me to accept her generous offering. Knowing I should resist, I wasted no time and bit into it, which triggered another blast of white light. And just like that, I was back in reality. Time had passed so slowly in my fantasy dimension.

"Take off your shirt."

"What?" Aria gave me a look of confusion, placing one foot behind her.

"Take it off—everything—*now*," I demanded, moving closer like a maddened, hungry wolf. But she didn't move. "Have I not made myself clear?" I reached for the buttons of her jeans and unfastened them, unzipping her fly and pulling her pants down aggressively. I was more beast than man at the moment.

Her obedience pleased me as she pulled off her shirt and stepped out of her jeans.

"You win, Aria." I set my conscience on fire, lifted her over my shoulder, and walked into the bedroom. She gasped as I threw her down on the bed and effortlessly ripped her panties off.

Fuck, she's waxed. That can only mean…

"You little liar—you said you're a virgin."

"I am!"

"Well, I guess I'm about to find out."

"Daddy, please—"

"What did you just call me?" I slit my eyes at her. "Daddies don't fuck their daughters, Aria. If you want me as your lover, then say my name," I commanded. "Say my fucking name!"

I was power tripping.

"Noah, please…" she weakly uttered.

Knowing another man had been inside her was making me crazy. I needed to claim her—*all* of her. Quickly disrobing, I wasted no time and parted her legs, leaning into her sweet spot. I needed release.

Breathing heavily, she looked up at me with those innocent eyes. No, they weren't innocent—far from it. I had to teach her a lesson… one she would never forget. She seemed to read my mind as she spread her thighs while I grabbed my cock and shoved it inside with one forceful thrust. Skipping foreplay, I went straight to penetration because the wolf within desired it. She screamed as soon as I buried myself in her. And that's when the crushing reality hit me hard. She wasn't lying. I had trespassed forbidden territory and ripped through that curtain of flesh that separated a girl from a woman. Her chastity stolen. I had carelessly destroyed it. My body was quivering in so much pleasure that I could hardly breathe.

"*Fuck me*—you're so tight…" I panted, slowly stretching her vulnerable opening. It was too late to stop and turn back. I needed to take her.

"Noah, it hurts," Aria whimpered, tears filling her eyes.

My inner wolf backed away, satisfied with his conquest as the man emerged from behind him, taking control of the beast. I lowered my lips and tenderly kissed her face while I gently slipped in and out of her tight, slick entrance. She locked her arms around my neck, pressing her soft lips against mine; they felt so familiar, making me desire her more. Parting her sensuous mouth, she invited my tongue inside as I drank her soul in a heated kiss.

"Don't you... [*kiss*]... dare... [*kiss*]...leave me... [*kiss*]... Aria." I kissed her with unrelenting passion, biting and tugging on her lower lip before devouring her with my powerful thrusts. If this was a sin, then we were sinking in it like quicksand.

Holding my face, she seductively stared into my eyes. I was on the verge of exploding and claiming her.

"Harder..."

"What?"

"Fuck me harder," she breathed.

That magic word was all it took to unleash my darkest half from its cage; he was more than willing to satisfy her forbidden request. Her cries of pain and pleasure echoed around me as I filled her to the hilt, thrusting harder and faster, slipping into hedonistic euphoria. It was the most erotic pleasure I had ever felt in my life. She was going to be an addiction that I wouldn't be able to kick. The rushing high I felt rivaled any drug-induced high I had ever experienced in the past. There was no way to rehabilitate myself after this. I would only want more, like a junkie addicted to methamphetamine. She was going to be the death of me.

Her shallow breaths felt hot against my skin as she dug her nails in my back and rocked her hips into me. I hid my face in the crook of her neck, groaning in pleasure and biting on her shoulder.

"Please don't leave me, Noah."

"Never." I looked into her eyes. "Never again, baby."

"You feel so good inside me." Aria moaned. "Don't stop."

"Are you on the pill?"

Fuck, I was close.

"No."

"I need to pull out."

"Not yet…"

"If I don't, I'll get you—"

"I don't care."

Fuck-fuck-fuck!

I was ready to flood her, leaving the evidence of my passion pouring down her pretty little…

"You belong in me."

She read my mind.

"What are you doing to me?" I pulled back and stared at her.

Her cheeks were flushed, and there was perspiration around her forehead. She smirked and wrapped her arms around my neck, pulling me closer and licking my lips. I caught the tip of her tongue and sucked it back before she could tease me. Our mouths moved in unison while I supported my weight above her, kissing her with no restraint. This was wrong. It was so wrong, but it felt *so good*. It felt so right.

"Tell me you love me, Noah."

"I do," I said between needy kisses. "I fucking do, so much." Picking up my rhythm, I ignored all the risks.

Her pleasurable cries never stopped as I worked toward release. And just as I was about to come, I heard my cellphone ring. Ignoring it seemed impossible; it sounded like it was ringing next to my ear.

What the fuck?

"Oh God, Noah…" Aria softly moaned, making me crazier. I was about to take her over the edge with me when the ringing started again.

"Do you hear that?"

"Hear what?"

"The ringing."

"I don't hear nothing," she said as I slowed down.

Something kept vibrating on the nightstand. Expecting to find my cellphone, it wasn't there when I turned my head.

୧୫

Suddenly, my eyes snapped open, and I found myself fully clothed, sleeping next to my daughter in bed, spooning with her. She was still under the covers while I lay over them. Half asleep and rock hard, I reached back to grab my cellphone. It was almost four in the morning. My buddy, Andy, had called me—most likely drunk off his ass. He typically called or drunk texted in the middle of the night. He led a "live fast, die young" sort of lifestyle. When I checked my text messages, my suspicions were confirmed. I couldn't make sense at all of what he was trying to say. I always joked with him and told him that a monkey could text better than him while intoxicated.

Feeling thankful to have woken up, I crept out of bed and made my way toward the bathroom. My mind was all over the place. I felt sick to my stomach, as an intense feeling of guilt washed over me. What kind of father was I, dreaming about sex with my daughter? And it wasn't just any kind of sex—I was rough with her. I'd fucked her in my dreams and had woken up fully aroused, still thinking about those images that shouldn't have been there. It was shameful, disgusting.

Aria's feral moans echoed in my consciousness as I stood in front of the mirror and smacked myself in the head three times in a fit of rage. But self-inflicted punishment didn't make the feelings disappear. Turning on the tap, I washed my face with cold water, refusing to jerk off because my conscience was marred with guilt.

When I calmed down, I exited the bathroom and left Aria to sleep in the bed without me. I must have fallen asleep while telling her that story. Why I even dreamed about having sex with her was beyond me.

Lying on the sofa, I felt an overwhelming sense of relief. There was no explanation why my dream was so graphic and wrong, but I was thankful to God himself (whom I had a hard time believing in) that it was only a dream. No, not a dream, a *nightmare*—a sick, twisted nightmare that still had me standing at attention, which only added to my disturbed state.

What the fuck is wrong with me? I asked myself.

If this happened one more time, I was calling my shrink. There was no way I would ever have sex with my daughter. I'd rather be castrated, have my arms sawed off, and blinded with battery acid. She was my little girl—all right, my almost *adult* daughter. Despite that, I don't know how I subconsciously viewed her as a sex object. Perhaps this was God's way of punishing me for turning my back on Him. Maybe I needed a church intervention to become a born-again Christian.

No you don't. Just give in. True love liberates…

Closing my eyes, I tried to forget the sensation of being inside of her… how good it felt.

Fuck it. I was going to Hell.

CHAPTER ELEVEN
ARIA

It was a Monday evening, and I was in the kitchen with my mother while she prepared a chicken casserole for dinner. School had been excruciatingly boring. I was a little disappointed to come back to our shabby old apartment after having spent the night at Noah's lavish hotel room last Thursday.

"You're joking, right?" I said in shock. "Do you understand what I just asked you?"

"Yes, Aria, I understand. I think it'll be good for you if you live with your father for the rest of the year."

"Good riddance!" my stepdad yelled from the living room, glued to the TV, per usual, with a beer in hand.

I ignored his snotty comment and handed the black pepper shaker to my mom.

"Don't listen to him," she said. "He's just teasing you."

Right. I knew Rob was ecstatic about me leaving. Personally, I couldn't wait to leave New York. I wouldn't miss him, and I didn't think my siblings would feel my absence, since they had this special bond that had always excluded me. I guess it was a twin thing that I could never be a part of. Mom, Jade, and Ally were the only people I would miss. It kind of sucked switching schools during senior year, but I couldn't pass up this opportunity. The semester was almost over, which meant my transition would be easier. I wanted to be close to Noah. I wanted to know him and be a part of his life. He and I were bonding crazy fast. I couldn't turn my back on that.

⚭

Dinner was a total drag. It was hard to take my mind off Noah. I kept hoping he would text me, but he didn't. I guess he was busy. He hadn't called or texted the whole day. Was he mad at me? Did he have second thoughts about inviting me to come live with him? My all-consuming thoughts thrust me into a panic and made me lose my appetite.

"May I be excused?"

"No, sit down and eat your damn meal," Rob grumbled, chewing on his casserole.

"But I feel sick—I can't finish the rest."

My stepdad pounded his fist on the table so hard that the plates and utensils bounced and clattered. I wasn't sure why I triggered him so much.

"Eat your damn food! What are you teaching your younger sister? Goddamn anorexic…"

"I'm not anorexic!" I stood up, my hands shaking from anger. "And even if I was, who the fuck are you to judge? It's not like you would help me."

"Watch your fucking language!"

"Says the man who cusses back."

"Aria, sit down." Mom intervened. "Robert, please. It's been a rough day."

"You need to discipline her better, Natalie! She's *your* daughter!"

"*My* daughter? She's *our* daughter!"

"Not anymore, since that son of a gun has claimed his bastard child!"

They argued back and forth while I stood there, catatonic.

"You're hurting her feelings!" Mom tried to defend me.

"And she's been hurting my damn wallet for years!"

That was it—I couldn't take anymore. It was fight or flight. Seething inside, I grabbed a plate full of steaming mashed potatoes and stuffed it in his face.

Take that, *you jerk!*

"Aria!" My mother looked mortified, while the twins giggled at the comedy-classic scene I just re-enacted. Larry, Curly, and Moe would have been proud. A cold pie in the face would have been a kinder gesture, but he didn't deserve that.

"You—fucking—bitch! I'm gonna whip you for this!"

I dashed away from his clutches and sprinted down the hallway to my bedroom, slamming the door shut and locking it. My stepdad's heavy footsteps pounded louder while he cussed me out, making me panic. I knew that lock wouldn't hold. Rob was like a huge, angry bull whenever he saw red.

Pushing my dresser against the door, I tried to obstruct him. Seconds later, he started pounding his body into the barricade that divided the predator from prey. "Let me in, *now!*"

With trembling hands, I pulled out my phone from my pocket and sent Noah a text:

Can u plz come and get me? Im @ home. Rob has gone psycho!

My stepdad kept slamming his body against the door, nearly breaking it down while my dresser rocked back and forth. I was scared. I knew if he got in, he would take out his belt, hold me down, and flog me until I'd turn black and blue. He had done this to me many times, and my mother never left him.

"Robert, stop! Stop this now!"

"That fucking whore nearly burned my face off!"

"Please, just *stop!* Let me talk to her!"

Suddenly, Mom cried out in pain, which meant he had either shoved her away... or had struck her.

Please, please text me back, was all I could think as I stood there, shaking in panic.

But a text never came through. It was hard to ask for help; I always struggled when I needed it. However, this was an SOS situation for me.

Swallowing my pride, I dialed his number, praying he'd pick up while Rob continued hurling insults at me.

"Hi, you've reached Noah Hunter. Please leave your name and number, and I'll get back to you as soon as possible."

Shit! I hung up. Why, why did I have to be so stupid and piss off my stepdad like that? It was too late for take-backs.

The lock kept rattling. Rob was trying to break it. I had to think fast. Glancing at my window, I opened it and looked down.

Oh God.

I had no idea how I was going to get my feet on the sidewalk, but there was enough space for me to walk along the ledge to get over to the unit next to us. My only chance was to tap on the window and pray that the neighbors would let me in so I could escape through their apartment.

Wearing my black leather jacket, I shoved my cell and some cash in my pocket, and stepped out on the ledge with my sneakers on. I had to be my own superhero. No one was coming to save me. It was tempting to look down, but I avoided it and inched my body against the brick surface, sidestepping with precision.

Okay, I can do this. I can be just as bad ass as "Nikita," femme fatale, I thought. *Arrive alive… arrive alive,* I kept repeating in my head as I got closer to my window of freedom.

It didn't take very long to reach the neighbor's unit. They were an elderly couple, and I rarely ever spoke to the old woman. But whenever she saw me in the hallway, we would always exchange a smile. I tapped on the glass, catching their attention. My neighbor said something to her husband, and then a younger-looking lady with short red hair appeared out of the corner of the living room. She warily opened the window in confusion.

"What are you doing out here?"

My face and fingertips were freezing as I crouched down and tried to explain. *Wheel of Fortune* was playing on their television. The woman seemed to hear my stepdad's outrageous cursing before she connected the dots and helped me inside. Now she understood why I was standing by the window like a convict on the run.

"Do you want us to call the police?"

"No, please don't." I didn't want to get my mom in trouble. I was so close to leaving this shithole. Tonight was my fault—I'd provoked Rob.

After apologizing to my neighbors, I ran out of their place and bolted down the hall. The elevator was taking forever to arrive, so I took a flight of endless stairs, until I reached a door at the bottom and pushed through it. A gust of wind hit my face as my feet hit the pavement.

Freedom, at last.

Racing away from my building, I stopped in an empty alleyway to catch my breath. Hopefully Rob wouldn't come after me, I thought.

My breath was visible in the night air as snowflakes floated down on my head. Pulling out my phone, I tried Noah again. It rang repeatedly and went straight to voice mail. I was about to leave a message when technology trolled me. My cellphone had shut off.

Cursing out loud, I started walking. There was no way of reaching him now—unless a payphone magically appeared. They had taken most of the payphones out in my neighborhood.

Stepping onto the street, I signaled a taxi with a clear destination in my head.

CHAPTER TWELVE
NOAH

My evening was horrible… just… bad. I'd had dinner with an old college buddy from law school, Kevin Ikeda. He was Japanese American—an upstanding guy who was hilarious and incredibly intellectual. He graduated at the top of our class at Harvard. I had errands to run earlier in the day when he'd called and offered me a job at his firm. I told him I was happy with my position in LA and was in NYC only for short-term personal business. He insisted we catch up over a celebratory dinner, since they had promoted him to senior partner. We had dined at a high-end restaurant, discussing one of his cases—consumer products liability. The conversation was mostly work related, and the food wasn't the best, but that wasn't what made my night so disastrous.

When I had got in my car after dinner, I realized my phone had been on silent. There were two missed calls from Aria, and my heart dropped as soon as I read her text message. My daughter was in a crisis, and I hadn't helped her. I had killed two hours like nothing was going on. I'd failed her when she needed me most. Calling her back was useless because her phone was off, which only worried me more, so I turned the ignition, pulled out of parking, and floored it to that prick's apartment.

ꙮ

No one answered when I buzzed in at the lobby, and Aria's phone was still off. I was about to call Natalie when someone left through the lobby door, giving me a chance to slip inside. Taking the elevator up, I rushed down the hall and heard the dysfunctional pair arguing so loudly that the neighbors should have called the cops. My daughter was all I could think about as I pounded my fist on the door.

There was momentary silence, and then it unlocked. Natalie looked like she had been crying. This was bad—really bad. I let myself inside and scanned the perimeter of the suite. It was a mess… laundry everywhere, dirty dishes. I noticed some children's toys scattered over the sofa and carpet in the living room, but the apartment was eerily quiet now, which made me think their kids weren't home.

"Where's Aria?"

Rob appeared from the kitchen and got in my face. "Who the fuck do you think you are, barging in uninvited?" He was a big guy, all right… as in all his weight was in his belly. The man had a beer gut the size of a nine-months'-pregnant woman.

"Where is my daughter?" I ignored the fuckface and frantically searched the room. There was a door at the end of the hall that looked demolished by a baseball bat.

"Noah!" Natalie called out. "Noah, she's gone!"

My world came crumbling down when I walked into Aria's vandalized bedroom. It was small… like the size of a mini walk-in closet. The one in my wife's home office was even bigger than this.

This is where my daughter's sleeping? A prison cell?

I felt fucking horrible.

Her books were all over the floor. I noticed various classics by Edgar Allan Poe, Charlotte Bronte, Jane Austen, and Dante Alighieri. Her laptop was smashed to pieces. What angered me most was when I read "STUPID CUNT" spray painted in black over the walls. That abusive asshole did this. The concrete evidence was enough for me to orchestrate exactly what took place earlier. I felt like a P.I., standing in a crime scene. All I needed was yellow tape and a forensics team. I would've made a shitty detective, though; I was incapable of keeping a level head.

Panicked, I leaned out the window, praying to God I wouldn't find my daughter's body lying dead on the ground. I was relieved to see only a half-filled dumpster below, though it wasn't enough to lower my simmering rage.

Tick. Tick...

"You motherfucking bastard!" Striding past Natalie, I targeted the coward who stood next to her. I would teach him a lesson he would never forget.

"Noah! No..."

Grabbing the SOB by the collar, I pulled him into the closest bedroom and dodged his punch before I swung with my right fist, smashing the bones in his face. I couldn't feel the pain; all I could feel was fury. Swinging again, I punched him in the nose. The attack stunned him and allowed me to strike another blow to his gut. He keeled over as I kicked him to the floor. I wasn't satisfied yet, far from it. Unleashing my inner psycho, I got on top of him and punched his face in alternating fists. My training in boxing and martial arts gave me an advantage. This guy couldn't throw a punch to save his life. It was easier for him to beat on a helpless female.

"You're gonna kill him!"

All I could see was black as Natalie tried to push me off. Rising to my feet, I circled the bastard like a vulture, taunting him. It took *a lot* to get me to explode. But when I did... it was scary.

"STOP!"

I couldn't. Rob's face had become unrecognizable, bleeding profusely from his mouth and nostrils.

"Who's a tough guy now, huh? You abusive fucker! This is the last time you ever see your wife and kids again!" I kicked him hard in the ribs in one direct blow before I repeatedly assaulted him.

"*Please, stop!*" Natalie cried hysterically.

"Get the fuck out of the room, Nat!" I was getting crazier by the second.

"I'm begging you to stop! I don't want the cops to show up!"

"Why? Does he have a record? Let me guess—assault and battery. You married a fucking criminal?"

Rob groaned in pain and clutched his ribs, coughing up blood on the cheap carpet. It was only then that I realized I was in their bedroom. A long brown belt caught my eye on the bed before I looked down at his trousers. It didn't take long to connect the dots. He had planned on using it as a torture weapon on my daughter (if he hadn't already). Whatever self-control I had escaped me, as I grabbed the belt, coiled it around his throat, and pulled his weight upwards. Sitting on the edge of the bed, I choked him from behind like the psycho I had become.

"Say hello to the Grim Reaper, asshole!" I tightened my grasp on the leather belt, pulling while he choked and tried to break free. Natalie was screaming and yanking my arm, but I wouldn't release him from my death grip.

"Dear God… *please!*" she begged. "Let him go! He can't breathe!"

Good.

"Slap him," I growled. "Slap him across the face!"

"What? No! Just let him go!"

"I said, *slap him* now or I kill him!" Squeezing my grip on the belt, I watched her face go pale with fear. She cried with pleading eyes, begging me to show some mercy, but I wouldn't show any. All I could feel was sadistic pleasure.

"I can't believe you would allow him to raise a hand to our daughter!"

"He didn't hit her! She ran away!"

"How can you defend this scumbag? Did you see her room?" I screamed at her. "Slap his fucking face!"

Finally, I had pressed the right button, giving her just enough of a push to surrender to my will. She slapped Rob across the face, screaming and crying at the same time. If she was doing this to keep him alive, it didn't matter to me. I was relishing the moment.

"Harder!" I tugged on the belt, taking gratification from his garbled breaths. "Now, tell him what a fucking failure of a father and husband he is! Say it!" I was livid, staring her down with murderous eyes.

"Noah, please…" Her mascara was runny, and her dirty blonde hair looked like a tousled mop on her head.

"Slap him and say it!" I yelled so loud, I nearly hurt my throat.

She eventually succumbed and slapped the lowlife across face, repeating whatever mantra I told her to recite like a submissive slave.

"You're a failure! You failed me! You failed us!"

I felt as if I had possessed her mind and she was finally giving that worthless prick the punishment of his life: humiliation. Feeling high with dominance, I was truly in my element—complete, unrestricted power and control. It was a rush.

"You had no right to hurt Aria, ever!" Natalie screamed. "You have no right to hurt me and hit me!"

Why am I not surprised?

Her confession only fed my rage more. I didn't like my ex, but violence against women was just plain wrong. Any man who raised his hand to a woman wasn't a man at all. The SOB continued to choke while I fastened the belt around his neck like a collar and dragged him across the floor out of their bedroom. Rob had turned beet red, bloodied from the beatings.

"Are you enjoying this, Robbie boy? Christmas has come early for you this year, and I'm here to deliver." I couldn't recognize my voice anymore. A twisted version of my former self had taken over—my darker half.

Desperately, he tried to free himself, but I wouldn't let him escape. I continued dragging his fat ass down the hall into Aria's bedroom.

"Okay, asshole… let's re-enact a scenario that happened in this room many times during my absence." I grinned wickedly, loosening the belt and unraveling it from around his throat.

Averting my gaze, Rob frantically gasped for breath. I kicked him to the ground and ripped his greasy under shirt in half.

Rrrrrrrip!

His back was now exposed, and I was ready to unleash my wrath on him. Curling the belt around my palm, I whipped the bastard, flogging him relentlessly as he cried out in pain. Every time he tried to get back up, I kicked him with a hard blow to the rib or spine. My adrenaline had cranked into overdrive. His painful groans were like music to my ears. I didn't want to stop. I felt like a maestro conducting a beautiful symphony of pain, and once I was done performing my masterpiece, I'd receive a standing ovation from a crowd full of women and children who had suffered domestic abuse.

"Don't you ever, *ever* lay your grubby hands on my daughter again, you sick fuck! I won't even give you the opportunity! If I find out you've laid a finger on your wife and kids, your ass is going behind bars. Do you hear me?" I flogged him until bloody welt marks appeared on his skin.

"*You're* the sick fuck!" he sputtered.

I had zoned out into my universe of carnage. I wanted to kill him.

"Noah! Stop this!" Natalie's trembling voice echoed in the background. "My kids have arrived home! Please don't do this in front them, I beg you!"

"Mommy… what's happening?"

"Go to your room, Terry!"

The voices kept fading in as I reluctantly dropped the belt. I was out of breath, pushing my raging demon back inside his padlocked cell. I had gone completely berserk.

"Get the hell out of our apartment!" she yelled.

There was no point in asking her where our daughter was—it was clear she didn't know. Abandoning the bludgeoned meat slab on the floor, I ignored the pain in my bleeding fists. I was angrier that my freshly laundered suit was all stained with blood and sweat.

"I'm pressing charges, you bastard!" Rob called after me.

"Do it. I dare you!"

That asshole had finally grown a pair now that I was a safe distance away. Typical coward.

I had no desire to go back and beat him again. My job here was done. His threats were meaningless. I had put him in his place; it sated my bloodlust. All I had to do now was find my daughter. Like a man on a mission, I left the apartment, cursing Natalie and Rob in my head.

CHAPTER THIRTEEN
ARIA

I made myself comfortable when I entered Noah's hotel suite. Unfortunately, the concierge hadn't recognized me when I'd walked into the lobby. Noah always introduced me as his daughter to people who were talking to him. The hotel manager had been present when we checked in, and Noah had briefly told him about how we'd reunited. The manager was a friendly middle-aged man who seemed happy for us. He'd given Noah his business card in case he ever needed anything. I was lucky he was there when I arrived at the hotel lobby this time. The other employees would not let me go up that easily. I had told the manager that my cellphone was dead and that I was trying to reach my dad. Immediately, he called Noah and left him a voice mail to let him know I was waiting for him at the hotel. He was also kind enough to give me a room key and escort me to Noah's suite.

Sitting on the sofa, I considered TV distraction while I waited for him, but I wasn't in the mood. I was still shaken up by everything that had happened earlier. Being in a safe environment made me feel grateful. I just needed to see him. I needed him to hold me and tell me I would never have to live with my mom and stepdad again. In the back of my mind, I was paranoid. All these what ifs kept swirling in my head.

☙❧

Almost an hour had passed since I'd entered Noah's suite, and I couldn't sit still. Growing impatient, I got up and paced near the window, praying he would walk in any minute. It seemed like a miracle when the front door unlocked. I was so relieved. There he was, in all his glory.

"Aria." He breathed my name, setting his briefcase on the floor. I said nothing and ran into his arms.

"I've been looking all over for you." Noah hugged me tightly. "I came back to the hotel as soon as I received the message from the manager." His body felt tense, but I didn't want to let go. I needed to feel his arms around me and breathe him in for as long as possible.

"I called you and sent you a text," I replied, "but you didn't respond, so I sort of… ran away." I buried my face in his chest.

"Why haven't you been answering your phone?" He held my shoulders and looked at me.

"My battery died."

I noticed the cuts and bruises when he dropped his hands.

"Oh my God… Noah, what happened?"

"Don't worry about it." He took off his trench coat and walked inside. There was blood on his shirt.

"Did you… get into a fight with Rob?"

His silence said it all.

"You beat him up, didn't you?"

"He had it coming," Noah muttered bitterly.

I grabbed his hands to inspect them, but he pulled away.

"I just need some ice and the swelling will go down."

"Um, no. You don't just need some ice; you need to clean those cuts first. Do you have a first aid kit?"

He studied my face, clenching his jaw before he answered, "Medicine cabinet in the bathroom."

"Let's get you patched up, then." I tugged his arm and led the way.

Noah took off his dark gray blazer and rolled up his white sleeves. A trip to the dry cleaners wouldn't have saved his clothing. He reached for his buttons when I stopped him.

"Here, let me. You're in enough pain." My heart skipped a beat as I unfastened the buttons… and quickly regretted it.

Holy muscles in my face!

I screamed like a lunatic fangirl in my head. His amazing body wasn't the only reason I was fangirling… he had my name tattooed on his chest.

"Well," Noah sighed. "I guess you found my ink."

He pulled his shirt back over his shoulders, revealing his flawless pectorals. A big black phoenix had spread its ashy wings above his heart, digging its talons into his skin. The tattoo artist had drawn some blood gushing out in red ink. It looked like the bird was trying to claw Noah's heart out. I couldn't hold back my tears when I saw my name inked in red capital letters on the breast of the legendary creature. The font was unique and beautiful.

"I got this when I was eighteen," Noah said. "You were always with me everywhere I went. I wanted to keep you closest to my heart, even though you were physically out of reach."

His words moved me in ways I never thought were possible. I wanted nothing more than to show him how much I loved and needed him. But first, I had to tend to his injuries. Calmly, I opened the first aid kit and sat on the counter while he stood across from me. The cuts around his knuckles were still bleeding as he rinsed it off under the tap. I was preparing to rub iodine on the wounds when he took the bottle from me.

"Hydrogen peroxide and iodine are safe," he started. "Rubbing alcohol makes it worse when the skin is broken. That's why doctors use iodine to clean an area before surgery. But when there's a cut, rubbing alcohol can be toxic to skin cells because they slow down healing. They're killing healthy cells. It stings because it's wiping out healthy tissue. The most effective way to clean a wound is to flush out the bacteria and debris with water."

I looked at him inquisitively. "Did you drop med school before you decided on a law career?"

"It's common sense, not rocket science." He chuckled.

"Well, I'll remember that next time." I matched his smile and put the bottle of iodine away.

Noah shook the water off his hands while I grabbed some gauze.

Nurse Aria to the rescue.

"Are these injuries caused by self-defense?"

"No." He exhaled and stared at his bandaged hand. "I instigated the fistfight. The damage done to your bedroom door was the first thing that caught my eye when I came looking for you. And when I walked in, I saw how he had demolished your room."

"It wouldn't be the first time."

Noah frowned. "I noticed you had moved your dresser to block off the doorway and… I lost it. I thought he hurt you, so I roughed him up badly."

"When you say *bad*, do you mean *hospitalized bad?*"

He met my gaze with a stoic stare. Those eyes were a health hazard to my heart.

"Probably," he answered wryly. "I don't regret it, though."

Noah seemed indifferent about the fiasco. Maybe in his mind it was an accomplishment, like a lifetime achievement:

Confront the stepdad: *Check*

Threaten him: *Check*

Beat the stepdad to a bloody pulp: *Check*

"I'm so sorry I didn't get to you sooner, Aria." He relaxed his tone, allowing the violent waves in his ocean eyes to settle into calm waters. "I should have been there."

I felt an overwhelming love for him. He was so protective of me.

"It's okay. It's not like you were expecting me to call you. I'm sure you want to know what really happened."

"Actually, no—and don't ask me what I did to him, either. Whatever you said or did, you don't deserve to be physically struck." The ocean went from calm to turbulent waves in a matter of seconds as I stared at him.

"I threw a plate of hot mashed potatoes in his face during dinner."

There was a brief silence, and then he threw his head back, laughing, which made me laugh as well.

"I won't even ask why." Noah snickered. "I'm sure he deserved it. We both taught that bastard a lesson."

Smiling, I finished bandaging his other hand. "I hate that you're hurt."

"Don't worry about it, baby. It doesn't even sting. I don't feel pain."

"That's impossible." I quirked a brow.

"I don't feel physical pain, just…" He paused. "A different kind of pain."

"I wish I could heal you."

"You do." He flashed a sad smile and caressed my cheek. "More than you'll ever know. But it's not your job to heal me. I'm the one who's done so much damage. I'm the reason you resent me so much."

"I don't resent you."

"You don't have to keep it from me, Aria. I know I messed up. I should have been there for you. It kills me you had to spend your life growing up with that no-good piece of…" He exhaled in frustration, as if to prevent a cursing tirade before he said, "I just feel so much regret."

For a moment, I tried to imagine this man raising me. But it didn't last long because I honestly couldn't envision it.

"I don't want you to go back there. Ever." Noah was dead serious.

The air shifted between us again as his eyes softened, warming me with his penetrating stare.

"But what about my things?"

"I don't care. I'll replace all of that with better stuff. We can leave as early as tomorrow."

"I can't just leave in between semesters."

"You'll be going to a private school. I'll get you organized. Don't worry."

I think that was his way of saying, money can buy you anything you want. *Almost.*

Hopping down from the counter, I hugged him.

"I'm sweaty."

"I don't care."

Every time I hugged Noah, all I could smell was aftershave, cologne, and body wash fused in one. He wrapped his arms around me, sliding his hand up the back of my shirt. My breath caught when he rubbed the dimpled area below my spine. Maybe it was by accident, but I only hugged him tighter. Being affectionate with each other felt so natural to us.

Exhaling, he kissed the side of my head and whispered, "You terrified me tonight."

"I'm sorry," I whispered back. "I didn't mean to."

"I don't know what I'd do if I ever lost you again, Aria."

The vulnerability in his voice brought me to tears. I blinked them away and withdrew. "You just got me back." I held his handsome face and stared up at him, losing all sense of time. "You won't lose me."

His pensive smile caught my attention as he caressed my cheek with his thumb and grazed it over my bottom lip. It was so erotic. I wanted to kiss him so badly, and I knew it was wrong. Ignoring it was impossible. An electrical energy was buzzing between us, like a magnetic field pulling us closer to each other. Or maybe it was all in my head? The way Noah stared at me made me feverish.

"I'm glad you came here," he said. "I was ready to call the cops."

My chest filled with love, sadness, and confusion while my body awakened to lust, desire, and arousal.

"I need to hold you." His deep voice made my tummy tighten as he led me into the bedroom. "Wait here, I'll be right back," he added.

Lying on the mattress, I tried to calm my nerves before he returned. The minutes passed, which concerned me. Hopping out of bed, I peered outside the bedroom door and found him drinking tiny vodka bottles near the minibar.

Is he getting drunk?

Maybe he was in serious pain and needed the liquor to relax, I concluded.

As he approached, I bounced back in bed, assuming the same lazy position. He didn't look intoxicated… yet. Secretly, I prayed he wouldn't cover that amazing body with a shirt. And fortunately, he didn't.

Noah sat on the edge of the bed and reclined on the mattress, resting his head on a pillow. I caught him off guard when I mounted him and leaned forward to kiss the tattoo on his chest. His skin felt cool against my warm lips. He breathed out deeply when I kissed him there. I was shamefully turned on, but I couldn't help it. I was attracted to him, and I couldn't hide it from myself. I kissed his phoenix tattoo like it was a lucky charm.

"I love you, Aria." Noah tucked back a strand of my hair behind my ear, staring into my eyes. My lips were burning. I needed him to touch me. I wanted him to kiss me.

"It's hard to believe you're my father."

"Why's that, sweetheart?" He frowned and sat up, resting his back against the pillow.

I couldn't form a sentence. All I could think about was the growing intimacy between us.

"Because you're young," I finally replied.

Noah grabbed my thighs and pulled me closer. It felt so good to feel his fingers floating through my hair.

"Hardly." He leaned forward and kissed my lower jaw. "I think you're talking about yourself." He grazed his lips across my crimson cheek, which only worsened my chronic blushing.

"I'm old enough."

Noah wrapped his arms around my waist and breathed me in, burying his face in my neck. I tried to slow my heart rate as he caressed my lower back. I didn't want him to stop.

"Not in my books, you're not." He smirked.

His eyes were seductively intense and alluring, yet dangerous like a strong ocean current pulling you into the deep end. Before you knew it, you'd drown. I beamed when he kissed my chin. No one had ever shown me affection like this. I wanted to kiss him, but I was too afraid to even attempt. Dragging my hands down his shoulders, I rubbed his chest as he shut his eyes and sighed while I traced his hard muscles.

Fathers and daughters were *not* supposed to touch each other this way, but I didn't care. It didn't bother me. In fact, I wanted more, so much more with Noah. He didn't feel like my father. He felt like a celebrity crush. I was caught off guard when he leaned in and kissed the center of my chest, right between my breasts. It wasn't like he kissed my skin—I was wearing a shirt—but still... it was hot.

"I love you so much." His bright blue eyes stared into mine, warming my body with his spellbinding gaze. My heart desperately wanted to say it back, but I was afraid to say it out loud. If there was such a thing as reincarnation, I was positive that someone as attractive as Noah would walk this earth only once every thousand years.

He pressed his forehead against my chest as I glided my arms over his shoulders, kneading his hair with my fingers. A sexy groan rumbled through his chest.

"Why do I feel this way about you?" he asked.

"What do you mean?"

Noah grabbed my hips and caressed them. "I wasn't expecting you to be so... perfect," he sighed. "You're perfect, Aria."

"No, I'm not. Really, I'm not."

Holding my face, he kissed my cheeks, then my forehead, nose, and chin. His lips felt warm and made my skin tingle. I felt silly for smiling so much.

"You have no idea how much power you possess over a man."

I want to possess you.

"I feel sorry for the boys at your school."

His comment flattered me. "I didn't expect to feel this way about you, either."

Noah's eyes sought mine for the longest while before he said, "Lie down. Let me hold you."

Shifting off his lap, I got comfortable and lay next to him. He moved in closer and spooned me, pressing his naked chest against my back. I trembled when his hand caressed my hip, traveling over my stomach, freeing a swarm of butterflies that fluttered inside me. Noah kissed my shoulder; I shivered when he brushed his hand up and down my midriff. My nipples pebbled beneath my shirt—it was embarrassing.

"So, tell me how you feel, exactly," he murmured in my ear, sending goose bumps down my arms.

I took a moment to think. Being in his arms like this was the closest thing to paradise, and I didn't want to be kicked out of there just yet.

"I feel something… between us."

Panic, anxiety, fear… all at once. He pulled me to his body and stroked my hip with a lazy hand. Shutting my eyes, I tried to breathe as he slid his hand up higher, resting his fingertips beneath my ribcage. There was a part of me that wanted to turn over and kiss him hard on the mouth, but I rolled on my back and stared up at him.

"I feel something too," Noah confessed. His eyes were heated, swirling with seduction as he rubbed my tummy. I couldn't deny the sexual attraction I felt toward him any longer. My desire for him to consume me was overriding my moral judgment.

"I'm the luckiest father in the world."

My heart sank when he said this, because for a sweet moment, I'd believed he felt what I felt. But I was wrong.

If only you'd move your hand up an inch more, then it would land directly on my…

Why was I thinking these things? My body craved his touch in places that made me ashamed. Did he desire me too? Was this his way of harmlessly trying to cuddle me? Maybe the alcohol was getting to his head. Or maybe the reason he downed all that liquor was so he could do this with me. No. I was pretty sure it was my sick mind making these conclusions.

"Noah…"

"Yes, baby?" His voice sounded so relaxed.

"Do you believe in love at first sight?"

My question made me shy as I turned away from him and snuggled his body, hoping he would spoon me again.

"I've never experienced love at first sight, though I can't say the same about the women who've come across me." He chuckled.

"That's cocky of you to say."

"To be honest, it's always been *lust* at first sight."

"What about when you met your wife?"

My jealousy was poking its ugly head out of the closet.

"I was attracted to Vanessa when I met her, but I wouldn't say it was love at first sight. I believe it takes time for love to grow between two people."

Was that what was growing between us: *love*? And if it was, what kind of love was it? How was he able to control my feelings so much with just one look?

"Why do you ask, Aria? Is there someone you're in love with?"

I shook my head.

"Come on, you can tell me. What's his name?"

Biting my lip, I released it and took a deep breath. "He's older than me." I imagined Noah knitting his brows together upon hearing this.

"How much older?"

He didn't sound too pleased.

"Um… about five years."

Okay, so I lied. Noah was sixteen years older than me, but I swear if you placed us side by side, you wouldn't notice a huge age gap.

"Where did you meet him?"

"It doesn't matter. It's just a dumb crush, anyway."

He kissed my shoulder and caressed my stomach.

"Sometimes even the smallest crush can be agonizing," he said. "When you're in love, your entire world suddenly revolves around that person. They're in your mind twenty-four/seven. And as euphoric as it is to be around them, it can be heartbreaking too when they don't return your feelings or have no clue how you feel about them.

"I'm not sure what your history is with this guy, but you're young, Aria. You should date boys your own age. I know I can't dictate to you to feel a certain way. In life, you may encounter moments where you feel a bond with a person who's completely wrong for you, but your heart can't help it."

I definitely couldn't help it.

"Can you tell me about him?"

"No, I'd rather forget about it."

Noah seemed reluctant to let it go. "I'm always here for you if you need to talk."

"Thank you," I murmured.

"Don't mention it. You need to get some sleep, though. You've got school tomorrow."

"Can you sleep next to me?" I turned around and looked at him. His face was inches away from mine.

"I don't think that's a good idea."

"Why?" I sulked as he sat up and got off the bed.

"*Because, Aria!*"

Whoa.

That angry outburst came out of left field. One minute he was sweet and affectionate, and the next minute he was explosive and mean.

"I'm gonna take a quick shower," he grimly said. "Get some rest. Goodnight." All the warmth had drained from his voice. Noah disappeared into the bathroom before I could say anything else. Tearing up, I sat there, feeling confused and rejected.

What just happened?

⚜

Lying on my side, I hugged a pillow and silently sobbed in the darkness. The city lights were visible from the window across from me. Suicide whispered in my mind, painting a horrifying image of me jumping off the balcony. I battled suicide ideation for much of my life, but I was still here. Telling Noah about it was out of the question; I was too ashamed, afraid he would judge me. I had already faced persecution from family members on Mom and Rob's side. People just loved to project their own bullshit onto me. I seemed to trigger that out of others.

Why is this happening? I depressingly thought, thinking of Noah. *Why can't I feel what I'm supposed to feel toward him?*

Self-inflicted torture, that's what it was. I played back the negative thoughts on repeat like a broken record. It was hard falling asleep when my mind was a mess, but at least I was physically comfortable. We should be grateful for the little things, right?

He had lent me his Harvard shirt and shorts the last time, but I didn't want to wear his clothes. It would have felt like I was wearing *him*, so I stripped down to my T-shirt and panties. Lying in bed, I shifted from gratitude to feeling sorry for myself. Noah's affectionate side made me feel so close to him. I needed physical contact. His warmth was just… out of this world. It hurt when he pushed me away. Loneliness was something I had adapted to. It was harder to cope after discovering what it felt like to be so close to someone. This was something I struggled with when Trevor left me.

Noah's shower was taking longer than he said it would. The faint sound of pressurized water hit the tiles, and my imagination wandered… his naked body under the water, his hands lathering his muscles with soap… shoulders, arms, chest, abs, leading to the mysterious length of his…

The bathroom door suddenly swung open, filling the room with white light. I raised myself up to look at him, noticing a white towel wrapped around his waist, showing off the attractive grooves of his Adonis belt. Water dripped down Noah's chest and stomach as a cloud of steam evaporated off his toned physique. How did he not have a modeling career? He looked unreal.

"I'm sorry, did I wake you?" he asked.

"No."

My curious eyes followed him across the room, watching him grab another towel to dry off. Noah started toward me, and I instantly turned away, rolling on the other side. I just didn't want to talk to him while I was still so upset.

He sighed and grabbed the extra pillow that laid beside me. "Sleep well, Aria."

Staying quiet, I stole a peek at him as he hovered near the dresser, taking some clothes before he switched off the bathroom light and walked out. I was alone again and frustrated. Maybe I was mad at myself for developing an emotional dependency on him. Feeling confused, I closed my eyes and tried to force my body to shut down and sleep, regardless of my new list of anxieties.

⋘⋙

Something pulled me out of my dreams when I felt the edge of the mattress sink down on one side. The covers were pulled back before a warm body moved in beside me, sliding a muscular arm around my waist. The familiar scent of body wash delighted my senses. I felt his chest against my back, making my heart speed up.

Noah.

I was disappointed when he withdrew. I guess he'd realized that I had nothing covering my waist down, except for a cute pair of lacy panties. He kissed my shoulder and placed a gentle hand on my hip.

"I'm sorry, angel," he whispered in my ear. "I can't fall asleep knowing I've upset you. It's been a stressful day for me. I shouldn't have got short-tempered with you."

His confession only brought on the waterworks even more. I sniffled and felt him reach over to wipe my tears away. I had no idea why I was crying, but I needed his comfort. Turning to face him, he held me in place.

"Don't—just let me hold you."

I obeyed his command and enjoyed the way he cuddled me. He seemed determined to keep his lower body from coming in contact with my curvy bottom.

"Close your eyes, beautiful."

My deepest desires would have to wait before they could come to life. The last thing I wanted was to anger him and make him leave again. There was a huge hole in my heart when Noah was far from me, and it would immediately fill up when he was close. Any kind of affection was better than none. It was all I could think about as I closed my eyes and surrendered to sleep.

⋙⋘

For the first night in a long time, I rested well. Sleeping beside somebody was something new to me. I wasn't allowed to stay over at Trevor's, and the same rule applied to him—apart from that one time we broke the rules and got caught. I did my best to erase the memory and focused on Noah.

His breathing was shallow, but he didn't snore. My stepdad snored horrendously loudly. It surprised me the neighbors didn't complain.

Reaching for my phone, I glanced at the time; it was almost six in the morning. I still had half an hour before I had to get up, shower, and get ready for school. It wasn't my body clock that woke me earlier than expected, nor the city traffic below. Something hard was poking and grinding against me. I couldn't move. Noah had tightly locked me in his arms. The disturbing part was that I didn't even want to get up.

How did we end up like this?

It didn't matter. He was in a deep sleep, and I didn't want to move or breathe in a different rhythm. I just wanted to enjoy this moment.

Strap me in a straitjacket and ship me off to the psych ward!

Not really. I did *not* want that to happen. But I felt crazy for being attracted to Noah.

He mumbled in his sleep, grinding harder into me, making me shiver when he rubbed my tummy and slid his hand up my breast… grabbing it.

Oh. My. God.

My pulse was racing, turned on beyond comprehension. I wanted him. I wanted him badly, and my body surrendered to my secret impulses, as I started grinding back on him. A pleasurable groan escaped his lips while he squeezed my breast like a lover.

"Mmmmm… Nessa…"

My sinful desire quickly vanished. I felt a twinge of jealousy when I heard him mutter her name again. I hadn't even met this Vanessa woman, and already I felt an extreme dislike of her. Envy brought out the worst in people. At least I could admit this shadow side of me. The worst thing is when you're not even aware of your own dark side and you project that onto others. I was a work in progress. Feeling annoyed, I moved his hand away and fled from his arms.

What a great way to start my morning.

This really put me in a downer as I headed to the bathroom to freshen up.

CHAPTER FOURTEEN
THANKSGIVING

November 24, 2010
New Castle, New Hampshire

Thanksgiving at the Miller residence was always an important holiday for John and Rose Miller. It was a time of celebration, to be close with family and give thanks for all their blessings, yet Aria couldn't find anything to be thankful for that year. She was staying at her grandparents' home for the weekend with her family. Her grandmother had cooked a delicious stuffed turkey, green beans, peas, mashed potatoes, and fresh-baked cornbread. Aria loved her cooking, which was the only thing to look forward to whenever they came to visit.

Her granddad was fond of board games; Scrabble and Monopoly were his favorites, and Aria enjoyed playing with him, but that year she was tired of the tradition. She wasn't ten years old anymore. As tedious as the games had become, she didn't have the heart to say no to her grandfather that afternoon.

By the end of the evening, her grandparents retired early to bed with the rest of her family. It was a four-bedroom house, and Aria always slept in her mother's old bedroom, which had remained the same since the time she had moved out. The walls were covered in pink floral wallpaper, and all the bedroom furniture was white. The beige carpeting direly needed removal, and the tacky flower-print curtains were outdated. Regardless, Aria was thankful she didn't have to share a room with her younger siblings.

Staring out the window, she noticed a full moon in the sky, glowing in a dark canvas of stars. It was a quarter after eleven, but Aria was sleepless. She turned on the bedside lamp and pulled out a book from her duffel bag.

"Hey, are you still awake?" Natalie asked, stepping inside.

"Yeah, I was about to do some reading."

She walked over to her daughter and sat on the bed. "I just wanted to check on you and make sure you're okay. I know your father upset you tonight."

"Mom, stop calling him that. He's not my dad."

"He's all you've got, sweetie."

"Whatever." Aria rolled her eyes.

"Anyway, I appreciate the way you handled yourself. I know Robert was out of line with what he said about you—but thank you for being mature and not provoking him further."

"I only did it for Grams. I didn't want to ruin Thanksgiving. She hardly sees us, so yeah…"

Natalie kissed her daughter's head and stood up. "This place always brings back so many memories." She hugged her chest, pacing the bedroom. "It's all so… nostalgic."

"You didn't lose your virginity in here, did you?" Aria teased.

"What?" Her mother went red in the face. "Are you kidding? I wasn't even allowed to have a boy call me." She stepped toward the window and looked outside. There was an enormous oak tree with an old tire swing hanging off the branch. Smiling to herself, she exhaled loudly. "Did you know I buried a time capsule in this backyard when I was your age?"

Aria lowered the book she was reading and glanced at her mother. "Really? What did you put in it?"

"My most precious memories."

"Which were?"

"Love letters mostly."

"From who?"

Natalie turned around with a saddened smile. "Noah."

"Oh. Well, we could always dig it up tomorrow…"

"Absolutely not." She shook her head. "There's a reason the past should stay buried."

"Mom, come on. I want to know what you were like when you were sixteen."

"Isn't it obvious? I was young and foolish. Who in their right mind would want to be a teen mom?"

A crestfallen look appeared on Aria's face. Natalie felt bad.

"Honey, I'm sorry, that's not what I meant. Of course, I'm happy that I had you and kept you, but—"

"Mom, it's fine. You don't need to explain." Feeling slightly injured, Aria quickly brushed it off. "I get it. I would hate to be pregnant at that age as well."

Natalie sat on the edge of the bed and caressed her daughter's face.

"Sometimes I think you resent me because I'm Noah's child."

"Sweetheart, don't be silly. I never feel that way."

If anything, whenever she looked at her daughter, it always reminded her of the greatest love she had lost, which often made her sad. "You are my first-born, and you know how precious you are to me. Your sister looks up to you. Have you not noticed?"

"Yeah," Aria mumbled.

"You're a very important part of this family. We all need you. You can always talk to me if something's on your mind—you know that."

"I know, Mom."

"Good. I'm gonna get some rest. Don't stay up too late."

"I won't." Just as her mother was about to leave, she asked, "Hey, Mom, can I bury my own time capsule in the yard tomorrow?"

Natalie gave her a warm smile and nodded. "Your grandma's got some empty shoeboxes in the attic. We can bury it together tomorrow."

"Great."

"Goodnight, sweetie."

"Night, Mom."

As her mother closed the door, Aria opened her book bag and pulled out a notepad and pen. She propped a few pillows behind her on the bed and sat with her knees bent up, placing the notepad in her lap. Tapping the pen on the paper, she clicked it and started writing:

November 24, 2010 11:30 p.m.

Dear soulmate,

My name's Aria Hunter. I'm fifteen years old, and I'm sitting in my mother's bedroom at my grandparents' house right now, writing to you. I know you don't even know me, and I have no clue who you are, but I want to believe that someone out there is thinking of me too, and possibly writing an anonymous love letter addressed to me, even though they don't know my identity yet. Okay, yeah... that sounds mega confusing, I'm sorry. I always ramble on and get lost in thought when I write. It's sort of like stepping into "Wonderland." Maybe I'm Alice reincarnated.

This is the first love letter I've ever written to anyone, and it's funny that I don't even know who you are, what you look like, and where you live. Maybe you're someone I might meet when I travel to Ireland, Brazil or France. It's possible that I might even have to travel farther than that... Italy, perhaps? Spain? Mexico? If that's the case, then I should learn Italian and Spanish. But I really hope you speak English too, because language barriers suck!

I'm not sure when I'll meet you, but I hope it's before someone breaks my heart and jades me forever. How much would it suck to meet you one day and let the opportunity to fly right by because I'd be too afraid to get involved with you? Isn't that tragic? Hopefully, that won't happen. I'm still an optimist. Maybe I'll run into you at a café in Paris and let my book "accidentally" drop off my table to catch your attention. I imagine you'll pick it up for me like a gentleman and find yourself entranced when you look at me. No, I'm not full of myself, but I have nice eyes. I'm sure you will love them. Or maybe I'll meet you somewhere local, like New York. I'll be walking through Central Park and a destined gust of wind will unravel my scarf from around my neck. I'll chase after it, but it crosses your path... you'll bend over and pick it up. And once we lock eyes, it's over. We'll both know that we have found our missing half. I know I'm a hopeless romantic, but I'm sure you are as well. We're soulmates after all, right? I assume that means we have many things in common.

I've never been in love before. I've had many crushes, but it's never been love… and I'm still a virgin. I hope that once you meet me, that won't turn you off. Guys get bored with girls who are sexually inexperienced (from what I've heard). I'm not trying to wait until marriage. I'm just waiting for <u>you</u> because I believe you're worth it. I have faith that you'll always love me and would sacrifice for me just as much as I would for you. We haven't met each other yet, but I know you'll read this one day, and when you do, I want you to know that I waited forever for you. I love you more than words can describe, and no matter what has happened to you in life or the things you have done in your past, it doesn't matter to me. I love you for who you are. I love your soul, and I always will, regardless of the way time will age you. Just know that you won't be alone, because I'll be by your side, aging with you, growing with you, and loving you always.

Yours forever,

Aria Hunter

Skimming through the letter, she folded it and felt lighter after getting all that off her chest. The room was stuffy, Aria noticed, as she rose from the bed to open the window. She paused for a moment and looked up at the sky, noticing the twinkling North Star.

I hope you're thinking of me right now, at this moment, wherever you are. She smiled to herself.

The next morning, Aria buried that letter along with her old diary in a shoebox near the oak tree in her grandparents' yard.

CHAPTER FIFTEEN
ARIA

I've discovered that you don't need to be a celebrity to live in Beverly Hills—you just need to be hella rich. My life drastically changed overnight when I moved to LA. I remember seeing palm trees for the first time when Noah drove us home from the airport. It was a sunny afternoon as we pulled up to the gated property. His home was too amazing to be real… it was so different from the environment I had grown up in (which was almost like living in the projects, to be honest). Noah lived in what I considered a mansion, probably worth millions. He had mentioned something about inheritance money. His father was a billionaire. Apparently, the house had gone through an expensive renovation. The home had a stunning 270-degree city and ocean view and an open floor plan. I loved the kitchen; it was massive with stainless steel appliances that would have impressed any chef. The family room was generously large, including a formal dining and gathering area. Almost every wall on the first-floor level was made of glass.

The patio doors opened to a large terrace with jetliner views. Noah gave me a full tour of the six-bedroom home on my first day there. His master bedroom had a Venetian theme, decorated to Vanessa's liking (he preferred "modern meets rustic"). I liked the fireplace, skylights, and my stepmom's walk-in closet. It was big enough to be another master bedroom.

The guest wing offered three sun-filled bedrooms painted in a vanilla color with separate baths. The interior décor of the home was contemporary with earth toned modern furnishings. I was in shock when I stepped into my bedroom. It was painted in lavender with silver Victorian-style wallpaper on one wall behind my bed. I loved the big bay windows and cushioned window seating—that was something I always wanted since I was a secret bookworm. My bed was upgraded from a single to a queen-size mattress. I had two bookshelves stocked with books, a crystal chandelier hung from the ceiling, and my mirrored vanity was covered in brand-new cosmetics and gift baskets. In the corner of my room was a long white desk where I had a brand-new laptop and iPad. Noah hadn't been kidding when he'd said he would get me new stuff.

The basement had a temperature-controlled gym with a variety of gym equipment—some of which I had never even used before, but I liked the idea of Noah training me. The backyard was professionally landscaped. I couldn't wait to dive in the pool on a hot summer day and soak in the hot tub in the evening. The outdoor fireplace, patio furniture, and cabana were straight out of a home gardening catalogue. There were palm trees on the property, and a five-car garage. My words fell short with describing the detail and craftsmanship that went into creating this dream home. It was worthy of being aired on *MTV Cribs*. The city view at night was just gorgeous.

I'd been rescued from my former life and felt like a modern-day Cinderella. The only difference in my tale was that I had been living with my evil stepfather instead of a stepmother. My mom wasn't perfect. I didn't want to believe that she didn't love me. And yeah, there were other blatant differences too... Okay, I was seriously bending the shit out of that fairy tale, but you get the idea.

Vanessa hadn't been around when I first arrived, but I got to see her later in the evening. She seemed overly enthusiastic about meeting me, and it was awkward. I felt like she was trying so hard to be nice. It just didn't feel genuine. Maybe I was projecting my own fears. I figured she was just nervous, so I didn't make a big deal out of it. Most days, I rarely saw her. She was typically busy with shopping or work. Noah told me that when they got married, she quit her job as a legal secretary and started her own swimwear company (with his financial help, of course). Vanessa was three years younger than him, but Noah had more of a youthful face in comparison. All that plastic surgery she had done to her face and body took away from her natural beauty. He had shown me some photos of her before her procedures, and she was so beautiful. I couldn't understand why she had gone under the knife. But I guess we all have our insecurities in different ways. Our perception of reality, including ourselves, is entirely subjective.

I got along fine with Vanessa… for the first three weeks. After that, my "friendship" with her turned sour. I couldn't understand it, but every time Noah and I grew closer, she seemed bothered by our bond. I could only assume it was because of jealousy, which was so bizarre… I mean, she was married to him. But maybe it was all in my head. Maybe *I* was the one who was jealous and demonizing my stepmom. I couldn't find anything in common with her. It's not like she really tried to get to know me. I felt like I was just a temporary accessory added to her house, like an object or a doll—fun to dress up and look at, if only to match her superficial world. If my stepmom had a theme song, it was "Barbie Girl" by Aqua. In fact, she should've starred in the music video. Her entire persona would have been an accurate depiction of the lyrics.

My transition to a private school was more difficult than I thought. It was a tremendous change of social scene, and the teachers taught differently. The classes were harder, and expectations were higher. Switching between semesters was not something I wanted to do, so I convinced Noah to let me finish up the semester in New York before I moved in with him. Of course, he had a hard time flying back knowing I'd be staying with Mom and Rob, but my stepdad gave me no trouble ever since Noah beat the crap out of him.

I had no problem making new friends. Although, I wasn't sure if the popular girls befriended me because they were genuinely interested in getting to know me or because they'd discovered that the hot guy that had picked me up was my dad. It seemed odd that the popular clique of chicks who had avoided me on my first day of school suddenly became my best friends. Whatever the reason, it was better than being a loner.

Three months had quickly gone by since I moved to LA, but I kept in touch with Jade and Ally. I was looking forward to their visit in the summer. But somehow, I didn't think they would like the people I socialized with. We used to make fun of the snobby rich kids at my old school. At present, not only was I associated with those kinds of people, but I was BFFs with a majority of them. My life had taken quite a twist. I was much happier, though. It was better than living on the grungy side of NYC with my abusive stepdad.

What was my relationship with Noah like? If there was an award for the best father of the year, he'd have won it. Moving in with him only intensified my feelings for him. I still couldn't feel that father-daughter bond, although he tried his best to develop that between us. The only person who distracted me from those feelings was Ryan Taylor, a tall, handsome, gray-eyed jock at my high school. He was captain of the football team, and definitely boyfriend material. Ever since I'd gone to one of his games, he couldn't take his eyes off me (even though he was seeing someone at the time). My friend Jessica told me he dumped his girlfriend the next day, and that there were rumors circulating that he wanted to pursue me. She encouraged me to date him because she had a personal vendetta against his ex, but I told her I wasn't one to rush into things—plus I didn't particularly like that he had a wandering eye while in a relationship. The guy was hands-down hot, but he could never measure up to the perfection of the man I was living with. Noah was just so heart-crushingly handsome, and I confess this with a heavy, swooning sigh. If I had rose-tinted glasses on, I didn't care. The two of us had strengthened our trust. I'd say it had even grown stronger than my relationship with my mother. It amazed me how we had got so close in such a short amount of time.

Noah had this tendency to show up randomly while I was at school. He'd pick me up during lunch hour or whenever I had a spare and take me out to eat, surprising me with little gifts, and spoiling me at every opportunity. He made me feel so special and loved. I felt this new sense of pride in him as his daughter. It was kind of like, *Wow, this is my dad. He's amazing. There's only one of him, and he's mine.* I did my best to adapt to my new environment and lifestyle. Most of all, I wanted him to be proud of me.

My girlfriends frequently came over. At first, I thought it was because they were in love with the house, but it was obviously because of Noah: hot dad, hormonal teenage girls, all in the same room—what do you get from that equation? Obnoxious flirtation. He usually locked himself in his office or gym whenever my gal pals dropped by.

California felt like home, like I really belonged there. I was so happy to have escaped the chains of my life in New York. Rob couldn't hurt me anymore. Noah would never let him hurt me again. I found it hard to trust in masculine figures, but I was slowly getting there. Noah's patience meant everything to me.

∞

It was mid-March, and I was in my room studying for a chemistry test. Even though I knew about ninety percent of the material, my mind was elsewhere. All four universities I had applied to had accepted me on the condition that I maintain my grade point average. The deadline to accept my offers was on June 2nd. I was torn between Berkeley and Columbia. I wanted to stay in Cali to be close to Noah, but I also wanted to go to Columbia with Jade and Ally because it was something we had been planning forever. The thought of leaving him gave me severe separation anxiety.

"Are you ready to hit the beach?"

Speak of the devil.

"The beach?"

"Uh—yeah. Come on, take a study break."

I placed my binder down and looked up at Noah. He flashed that irresistible smile that always left me speechless.

"Don't you have dinner plans with Vanessa?"

"Plans have changed." He slid his hands into his pockets. "Let's go. The weather is beautiful. I'll let you drive the Mercedes…"

He didn't need to bribe me with fancy cars. I was happy just to go grocery shopping with him.

"I'll get changed real quick," I said.

"Meet me in the garage when you're ready." He kissed my head and walked out of my bedroom.

I loved cruising around LA with Noah. It was spontaneous and fun. Every time he took me out for a drive, we wound up going some place new, either for a bite to eat or for a simple smoothie. No matter what we did or where we went, I always had a great time because I was with *him*.

Recently, I had picked up a habit of trying to match my wardrobe to whatever color scheme he was wearing. I changed into a pair of faded blue shorts and a white crop top that showed off my midriff. The California sun had done wonders to my pale complexion. I looked more sun-kissed than usual as I examined my figure in the mirror. My hair had grown longer since I'd moved here. Loosening my ponytail, I shook my wavy brown locks before I brushed on some gloss and mascara. Noah said that I didn't need makeup to look beautiful, but I enjoyed experimenting with different eyeshadow pallets.

An elephant stampede was unleashed in my stomach when I stepped through the garage door and approached the silver Mercedes. It was a brand-new convertible, and Noah looked so sexy behind the wheel. The engine roared to life as I got in beside him and strapped on my seat belt.

"I'll let you drive on our way back," he said. "I want to test out this new sound system—you'll be impressed." He smiled and turned on the Bluetooth on the stereo.

Boys and their toys.

"Sit tight, beautiful." He pulled out of the driveway.

A blast of bass suddenly vibrated through my body.

"You listen to Dash Berlin?" I couldn't hide my smile.

Noah glanced at me and shouted over the music. "You forget I'm not that old, Aria!"

ഇരുന്ന

Convertibles are fun for a reason. Driving on the road with the top down was amazing; it was freeing. I closed my eyes and felt the wind dance through my hair as we hit the freeway. Edward Maya's song "Stereo Love" was blasting from the stereo speakers, giving me the chills. I was pleasantly surprised by Noah's music selection. He listened to pretty much everything I loved, which was awesome. I didn't feel like I was riding in a car next to my dad. If anything, I felt like I was sitting next to my best friend, someone I was badly crushing on. Was this what being in love felt like? Or was I just high on house beats? I couldn't tell anymore. All I knew was that in those brief minutes, nothing and no one else mattered. It was just me, Noah, and the sunset on the horizon.

There was something I had been dying to get off my chest, but I was too chicken to say it out loud.

Just tell him already.

Noah suddenly switched gears with the stick shift and sped past an SUV. The sound of the engine overpowered the music.

Say it…

I looked down at his hand resting on the gearshift and slowly started tracing on his skin with my index finger: I… ♥… U…

The corner of his mouth tugged into a smile as he took my hand in his and raised it to his lips, leaving a sweet kiss before he started tracing a response on my left thigh:

I…♥…U… MORE.

Goosebumps instantly prickled my skin. I couldn't control the way my body reacted to his touch. It all came so naturally, even though it was disturbingly wrong. Elated with happiness, I was dangerously losing myself in a delusional fantasy where Noah was my boyfriend and I was his secret lover. This alternate universe was much more appealing than my present reality.

We drove for the longest while, cruising along the coast, headed toward Laguna Beach. I enjoyed every moment I spent with him. My stepdad rarely made time for me. He never took an interest in any of the things I cared about. He didn't give a rat's ass about me because I wasn't biologically his.

Don't think about Rob, a voice whispered in my head.

After an hour on the road, we arrived at the beachfront and pulled into a parking lot. Noah shut off the engine, lifted his shades, and looked at me.

"Are you hungry, beautiful?"

"No, I ate earlier."

Glancing at my Chanel wristwatch, I got out of the car; it was half past seven. There was a three-hour time difference between LA and NYC. Typically, at this hour, I would have been in bed, staring up at my ceiling and fantasizing about my life as an actor or a high-fashion runway model. Deep down, I felt these dreams would never materialize. At almost eighteen, I still had so much self-discovery to do. What did it mean to achieve my highest potential? Why was I here? What was my purpose? I questioned these things every day like a lost soul wandering in life.

"Do you feel like ice cream?" Noah asked, resting an arm over my shoulder. "I've got the biggest craving that's been nagging at me all day."

"Now that you mention it, a strawberry cone sounds tempting."

ᘒ

The beach strip wasn't too crowded, but there were enough people scattered around the sand, basking in the last few rays of sunlight. Noah and I stopped by a tropical tiki hut for ice cream before we ambled along the shore together.

"California sunsets are so beautiful." I glanced at him, shying away before he met my eyes.

"Yeah, I love living out here."

My mind wandered as I looked out at the ocean. I was so lost in thought that I didn't even notice the football that was heading straight toward my head.

"Watch out!" Noah stepped in front of me and intercepted it.

"Sorry about that!" a young guy shouted from a distance.

Noah threw back the ball while I stood there, feeling dazed.

"Idiots," he muttered under his breath. "They can't even toss a football properly." He brushed the hair out of my face. "You okay?"

"Yeah… I just didn't see it coming."

"I have fast reflexes."

"I noticed." I nervously chuckled.

He took my hand and held it. I wanted to cry from guilt because his touch felt amazing. He had a warmth I could never get over. My situation was tragic. What had I done wrong in life to meet such an ill fate? To be in love with my own…

"I'm gonna take you out on my boat this summer." Noah turned his head and looked at me. "Would you like that?" A warm smile spread across his lips.

I nodded, beaming.

"Have you decided what you'd like to do for your birthday?" he asked.

"That's like three weeks away."

"Yeah, so? I'd like to plan the big event ahead of time." He raised my hand to his lips and kissed it.

I hated blushing around him. It was embarrassing.

"I don't know—I'd like to have something small."

Birthdays were never a huge event in my family. Rob wasn't a fan of spending money on cakes or presents, so my mom usually baked me a chocolate cake and personalized her gifts. Jade and Ally always made my birthdays feel special. But I wasn't in New York anymore. I was in sunny California.

"I guess I'll have to plan your party myself," Noah said. "And just so you know, I suck at organizing special events, so I'll have to hire a party planner. Would you like a band?"

"A band?"

That took me by surprise.

"Yeah, you know… drummer, guitarists, and I think there's also a person who stands behind a microphone and sings," he teased.

"Obviously, I know what you're referring to."

"Name your favorite band and I'll have them booked for your party."

"Oh my God, Noah! You don't need to do that."

Suddenly, I saw myself sitting on the sofa, watching an episode of *My Super Sweet 16*. I remember the first time I saw that show. The lives of those rich teens were so different from my reality. It's funny how I still watched that program now and then, even though it infuriated me sometimes. Those girls lived under a sky from which money rained down on them. Nothing but cold, wet rain poured down on *my* head, not cold, hard cash. That was my reality in New York, but Noah had changed all of that with a snap of his fingers.

"I'll figure something out," he said. "There's no way I'm gonna let you do something small this year."

I was grateful that he cared so much. I would have been content with spending my birthday with him, but of course he didn't know that.

Yearning for contact, I hooked my arm around his as we strolled along the shore. I didn't feel comfortable discussing my birthday, so I took the focus away from myself and brought up the subject of his ever-doting wife.

"How are you and Vanessa doing? I hardly see her around the house."

It took him a while to answer. "We're doing well, Aria."

The eternal poker face. He couldn't fool me.

"She's just busy launching her company," he added.

"I know I don't have your years of experience, but I'm here if you ever need to talk… about anything."

"Thank you. That's sweet of you." Noah kissed my head and moved his arm over my shoulder.

I hugged his waist and was happy he didn't recoil. It was all so natural; even the movement of our bodies brushing side by side felt so fluid. We walked like this for the longest while until I got playful and removed my flip-flops.

Stepping in the water, I splashed Noah with my legs.

"Hey!" He laughed, kicking off his slides and lunging toward me. I tried to dodge him, but he grabbed my waist.

"Don't drop me!" I screamed, giggling as he spun me around.

"Maybe I should—you got me all wet, you naughty girl."

"No, no, please!" I begged, unable to control my laughter.

Noah chuckled and carried me deeper into the ocean. I held on to his arms and raised my knees up to avoid the water.

"You wouldn't dare."

"I *so* would," he whispered wickedly in my ear. "All I have to do is let go." He shifted me in his arms and carried me the way a groom carries his bride to their honeymoon suite.

"One… two…"

"If I go down, I'm taking you with me!" I locked my arms around his neck.

He seemed hesitant. I kept waiting for that unexpected moment when I would finally fall in the water, but something had changed in his eyes. They weren't wild and playful anymore—they looked sincere.

"I wouldn't drop you, Aria." He paused. "I'd catch you. I'll always catch you."

We stared at each other for a moment as the waves crashed onto the shore. I loved that sound. It was so relaxing. What was he thinking when he looked at me this way?

Why, God? Why have you brought this man back into my life only to cause me to feel things no one could understand? How could anyone empathize? I would be burned at the stake and considered sick and psychotic. I felt so isolated in my emotions.

"I'm holding you to those words forever, just so you know," I said.

"Good—you should." He flashed a subtle smile, carrying me out of the water.

I loved him, but… I wished I didn't. It would have been easier to hate him than to feel this way.

"So, shall we keep walking?" Noah placed me back on my feet and slipped on his slides.

"I want a piggyback ride."

"You serious?" He laughed.

I nodded with a cheery smile.

"Well, I guess I have years of making up to do." He bent over. "Hop on."

I jumped on his back, and before I knew it, he had taken off, kicking sand behind him like the Road Runner. It was comical in my mind as I held on for dear life, laughing and screaming.

"Let me off! Let me off, Noah!" I thought he would lose his balance, but he didn't. I'm sure if there were marathon hurdles in front of him, he still would have been able to clear the jumps while carrying me like a superhuman athlete.

"You're the one who wanted a ride!" He sounded out of breath. "I just made it worth your while."

When we suddenly stopped, my body jerked forward, and I gasped. My inner child was happy. Rob had never made time to play with me in my younger years. He was playful with my siblings, but not with me.

"You ready to get off?"

"That was fun!" I giggled as Noah slipped my thighs down his hands. I was safely back on the ground.

"My body is not an amusement park, Aria." He smirked.

"I never assumed it was."

But I'm sure it's the best thrill ride in the bedroom, I deviously thought, feeling my stomach twist into a hundred knots.

The things I would have done to him, if only he'd let me. I entertained my fantasies for a while as we walked up a ramp that led to the docks. Noah seemed like he wanted to say something, but stopped.

Why is he frowning? I wondered, looking at him.

We walked past a group of guys as they whistled at me. Funny how I hadn't noticed them at first. A celebrity could have passed us, and Noah still would have had my attention. It's a good thing he wasn't an actor. He would have had millions of Instagram followers, women mailing him their panties and who knows what else. Oh, I forgot... can't exclude the demographic of gay men who would hang his posters on their walls and worship him. I knew I was idolizing Noah, and maybe that was unhealthy, but I couldn't help it. I was seventeen. I could act my age—at least in my head.

"I shouldn't have let you come out of the house dressed like this."

I rolled my eyes and took his hand. "Let's keep walking."

There was nothing wrong with my attire; it was suitable for this weather. A guy with a red mohawk lewdly flicked his tongue between his fingers, making Noah snap.

"Wait!" I tried to stop him, but he was already in the guy's face.

"Do you always look at every girl as some piece of ass?"

"Nah, just the ones that look fine as hell, like *that* sweet ass right there…" mohawk man nodded at me, flashing a creepy grin. "Wassup, li'l mama?"

"She's not even eighteen, you piece of shit!" Noah was angry. I hadn't seen this protective side of him. Rob never defended me against anyone. If anything, he always blamed me.

"Noah—"

"Get back to the car," he demanded, handing me the keys while locking his murderous gaze on the punk who was provoking him.

"Let's just go, it's not even worth it," I reasoned.

That idiot had an entourage of morons sitting next to him. Noah would be unfairly outnumbered if a brawl broke out.

"Come with me," I said, refusing to leave. But he wouldn't budge, despite my efforts to tug him back. It didn't help that those guys were still antagonizing him.

"Why don't you leave your lame boyfriend and chill with us? We'll show you a good time, cutie. I'm *big enough* for it." Mohawk man groped his crotch and winked at me.

"She's my daughter, you fuckface!"

Just let it be, I groaned in my head.

"*Oooooh, snaps… day-um!* Maybe you should pimp her out, bro. I'd pay top dollar for that."

Stepping in front, I forced Noah back before he could throw any punches.

"Please don't make a scene here," I said, lowering my voice. "They could have guns and knives for all we know."

"They deserve to be castrated," he replied in a taciturn tone.

"Let's go." I turned and addressed the pervs. "It's been fun, guys. Bye!"

Grateful that Noah followed me, we walked away from a potentially dangerous situation. The assholes continued to catcall at me, while I prayed Noah wouldn't turn around and beat them to a bloody pulp. Thankfully, we got far enough from the gang of losers. I'd lost count of all the times we were mistaken for a dating couple. It didn't bother me, though. I was always flattered.

"Are you all right?" I asked, breaking the silence.

"Just keep walking." The warmth in Noah's voice had turned ice-cold… borderline scary.

Maybe he was just trying to calm his temper, I concluded.

We eventually stopped by a guardrail, and I studied him as he looked out at the water. He was so handsome it hurt.

"I'm sorry I get so temperamental, Aria." He sighed.

"It's okay."

"It's not. I used to really lose my shit back in the day—not proud of it."

"You kept your cool. You're fine. The past is the past," I said, resting my elbows back on the cold steel.

I knew what it was like to have bursts of anger, or a burning homicidal rage within. Anger was just masking deep hurt and sadness.

"I can't stand the idea of anyone looking at you like a sex object."

His confession made me blush, not because I didn't know that I had sexual prowess, but because he recognized it.

"You can't control the way people think," I answered.

"No." He half smiled. "But I can control how you dress. Perhaps a more modest selection of casual wear next time?"

My jaw dropped. "You're kidding me, right? Look around you. I'm not dressed in a skimpy bikini—not that there's anything wrong with that. A crop top and shorts are a reasonable choice when the temperature is this hot." I folded my arms defensively.

Noah's eyes cascaded down to my bare stomach.

I shivered.

"Maybe next time"—he touched my tummy—"you should cover up this flawlessness."

My breath caught, and my skin heated from contact. The way he said those words sounded so seductive. It was wrong of me to even think he was trying to sound sexy on purpose. I couldn't look away from his hypnotic gaze until he pulled me into a hug.

"I love you, Aria."

Noah's voice was like music to my ears. He often told me he loves me, yet I never had the courage to say it back. Expressing affection wasn't common in the household I grew up in.

"Don't get all mushy on me," I joked.

"You're never gonna call me 'Dad,' huh?"

I shrugged, smirking.

"Let's head home." He tossed me the keys. "You're driving."

∞

My stepmom flung herself at the sex god as soon as he walked through the door. I couldn't help but feel jealous, but at least I had it in check. She was his wife. I had to learn to manage my emotions better, even though I struggled.

"Finally, you're back!" she gushed. "I missed you!"

"Missed you too, honey." Noah hugged her and kissed her swollen lips.

It kind of grossed me out. She needed to quit the lip fillers.

"I feel tired," I said, glancing at the blissful couple. "I'm going to bed. Thanks for taking me out for a drive."

"Oh, okay, sweetheart," Noah answered.

I think he wanted to hug me, but I was irritated, so I walked off.

"Is everything all right with her?" Vanessa asked.

"Yeah, she's just tired and stressed out over a chemistry test."

It took every ounce of effort not to slam my door shut when I heard them chattering about me. I wasn't sure why I was so triggered. I'd had a perfect evening with Noah. Vanessa was always nice to me. I felt horrible for being jealous of her relationship with my father. I had wounds inside I needed to heal, but didn't know how. And the thought of opening up to

Noah about these feelings terrified me. Vanessa wasn't to blame. I was just fucked up hell spawn.

Desperate for catharsis, I spent half an hour writing in my diary before I opened a book to help me fall asleep. I loved *Wuthering Heights* by Emily Bronte. I empathized with Heathcliff.

CHAPTER SIXTEEN
NOAH

Vanessa was driving me insane. What I had hoped would be a romantic evening between me and my wife had turned into a typical argument. I guess it shouldn't have surprised me.

"Really, Nessa? Don't you think it's about damn time you quit all these costly cosmetic procedures? They're completely unnecessary!"

"Keep your voice down!" she hissed.

"No, I will *not* keep it down! I'm so damn sick of this! It's never enough for you. You're addicted to plastic surgery. I didn't sign up for this marriage to help you destroy the woman I married!"

"Don't you understand I need it? It's just a brow lift and lip filler. What's the big deal?"

"Are you really gonna stand there and ask me that question?" I was beyond outraged.

"Uh—well, I just did."

Christ, enough with the attitude.

"You need help, Vanessa. I'm sleeping on the couch tonight."

I could have slept in a guest room, but I usually preferred to fall asleep in front of the TV.

Grabbing a pillow, I controlled my anger and walked out on my wife. She knew not to provoke me further. There was no point in arguing. I knew she would go through with the procedure, whether I liked it or not. I didn't think she realized how rocky our marriage had become.

"You're wrong about this, Noah!" she called after me.

Rolling my eyes, I was thankful when she finally shut our bedroom door. The rest of my night was going to be a long one, and I was ready to tough it out with some re-runs of "24" when something caught my eye down the hall. Aria's bedroom lights were on. It was almost two in the morning. I made my way down the hall and gently knocked on her door.

"Aria? You still awake?"

"Come in."

She was sitting at her desk with a stack of textbooks in front of her.

"Hey, beautiful, what are you doing up so late?"

"Studying."

"You need your sleep. Otherwise, all these long hours will go to waste."

She looked at me, puzzled. "What do you mean?"

"We sleep to remember. Sleep helps us remember things. It's important for the brain."

"There are lots of things I wish I could forget," she mumbled. "Unfortunately, I always remember. Sleep or no sleep."

Even the faintest smile on her lips was so beautiful, but her eyes revealed nothing but sorrow in that moment. I instantly felt like crap because I should have provided a better life for her much sooner.

"Is everything okay with you?" she asked. "Why aren't you catching some Zs?"

I'd been hoping she wouldn't ask me that.

"Insomnia, and I'm also working late."

"I guess we have that in common."

Very true, even though I fibbed a little.

"Anyway, I just wanted to check in on you. I'm gonna try to get some shuteye." I kissed her on the head, forgetting to breathe when she stared up at me. Her white camisole was extremely transparent. I had to avert my gaze.

"I feel like something's wrong." Aria frowned. "You're upset about something."

Was she also psychic?

"Everything's fine."

"But I heard you arguing with Vanessa."

That explained it.

"It's nothing to worry about. We were bickering over stupid things. It'll blow over by morning."

That was highly unlikely, but I would not drag my daughter into my marriage problems.

"I don't like to see you sad." She pouted, tugging at my heartstrings. I never wanted to be the reason for her sadness.

"I'm not sad," I said. "I'm just frustrated."

Not just emotionally, but sexually as well. Things had been quite frigid between me and Nessa.

"You know you can talk to me," Aria said.

"I know, and I love you for that, but some things need to stay between us grown-ups. Besides, you have better things to worry about." I cupped her face and lightly kissed her forehead, intoxicated by the scent of her shampoo.

"Mom would always share her problems with Rob, including their intimacy issues. Apparently, he always wanted threesomes, and she didn't."

"Are you kidding me?" I was shocked in outrage. "How old were you when she told you this?"

"Fifteen."

"That's oversharing and emotionally dumping on a child."

Who the fuck shares their sex life issues with their own children? I was angry. If Nat was here, I would've given her a piece of my mind.

"I'm so sorry you had to deal with all that," I said, staying calm. "I'm really starting to dislike your mother, given all the abuse you've had to put up with. Has she ever been in therapy?"

"No."

I took a moment to reflect.

"I'm sorry," said Aria.

"For what?"

"For just randomly burdening you with that information."

"Aria, you don't burden me. I'm your father. You can talk to me about anything."

She tried to smile, but I could still see traces of pain in her eyes. I felt responsible for her harsh upbringing. Sometimes my guilt was unbearable.

"Anyway," I sighed. "Bedtime. Sleep well, sweetheart."

"Goodnight."

Leaving her room, I walked down the hall and headed for the couch, where I slumped down and turned on the TV. I lowered the volume enough to help me fall asleep. This was my typical routine whenever I couldn't get my mind to shut off. I was halfway through an episode of *CSI*, and unfortunately, late-night TV didn't seem to cure my insomnia. I hated going to bed angry at my wife, but by that point I had gotten used to it. Lately, all we did was fight and argue over the same shit. The fucked-up part was, if I were to cheat on her and admitted my infidelities, she still would have blamed herself and believed that I didn't find her attractive anymore, which undeniably had some truth to it—but only because the plastic surgery had botched her appearance. She was so beautiful when I married her. Now I hardly recognized her. No amount of surgery could have restored her face to what it once was.

I thought about booking an appointment with a marriage counselor—that's how severe the situation had got. Vanessa may have been in denial, but I wasn't. We were in troubled waters. I wondered how this was affecting Aria. I worried that my wife's obsession with perfection would rub off on her, and by the time she'd turn eighteen, she'd be begging me to fund an expensive boob job or God knows what else. Thankfully, she hadn't been showing any symptoms of body dysmorphia… yet. My problems with my wife had to be taken care of.

Aria might have been safe from Vanessa's influence, but if Nessa and I were to have a child together, then psychological trauma would surely follow. Parents are usually the ones who fuck up their kids. I didn't want to be one of those parents. I already felt like shit about abandoning my daughter the way I had, but I was trying to atone for my mistakes. It was a miracle she had turned out the way she did. Since the moment Aria had moved in with us, I felt so much happier, like there was actual life in this big house. Every morning I'd wake up looking forward to seeing her beautiful face, driving her to school before going to work, thinking about her while I was at work. I took comfort knowing she'd be right there waiting for me when I got home. It was nice knowing that someone was happy to see me and loved me enough to have dinner prepared on the table. Sometimes I'd get takeout, but on the evenings when Aria would cook, she would text me ahead of time to let me know she was making dinner. That always put a smile on my face. She was an amazing cook. I was so proud of her—I couldn't even express how much.

Drifting off to sleep wasn't exactly going as planned, since I couldn't shut off my thoughts. I felt like my skin was suffocating in my slacks; I took them off and lay under the throw blanket in my black boxer briefs.

Counting sheep got sidetracked when I heard footsteps down the hall. Opening my eyes, I noticed my daughter hovering over me.

"I can't sleep." She rubbed her arm. "Can I cuddle with you for a bit?"

"Of course." I shifted over.

She snuggled in next to me as I shared the blanket, sliding my arm under her neck. I was about to switch off when she turned and looked at me.

"Everything okay?" I asked.

Nodding, she moved in closer, hugging my waist. I could sense she needed me. Maybe she knew about why I had been fighting with Vanessa.

"Noah?"

"Mhm?"

"Am I beautiful?"

I was right. My wife's superficial beauty practices had been affecting her. This was not good. Time for damage control. Kissing her forehead, I ran my fingers through her hair.

"Your beauty is unmatched, Aria. I'm sure all the boys at your school are lining up after you."

She smiled, which implied there was truth in my statement.

"Well, yeah," she began. "I'd be lying if I said there weren't any guys interested in me. But I wanted to know if *you* think I'm beautiful."

It touched me to know she held my opinion in high esteem. "That's not a hard question for me to answer, because the answer is obvious." I smiled and caressed her cheek. "I'm so proud that you're my daughter. I never want you to change a single thing on your body or pretty face. You are perfect the way you are."

"Then how come Vanessa keeps changing her body image?"

I'd hoped she wouldn't ask me that question.

"Because she doesn't believe she's beautiful the way she is. I'm trying to help her accept herself."

"So, you don't think I need lip injections and other procedures? Some girls at my school are planning to get those done."

"Aria, please promise me you won't ever go under the knife unless the problem is life threatening. You don't need any sort of enhancement, sweetie. I love the way you look." I brushed my thumb over her perfectly arched eyebrows. "And *these* are perfect. I adore them. So are your sensuous lips."

Sensuous? Fuck. I should have kept that to myself, but at least I got her smiling.

"I love the way you look, too." Her hand slowly moved down my chest, and my heart stopped beating for a second, only to pump blood through my valves at an erratic rate. I couldn't understand why her touch had this effect on me. I was sexually frustrated. (Not that I would ever try anything on my daughter—I would never cross that line.) I just needed to heal my intimacy issues with Vanessa.

"I want to work out with you," she said, caressing my abdominals.

"You don't need vigorous exercise, though. I don't want you all skin and bones."

"I know, but your abs are amazing—they're super hard. I'm kind of jealous."

If she keeps touching you like that, something else *will be super hard,* my conscience warned.

"Are you telling me you want a bodybuilder's masculine physique?"

I know I'd probably get crucified by a handful of feminists if I voiced this opinion publicly, but I strongly believe that women should maintain their femininity. Pumping iron and injecting steroids only makes them look like men with vaginas.

"No, not masculine." Aria laughed. "I just think I could learn a few tricks from you at the gym—and don't be so sexist! If a woman wants to work out and be a bodybuilder, that doesn't make her masculine! It makes her a strong woman—femininity intact."

Someone read my mind… *again.*

"Lifting isn't limited to men," she added.

"All right, all right, I get it." I chuckled. "I didn't mean to discriminate against your gender. My apologies."

"You are forgiven."

I felt her lips on my chest and something down below responded with a throb.

Not good.

Gliding her leg over my hip, she moved in closer, pressing her crotch against mine. I'm sure it was innocent on her side, but how do you even explain to your daughter that any kind of stimulation down there would cause an erection?

"Just train me with the weights," she said. "It wouldn't hurt to sculpt and tone a bit."

No way. She was sculpted enough. Every time I saw her in a pair of skinny jeans or shorts, I had to look away because… well, let's just say it showed off one of her best assets.

"You want to work out with your old man, huh?"

"You're not an old man—stop saying that."

That comment bothered her, despite my humorous delivery.

"Fine. I'm a charismatic, attractive young man. Is that better?"

Smiling, she kissed my cheek. God, I loved her so much.

"Noah?"

"Yes, baby?"

"Can you rub my stomach? I'm cramping a little."

"Is it that time of the month?"

"Almost."

I placed my palm on her tummy and gently massaged her in a soothing motion. She sighed and stared at me like she was searching for something in my eyes.

"Does that feel better?"

"Much."

My hand slid under her shirt, not of my own free will; Aria moved it there. I was suddenly tense as my palm brushed against her soft, warm skin.

"Hey," I said, "are you eating enough?"

"Mhm, why do you ask?"

"Well, because your stomach is just so…" How could I say this without offending her? "… flat."

"I guess those PE classes have been paying off. I'm working out a lot. You're not the only gym buff around here."

"No, I guess not."

Brushing my fingertips over her stomach, I kissed her forehead again. She was so damn beautiful. She was my angel. I caressed her like this for the longest while until her eyelids slowly drooped shut and her breathing became slow and shallow. It was probably best to get her back in bed, I thought, lifting her in my arms and carrying her to her bedroom.

Where were you when she needed you most? Were you there to take her to a doctor when she caught the flu? Were you there to hold her and chase the monsters away when she woke up from a nightmare? Where were you, Noah?

My guilt was self-inflicted, and I felt the pain every time I removed the bandages. I realized right then that these wounds would not heal on their own.

୦୨୫୭

Aria stirred awake when I placed her on the bed, looking sleep-drunk.

"Go back to sleep, sweetie," I whispered.

"Don't go." She slung her arms around my neck, pulling me close. "Just stay with me a little while longer."

Smiling, I moved in beside her. She wrapped herself around me so fast that escaping was virtually impossible. I didn't know why I felt on edge, but it only increased as Aria molded herself into me while I lay on my back, looking at the ceiling. She hummed and slipped her arm over my stomach. The house was still, and the only thing I could hear was the rhythmic sound of my heartbeat, which refused to slow down. The last time I'd felt this way was when I was fourteen. Someone had thrown me in a closet with the cutest chick at school, and I had no clue what to do or how to kiss. I'd almost pissed myself from nervousness. Yeah, it wasn't the best experience.

Minutes went by, and the silence lingered between us. I kept hoping and praying she had fallen asleep because I needed to get out of her room ASAP.

"Noah?"

So much for praying.

"Yes?"

"Can you look at me for a sec?"

Reluctantly, I turned my head and faced her. My eyes had adjusted to the darkness.

"What's up, beautiful?" I asked, battling my nagging conscience; it was shaking its righteous finger at me, telling me to get up and leave—as if I was doing something wrong.

"Do we have… something going on between us?"

My heart was in my throat. I had no clue how to answer her.

"Um…" I breathed out slowly, staring into her big blue eyes. "I don't…"

Why the hell am I so nervous? This was ridiculous.

Okay, she was a teenager—a girl with sensitive feelings. With that in mind, I replied, "Yes, we have something between us, Aria."

She's my daughter and I love her. Why did I keep repeating this in my head?

"I feel so close to you." She touched my chest. "You've really become my best friend, not just a father to me."

What could I say to her? It was like she was reaching out to the most secret part of me that I had locked away forever.

"I'll always be here for you, angel."

I meant it. There was no way I would abandon her again. Never.

"I think I figured out what I want for my birthday," she said.

"Tell me."

It took her a while to respond, and I wondered if she was going through an internal struggle. Maybe it was emotionally triggering for her. Pulling her closer, I gently caressed her hip. She was wearing dark blue shorts. I was thankful. Her camisole wasn't long enough to cover up her panties.

What the fuck? Why am I even thinking about all this right now? I yelled in my head.

"I want you to take me on a trip."

"A trip?"

"Yes, just the two of us."

A father-daughter vacation. I liked that idea—definitely doable. "Where to, beautiful?"

"Italy. Do you think you can take time off from work?"

"Yes, that won't be a problem. But it will have to be a much later birthday present since you're still finishing school. We can fly after you graduate. I can book our tickets tomorrow."

"I would love that."

"Are you sure you don't want a party? I was looking forward to that—Vanessa especially. She loves planning big events, and to be honest, she's been already arranging it."

Aria took a moment to reflect. I could see a look of panic in her eyes before she sat up.

"Hey, what's wrong?" I touched her back, confused and upset.

"I really don't want a party. Please tell Vanessa to stop."

Did she have an irrational phobia of pleasant surprises? I knew there had to be something that was triggering her anxiety. "Sweetie, don't worry. If you don't want a big thing, I won't force it on you."

Knowing Vanessa, she would obsess about the party planning, but I was sure I could convince her to scrap the ideas.

"On my sweet sixteen," Aria began, "I had a party because Rob wasn't gonna be home that weekend. He and Mom had had a huge fight two weeks prior, and she kicked him out because his drinking had gone out of control. He'd been staying at his friend's place because Mom said she needed some time apart, and he respected her wishes. On the day of my party, Mom took Terry and Tiffany to stay with her best friend for the evening while she chaperoned.

"I felt relieved because at least Rob wouldn't be there to embarrass me and ruin my evening. My friends came over—about fifteen people, and everything was going smoothly. I was having fun… but it all blew up in my face. Just as I was about to blow out my candles, Rob stormed in through the apartment door, stumbling around like a drunk. He started yelling at my mom, saying how this was his damn house too, and refused to live under someone else's roof any longer.

"He humiliated me in front of all my friends. Mom had tried to do some damage control by taking their argument outside of the apartment, but he crashed my party, stuck his dirty fingers in my birthday cake and made a huge scene. I'll never forget what he said to me: 'It's such a waste to buy you a cake. You're just gonna puke it up later.'"

I was afraid to ask my next question. But I had to. "Were you battling Bulimia?"

"No. I got nauseous often because of the anxiety of living with him. I had a period where I couldn't keep my food down for a month. He was very abusive and unpredictable. He used to hit me—a lot."

Now I regretted not killing the bastard.

"Anyway, that wasn't the worst of it," she said. "When Mom pulled him into the kitchen, they started arguing and he lost his temper. The next thing I knew I was sitting there listening to him breaking dishes and degrading my mother. All my friends got freaked out and felt awkward, so most of them left, except for Jade and Ally. They stayed behind because they were worried about my safety, but I urged them to leave."

Now her reservations made sense. "I'm sorry you had to go through that, Aria. I promise you that won't happen here. That piece of shit won't ever come close to you again. Turning eighteen is a big deal. It's another milestone."

"I understand that you and Vanessa want to go all out, but I'm honestly not ready for it. The memories are still too fresh, and it's very triggering for me. I basically told you the summarized version of that evening."

I knew what it was like to live with triggers, which was why I respected her decision. "You know what? It's supposed to be your special day. Whatever you want to do, tell me and I'll make it happen—no complaints from my side."

The softest smile touched her lips. "I just want to spend the day with you."

"Done."

Of course, I would shower her with gifts and take her out to a nice dinner, at least.

"I can't wait," she said, tangling herself around me.

"I love you," I whispered, hugging her close. All these months, I kept hoping she would say it back to me. Sure, she traced those words on my hand, but hearing it was different. Regardless, I understood she needed time to trust in my feelings for her.

My daughter looked up at me with those glowing sapphires, and I was suddenly in a trance. I couldn't focus on anything else aside from her being in my arms; our bodies were dangerously close. I brushed a strand of hair out of her face and carefully tucked it behind her ear. My intention was to shift my gaze away from her enchanting eyes, but before I could think of another diversion, she captivated me, and I couldn't look away.

Like a madman, I desperately tried to sift through the chaos in my head. She was edging closer to me. Our faces were inches apart...

What the fuck is going on?

Her lips were so close to mine, driving me crazy with the scent of her vanilla lip balm.

This. Isn't. Happening right now.

I had to get my ass out of bed, but my body was paralyzed.

That's when it happened… vanilla and mint collided. She kissed me. It wasn't a full-out passionate kiss. I wouldn't even say it was sexual, but it left me feeling… confused. Aria's lips lightly pressed against mine, igniting an attraction between us. Time seemed to stand still as I closed my eyes. I hadn't moved my mouth to reciprocate her affection. I couldn't. Her lips seemed unsure of my reaction, but confident in their intent. When she slowly pulled back, all I could hear was her shallow breathing. Was she trying to decipher my expression? I gave nothing away. My heart was beating so fast it made my chest vibrate. A darkness was growing inside me, shrouding my logic.

Staring at her, I froze in panic. I was never so aware of the demon sleeping in my head—not until she kissed me, as if her lips were the deadly catalyst to a toxic chemical reaction. My brain chemistry had shifted, and I was all animal instincts, carnal and predatory. This wasn't good.

"You should get some sleep," I said, brushing off the kiss. "Goodnight, Aria." I mustered every ounce of strength to pull away and stand up, leaving her alone in her room.

This didn't happen. I tried to calm myself as I walked back to the sofa. It was a poor substitute for a bed.

Please don't follow me out here.

My lips were still tingling. That part when I said her kiss was anything but sexual? I take it back. This was the first time I had ever been kissed so innocently and felt such intense arousal. I couldn't understand it.

Take a cold shower—it'll go down.

Just jerk off and you'll feel better.

Two speakers, distinct personalities, same voice. And that voice belonged to *me*. I battled my psychological turmoil until I finally stood up and headed to a bathroom downstairs.

Cold shower, cold shower…

Pulling down my boxer briefs, I let the weight of my cock hang freely.

You're turned on because you're sexually frustrated. It's not about Aria. Just think of the wife and rub one out real fast. You'll finally be able to sleep.

The justifications were sinful as I wrapped my fingers around my shaft and slowly stroked it. Closing my eyes, I tried to focus on Vanessa—her body, her face, our lovemaking. But those images were forced away and replaced with a fresh memory: Aria kissing me. The harder I tried to erase that image, the longer it lasted in my head, taunting me with its sick meaning. I felt enslaved to indescribable pleasure. I had sealed my fate and accepted that I was Hell bound.

One simple decision was all it took to chain myself to the sorrow and guilt that I would feel once I'd accomplish what I biologically needed. My body was almost convulsing as I stroked my length faster, breathing harder, while beads of sweat dropped down my forehead and chest. It was all happening in flashes in my mind. X-rated graphics assaulted me; they wouldn't disappear. Everything was Aria now, as if a virus had entered my system and wouldn't leave. Her eyes, her lips, her breasts, her toned legs… I kept replaying every moment I had shared in her presence. Every moment she had hugged me, sat on my lap, cuddled me, kissed my cheek, or touched my chest. No memory was safe anymore. No longer were they stored inside my vault of innocence: the demon within had confiscated that purity by contorting and manipulating the memories into everything lustful, sexual, and immoral.

Masturbation was not part of my routine in life, but I couldn't help myself as the room seemed to spin while I shamelessly stroked my cock. Steadying my balance, I held the edge of the vanity and opened my eyes, hoping her innocent face would fade away. But it didn't. My pleasure only intensified and I couldn't stop myself. A ravenous beast had taken over, and it wouldn't cease its possession until it was satisfied.

"Fuck!" I held my breath as every muscle in my body tensed up before I finally released an unbelievable load, leaving a mess all over the toilet.

Twenty seconds of the most intense pleasure, only to be left with unbearable shame.

Was it worth it?

Once again, the taunting voice in my head berated me as I reached for some tissues to clean up. If psychically impregnating a woman were possible, I would have achieved it.

My body finally relaxed and my demon was satiated as he shackled my wrists to a wall, goading me. He was my evil twin, someone I thought I had killed long ago. Behold his resurrection.

On the verge of a breakdown, I fought my tears while I washed my hands. The shame I felt was too much to handle. I couldn't even look at myself in the mirror.

What kind of father am I? How could I allow this to happen? How could I be so weak and perverse? They should lock me up. I should turn myself in tomorrow. How the hell could I fantasize about my daughter? I needed help.

There was no way I could forgive myself. The deed was done. Raising my head, I finally stared at my reflection: Noble Noah versus twisted shadow Noah. I was drowning in the guilt of what I had done, and I hadn't even touched her. Crossing that line in my head for the past five minutes said enough. The man who was staring back at me was unrecognizable, and I was suddenly afraid of myself because I couldn't identify with my reflection.

You just murdered the salvation of your soul. Welcome to my world.

I had split myself in half. Who was I? Had I always been this person? Was this shadow of a man always present? Or was I just oblivious to his existence? Nothing made sense to me, and no matter how hard I tried to rationalize, it still didn't take away the heavy burden of shame. My temper suddenly shattered, and I felt a surge of anger through my body as I resisted the urge to punch my fist in the mirror. Pushing back remorseful tears, I made a mental note to call up my shrink in the morning. It wasn't too late. I could fix this. There had to be a reason for all of it, and I had to believe it was fixable. Nothing was destroyed, and I would never lay a hand on my daughter sexually—ever. I'd rather kill myself.

Being vulnerable had never really been my deal. I had been through a lot of shit in life, but I'd never felt comfortable crying in front of anyone, or on my own. The fact that my daughter could get so close to me and make me feel this emotionally exposed scared the fuck out of me. I didn't know how to deal with these feelings. It was too much to handle, and I felt so overwhelmed. I knew I had a spot reserved in Hell after what I'd done tonight, but I would never drag her to Hell with me. I would never do this again.

Take it easy. You were frustrated. You haven't had sex with the wife in a while. Give yourself a break. It's nothing serious. You were in the wrong place at the wrong time. No need to call that decrepit old shrink. You love Aria the same way any protective father loves his daughter, nothing more. Relax.

I desperately tried to comfort myself as I walked out of the bathroom into the darkness. The fucked-up part was that it wasn't "Noble Noah" doing the consoling in my head; it was my evil twin, slapping my shoulder and mocking me with a gloating grin that was supposed to pass for a sympathetic smile. I wished I was a blissfully ignorant person. Maybe my life would have been easier.

CHAPTER SEVENTEEN
ARIA

I didn't want to wake up that morning. It had been impossible to fall asleep after what happened the night before. I had kissed Noah… not full-out tongue action, but… I kissed him… on the lips, and he had walked out of my room like nothing happened. I probably embarrassed him and freaked him out. I'd felt way too humiliated to go after him. His departure felt like rejection. What was I thinking? I knew I wasn't supposed to cross that line, but I couldn't fight the attraction between us. There was something about him that pulled me closer while we lay together. It seemed useless to avoid or resist it, so I gave in.

Having already showered and styled my hair, I quickly fixed my face with some light makeup and sprayed on some D&G before I put on my school uniform. The girls at my school always hiked up their skirts to look sexier, leaving a couple shirt buttons undone to show off some cleavage. I could get away with the shorter hemline, but whenever I attempted to unbutton my shirt a bit, Noah gave me a hard time. He wouldn't let me leave the house looking so provocative. It wasn't an issue for me, though. Conforming to popular dress code was much easier once I got on school campus. Pretty sneaky of me, I know, but I just wanted to fit in.

Grabbing my schoolbag, I walked out of my bedroom and quickly checked my phone for text messages. Vanessa and Noah were already up. She was fixing a cup of coffee, and he was sitting on a stool by the island.

As I brushed past him, I glimpsed at the sports article he was reading on his iPad.

"Ah, look who's finally up!" my stepmom greeted me in her annoyingly high-pitched voice.

"Good morning, Aria." He kept his gaze on the article.

"Morning."

Noah's eyes remained glued to the screen while I placed my book bag on the floor. Normally, we would hug or I'd kiss his cheek, which had become a morning ritual between us. But today, I felt insecure, and I wasn't sure why. Maybe I was afraid of being rejected again. It would have mortified me if he pulled away from my hug and cringed at a simple peck on the cheek. I avoided it altogether.

"Slept well?" asked Vanessa, sipping her coffee.

"Yeah, more or less."

"Good, at least one of us did in this family." She sounded patronizing and kept glaring at Noah, throwing invisible daggers at him with her eyes. I guess she was secretly trying to get her point across. Although I don't think it worked, because he continued to ignore her without giving the slightest glance.

Shaking some Cheerios into a bowl, I poured some milk while stealing secret glimpses at Noah every five seconds. He was wearing a dark gray suit with a white shirt, navy blue tie, and smart black shoes. I noticed how he always wore this wicked band on his right wrist. It was a leather woven bracelet, braided like rope. The leather was dark espresso, and although the accessory didn't seem to fit with his formal attire, it gave him an edge, which was kind of mysterious. Noah wasn't just another suit at the office—he was so much more than that.

There was an uncomfortable tension between Vanessa and him. I wasn't sure if my presence only added to the agonizing awkwardness.

"I'll be home late tonight," Vanessa announced. She placed her mug in the sink and looked over at Noah. "Just thought you should know."

We were all dressed except for my stepmom, who was still in her pink silk night robe. My guess was that she was starting a much later morning than us.

Noah stayed silent as he swiped his fingertips across his iPad. Ignoring his irritated wife seemed like an effortless task for him.

"And that means I won't be able to make dinner this evening," she added. "You should probably order in."

"As usual," he muttered.

"What was that?" Vanessa whipped her head around. She angrily tapped her long red nails on the counter.

"I can cook," I blurted out.

Noah's eyes were on me. It was hard to read his face, but his piercing blue eyes darted over to my stepmom before he spoke.

"I was just saying," he paused and smiled at her, "that's no surprise, honey."

Could he sound any more sardonic?

"Stop giving me a hard time so early in the morning, Noah. You know I'm busy trying to launch this new swim line."

"Yeah, well, it's nice to know you're busy with better things than constantly visiting your incompetent plastic surgeon."

"He's not incompetent!" She glared at him, resting her hands on her hips. "Doctor Fielding has worked miracles on my face and body, and I'm always happy with the results."

"Vanessa." He stood up, walking toward her. *"Dear..."* He placed a consoling hand on her shoulder. "The man's incompetent because he should have known enough was enough when he reconstructed your nose three times. And evidently, you're not happy with the results, since you keep going back to him." Noah sighed. "I'm filing for divorce if you go through with another cosmetic procedure."

I'll admit, I would have hated being my stepmom at that moment, because it almost sounded like he was belittling her. But I knew him better than that. He was just giving her a painful dose of honesty, and sometimes the truth really hurt.

"You're bluffing."

"I dare you to try me."

Vanessa seemed to contemplate a comeback. I stayed quiet and grabbed my bowl before I walked out of the kitchen. Confrontation made me uncomfortable.

"So," she finally said, "are you saying you're done with this marriage? Is that what you're trying to tell me, Noah? Because I'm trying my best here!"

"Please do me a favor and save your crocodile tears. You look ridiculous when you cry anyway, and you can thank your surgeon for that."

"How can you speak to me this way?" she shouted.

Things were getting destructive between them as they exchanged harsh words. Noah wasn't cussing her out, but insults had the power to leave emotional scars. I had experienced this firsthand by living with Rob.

"I never complain when you devote all of your time to those cases!"

"I've always been a workaholic! You knew that while you were dating me, and you knew it when I asked you to marry me. I'm not the one who's changed here, *you* have! And I'm not happy, Goddamn it!"

"Everything I do is to make you happy!"

"You've got it badly twisted, sweetheart, because lately, everything you do is just the opposite. I've tried polite interventions with you. I've tried tough love, and nothing works. You've got two options here: get some therapy or hammer the final nail into the coffin and end this marriage."

I could hear her crying, and it made me feel bad. I wasn't exactly Vanessa's biggest fan, and we weren't close, but I've always had this ability to empathize with others. Noah didn't seem to understand her insecurities.

"I can't believe you would say all these hurtful things to me in front of your daughter!"

"Don't drag Aria into this—stay on topic. At least she was mature enough to leave and give us privacy to argue like children without the humiliation of having her witness it. Shame on us, right, honey?"

"Oh, shut up! You condescending asshole!"

"Ouch, darling. That hurt. Wanna throw another punch?"

"Get out of my sight!"

"Gladly, thanks for reminding me—don't want to be late for my meeting."

I was expecting her to say something, but all I heard was glass breaking, feet pounding up the stairs, and a door slamming shut. It made me jump. Afraid that she had hurled something at him, I ran into the kitchen.

"Is everything okay?"

Noah was staring off into space. He snapped back to reality when he heard my voice.

"No, but it will be," he casually replied. "You ready for school?"

I looked down at the broken glass.

"Don't worry about it." He exhaled. "The maid will clean it up later."

"Some messes just aren't nice to leave for other people to tidy, regardless of whether Irene's on your payroll—and leaving broken glass on the floor is irresponsible and dangerous."

Irene was our maid—an extremely kind lady. She taught me a lot of Russian words. I felt like the parent in this scenario as I grabbed a broom and swept up the glass. A pair of icy blue eyes followed me. My temperature started rising.

"Don't grow up so fast, kiddo."

"I'm not a kid. Stop calling me that." I wished he could see me as the grown-up woman that I was.

"All right, you're a mature young adult who's taught her father a lesson in the rules of responsibility this morning."

"Well, I'm happy to have taught you something valuable," I said with a smirk.

"Smart-ass—give me that." He grabbed the broom from me. Our fingers gently brushed against each other, making my stomach flip. There was an immediate exchange of electrical currents through our fingers when we touched.

"I don't want you to cut yourself," Noah expressed with concern.

I could smell his cologne, and it made me light-headed again with overwhelming emotions. He was unreal. This man was flawless in my eyes. Even his most blatant imperfections were perfect to me. I didn't care that he had a fiery temper. I didn't care that he had the power to raise people up and smash them down within seconds. None of it mattered to me, no matter how intimidating he was, or whatever demons he had battled in his past. Noah stood before me as a powerful Titan, and I realized I had placed him so high on a pedestal that not even I could reach him. He was going to be my undoing. I was fully aware of it.

Offering a hand, I helped him sweep the glass into a dustpan before he discarded the debris in the bin.

"Get in the car," he said. "I'll be out in a sec."

I think he wanted to reconcile with Vanessa, but I didn't stick around to find out. Following his command, I grabbed my bag and marched out of the dream house.

ဆာလ

The car ride to school was quiet. I tried to start some conversation, but Noah kept giving me short answers, which made me feel like he either wasn't interested in the topics I brought up or didn't want to talk at all. Eventually, I gave up and let the radio play instead. My mind wandered, and I thought about my life back in New York. I hadn't spoken to my siblings in a while, and I felt bad for not keeping in touch very often. Mom and I emailed each other a lot, and I talked to Jade and Ally regularly on Facebook and FaceTime. I missed those gals. The only person I hadn't communicated with since moving here was my stepdad. It wasn't like he tried. He was dead to me.

After dodging the morning traffic, we finally pulled up behind my school. Noah usually dropped me off in the front, but today we had stopped at a gas station on the way and took a different route. I wanted to lean over and kiss his cheek before getting out of his sexy sports car, but the vibes he was giving off made me feel like hiding under a rock. I worried I'd made things weird between us because of the night before.

"You should invite some of your friends over for dinner," Noah said. "I'm sure you're sick of it being the two of us all the time."

I was right. He didn't want to be alone with me anymore. I hated myself.

"Um… sure. I'll extend the invitation."

"And you don't need to cook this evening. I'll order in."

"I don't mind cooking."

"Aria." He sounded annoyed. "Let's keep it simple tonight. How about some Chinese? Pizza?"

"Pizza's fine." I tried to be agreeable.

"Great. I'll see you at home, then."

Unfastening my seat belt, I slung my schoolbag over my shoulder and reached for the door handle. I was about to leave when I paused and looked back at him. He had one hand on the wheel, and his other elbow was bent on the edge of his window, resting his head in his hand.

"Noah…"

His gaze found mine.

"Are you okay?"

"I'm fine, sweetheart." A ghost of a smile appeared as soon as the ice in his eyes liquefied. "I didn't plan on starting my morning that way. I sort of lost it—sorry you had to hear all that."

"Maybe if you suggest couples' counseling to Vanessa, she'd be on board."

"Has anybody ever told you that you are way too wise for your age?"

I couldn't help but smile. "I've heard it too many times to count."

"Come here—I need a hug."

He gave me the world when he said this to me. All my fears and insecurities suddenly vanished. Leaning in, I wrapped my arms around his neck and hugged him closely. There wasn't anyone around us, and even if there had been, they wouldn't have been able to see anything through the tinted windows.

I wanted to confess my love for him, as if it was my last day on Earth and I'd never have the chance to say those three words again. But I couldn't. I just couldn't.

"I love you, baby." He held my face, staring deeply into my soul before kissing my forehead. Holding my breath, I slowly exhaled when he withdrew.

Memories flashed before me. I remembered the way his lips had felt when I had kissed him the night before. I had to resist the need to do it again, but Noah was just intensifying those urges.

We locked eyes, and once more, I felt that impulse—that strong desire to close the space between us. But I chickened out. Our midnight encounter had left me feeling sad and confused, and I lacked the confidence to make a second attempt. A part of me wanted to yank him by the tie and feel his lips crash down on mine, surrendering to me, allowing me to explore his mouth with my tongue. I knew better, though. These steamy events would only transpire in my mind, not reality.

"I'm gonna miss you." I don't know why I admitted this, but I blushed right afterwards.

"You're such a sweetheart." He tilted his head to the side, half smiling.

"I mean it, though. I'm not just saying it to be sweet to you. To be honest, I didn't expect to grow this close… not used to it."

Noah gently touched my cheek, and before I could stop myself, my hand was on top of his. I softly kissed his palm, maintaining eye contact. He blinked a couple times as if to break free from my compelling stare. Maybe he was receptive to my touch, after all. Silently, I begged him to release me from this torture. My heart was pounding so hard I was sure he could hear it if he leaned in.

Moistening my lips, I left them slightly parted as Noah pressed his forehead against mine. Did he feel what I was feeling, too? I closed my eyes and listened to my breathing as a scorching heat spread all over my body. Bravely, I placed my hand on his chest, right at his heart, just so I could feel it thudding against my palm. I needed to feel some sort of vibration. I needed physical evidence as proof that he was just as affected as I was.

"Aria." His voice sounded husky, like a hushed whisper, giving me chills.

Our foreheads were still touching, and when I looked at him, his eyes were closed. All he had to do was tilt his chin up and kiss me. One subtle movement, and I would dominate his lips.

Oh, God… why am I thinking this way?

"Aria…" he whispered again, gliding his fingers through my hair. My desire to kiss him was so strong that it was making me hurt inside. Holding back was painful.

Bravely, I sloped my chin up and leaned in closer, gently brushing my lower lip against his. A sizzling spark ignited upon contact. It was enough to make me abandon all self-restraint as I tried to taste his lips again, praying he would kiss me back. But he didn't make a move. My heartbeat thudded in my ears as I moved another inch, barely touching his lips.

Why am I so attracted to you?

Breathing slow, I steeled myself for my next move, when suddenly, he dropped his hands from my face and held my arms.

"Stop." Noah rested his forehead against mine.

I wanted to cry because I knew there was no way I could make him understand these feelings I had for him. There was no happy ending for me. I was a desolate character from a Shakespearean play, destined to carry out an ill-fated life that would only end in heartbreak and inevitable tragedy. *Hamlet,* oddly, came to mind. I felt like Ophelia, suffering from melancholy and erotomania—the delusion in which you believe another person is in love with you. I might as well have labeled myself psychotic, schizophrenic, and a sex-crazed nymphomaniac, too.

Noah may have loved me, but there was no way he would ever *fall* in love with me. I was fooling myself.

How could I even classify my disease, this sickness that wouldn't go away? There was way too much hypersexuality in my head. I didn't think it was normal—especially since I kept fantasizing about sex with my father. I needed professional help before I lost him for good.

Regardless of the warnings, my body refused to listen. Leaning toward him, I grazed his lips with mine, ever so gently. My breathing had become more labored, despite my efforts to control it.

"Don't." He pulled back, stopping our mouths from colliding. "Don't move." Noah held me in place. "Aria, what… what's going on here?"

"I don't know."

I think he needed me to convince him that nothing was going on between us. But I couldn't do that. It would have been a lie.

Please tell me what you're thinking. I felt anxious.

"Did you… just try to kiss me?"

Wasn't it obvious? I opened my mouth to speak, but no words came out. On the verge of panicking, I tried to calm myself. Being around him only triggered my anxiety more. Embarrassed and emotionally exposed, I had to get out.

"Listen, I'm sorry." He frowned. "I'm confused. I don't mean to make you cry." Noah brushed my tears away with his thumbs. "We should talk about this later."

But I was too stubborn to listen, and my pride was too wounded to handle things maturely. "You didn't make me cry. I'm just going through stuff. It's not a big deal. I'll handle it solo, always have." I forced a smile, picked up my deflated ego, and opened the passenger door.

"Wait—"

"See you later."

"Aria!"

His words fell on deaf ears as I slammed the door shut. I couldn't handle sitting in that car any longer; it was too overwhelming. It didn't help that I had a math exam in twenty minutes. All I could think about was the *aftermath* of that almost kiss instead of algebra equations.

Fuck. My. Life.

CHAPTER EIGHTEEN
NOAH

Nothing seemed to help me at the moment. Whatever I did, I couldn't get her out of my head, nor could I stop obsessively thinking about what had happened in the car earlier. I was supposed to be on my lunch break, but I was still at my law firm, sitting at my desk, squeezing a stupid stress ball in my hand. Last night's events looped in my mind. It was a good thing I hadn't lost control with Aria. I knew exactly what was happening. Thankfully, I'd backed off just in time. Was it possible that she was attracted to me? I was her father, for Christ's sake. Why the fuck did I even feel this way?

You wanna bang her brains out, penetrate her and teach her a...

I had to cut off that twisted voice in my head. My demon was still alive in there, and all I felt was disappointment. This attraction couldn't happen between us.

I created her. She's a part of me, and we're not supposed to feel this way.

Shit.

Well, I had said it... "we." The answer was crystal clear.

Aria was not just my daughter; she was my world. My self-destructive days were done, and I did not want to go back. Rotating the rubber ball in my hand, I sighed in irritation. My mind was a fucking mess, my marriage was in crisis, and to top it all off, I was working on my biggest case ever with a cocky client who refused to listen to my legal advice. What the hell was I hired for, then? To make matters worse, my teenage daughter was emotionally confused, and now I was failing as a father because I was too busy dealing with my own problems. Maybe I was over analyzing things too much. I had to simplify it. Life didn't need to be that complicated.

Divorce the wife while you still can before you've got a baby on board. Drop that dumbass client, and just give in to your desires regarding Ar—

Nope, didn't want to hear her name, as I struggled to dominate my darkness within. Was this how it was always going to be now, living life through the eyes of Jekyll and Hyde? I squeezed the ball harder, hoping it would stop my paranoia.

I'm going crazy.

I would have volunteered to be in a padded cell for God knows how long until I was cured of this… whatever the fuck it was. It wasn't normal, and I felt ashamed about the night before.

No, you don't. It felt good—admit it. When was the last time you ever blew a load like that? Never.

Snapping, I hurled the stupid stress toy at the wall, then stood up and paced my office.

Noah, you want her. You wanted to kiss her in the car. You wanted to kiss her last night. And trust me, you want so much more than that. Shall I list the fantasies?

The thoughts were pure torture. I couldn't tune them out.

I'm not trying to torture you, pal. I want you to be honest with yourself.

Why the fuck was I talking to myself?

You're not, I'm talking to you.

What the fuck?

Pour yourself a glass of whiskey and wind down for the afternoon. You need it.

I was losing it. Desperate to get a grip, I picked up the phone and dialed my assistant.

"Diane, I need you to make an appointment for me with Doctor Grey… Any available time is fine… I can clear my schedule." I hung up, and minutes later she called me back confirming my ten o'clock appointment on Wednesday next week.

Alexander Grey was a phenomenal psychiatrist, specializing in cognitive therapy. He had counseled me before, when I was struggling with my drug addiction. I was referred to many doctors during that time, and the only one who seemed to make a difference was this guy. Coincidentally, I had discovered last year that he had moved to LA. One of my colleagues had mentioned his son was seeing him for counseling, which is how I had found out. I had paid him a visit before the new year, just to say hi and see how he was doing. He had given me his card and told me to call him if I ever needed someone to talk to. I had faith in Grey's methods of healing. I wouldn't settle for less.

So, you're just gonna march into his office, make yourself comfy on his couch, and tell him you want to fuck your daughter?

There it was, that taunting voice, laughing at me once again. I guess he took pleasure in my torment. The only person I could be angry at was myself. Split personality or not, that demon within me existed and wasn't going anywhere. I needed answers. I needed to find out *why* I was like this, and the only way was to open that door that read DO NOT ENTER. Grey would have to be given access to look inside and assess the damage.

I didn't want to do it alone.

A knock at my door suddenly sucked me out of my personal purgatory. Clearing my throat, I adjusted my tie before saying, "Come in."

My colleague Amir stepped into my office in a sharp navy suit and a fresh buzz cut. He was tall and in good shape, with green eyes and a goatee. The man was happily married with kids and one of my best friends.

"Good, you're not with a client," he said. "What the hell are you doing cooped up in here? Let's grab lunch—I'm starving, my treat."

I abandoned whatever warped reality I had traveled to and plastered on a winning smile. There I was: my cheerful self again, pretending as if I wasn't unraveling at the seams.

CHAPTER NINETEEN
ARIA

The house was empty when I came home from school, which wasn't surprising because Vanessa was rarely around. I'd had an average day full of the usual boring stuff, so I livened up my evening by inviting some friends over for dinner. Jessica was the only one who said she would make it—the other girls had cheerleading practice.

Lives of the Beautiful and Popular: that would be a cruddy title for a soap opera. Where would I even fit in? I wondered. My stomach churned every time I thought about Noah. For once, I wasn't looking forward to seeing him.

You've officially made things awkward now. Great job!

Dragging my feet to my bedroom, I tossed my bag on the floor before I collapsed on the bed. The ceiling was my only focal point as I stared up at it for the longest while. I needed to erase the memory of what had happened between me and Noah in the morning. But it was impossible.

After what seemed like forever, I turned on my iPod and listened through a playlist. I was in the mood for some '80s tunes. That era was the most fashionably confused. Shoulder pads, parachute pants, mullets... I was thankful the fashion industry had abandoned retro fashion, locking it away forever in the fashion hall of shame. However, I loved '80s films like *Pretty in Pink, The Breakfast Club, Sixteen Candles,* and *When Harry Met Sally*—oh, and *Dirty Dancing.* I was a sucker for those chick flicks.

Finding my favorite track, I turned up the volume and relaxed. The only thing getting between me and my math textbook was myself. Procrastination was a bitch.

⋘⋙

I had already changed out of my school uniform when Jessica came over. It was almost five, and we were hanging out in my room until Noah would be home with dinner. Jess was your typical all-American teenager, standing at five foot five, hazel eyes, thin frame, with long, dirty blonde hair. Almost everyone in this state had cinnamon skin because of the California sun.

"I so need to go on a diet," she said.

"Jess, seriously, I'm not gonna repeat myself. You don't need to—you're already skinny enough."

"Yeah, but I think if I lost ten more pounds, Jake would ask me out."

I rolled my eyes and dropped my pencil in my notebook. "If Jake hasn't asked you out by now, that should say enough. He's probably gay."

"Definitely not!"

"You're so pretty. Don't be so shallow-minded and don't settle for shallow guys. They're not worth it—not even mega dream jocks like *Jake Matthews*."

She was quiet. I took it as a good sign. Hopefully, my advice was sinking in.

"How come you won't give Ryan a chance?" Jess finally asked. "You've got the guy wrapped around your little finger."

I wasn't sure how to answer that. "I don't know… I'm taking my time. I'm not one to commit to anything serious so soon."

"Is it because of your mommy and daddy issues?"

My face went bright red.

"Oh—shit," Jess gasped, covering her mouth. "I really don't have a good filter sometimes. I'm sorry, Aria." She frowned. "That came out sounding insensitive."

"No, it's fine." I tried to smile. "You're right. My commitment issues are because of my parents. I have this fear of getting close to people, especially guys. Nothing ever lasts. I mean, my mom and dad are a prime example of failed high school relationships, and they were supposedly 'sweethearts.' It's obvious I wasn't a planned pregnancy."

"Still, it must be way cooler having younger parents. Mine are in their 50s and unbelievably boring. But your dad is so frickin' awesome, not to mention a total hunk!"

"Jessica!"

"Sorry! I'm just being honest! I'm sure it's not the first time you've heard he's total eye candy."

It wasn't, but it annoyed me how all my girlfriends were crushing on him. My jealousy was pointless. To what end? The question depressed me. Envy does nothing but make you suffer. You waste your time and precious energy by creating more misery for yourself. I guess it was a universal vice that we all had to conquer.

"I've got some *juicy* gossip to share with you." Jess rolled onto her tummy, swinging her legs back and forth. "Technically, I'm not supposed to tell you this, but oh well." She giggled. "I pledged no loyalty to Steph, so…"

"What do you mean?" I arched an eyebrow.

"She told me today the next time you invite her over, she's gonna put the moves on your dad."

"*What?*" That shouldn't have surprised me.

"She's so hot for Noah. It's insane. She's got some serious plans to seduce him."

"Oh, really?"

I hid my anger.

"Yeah, she went through all these fantasy scenarios… wearing something skimpy… being alone with him…" Jess started cracking up. "And she said she wants to suck his—*you know*…" She threw her head back, giggling harder than ever.

"Oh, my God! Okay, enough!"

The sheer thought of snobby Stephanie Cohen getting it on with Noah made me want to puke. I was irritated, but I didn't show it.

"I just think it's funny," Jess said. "I've been over here so many times, and Noah's amazingly sweet—not a creep like Steph's dad. I wouldn't worry about her, though. She's lost in some crazy delusion."

My mind spiraled into insecurity. Steph was the "hot girl" at school. All the popular guys wanted to date her. I didn't want her over anymore when it was clear she had ulterior motives.

"Besides," Jess added. "I think she's way too chicken to *actually* put these plans into action. Your stepmom's got the body of a porn star. I doubt our deluded friend would be an ideal lay for him."

This conversation was making me uncomfortable. I wanted to close the subject before I'd slip up and vent about Noah's marriage problems, but Jess got there first.

"Let's take a break! My brain's fried from all these assignments."

She'd read my mind as she got off the bed and walked over to my iPod dock.

"I downloaded this song yesterday." She swapped our iPods and cranked up the volume. "I can't stop listening to this—it's a sick remix of 'Beautiful, Rich & Horny.'" Jess grinned. "Get up! Let's dance!"

I laughed, watching her sway to the electro house beats while singing along to the lyrics, which were… interesting. The worst part was when I started singing with her.

"We have to choreograph this and make a video!"

"Are you kidding me?" I laughed. "We are *so* not uploading this on YouTube."

"We *so* are! Seriously, Aria—have some fun for once!"

I was tired of being the responsible teenager all the time. I just wanted to do something dumb and potentially reckless. I wanted to act my age.

"Tie your shirt like this." Jess walked over to me and rolled up my red tank top, tying it in a knot. "See? Show off those abs!"

Abs?

I didn't think I had any.

"Now, pull down the front a bit—I wanna see some cleavage."

I followed her instructions like a virgin learning the art of seduction. (More like the art of turning into a video vixen.)

"Let your hair down."

I yanked on my hair tie and shook my locks free.

"*Way* sexier. Unfasten your jeans."

"Definitely *not*."

She rolled her eyes and tugged my pants down to my pelvic bones.

"Cute thong!" Jess giggled. "And it's black... You know what that means, right?"

I shook my head.

"You're so ready to get laid."

The only meaning I attributed to that color was creativity. All thoughts spawn from the darkness before they can materialize in reality.

I hadn't told Jessica about my tragic relationship with my ex. She emulated my new wardrobe change and placed her laptop on my desk. We choreographed a dance routine full of booty popping and twerking before we were confident enough to sing along with the lyrics. Jessica sang the first four verses, and then it was my turn. I got in front of the camera and lip-synched the explicit lyrics with her.

Yeah, I'll admit it, I felt "super slutty" dancing the way I was, but I didn't care. Why did slut shaming even exist? I had read a book on tapping into your inner dark goddess. It was extremely enlightening. It honestly felt good to let loose and just move my body. Jessica started grinding on me while I thrust my hips into her, as if I had an invisible... You get the picture. It was more comical than sexy. When she finally turned around, her face went flush as she dashed for the iPod and turned it off.

"Why'd you kill the tunes?" I asked in confusion.

Looking panicked, she quickly untied the knot on her shirt and plastered on a smile.

"Hi, Mr. Hunter."

Oh crap.

I didn't want to turn around and face him. How long had he been standing there watching us dance like strippers? I was equally embarrassed as Jess.

"Hello, Jessica." Noah smiled amusingly, folding his arms in his chest. "I hope this isn't something you're planning for the school talent show."

"Absolutely not!" She laughed. "We were just messing around, right, Aria?" Jess quickly shut my laptop and fixed my shirt since I was still paralyzed.

At least our video footage wouldn't make it online.

"Hello?" Jess snapped her fingers. "Anyone alive in there?"

Noah slid his hands into his pockets and pushed his weight off the door frame. He stared at me while I stayed tongue-tied.

"I'm gonna order pizza. Do you girls want the usual?"

"Veggie sounds great. Thanks, Mr. Hunter."

"Please, call me Noah."

"*Makes you feel old to be addressed so formally*—we know!" I slammed the door in his face.

"Aria!" Jess looked annoyed. "What the hell?"

"I just want some privacy."

"Your door was open, so it's not like he was intruding."

"*Whatevz.*" I slumped back on my bed.

I had rudely ended our conversation. I just couldn't handle him being in my space at that moment. Noah's facial expressions were hard to read; it was frustrating. The way he had stared at me… I couldn't tell if he was mocking me in his head or checking me out. Being walked in on like that had left me mortified.

80C03

Once the delivery guy arrived, Jess and I left my bedroom and joined Noah in the kitchen. He had changed out of his suit and was wearing a pair of faded blue Levi's and a black tank top. Jessica couldn't stop staring at his arms. I couldn't blame her. Noah was fit, and he worked damn hard to stay in shape. He didn't get those bulging biceps and six-pack overnight. I remember when he showed me a photo album of his younger years. He was a skinny little kid then. Puberty is an amazing phenomenon.

"How's the pizza?" Noah asked, helping himself to another slice.

"Delicious," Jess answered with a smile.

I could feel his eyes on me, radiating an invisible heat wave. He observed my every move as if I were a test subject. My face felt feverish. I was still embarrassed about him walking in on our sexy dance routine.

"Aria, you're quiet this evening," he stated.

"Don't have much to talk about."

Jess looked at me, and then at Noah. "Well, *I* have plenty to talk about!"

She was so quirky and extroverted—the opposite of me. Jess went on about her plans to fly to Europe in the summer with her cousins. I tried to stay interested, but Noah was distracting me with his flawlessness. He gave Jess his undivided attention, occasionally glancing at me now and then. I hated being so attracted to him. It wasn't fair.

"… sounds like you'll have a blast!" he said to Jess. "Me and Aria are going to Italy this summer as well."

"Say what?" She glared at me. "You mentioned nothing about that!"

"That's because I changed my mind." I stood up and carried my plate to the sink.

"Funny," said Noah. "I wasn't aware of this."

"Sorry—maybe next summer." My condescending grin spoke more truth than my words. "Jess, are you done? We still need to finish that project."

"Yeah, I'm done eating. Thanks for the pizza, Noah."

"You're very welcome."

Charisma just oozed off him every time he smiled. His presence alone was enough to make a woman faint. But again, I was overdramatizing things in my mind. My fantasy world was typically sexy and comical, mirroring the shy but hilarious nerd I had locked away. Impatiently, I hooked my arm around Jessica's and pulled her forward before she could start more conversation with the man of my dreams.

ڃڀ

Studying was nearly impossible since Jess wouldn't drop the Noah subject.

"Are you two fighting or something?" she asked.

"No, what makes you say that?"

"I don't know. You're acting weird around him."

"How so?"

"You're usually affectionate and sweet. What's going on?"

"How observant of you," I sarcastically replied.

"That's it? You're not gonna tell me?"

"There's nothing to tell, Jess."

"I'm your best friend—you know you can talk to me."

She was the only person at school I was closest to, but best friend status? No, not yet. Jade and Ally were my true blues. I missed them a lot.

"We had a dumb argument this morning," I said. "No big deal."

"Well, clearly it *is* a big deal and you're not over it since you canceled your trip to Italy—unbeknownst to Noah, of course."

"I don't want to get into it. Let's focus on this project."

She studied me for a while, and then eventually gave up.

"Okay, fine."

80C03

Jessica left my place around nine-thirty that evening, and my stepmom still wasn't home yet. Shutting myself in my room, music was the only good distraction. I was listening to Radiohead while I sat in front of my mirrored vanity doing my makeup.

Maybe if I look older, he'll notice me, I thought, tears running down my cheeks, leaving track marks on my foundation.

Brushing on some red gloss, I peered at my reflection.

Who am I? I hardly recognized myself. I was a hot mess, that's for sure. I felt like I was having an identity crisis.

Frustrated by my mood swing, I stood up and pulled off my shirt. All I had on was a black push-up bra and dark skinny jeans. Glancing at my figure, I twisted my body, searching for flaws from different angles. My chest was nowhere near the size of Vanessa's, but I was a decent B cup. I touched my navel and thought about getting it pierced. Ally had got hers done the year before, and I had gone with her. It looked painful, but she had soldiered through it.

Brushing my hair to the side, I tried to see if it improved my look.

Nope.

Sigh.

I ran my fingers through my locks like a madwoman. It was hair-spray overkill. I had sex hair going on, but I wasn't ashamed.

Maybe he'll think it's sexy.

Stepping into my walk-in closet, I rummaged through clothes and put an outfit together. My shoe rack was filled with a variety of designer heels; Prada, Louboutin, Valentino, Giuseppe Zanotti, Gianvito Rossi… These designers knew how to make amazing shoes for women. Grabbing a pair of black pumps, I slipped them on.

Hot. I snapped a selfie, taking another picture while blowing a kiss before I sent it to Ryan.

A few seconds later, my cellphone vibrated.

Damn, Aria, you are fine as HELL.

I smirked triumphantly, but felt anxious inside. The last thing I wanted was a provocative photo of me trafficked through hundreds of cellphones at school. I hadn't sent him a topless nude—just in my bra.

"Aria?"

There was a knock at my door, and I knew exactly who was standing behind it.

"Can I please come in?"

My music was blasting, so I turned it down.

The Noah Hunter side effects were beginning to physically afflict me again as my heart rate picked up. Not bothering to put on a shirt, I overlooked my indecency and just stood in the middle of my room, partly naked, dressed like… a hooker?

"Come in."

The door slowly swung open as I held my breath. Noah's eyes scanned my body from head to toe, and it made me shiver. I rubbed my arm out of habit like a nervous tick.

Shit. Why did I do this?

I felt shamefully naked in front of him and was worried that he'd mistake my wardrobe experiment for desperation. Was I truly desperate? I mean, why was I even doing this? Maybe I was in denial.

Acting out, I told myself.

The music only heightened the seduction in the air as he stood before me like an ageless vampire who could make me surrender to his will. But Noah wasn't a vampire, he was very much human. The way he made me feel was dangerous to my psyche.

"Aria," he murmured, stepping forward.

My skin was flaring up.

"Sweetheart, why do you have all that makeup on? Are you going somewhere?"

I strengthened myself and convinced my wounded ego to stand tall. "So what if I am? What's it to you?"

"Put a shirt on, please." He frowned.

"No."

Folding his arms in his chest, he arched a *very* sexy eyebrow at me. Yep, this was totally a challenge.

Bring it.

"You're in *my* room. If you don't want to see me in a bra, then leave."

"Is that right?" He took another step.

"Yep."

"You really love to test my boundaries, don't you?"

"From what I've observed, you *love* having them tested, especially by me."

"You're such a brat."

"And you're a domineering control freak."

"Who is your *father,* which means I have max authority in this household, Missy."

I wasn't backing down as we scowled at one another.

"If you refuse to cover up, then I'll just cover you up myself." Noah pulled off his tank top.

Closing the space between us, he slid his shirt over my head and gave me a stern look. It was a useless effort because I pulled it right off and threw it on the ground. The next accessory to go was my heels, as I kicked them off and stared up at him. Now we were both barefoot, with no shirt on. Noah's naked chest was… *lickable.* I couldn't help but undress him more in my mind. Gazing at his body, I glanced at the rippled muscles beneath his abs. He had the sexiest nipples, and I could have sworn he had flexed his pectorals on purpose, but maybe that was my perverted imagination playing tricks on me.

"We need to talk, Aria."

"I don't wanna talk. There's nothing to talk about."

He sighed and stared deeply into my eyes, as if they held all the answers he was searching for.

"Why have you changed your mind about Italy?"

I shrugged. "I want to go back to New York for the summer. I miss my friends. I miss Mom and the twins." It wasn't entirely a lie.

"I don't want you living with that asshole again." Noah clenched his jaw.

"I don't think Rob will be a problem after what you did to him last time."

"I don't care. Look, if you want to spend the summer in New York because you miss your family and friends, I understand. We can cancel the trip. But I would feel much more comfortable setting you up in safer accommodations."

His offer was sweet. Why did he always have to be so nice and understanding? I was angry because I wanted him to give me every reason to hate him, not love him more.

"At least let me come and stay with you."

"No."

"Aria, please don't push me away like this." There was a faint sadness in his eyes as he held my face. "You have no idea how much it hurts me when you keep me at arm's length. It's not even that short of a distance with you at the moment. You've got me standing behind a brick wall, and you're on the other side."

Trembling, I rubbed my arm again, hoping the goosebumps would disappear. It was difficult to process any rational thought because the only thing my brain registered was:

1. Noah is standing inches away from me with his shirt off.
2. I'm standing across from him with my shirt off.
3. This music's turning me on.
4. *He's* turning me on.
5. I want him.
6. I'm in love with him.
7. I shouldn't be.
8. I want to kiss him.
9. I want him all over me.
10. I shouldn't feel this way.

All right, so it wasn't just *one* thing, it was a list.

"That's hardly an appropriate metaphor to use, Noah. I'm standing right in front of you, minus a brick wall and a shirt." I pointed out the obvious.

"You know what I mean." He dropped his hands from my face.

Neither of us moved, never taking our eyes off each other, alone in our messed-up universe.

"You really don't need all this makeup." He reached out and rolled his thumb over my bottom lip, wiping off the red gloss. My stomach tightened. I could have smacked his hand away, but I didn't. Instead, I asserted myself through useless verbal combat.

"Don't tell me what to do."

"I'm your father." Noah cocked his head to the side. "I'm supposed to tell you what to do."

"Maybe I don't want you to be my father anymore." I sounded as cold and venomous as he had in the morning.

Expecting him to roll his eyes, he stayed quiet for what seemed like the longest five seconds of my life.

"You really know how to cut me deep," he finally said. "And that scares me. I hope you didn't mean that."

I definitely meant it—only because I didn't know how to make these feelings disappear. It was virtually impossible for me to carry out a normal father-daughter relationship with him. There was no way of making him understand as I stared into his eyes and saw the tide turn, submerging me in his sea of sorrows.

"It doesn't matter," I mumbled, catching his wandering gaze toward my cleavage.

"I'm sorry if I'm not doing a wonderful job in the 'daddy department.' I'm trying my best, Aria. I—"

"Stop it! Stop being the nice guy! I don't want to love you any more than I already do!"

After months of restraint, I had finally said the "L word" out loud. I was tearing up and hated it. I didn't want to cry. Wrong place, wrong time.

Noah looked at me with compassion, and I felt my heart squeeze inside my chest. The waterworks were starting again as I struggled to fight back tears.

"And please... *please* don't look at me like that."

"Like what?" He sounded confused.

"Like... like *that*," I stuttered, switching glances from his eyes to his lips.

"I don't know how else to look at you, Aria." His voice was low and seductive.

This man made me believe that behind those eyes was a promise: a promise that he would reveal his soul and allow me to see his true self. But it was all in my head... a figment of my imagination. *This* was his true self: an amazing man who loved his daughter like any good father would. My erotomania had fooled me into thinking he loved me differently, deep down. It was part of my "disease."

"Aria..."

My body was on fire. I wanted him to touch me so badly, but neither of us moved. We were teasing each other while our demons danced around us, taunting us, whispering temptation in our ears. One sinful act was all it took to bind them to our bodies, claiming our identities as their own… possession. They would drink our souls to unsalvageable nothingness.

"I don't want to argue with you," Noah whispered.

My skin tingled when he stroked my hair and brushed his fingertips up my arm, guiding my fallen bra strap over my shoulder. His touch was magic, sending electrical currents through my body. He was just too damn beautiful. My heart seemed to shatter and revive itself in his presence like a curse and blessing. I was grateful to have him in my life, but it depressed me knowing I had half his DNA. I would never be content with that fact.

The music wasn't helping. There's a reason religious fanatics ban "ungodly music": it puts you in a trance. And when you achieve that trancelike state, thoughts and images manifest in your mind. Doesn't the Bible imply Lucifer took part in some sort of musical worship? Maybe Satan was to blame. Maybe I was hell spawn. But how could I be a product of the Devil when a hybrid angel contributed to my creation? Noah wasn't evil, and my mother didn't possess an ounce of wickedness. She was just traumatized by life. I couldn't understand how this corruption had deeply rooted itself inside me. Where was its origin? Perhaps there was satanic intervention when my mom got pregnant—like that horror flick *Rosemary's Baby*. For a second, I imagined myself as a succubus with hell horns, looking back at Noah. White feathered wings would open from behind his shoulder blades, arcing in magnificent glory, like the angel I believed he was. Was he my only chance at salvation, or was I too corrupted to the core to be saved? All I wanted was to give in to temptation and contaminate him as well. But you can't corrupt an angel. The only being who stood as Biblical proof that there was any flaw in creating the angelic species was Lucifer himself. Noah wasn't Lucifer. He wasn't evil. But *I* was.

My iPod switched tracks and randomly played something slower, "Body Close" by Lyves X Synkro. It had captivating lyrics with a rhythmic bass drum.

As if the sexual tension isn't bad enough.

"You should go," I said. "Vanessa will be home soon."

"Why are you so adamant about pushing me away?" Noah scowled.

The space between us was so small. I could feel his body warmth.

"I… " My voice cracked. "I'm not trying to."

He was breaking through my barriers, and I was freaking out inside because I didn't want to break down in tears.

"Just talk to me, please." He held my hands.

Looking down, I loved the way his fingers intertwined with mine so organically. My hands were freezing, but his were brilliantly warm. How could I ever communicate these feelings to him without losing him? I never could.

The song lyrics were getting to me, as if fate were mocking me. Whatever powers existed above were clearly laughing at my expense. My palms were sweaty, and I wanted to pull away, but Noah stopped me.

"It's okay—I don't care." He firmly squeezed my hands. "I know you're nervous."

Apparently, he was a master of body language, too.

Great.

"Whatever's bothering you, you can tell me. You know I love you."

Hearing him say those three words resurrected my heart back to life, and then I cried because I knew he didn't mean them in the way I wished he would. His eyes were sad. I tried to compose myself, but the tears kept on falling.

"Sweetie, please don't cry… Aria," he whispered. "Come here." Noah guided my wrists around his waist and wrapped his arms around my back.

I was hugging him now, and it felt like heaven when he enveloped me with his masculinity. Black tears fell on his naked shoulder as I sniffled and tried to stop sobbing.

"Hey, *shhh…*" He caressed the small of my back. "It's okay, baby. Don't cry."

I snaked my arms around his shoulders with a desperate need and held on to him, as if my life depended on it. He slowly rocked me side to side in rhythm with the music. It was soothing, comforting, and erotic at the same time. I found comfort in his radiating warmth. I don't think he realized how his gentle rocking had turned into an intimate slow dance. It all happened naturally.

As I turned off the tap on my emotions, I noticed Noah's shoulder and rubbed off the wet mascara.

"Don't worry about it." He glanced at the black smudges. "You're so beautiful." He smiled. "I swear, you don't need any makeup."

"I know it doesn't define my beauty. It enhances it."

"Okay, now *that* is a lie." Noah chuckled as we moved side to side.

Why did he always have to smell so good? I rested my head in between the crook of his neck and breathed in his scent, wondering what Vanessa would think if she walked in on us. Maybe she wouldn't care. Sometimes, I didn't believe she really loved him; she seemed to love herself more.

Vulnerable narcissist?

"Aria."

"Yes?"

"I love you."

"I love you, too," I whispered back, placing the softest kiss on his throat.

"Are you gonna tell me what's going on with you?" Noah murmured in my ear, sending chills down my spine. "Well?"

I shook my head.

"All right, but I'm not letting you off the hook that easily. You're only getting a 'Get out of Jail Free card' tonight."

Pulling back, I looked at him and fantasized about him slamming me against the wall and devouring me. Having sex with Noah seemed like the only way I could ever transition to true womanhood. My past with the ex was nonexistent in my mind. The things I would do to Noah's flawless body… if he only knew. He'd probably think I was a porn star in training.

I was guilty of having X-rated dreams of waking Noah with some spontaneous foreplay… slowly sucking him off in his sleep. By the time he'd realized what was going on, he'd already be exploding, releasing wave after wave down my throat… too late to stop. I had countless dreams of him penetrating me in so many positions: spooning, missionary, lotus, reverse cowgirl. I'd wake up stimulated, bordering on an orgasm—

especially when I'd dream of him going down on me in my sleep, licking my slick, wet folds with his warm tongue.

Fuck.

I had to stop these sexual thoughts.

"Are you okay?" Noah asked.

"Yeah, I'm fine."

The music slowly faded out, ending our intimate encounter.

"You need to get a shirt on." He reached down to the floor and picked up his shirt. "And I need to finish up some work."

I couldn't help but steal a last glance at his flawless physique before he covered it up again.

"I'll be in my study if you need me."

I nodded.

"All right." Noah exhaled. "Going now." He couldn't take his eyes off me as he backed away. "Goodnight, then."

"Goodnight, Noah." I smiled.

Halfway out the door, he stopped in his tracks and turned around, as if he were struck by a revelation.

My heart pounded when he headed toward me, took my face in his hands, and kissed me softly. This set off a grand finale of fireworks in my chest. I was happy and disappointed at the same time because I wanted more. His unprompted affection had triggered that same urge I felt in the car with him that morning. My hands took on a will of their own as they slid along his jawline before my lips left a trail of kisses near the corner of his smile. I didn't want to pull back, but when I did, Noah's hypnotic eyes were on me. I surrendered and lost myself in his ocean.

Please don't leave. Please kiss me back.

"I love you."

"I can feel it," he said in a husky voice.

The energy between us was emotionally charged. I wanted to kiss him, but I was too shy to make a move. He seemed to mirror my desire as he glided his thumb down the curve of my jaw, rolling it over my bottom lip before it bounced on release. Licking his lips, he leaned in while I closed my eyes in anticipation. But our mouths didn't touch. He left a lingering kiss on my forehead, which left me disappointed. All that buildup… tension…

"I'll get out of your way now," said Noah. "Sleep tight, beautiful."

"Night."

He turned and left, leaving me sexually frustrated. I didn't know what to do with myself. Was this what a *real* sexual awakening was like? Why did it have to be him? Why was I so attracted to him? I hated myself. My self-loathing intensified when I finally went to bed and had back-to-back fantasies about sex with Noah.

♋

Lying in the darkness, I had stripped down to a white bra and panties since it was too hot for PJs. An hour had passed, and I still couldn't sleep. I needed to clear my head. Trying to relax, I focused on my breathing. But as soon as I placed my hand on my stomach, it moved downwards, as if an external entity had possessed me and was moving it for me. Noah's deep voice suddenly faded into my consciousness.

If you refuse to cover up, then I'll just cover you up myself.

I couldn't get his words out of my head. The disturbing part was how turned on I was when he'd said it.

Stop thinking about it. He's your father!

The images only brightened and zoomed in on graphic areas of his body. My fingers slid under the edge of my panties, searching for that swollen bundle of nerves that desperately needed stimulation. The first time my mother walked in on me engaging in self-pleasure, she nearly lost her shit. I was young and I guess I triggered her into thinking I'd wind up as a teen mom. Crazy how our parents seem to project their own fears and BS onto us. But this didn't hold me back as I writhed in the dark, stifling a breathy moan while imagining a naked Noah standing in front of me, watching me touch myself. My inner demon was wide awake as she painted a steamy image of him stroking himself while reaching for my sweet spot. Obscene as it was, I wanted him to break the rules, abandon his moral code, and glide his length into me, skin-on-skin.

I couldn't end this sick fantasy. Not when it felt *so good* to fuel it more with my darkness. My wrist was sore, but I was desperate for sweet release. The sensations were intense, as if Noah had claimed my sex drive. Nothing and no one could stimulate me, only him. I was cursed. My breath hitched as my toes curled into the mattress. Why did I sexually crave this man? His hard body was engraved in my mind forever, transforming into a lustful god of sex.

My imagination kicked into overdrive as I felt something wet spraying over my stomach. Slipping his fingers between my folds, he invaded a territory he had yet to conquer. I moaned at his intrusion, eyes locking, as if our energies had opened a cosmic portal for our souls to merge.

Yes… yes…

Panting uncontrollably, my body quivered when I finally achieved a mind-numbing climax, biting on my arm.

Sick, sweet release. A minute hadn't passed, and my conscience was already harassing me.

Was it worth it? You should be ashamed of yourself.

I was. Shame was all I could feel whenever I gave into these dark impulses, like I was an evil, fucked up person. It was depressing. I didn't want to feel this way. Life would have been much easier if I *didn't* feel this way, but sadly that wasn't the case. I didn't know whether to be elated over my little conquest with Noah earlier or to cry tears of agony for seducing him and corrupting his soul. I couldn't even trust myself anymore, especially not around him.

CHAPTER TWENTY
NOAH

What the hell was happening between me and Aria?

She kissed you again.

Not on the lips.

It was close enough.

That familiar voice patronized me in my head as I paced my study, shutting the blinds before I sat at my desk.

You didn't pull back...

I wasn't sure if it was my conscience speaking this time or the same guy who walked through that forbidden door last night: Noah 2.0, reprogrammed for destruction.

You wanted *to kiss her.*

My mind was racing. I couldn't calm down. I had to get away from her, otherwise I would have—

Lost control? Oh, please, she wants you. It's obvious, don't you think?

It wasn't like there was someone else in the room finishing my sentences—it was just that my voice sounded so foreign to me, like another entity was saying the words, impersonating me in my head. I sounded crazy. Maybe I was... Probably a good thing I'd made that appointment with Dr. Grey.

Taking a moment to breathe, I propped my feet up on my desk and folded my hands behind my head. Aria's lips had left a permanent impression on mine. I could still feel the tingle. A full twelve hours had passed, yet I could still taste her kiss… the sweet scent of vanilla gloss. I found it challenging to be in her presence lately, especially yesterday, when she had her friend over. I couldn't stand the way my daughter was behaving around me. She was pushing me away. I didn't want any distance between us. Not anymore. I knew she had abandonment issues, but so did I. Losing her again terrified me. I could handle losing everything I had worked hard for, but to live in a reality without Aria made me want to die. She had to know this.

You walked in on her dancing, and all you could do was ogle her body.

I exhaled loudly and faced the shadow standing before me.

You want her, you sick fuck.

No. I refused to believe his accusations. It was self versus self, battling it out. The sad part was that once my denial faded, all I could do was hang my head in shame. I would have begged my unyielding opponent to show some mercy and lock me up forever, but the more I tried to stop thinking about Aria, the longer she lingered in my head. There was no escape. Burying myself in work wasn't helping either since I couldn't focus.

Keep it together.

My appointment with Doctor Grey was next week. I could finally let my ugly demons out and trust that he'd help me.

Grabbing my phone, I was about to text Amir when my wife entered my study and shut the door behind her.

"I know we're not on good terms right now, but I need to talk to you. I've done a lot of soul searching."

"Vanessa, I think—"

"Hear me out, please?"

I wanted to apologize for losing my temper, but she cut me off again.

"Let me say what I have to say, and then I'll zip it and listen. I promise."

Dropping my feet off the desk, I exhaled. "I'm listening."

"My assistant, Phoebe—her husband dropped by at work today and surprised her with a big bouquet and chocolates. It wasn't anything expensive like the Belgian chocolates you buy me and designer jewelry, but the romantic gesture itself was so sweet. It made me realize how I've been making you feel like I take you for granted."

I wanted to respond, but she had the floor at the moment, not me.

"Noah, you always go above and beyond for the people you love. You basically own my company, and if it wasn't for you, I never would have been able to launch it. I've always been a prideful person. It's hard being vulnerable… so when you threatened to divorce me this morning, all you got was a stuck-up, egotistical bitch in your face."

At least she was honest.

"I don't want to lose you, and I don't want to end our marriage. I understand I've damaged it by ignoring your feelings about what I'm doing to myself with all this plastic surgery. I was bullied and picked on a lot through school… even my family"—she teared up—"I never felt pretty. Every time I looked in the mirror, all I saw were flaws. My cosmetic procedures are an attempt to rescue myself from the pain of living in an avatar I hate."

"But why?" I blurted out. "Nessa, you were so beautiful before. You never needed these procedures."

"That's not how I feel about it."

"I wish you could see yourself through my eyes."

"I can't. What I'm aware of now is that I definitely need therapy for the bullying I experienced growing up. You were right. I'm ready to get some counseling and save our marriage. I love you so much. You're such a supportive husband, and I know you're worried about my mental health. I'm sorry I've been selfish."

Did she switch her brain with someone else for twenty-four hours?

"Please don't give up on me… please." Vanessa wept.

I felt bad for hurting my wife. I hated arguing with her, but I respected her for coming to terms with her deep-rooted issues.

"Come here." I stood up and hugged her. "I'm glad you've agreed to get some help. I want to save our marriage, too. I haven't given up."

Have I?

∽◌∾

After what had felt like ages, we were finally intimate when we went to bed. It felt good to reconnect with my wife with some slow makeup sex, but that connection immediately interfered the moment I shut my eyes and fell victim to intrusive thoughts. I wasn't making love to Vanessa anymore… Aria's face had appeared before me. My nightmare had come to life. There was a part of me that wanted to stop, but the fact that I didn't want to open my eyes and look at my wife said enough. She was kissing me while I fantasized about Aria's sensuous lips caressing mine. It was twisted how I could conjure up such sick fantasies.

"Oh, God… fuck me harder, Noah…"

Revulsion seeped into my psyche after I came down from an explosive release. We were finally satisfied and breathless, entangled in each other beneath the sheets. Vanessa wanted to cuddle, but I wasn't in the mood for that as I pulled away.

"I need to clean up," I said. "Be right back."

It was an excuse, but my guilt was all-consuming.

Standing across the bathroom mirror, I stared at my reflection, alone with my demons at last. Nothing made sense anymore. Six months ago, I was so happy to have found my daughter again. I was grateful she wanted me to be a part of her life. Now I was racking my brain, trying to think of all the alternatives if Doctor Grey couldn't cure me of this… illness.

Should I push her away? What if she's better off living with her mother?

Fuck. No.

Natalie was still married to that asshole. There was no way I was going to let my daughter live with that son of a bitch again. I just couldn't figure out why Aria was trying to seduce me. My panicking thoughts were swallowing me whole when I heard Vanessa's voice.

"Noah, honey, is everything all right in there?"

I turned on the tap and splashed some water on my face.

"Yeah, I'm almost done. Be right out."

Switching off the light, I walked out of the bathroom and slipped back into bed.

"Come here, big boy." She giggled, wrapping herself around me. "I missed you. I missed *this*." Vanessa hummed. "We really needed some makeup sex."

Troubled by my damaged psyche, I stayed quiet and kissed my wife on the head before I shut my eyes and tried to sleep.

∞

The week had gone by agonizingly slowly. It looked like it was going to rain when I woke up on Wednesday morning. I left the house earlier than usual, which meant that Vanessa was driving Aria to school. This was a good thing. They needed to bond more. I just didn't want to be alone in the car again with my daughter. I didn't trust myself to be strong enough to resist temptation. It was getting harder to fight my feelings, but at least I was getting the help I needed.

I made a mental note of everything I wanted to discuss as I took the elevator up to Grey's office. The fateful morning I'd been dreading had finally arrived. I could have turned around and spared myself from humiliation, but then I remembered I was paying the guy to help me; and if I wanted help, I had to be honest.

Reaching the seventh floor, I got out and glanced at my watch. I wasn't late. Opera music echoed in the background as I walked down a narrow hallway. Grey's waiting room was empty, and there was no receptionist.

Maybe he gave her the day off, I assumed, making my way toward a big mahogany door.

I was about to knock when the door swung open, revealing Alexander Grey himself.

"Good morning, Noah." He smiled politely and stepped aside. "You're right on time."

He looked youthful for a man in his late forties. Standing only an inch taller than me, he still wore his favorite brown suit. Grey had moved to America with his parents when he was twelve years old. His father was British, which explained the surname. They emigrated from Denmark, and he had a tough upbringing. Money was tight and expectations were high in his family. But he turned out just fine. He had a hint of a Danish accent, but his voice was deep and soothing to the ears. I recalled telling him to start an ASMR YouTube channel for meditation if he ever tired of his gig as a therapist.

Just as I'd expected, his face was clean shaven. The only difference in his appearance was that he'd grown out his hair; it was lighter than mine— a caramel brown.

A pair of hazel eyes looked back at me before I was greeted with a smile. "Come on in, Noah. Make yourself comfortable."

Stepping inside, I scanned the room. His office was spacious—almost like a library, with bookshelves surrounding the walls, covered in books from corner to corner. The design was unique. I didn't feel claustrophobic. There were floor-to-ceiling windows on one side of the space with the curtains drawn back. He had repainted the walls.

"Love the new color," I commented, walking to the window.

"Thank you. Red adds warmth to a space and makes it more… inviting."

Nervously, I shoved my hands in my pockets and looked at him. He had a long brown desk resting on a red oriental rug, followed by two teal armchairs positioned across from each other in the center of the room. That's where he normally sat with his patients. Typically, I preferred to lie down on the black lounging sofa across the windows. I was glad he hadn't replaced it.

"Have a seat."

Sitting down was next to impossible for me at the moment. I needed to pace and move my energy.

"Do you mind if I stand and stretch my legs a bit?"

"Whatever you're comfortable with, Noah." Grey seated himself and pulled out a notepad.

"Do you need to update my file or anything? I've had a change of address since you last saw me."

"No need for that. Your assistant, Diane, already took care of it."

Right—he was always great at remembering names. I had to stop delaying the inevitable.

"You seem nervous," he said. "Relax. Remember the Vipassana breathing technique I taught you?"

Pacing the room, I found that it only heightened my anxiety, so I lay down on his lounger and closed my eyes.

"Inhale…" Grey instructed. "Exhale… Very good. Relax your mind. Focus your breathing on expanding your lungs and listen to my voice."

I stole a few minutes to breathe and clear my mind, focusing on my measured breaths.

"Do you feel more relaxed now, Noah?"

"Yes."

"Wonderful."

Patiently, I waited for him to direct me further when something suddenly flashed in front of me. I was in a tunnel, inhaling cold air as I walked in the darkness.

"Would you like me to turn off the music?"

"No, I don't mind," I replied, keeping my eyes closed. "I like it. Who's the composer?"

"It's one of my favorite operas. *Lakmé*, the Flower Duet, in Act One."

Lakmé, of course—now I remembered.

"But… we're not here to discuss my taste in classical music. Tell me what is troubling you, Noah."

I opened my eyes and stared off at space. How the hell was I going to talk about this?

"I think I'm going crazy."

Doctor Grey waited while I tried to gather my thoughts.

"What makes you say that?"

"Because I'm hearing things."

"Voices?"

"Yes."

"Multiple voices? Male, female?"

"No, just one—my own."

"Well, that's hardly a legitimate reason to label you 'crazy.' It's not uncommon to have conversations with yourself out loud or inside your head. Is this about your addiction? Do you feel the urge to use again?"

"No." I looked at him, watching as he removed his black-framed glasses from his breast pocket and put them on. There was a click of a pen before he started scribbling something down.

"I think it's safe to say I've conquered those demons," I continued. "I've been clean for ten years now."

"I'm glad to hear that, Noah."

"Thanks, Doc."

"Please, tell me, what seems to be the issue at hand?"

I paused, staring at the ceiling. "Do you remember when I talked about my daughter?"

"Yes."

"I got back in touch with her about six months ago."

"That's wonderful. How was the reunion?" he asked, crossing his leg over his knee.

"Better than expected. I have shared custody of Aria now. She's been living with me and my wife since December."

"I'm so happy for you. I remember you expressing how much it pained you to not be a part of her life."

A spell of silence passed between us as I sat up and leaned forward, resting my elbows on my knees.

"Is Aria getting along with the two of you?" said Grey.

"Aria's amazing. She's incredibly smart for her age and very mature. My daughter has adapted to her new life with me very well. She gets along just fine with her stepmom."

He readjusted his reading glasses and folded his hands in his lap. "Then what seems to be the problem?"

A phantom pain had suddenly afflicted me as I thrust my fingers through my hair and massaged the back of my neck. "I'm sorry, Doc, I just… I don't know how to open up about this."

Breathing out my anxiety didn't seem to help, and talking about it wasn't progressing well. I was too afraid to say the words out loud.

"You find your daughter sexually attractive," Grey blurted out.

I felt like someone had poured a bucket of ice water over my head as I looked up in disbelief and laughed off the excruciating awkwardness. My initial reaction was to yell out, *no!* But that would have been a lie. It perplexed me how well this man could read me; I hadn't admitted to anything.

"Wow… you're just… I can't believe…" I stammered, shaking my head.

"Apologies if I've offended you. I could be entirely wrong."

My snickering died down as I pulled it together and looked up at him. *Time to confess my sins.*

"You haven't offended me," I replied, refusing to articulate the words in my head: *Yes! I'm sexually attracted to her!*

"Can I have some of water?" I pulled on my collar and loosened my tie. The room temperature was comfortably cool, but I felt like I was suffocating in my skin.

"Of course." Doctor Grey stood up and poured me a glass. I drank it all down in big gulps, placing the empty cup on a round table next to me.

"It just feels like I'm on trial here." My palms were sweaty. I felt a panic attack approaching.

"I'm not here to judge you, Noah. I'm here to help you and offer my professional advice. Whatever you tell me in confidence will never leave this office."

"I'm fully aware of the confidentiality agreement."

"Good, then please take some comfort knowing that I will not violate that agreement unless you prove to be a danger to yourself or to others. In which case—"

"The authorities will be contacted, I know."

We had been through this before. He offered a reassuring smile and waited for me to speak. I was booked for the hour. Glancing at the clock, I realized only ten minutes had gone by, which made me antsy, so I stood up and paced again, hovering by the window. It was raining. A pedestrian caught my eye on the street as they opened a red umbrella. I closed my eyes for a moment and listened to the soothing sound of heavy rain.

"I wasn't expecting this to happen, you know… It sort of—did."

"What were you expecting, Noah?"

"For things to be normal between her and me," I replied, staring at a red fire hydrant.

"Who?"

Isn't it obvious?

"Aria."

"How do you feel about Aria?"

How do I feel? Like a son of a bitch who should be locked up.

"I love her. She's my daughter—my only daughter and only child."

"How old is she now?"

"Seventeen going on eighteen."

I heard the quick movement of his fountain pen rolling on paper. I still couldn't look him in the eye.

"How old are you now, Noah?"

"I'll be thirty-four in August."

"So there's only a sixteen-year age difference between the two of you, and you've been separated from her since the time she was born, correct?"

"Yes." I heard his pen again while I fixated on a stop sign.

"Do you find yourself attracted to her?"

I think he left out the word "sexually" on purpose because of the way I'd reacted when he asked me the same question earlier. Taking my time, I struggled to respond, but my silence said enough.

"It's okay, Noah. Just be honest."

"Right."

After a deep breath, I finally confessed in a quiet voice that lacked my usual confidence and authority.

"Yes, I'm attracted to her."

"Physically, emotionally?"

I paused again. "Both."

"Which one is stronger? The physical attraction or…?"

I was slowly falling apart in my head as I turned around and faced him.

"I don't know, Doc!" I erupted. "I don't know why I feel this way! I just know I shouldn't!" My hands were shaking. I shoved them back in my pockets and leaned my weight against the wall.

Doctor Grey removed his glasses and put the notepad away. "This is not uncommon—what you're experiencing, I mean. There's a reason you feel this way, and there are contributing factors that have caused dysfunction and lack of growth in your relationship with your daughter."

"I feel like a sick, perverted bastard."

"Have you acted on the attraction?"

"No, of course not!"

"Do you think you're a threat to her?"

"What do you mean?"

"Are you worried you might molest or—"

"No! Christ, no, never! I'd rather castrate myself than to touch her in any indecent way. I would never cross that line!" I was livid with rage. "You said you wouldn't judge me."

"That's not what I'm doing here. I'm trying to better understand your current mental state and thought process."

"Well, you're speaking to me as if I'm premeditating a crime."

"There are strict incest laws in the state of California. According to 'Penal Code Section 285, committing incest may lead to serious criminal charges.'"

Being a man of the law, I already knew this. I needed a smoke. Badly.

"Are you experienced in this topic or something?" I asked.

"I've had several patients—siblings who've encountered the same problem you are facing. Their situations were like yours: estrangement and separation at birth. Are you familiar with GSA?"

"What's that?"

"Genetic sexual attraction."

How could he remain so calm about this? All morning I had played out various outcomes of this visit with Grey. No matter how I replayed it, I always ended up walking out of his office in handcuffs.

"GSA," Grey said, "is a sexual attraction between biologically related family members. By this I mean siblings, a parent and progeny, or first and second cousins that have lived separately from childhood and meet later in adulthood."

Gaining my composure, I stepped toward the chair across from him and sat down.

"In your case," he continued, "given the unique circumstances that have occurred in your life, I can only conclude that a proper paternal bond did not develop between you and Aria because of your absence during her primary stages of growth.

"You missed out on changing diapers and feeding her. You missed the first steps she took as a baby, her first word, her first scraped knee from a playground tumble, countless birthdays… You've been absent for much of her life, Noah—so much that it's prevented you from nurturing Aria the way you should've when she was a child. Now that she's a grown, young woman, you find it difficult to develop a functioning paternal relationship.

"And the reason for this is that you didn't raise her from birth. The bond between father and daughter did not develop naturally between you two and run its course according to society's rules and expectations. I believe if you had raised her as a child, you would not have sexually imprinted on her in later years like you are currently experiencing right now."

"So, let me get this straight… You're saying that I want her— *sexually?*"

"Well, do you desire her sexually?"

I paused and rubbed my temples.

"Stay honest," he said. "The more honest you are with yourself, the better I can help you."

I exhaled my frustration. "Yes. Shamefully, yes. But it's not on purpose, I swear. I'm a married man and I love my wife. I don't want to feel this way about my daughter."

"Let's focus on investigating *why* you feel this attraction, instead of burdening yourself with negative thoughts. Clearly you have self-control, and you've stated that you would do nothing to harm Aria."

"I would take a bullet for her. I'd rather have my arms hacked off than lose her." As graphic as that was, I was dead serious.

"This is a good sign—well, not the self-violence. I would never encourage that. But what I mean is that you are self-aware."

"Then why am I constantly talking to myself in my head? I feel split in half."

"What are these conversations like, Noah?"

I was too embarrassed to open up about my fantasies the last time I jacked off… or what happened in my head when I made love to my wife—including that dream I had when I first met my daughter.

"It's just… I feel like I'm constantly battling right and wrong. There's a part of me, a darker half that wants me to…" I revised my choice of words. "… pursue Aria and give in to her advances."

"Wait, hold it right there." He gestured with his hand. "Has your daughter been seducing you?"

Scratching my head, I recalled the incident in the car.

"If attempting to kiss me on the lips is considered seduction, then yeah, I believe so."

"She started that all on her own?"

I nodded and summarized what had happened in the car and the night before.

"Hmm, interesting." Grey nodded pensively.

"I want it all to stop." I sighed. "It's wrong on so many scales, Doc. I'm sure you're aware of that."

"I am. But I would like to enlighten you about the general factors that contribute to GSA. You're not the only person in the world who's going through this."

"I feel like I'm bipolar or have split personality or something."

"I think you've opened a bit of a Pandora's Box here, and you're psychologically coping with it by dividing yourself from what you consider your 'evil half.'"

"So, I've fragmented good and bad?"

"Yes, precisely. We are not born evil. We come into this world as blank slates, but we have rebellious propensities. It's human nature. All three parts that develop your psyche seem at war. You're just exaggerating it in your mind."

That made sense.

"Any hallucinations?"

"No."

He jotted some things down and asked me about my marriage and Aria's relationship with her mother and stepfather. Grey listened attentively until I was done talking.

"Are you familiar with Sigmund Freud?" he asked.

"I've heard of him."

"Freud had devoted a lot of his studies to explaining the unconscious mind. He started psychoanalysis and believed a lot of our behavior comes from the unconscious mind. His specific area of interest was on sexuality, and this was because he grew up in the Victorian era where people in society were extremely sexually repressed. Anyway, according to his structured model: the id, ego, and superego play a key role in completing the psychic apparatus."

"That sounds confusing as hell," I responded.

"Well, the superego is predominantly preventing the desires of the id from manifesting into reality."

I guess that explained all the internal dialogue.

"The id is the disorganized part of your personality that holds a person's instinctual drives. And by this, I mean the needs that are present at birth. It's a primitive instinct that operates according to the pleasure principle. It is the source of our biological needs, wants, and impulses. Particularly our sexual and aggressive drives. I think you're doing your best to rationalize these thoughts and feelings, and the id and superego are boxing it out in your head, hence your internal warfare."

"You're certain that had I raised her, these feelings wouldn't have existed?"

"GSA is *very rare* between people raised together from early childhood. So yes, I believe that if she grew up with you, these sexual feelings would not have developed."

I let out a sigh of relief.

"Think about your sister for a moment."

"Breanne?"

Grey nodded. "Are you attracted to her?"

I twisted my face in disgust. "God, no! She's my *sister*! I mean, she's beautiful, but I love her the way a brother should. Nothing more."

Just the thought of labeling her as a romantic interest made me want to puke.

"And that's what I mean, Noah. You were raised together, so you both developed that bond as siblings. You and Breanne grew up in a safe, conditioned environment where you learned appropriate social interactions within your family unit. Had you been separated at birth and crossed each other's paths in adulthood, you would have never known you were related."

I couldn't imagine that scenario, but I knew what he was saying.

"How did you feel when you first saw Aria after seventeen years?"

Staring into space, I rewound to that November afternoon when I saw her in the courtroom. She was a vision of beauty. I was mesmerized, but I never processed my feelings that day.

"I… felt like I had died and came back to life when she looked at me."

How poetically tragic. I couldn't believe I'd said that.

"Were you aware of the physical attraction?"

"No, absolutely not. These past five months have been great between me and Aria. It's only recently I feel like my world's been flipped upside down."

"Hmm." Grey tapped his fingers on his armchair. "I think you were *subconsciously* aware of the attraction. You must have been repressing it or choosing to ignore it when you reunited with her. There must be something that triggered the id to become more vocal in your mind."

"Everything changed when she kissed me."

"I'm curious about how Aria feels regarding all of this, especially since she's engaged you in sexually subtle ways."

"Uh—I don't know. I tried talking to her about it, but she didn't seem to want to acknowledge anything or communicate with me. I think she's just confused."

"It's possible indeed." Doctor Grey nodded. "But I think you should consider a few important facts here. You mentioned that she's had a turbulent relationship with her stepfather. That's enough to say she doesn't truly know what it's like to have a real loving father figure in her life. When she met you, she did not know who you were.

"Her judgement of you was based on first impressions. You're a young, attractive, successful man. She may have felt attracted to you from the get-go but suppressed it. Maybe she felt as if her white knight had come to her rescue, and as she got to know you better, she discovered that you have all the admirable attributes she sought in a potential mate. You may have transformed into an idealized lover and father figure in her mind. She probably idolizes you."

Idolize me? No way. Not possible, I thought.

"Who am I to be placed on such a high pedestal?" I said.

"You are her father, and that's reason enough to place you so high above herself, including above other men. Is she dating? Do you allow her to date?"

"I've established some rules with her regarding boys, but I didn't forbid her to date. I just advised her to take it slow with love and relationships while she's still in school."

"And has she mentioned liking anyone in particular or brought anyone home for you to meet?"

"No."

Grey nodded again, as if he was making mental notes. "She could be infatuated with you."

"Well, I don't want her to be."

"Easier said than done. This is a complicated situation, Noah. With teenage girls, their feelings should be delicately handled, especially when it's your own daughter."

I nodded in agreement.

"On the other hand," he said, "we should consider the possibility that Aria may be experiencing the Electra complex."

"You've lost me again, Doc." This was uncharted territory for me.

"The Electra complex is when a child feels the impulse to psychosexually compete with her mother for her father's attention and affection. I find it unique because normally these feelings occur during the phallic stage of a young girl's psychosexual development."

"Phallic stage?"

"Ages three to six."

"Ah." I frowned, somewhat disturbed. "But she gets along well with Vanessa and her mother. I don't understand how she would compete with them."

"This could be the early stages. The hostility toward her biological mother or stepmother may manifest and reveal itself later on."

I tried to absorb everything Doctor Grey had explained.

"Is Vanessa aware of what's going on between you and your daughter?" he asked.

"No," I sighed. "I'd rather not discuss it with her. That's why I came here to see you. To get this—*situation* under control. Besides, nothing's really happened between me and Aria."

"Hmm, well, I suggest receiving some long-term counseling together."

"I don't want to make her feel like she's crazy by taking her from one therapist to another. I just got her back. I don't want to lose her again."

"That won't be necessary, Noah. I can counsel you both, together or separately. Either way, I recommend you sit down and discuss it with her. It may be awkward at first, but communication is always best. Should you choose to ignore her feelings, she may act out in more destructive ways, not only toward you, but toward herself. I'd like to prevent that from happening."

"I'll talk to her, even though it won't be easy."

"Just tell her you love her and that you want to have a healthy relationship with her. Make sure you express how happy it would make you if she agreed to get some counseling with you." He glanced at his watch and rose to his feet. "Unfortunately, our hour is up. I want to see you regularly. I believe I can help you through this."

"You helped me before. I'm confident you can help me again."

"Let's schedule your next appointment." Grey walked to his desk, pulled out his agenda, and opened it. "Are you free next Thursday?"

"Yes, but preferably in the evening."

"That's fine. How does seven o'clock sound?"

"Perfect."

He penciled me in and smiled. "It was good seeing you again, Noah."

"Good seeing you too, Doc." I shook his hand.

"Please don't torture yourself with shame," he added. "I honestly empathize and can fully understand the circumstances that happened in your life. I assure you, it's not uncommon."

Uncommon or not, I wanted to be cured of this. "Well, I won't take up any more of your time. Thanks for the session. I'll see you Thursday."

"You take care of yourself—and speak with Aria about what I mentioned."

"I will." Smiling politely, I said goodbye before leaving Grey's office.

How the hell am I gonna talk to her about this? I tried to re-enact the conversation in my head.

ⅎ⅏

The rain had stopped when I stepped out on the sidewalk. I did my best to remember all the important advice Doctor Grey had given me when suddenly my cellphone vibrated:

I miss u.

I couldn't help but smile. She always had this effect on me, making my heart bloom with life.

I miss you more, beautiful.

Cursing under my breath, I hit "send." I had to be more careful with how I expressed my affection to Aria. I didn't want to give her the wrong impression and confuse her any more than I already was.

Pick me up for lunch today?

Staring at my phone, I hesitated to respond while I held my breath, exhaling when my lungs couldn't take it.

Take her out. You miss her. You hardly got to see her this morning.

Remember what Doctor Grey said? If you take her out to lunch, you'd be doing it for all the wrong reasons, Noah.

This was the part where I was supposed to be aware of "the id and superego" boxing it out, one on one. I hated watching myself trying to choose between right and wrong, as if I had already pledged my allegiance to the dark side.

Feeling indecisive, I got in my car and turned on the ignition, when my cellphone vibrated again:

Plz?

She had a power over me I didn't exactly like.

Fuck's sake. Not emojis…

Releasing a sigh, I punched some letters on the screen and responded. It was impossible to ignore her. I didn't have the heart to do it. I was a big softie with her.

Okay, baby. Be there soon.

Id: 2
Superego: 0
End of round one.

CHAPTER TWENTY-ONE
ARIA

Chemistry class was a bore. Mr. Reese always cracked a joke right before dismissal. Today it was "What show do cesium and iodine love watching? *CSI!*"

Yeah… Hopefully, he didn't tell those jokes on dates. I was about to walk out of my high school when someone called out my name.

"Aria, wait up!"

Stopping in the hallway, I turned around and smiled. "Hi, Ryan." I suddenly remembered that racy selfie I had sent him.

Ugh. Why'd I do that?

He was tall with short, blond hair and cute dimples. All the girls wanted to date him because he was the "hottest guy" at school. I liked him because he wasn't a bully. Something about his gray eyes made me blush a bit.

"Are you going out for lunch?" he asked.

"Yeah. Noah—my dad's waiting for me outside."

"Oh, okay."

"Did you need something?"

"I was wondering if you'd like to go with me to the Sunset Festival."

Jess had already told me about it.

"Isn't that like, two weeks away?" I asked.

"Yeah, but I figured I'd ask you now before other guys did."

I was flattered, but I had other plans in mind.

"That's sweet of you to ask me, but I don't think I'll be in LA."

"Going somewhere?"

"I might fly to New York for my birthday to visit my family."

"When's your birthday?"

"April sixth."

"I should throw you a party at my place when you get back, or maybe even the weekend before."

"Please don't trouble yourself. I seriously hate surprise parties."

"Well, it wouldn't be a surprise since I already told you about it." Ryan chuckled.

"You get what I mean."

"Yeah, no worries." He offered a warm smile, walking in reverse. "Just don't get mad if you find roses in your locker."

What a sweetheart.

"I'll let you know if plans change," I yelled out. "Is that cool?"

"What does a guy have to do to get a date with you?"

I couldn't think of an answer fast enough, so I let out an awkward laugh and brushed off my embarrassment.

"Bring on the hoops of fire!" He winked at me and turned in the opposite direction.

A few seconds later, my girlfriends, Jessica and Stephanie, appeared behind me.

"Did you just turn down *Ryan Taylor*?" Steph asked in disbelief.

"Um, not really—I just told him I'm busy this weekend. Were you two eavesdropping?" I pushed through the double doors that led to the front entrance as my friends followed me.

"Well, *unbusy* yourself!" Jess hooked her arm around mine.

"Why?"

Steph chomped on an apple and tossed it behind her before she stopped me. "Okay, seriously, Aria"—she clutched my shoulders— "You're my bestie, and I love you, so I'm gonna tell you this straight up."

"O… kay." I scanned the parking lot to see if Noah was around, but he hadn't arrived yet. My raven-haired friend made a silent exchange with Jess and then fixed her piercing eyes on me.

"If you don't date Ryan or at least some guy, people are gonna think you're a lesbo."

"Well, what's wrong with being a lesbian?" I'd always been an advocate of equality for all, no matter their gender, sexuality, race, or religion.

"Oh, my God!" Steph gasped, releasing her death grip from my shoulders. "Jess, I was right. She's into girls."

Rolling my eyes, I shook my head. "I'm not. I'm just taking my time with dating."

"Is there someone else you like?" Jess asked. "Does he even go to our school?"

"Uh, no…"

"There is, isn't there?" Steph overdramatized almost everything with her highly animated facial expressions. "Is he loaded? How big is his cock? And when do we meet him? Details! Right now!"

Was sex the only thing she thought about? I questioned, relieved to see a black Audi convertible pull up.

"Sorry, girls—gotta go. Noah's waiting for me."

Slipping away from my friends, I speed walked to his car, skipping puddles. There was heavy rain earlier, but now the sun was out.

"Hey!" Noah turned down the stereo as I got into my passenger seat.

"Hi." I beamed, kissing his cheek before strapping on my seat belt.

He made a three-point turn and kept his eyes on the road while driving.

"So, where would you like to go for lunch?" he asked.

"Surprise me."

"Surprise you, huh?" He glanced at me, showing off that seductive smile that made me melt. "I think I know just the place."

Noah cranked up the volume and sped past traffic. I felt the wind in my hair and enjoyed the warm spring breeze. His cologne was intoxicating. It made me want to climb onto his lap and kiss his face off, just to feel his energy. He had the sexiest profile, but I couldn't look at him. I knew if I did, all I'd feel is undeniable chemistry that made no sense at all. But it made sense to me.

₧₧

Noah took me to a local restaurant called Ocean Avenue. It wasn't very crowded, as we sat on the patio and shared a basket of fries. The Smashing Pumpkins were playing in the background, but after a while, the song faded into Gwen Stefani's magical voice. I stole a secret glance at Noah now and then without him noticing.

Why does he always have to look so freakin hot? It frustrated me more than anything.

He was wearing a navy-blue pinstripe suit, and I could've sworn he had on a silver tie before he'd left the house in the morning. Maybe he took it off because of the heat. I quietly studied him as he drifted off in thought.

"You left for work early this morning," I said, stirring my straw in my drink.

"I had some errands to run before heading to the firm." He tapped his fingers on the table, avoiding my eyes.

"Is something bothering you?"

The tapping stopped as he looked at me and said, "Nope." He sounded distant.

Something wasn't right. Why was he closing off on me? His body language was a dead giveaway.

Please don't do this now… not after last night.

"So, how's school going?" He changed the subject.

"Good." I kept it short, like him.

"Has anyone asked you out to the dance?"

I had mentioned nothing about that, as I looked at him in confusion.

"I read it on the bulletin board outside, on campus," said Noah.

Ah.

"I got asked out, but I'm not going."

"Why not?" He seemed shocked, grabbing another French fry.

"School dances are dumb."

"Now, *that* is strange."

My gaze founds his.

"Most girls your age look forward to high school dances."

"I'm not most girls, am I?" I said with attitude.

"Clearly not." He finished his drink, smirking.

If he wanted to play head games, he had met his match.

"There *is* this guy…"

"Oh, yeah? Tell me about him."

Now I had his full attention. Excellent.

"His name's Ryan, and I think he likes me."

Noah was silent for a while, contemplating.

"Has he asked you out?"

I nodded.

"Do you like him?"

"Yeah, I think he's really cute and nice."

Was that seriously the best description I could give? Fail.

"Bring him over sometime. I'd like to meet him."

"Sure." I suddenly lost my appetite. "By the way, he's captain of the swim team—oh, and the football team."

"So, he's athletic," said Noah, chewing on a French fry. "That's good."

God. Even the way he ate was sexy. I fantasized about feeding him while sitting on his…

"Cocky?"

I nearly choked on my drink. "Excuse me?"

"Is he the cocky type?"

"No… but I forgot to mention he's an amazing swimmer, too."

"Which is probably why he's captain of the…"

Duh, Aria. This conversation felt so awkward. My vendetta to make him jealous was clearly not working.

"I was athletic in high school," said Noah. "I was also captain of my swim team, football, and track."

Of course. Noah was just annoyingly perfect in all things.

"You still have a lot to learn about me, Aria."

"I guess it's good that you have me so close to you now." That came out sounding more flirtatious than I intended.

"It's definitely… Good."

He looked at me with his soul-penetrating stare. I couldn't tell if he was being seductive on purpose or if my warped-out brain was interpreting it that way. Probably the latter.

"Have you and Vanessa made up yet?"

Noah smiled and brushed my hair out of my face. His fingertips grazed my skin, making me shiver.

"Yes," he replied, "and she's agreed to get some counseling, so I think we're gonna be okay."

"That's good. I'm glad."

I should have been happy for him, but a part of me felt… crestfallen. My shadow side wanted him all to myself. A couple of buttons on his shirt were undone, revealing his muscled chest. I had flashbacks of the night before, when he stood inches away from me, half naked. His body was perfect. I wished I wasn't so attracted to him. It wasn't like I enjoyed this—I felt like a slave to the feeling.

"Vanessa's sister will visit us soon—in two weeks," Noah said.

"What's her name? How old is she?"

"Her name's Vienna, and she's a year younger than Nessa. She's nice. You'll like her. She's not as… um… high maintenance as her sis, but she's down to earth and funny. We'll most likely go to the Sunset Festival on your birthday weekend."

"Do you keep in touch with your family at all?"

"No."

Stirring my straw in my drink, I waited for him to explain, but he didn't.

"Why not?"

"Because I blame them for interfering with my involvement—or should I say, *lack* of involvement in your life." Noah looked at me long and hard. "To be specific, I blame my mother."

"Do I have any aunts and uncles?"

My mom never liked to talk about Noah's family when I was growing up, so I had no clue who else I was related to.

"I have two older siblings. I'm the youngest."

"What are their names?"

He sighed in annoyance.

"What? I'm curious."

"Isaac and Breanne."

"Nice names." I watched his expression, but he gave nothing away. "You don't talk to them either?"

"No."

"But why estrange yourself from everybody?"

"I don't want to discuss it right now, Aria."

Noah: the authoritarian parent.

"Why are you so edgy?"

"I'm not," he replied.

"You are."

"I don't know what you're talking about."

"You're scratching the back of your neck."

"Is that a crime? I'm itchy."

"You do that every time you're lying."

"How vigilant of you"—he slit his eyes—"but you're wrong."

A server walked by our table, giving Noah the chance to ask for the bill.

"Just tell me what's going on," I said.

"Aria, it's nothing—it's all work related."

He skimmed the bill and threw a crisp hundred-dollar note on the table without asking for change. "Let's get you back to school."

I didn't want to go, but I knew I couldn't convince him to let me skip. He wasn't exactly in the best mood. Maybe I shouldn't have insisted he take me out to lunch. I didn't want to become a spoiled stereotype. I was just missing him badly and loved being around him. It hurt that he didn't share my enthusiasm.

ﬢﬢﬢ

The ride back to school was quiet. I tried to make conversation, but Noah kept giving me one-word answers, which left little for us to talk about. I didn't like being overly emotional. I felt cursed. When the car came to a halt, I was relieved. Now I could finally escape from this unbearable tension.

"I'll see you at home tonight." Noah put the gearshift into park and turned down the stereo. "Hope you enjoyed lunch."

"Thanks for taking me out. See you later."

Avoiding his gaze, I unfastened my seat belt.

"Aria…"

I didn't want to hear it as I opened my door and stepped out, noticing my friends waving at me. They were sitting by the fountain with some friends. I was about to approach them when Noah's voice echoed behind me.

"Aria, wait!"

Not wanting to argue in public, I steeled myself and turned around.

"Can you come here a moment, please?" he said, standing by the car. "I need to talk to you."

Sigh.

Stepping away from his Audi, he waited as I reluctantly followed. We stood in the shade under a tree. His eyes seemed unsure as he slid his hands in his pockets and said, "Are you mad at me?"

"Great question, Noah. Do I look mad?"

"Can you please leave Planet Passive-Aggressive and come back to Earth for a couple minutes? I know you reign high as the queen of sarcasm, but you need to take me seriously right now."

I rolled my eyes and shifted my weight onto my right leg.

"Are we ready for an adult conversation?" he asked.

We?

"Quit talking down to me, Noah—it's patronizing as fuck."

"Watch the cussing."

"Make me."

"Why are you acting up?"

"I'm not. I don't appreciate you infantilizing me with your 'daddy disciplining' moments. It's pissing me off."

"Well, get used to it."

"I don't know what your deal is, but you're acting weird today."

"How am I acting weird?" He frowned in confusion.

"You're such a hypocrite."

"Where are these random arguments coming from suddenly?" Noah looked shocked. "I'm a hypocrite now? What the hell is going on with you?"

I had angered him. I could hear it in his voice, but it kind of turned me on—that's just how fucked up I was. At least I was self-aware of my own fuckery. We received a couple of awkward stares as some students walked past us on the lawn.

"Are you trying to kill my social life or something?"

He grimaced, shaking his head. "I'm trying to talk to you, but you're being impossible. Why are you so fucking stubborn?"

"Who's cussing now?"

"Give me a fucking break."

I loved the way he said *fuck*. How could he not realize he was hurting me?

"I'm never letting you in again." I backed away.

"Aria, please…" Noah grabbed my arm and gently nudged me forward.

"You were begging me not to push you away last night, and here you are doing exactly that."

I hated being so sensitive.

"You've been misinterpreting my body language. I'm not pushing you away. I told you earlier I'm just stressed out from work."

"You're just using that as an excuse!"

"I'm not." He tried to sound gentle, but there was a raging undertone in his voice that betrayed his calm composure. "What are you, a professional polygraph examiner suddenly? Are you psychic, as well?"

I avoided his heated gaze and stared at a red Mustang parked across from us.

"Look at me when I'm talking to you."

It was tempting to provoke him further, but I eventually gave in and faced him. His cheeks were slightly flush, which was rare. I wasn't sure if it was because of the humidity… maybe he was just trying to hold back his volcanic temper. I started visualizing glowing, molten magma overflowing from his head.

Look out for Drill Sergeant Hunter. Everyone stand at attention or he'll rip you a new one. Well, he didn't intimidate me, so I continued to ignore him.

"God damn it, Aria—" he grabbed my shoulders, causing my schoolbag to slip down my arm. "What do you want from me?"

I stayed quiet.

"Why are you trying to pick a fight? Answer me!" he commanded in a harsh voice. His eyes were inflamed, setting my insides on fire. I felt like a medium affected by psychic energies that made me shudder. I blamed him and the invisible waves of aggression that seemed to respawn from his chiseled body. To say that Noah was angry was an understatement. My anger was just a mask. I was sad deep down.

"I'm not trying to argue," I finally replied, wiping a tear from my cheek. He seemed to back off as he softened his gaze.

You better feel like an asshole for upsetting me in public.

"I didn't mean to make you cry. I'm sorry."

"I'm not crying!" I looked at him, mirroring his glare of fury he'd given me ten seconds earlier.

Silence… staring… more silence… and more staring.

Noah was the first to surrender as he sighed and wrapped his arms around my body, forcing me into a hug. "I'm sorry if I seem distant," he whispered in my ear. "I just have a lot on my mind."

I couldn't understand my anger, but it was impossible to pretend to be an ice queen around him, especially when his body felt so warm and welcoming. He kissed the top of my head and soothed my stubborn pride with affection. It was hard to rationalize when his cologne and aftershave smelled so indescribably good. Noah was like a drug to me. I guess I was just depressed to know I didn't have the same effect on him.

"Why do we have such a bipolar relationship?" I asked.

He looked at me for a moment, his lips curving into a crooked smile.

"I don't know, sweetheart. Maybe we're both bipolar. It *is* hereditary…"

Mental health wasn't a joke, but we needed some comic relief. I laughed with him and took comfort in his amazing embrace. Some people gave dry hugs, but Noah wasn't like that. Every time he held me, I felt as if he was hugging me with his soul. Our energies seemed to harmonize every time we touched; it was euphoric. Maybe that was one of his gifts: magical hugs. All my anger had disappeared the moment he pulled me into his arms.

"I don't want you going to class upset because of me." He withdrew and held my face.

This argument was so pointless. I was feeling insecure because it hurt when he detached from me.

"I'm just afraid you're pushing me away." I looked into his eyes, desperately hoping he understood my feelings without me having to explain. My abandonment trauma was real; Noah was staring right at it.

"Why would I push away the reason for my existence?" His gaze never left mine as he caressed my cheek, making my heart explode in ecstasy every time he touched me. It was frustrating. How could he be so unaffected?

"Hey, now. No tears," he said with compassion.

I had met no one else who had eyes as expressive as his. It was no wonder he masked his emotions so well—he had to guard himself.

"Come here." Noah wrapped his arms around me again as a gentle breeze blew by. I didn't want him to let go, but the school bell rang, disrupting my secret moment in paradise. I was pulled back to wretched reality.

"I have to get going," he said, "and you need to get to class. Teachers don't like tardy students."

"With my grades, they'll be lenient with me." I kept fidgeting with the leather bracelet he wore around his wrist.

"You really like this, don't you?" He looked down at my hand.

"You always wear it. Is there a special reason?"

Suddenly, I dreaded the answer. What if his first love had given it to him? What if his first love was my mom?

Please don't tell me.

"A merchant sold this to me when I was in South Africa. He said that it would bring me good luck if I wore it every day. According to tribal legend, whatever I had lost would return to me—be it fortune or a lost love. Now, of course, I knew it didn't possess any magical powers—he was only trying to make a sale.

"But I think a part of me wanted to believe in the fantasy. At that time in my life, I needed a ray of hope, so I bought it and wore it every day since. Miraculously, just like that man said…" He stared into my eyes. "The person I love the most in this entire universe returned to me." Noah untied his bracelet and fastened it around my left wrist. "You came back to me."

I teared up.

"You don't know how special you are, Aria."

His bracelet felt a little loose, but just wearing a part of him on my body elated me.

"Thank you." I flung myself at him and hugged him, not caring if I wrinkled his suit.

"I love you," he kissed my forehead.

"I love you, too." And I meant it with all my heart as I reached down for my red messenger bag.

"I'll see you later tonight, beautiful."

I was about to turn around when he reached for my hand and stopped me. "Wait. Your—um…" Noah hesitated, glancing down at my uniform. "Buttons…" He pointed at his shirt to signal my wardrobe malfunction.

I rolled my eyes. "You should see my friends—their cleavage is much worse."

"You don't go to school to show off your cleavage. You go to school to educate yourself."

I hated how he was so annoyingly right all the time.

"You need to lighten up a bit, Noah. It's like a hundred degrees outside."

"You're my daughter. I don't want boys staring down your bra."

Is that what you're doing? I questioned, smirking at him.

"You're so overprotective."

"Aria, we don't have time to argue over this now. Please, fix your shirt."

No. I was enjoying this. I liked teasing him.

"Why don't you fix them for me, since *you're* the one who has a problem with a couple of buttons coming undone?"

Noah arched a sexy eyebrow. "Don't be such a spoiled brat."

"It's not my fault. You're the one who indulges me too much, so if I'm a spoiled brat, it's because of you."

"Stop being a smart-ass."

"Like father, like daughter."

"Yeah... a family trait, I see."

I teasingly unbuttoned my shirt a little more, letting him sneak a peek at my red push-up bra.

"Aria." He cautiously met my gaze.

"See, this is how the girls normally wear their shirts at school."

I felt satisfied knowing that he was staring at my cleavage; it was oddly empowering.

"You're being such a pain in the *you know what* at the moment." Noah shook his head and reached for my buttons. I bit my lip when his fingers lightly grazed the swell of my breast, ever so slightly. I'm sure it was by accident, though.

"There, much better." He quickly buttoned up my blouse and grinned.

"You know I'm just gonna unbutton them when you leave, right?"

"Is that what you do every day?"

"Maybe." I smiled deviously.

"Aria Sophia Hunter, you naughty, naughty girl."

A thrilling heat radiated from my thighs when he called me naughty—*twice*.

"What are you gonna do?" I said. "Ground me?" We both knew that wouldn't happen.

"Worse, young lady." He matched my smile with a wicked grin. "Much, *much* worse."

"Like?"

Our banter was turning me on.

Noah looked at his watch and said, "We're both officially late. You realize that, don't you?"

I nodded, smiling innocently.

"Get to class, Aria."

"No." I crossed my arms against my chest. "I'd like to know how you plan to carry out my punishment, if you don't mind—just so I can prepare throughout my day for this 'great disciplinary act' you'll be executing at home, I assume? Or do you have a secret 'daddy dungeon'?"

"Are you testing my power over you?" Noah's eyes were intense.

"You're the one who said *it's much, much worse* than getting grounded." I mocked him.

"Trust me, you don't want to know."

"I do."

He let out a short laugh and ran his fingers through his hair before he fixed his gaze on me. "Let's just say that if you keep up this little ruse of yours, I'll have no choice but to bend you over my lap and give you a *proper* spanking."

I liked that visual, disturbing as it was. I didn't mind a spanking, so long as *his* hand delivered it.

"I might like that," I bravely stated.

Noah shadowed his eyes, tilting his head. "Are you admitting you're a masochist?"

"Are *you* admitting you're a sadist?"

Cricket-chirping silence.

He chuckled. "How did we go from arguing over traditional parenting styles to S&M?"

"You're the one who wants to spank me."

"Yeah, well, clearly you've outgrown the spanking stage—and I was just kidding, by the way."

"Hmm… I dunno… somehow, I doubt it."

What kind of monster hid behind the sexy man who stood before me? I wondered.

The idea of him bending me over, pulling my panties down roughly, and spanking me was a shamefully hot fantasy of mine. I'd had many dreams about him doing exactly that before he shoved his steel-hard shaft inside me and banged my brains out. I'm hell spawn, I know.

We stared at each other for the longest while before he said, "Don't lose that wristband."

"I won't." I would guard it with my life.

"I'll see you at home, then."

I gave him one last hug and kissed the corner of his mouth, letting my lips linger for as long as possible. Yes, this was my idea of sneaky seduction. When our eyes locked, he smiled and told me to hurry along.

We parted ways, leaving our secrets behind to take root underneath that tree—buried possibilities of all the different ways our conversation could have transpired. It would have been so romantic if he'd kissed me, but he didn't. Maybe I was hopelessly holding on to a dream that would never come to life. I refused to believe there was nothing going on between us. There had to be something. There just had to.

CHAPTER TWENTY-TWO
ARIA

The weeks flew right by, and before I knew it, April was finally here. It was going to be a long weekend for me. I didn't have school next Monday because of an all-day staff meeting. Vienna had flown in on a Tuesday afternoon. She was a little shorter than my stepmom, and unlike her sis, she had dark brown hair, didn't hide her brown eyes behind blue contact lenses, and nothing was surgically altered on her face or body. Vienna was a graphic artist and had taken six months off from work to travel the world. Noah was right—she wasn't high maintenance at all. In fact, if you saw her and Vanessa standing next to one another, you'd never think they were sisters. I guess that was because of all the plastic surgery my stepmom had done to her face. Vienna didn't seem happy about that, either... I heard them arguing about it in the yard when she first arrived. My stepmom had brushed off her sister's concerns and insisted she wasn't going under the knife anymore. (Though I seriously doubted that.)

Vienna planned to make her visit short. She was staying only through the weekend and flying out to New Jersey to see her parents next week.

My Friday had gone by sluggishly, but things livened up toward the evening. I called Ryan like I'd promised and invited him over for dinner tomorrow evening, since Vanessa insisted on hosting a small birthday dinner for me. I was grateful for her kind gesture, but I really didn't feel like celebrating. I had invited Jessica as well, but she wasn't able to make it. She promised to take me out to lunch on my b-day.

The Sunset Festival was coming up, and Noah had plans to take us with Vanessa and Vienna. He'd told me it was okay to invite some friends. I also had the option of going solo with my gal pals, but he begged me not to leave him alone with Vanessa and his sister-in-law.

I was in my room, listening to music while doing my hair when I heard a knock on my door.

"Come in!"

"Do you ever not have that iPod playing?" said Noah, stepping into my bedroom.

"Nope—love music—can't live without it."

He sat on my bed and dropped his weight back on my mattress. He looked amazing as usual, dressed in a pair of dark denim trousers and a gray V-neck T-shirt. Anything he wore looked attractive on him. He had just got a fresh haircut, too. I often imagined running my fingers through his thick mane while kissing him. Noah could've sold anything with that killer body and charismatic smile. He had already won my heart from first glance.

"Something on your mind?" I asked, noticing his lengthy sigh.

"Not really." He folded his hands behind his head and stared at the ceiling.

"All right, talk to me." I finished with my lip balm and turned around, sitting astride my chair. "I'm all ears."

"It's nothing, sweetie." Noah rolled on his side, resting his head in his hand. "Just some stuff between Vanessa and me."

"Oh, okay." I wouldn't push. The last time I did, things hadn't turned out so well and I wasn't in the mood to argue with him.

"You're looking pretty this evening."

"Thanks." I blushed, making my way toward him. I was wearing a light blue denim skirt and a white halter top. My hair was wavy that evening. Women loved it when guys noticed the little things.

"You don't look too bad yourself," I flirted, sitting next to him.

"It's nice to know that at least someone approves of my outfit. Vanessa was hell-bent on making me wear this ugly purple polo shirt she bought while shopping with Vienna."

I laughed.

"She's still doing her makeup," said Noah. "She takes hours to get ready for a night out." He exhaled and rubbed his eyes before fixing his gaze on me. "I figured I'd give the ladies some time alone and come bug you instead."

I melted when he grinned.

"FYI, you don't bug me."

"That's too bad. I guess I'm not doing my job as a father, then."

I chuckled. "How so?"

"Because every dad is supposed to be annoying. At least mine was, from what I can remember."

He never talked about his father. All I knew about my granddad was that he had passed away years ago.

Stretching, I reclined on my back as we both stared at the ceiling in silence. My iPod switched tracks to an ambient tune.

"I feel like getting high."

Can I join?

"And I probably shouldn't be saying that to my teenage daughter."

Noah turned his head and looked at me. "Don't do drugs—and forget what I said about… you know."

"Forgotten." I giggled. "Don't worry."

"I meant weed, not hard drugs."

"I didn't make that assumption."

"I'd never touch that stuff again. It really messed me up."

"I know."

It saddened me knowing he had suffered from a drug addiction. If only I could have saved him from self-destruction, but I couldn't time travel. I was just glad he had got out of that nightmare alive.

"Are you okay?" I curled up closer to him.

"No point dwelling on the past, right?" He kept his eyes fixed on the ceiling.

"You got it."

"We just have to learn from our mistakes and move forward." He sounded tired, like he was exhausted from fighting a battle in his mind. Noah was like a complicated Rubik's cube. But then again, so was I.

"Was I a mistake?" I randomly asked.

Shifting his weight, he gave me a serious look. "You. Were *not*. A mistake. *I* was the one who made the mistake of not being there for you from the beginning." Noah eased his expression and caressed my cheek. "The guilt still eats me up every day." There was a palpable pain in his eyes.

"I don't hold a grudge against you, though," I said. "All that matters is that you're here now." I tried to comfort him with words, but I feared it wasn't enough.

"I know, baby." He slid his hand down my arm, resting it on my hip. "I'm never leaving your side again. I promise." Noah's voice was deep and modulated; it was addictive.

The song had reached its bridge, as I listened to the lyrics about love and trust. I couldn't tell if it was a coincidence or synchronicity. There couldn't have been greater forces at work. Feeling this way about Noah was wrong, and I was certain that God, angels, or whatever powers above were shaking their heads at me in disgust.

"I love you," I murmured.

Noah's face lit up with a warm smile. "I love you, too." He pulled me into his arms and made me feel like it was the safest place ever.

Breathing him in, I wrapped my leg over his waist, wishing he would kiss me and glide his hand up my leg, between my thighs, under my skirt, and… but that was wishful thinking. It would never happen. It felt nice to have my forehead kissed, though.

"So," Noah began, "Vanessa told me you're bringing that guy over tomorrow. What's his name again? Brian?"

"*Ryan*," I answered. "And yeah, I figured since you're so curious to meet him, I'd invite him to dinner."

"Okay, that's cool." He held my thigh in place over his hip while gently caressing my skin with his thumb. Our eyes locked. "I was just double checking."

God, so hot.

"Your birthday is tomorrow."

"Don't remind me," I sighed.

"I know you don't want to do anything big, and I promise there won't be any scary surprises, but we can have a barbecue if you like."

Hmm…

"It doesn't have to be anything fancy," I said.

"How are barbecues fancy? You throw some burgers and dogs on the grill, pull out some cold beers… Well, the alcohol would be for us adults. You kids can have carbonated or caffeinated beverages." Noah grinned, knowing I was annoyed.

"I'm not a kid!" I playfully slapped his chest as he threw his head back, laughing.

Pulling my leg back, he tightened his grip around my thigh and pressed it closer to his waist, thrusting me forward. Those clear blue eyes left me breathless every time they penetrated mine.

"You really hate it when I call you that, huh?"

"Yes, because I'm *not* a child."

"But you'll always be my baby."

"Oh God, Noah." I groaned. "Stop it, please."

He smiled, releasing my thigh before rolling on top of me in a flash. My heart was doing cartwheels in my chest when I felt his crotch push against me.

"Don't you want to be my baby forever?" he said, supporting his weight on his elbows and tangling his fingers through my hair.

I couldn't think. The only thing I understood at that moment was how his body was pressed against mine. The heat was unbearable. I was so in love with him; it hurt.

"Nothing lasts forever," I sadly muttered.

"A bond between a father and daughter does."

"I guess so."

"I *know* so."

The stimulating scent of Eternity permeated the air in my room. I loved that cologne on him. His face was so beautiful, mesmerizing me with its symmetrical perfection as I lightly traced his jaw to his chin.

"What are you doing?" Noah chuckled. His cheeks were reddening, which amused me.

"Tracing your face."

"It's just a face."

"Yeah, but it's *your* face." I brushed my fingers over the flawless arches above his eyes, as if I were blind, learning to identify him.

"Oh, yeah?" He smirked. "Tell me, what do you like most about it?" Noah twisted his neck. "My outstanding profile?"

I laughed.

"As amazing as that profile is…" I coaxed his head in my direction. "It's not your best facial feature."

"I'm curious to know what my daughter thinks of me, so go on." His smile unleashed a swarm of butterflies in my tummy.

"What's my best feature?"

"I'm staring right at it."

Silence…

"You know, you're really stroking my ego here, Aria."

"Is that dangerous?" I flirtatiously asked.

"Depends on the company."

My hands moved over his shoulders, winding around his neck, before I whispered, "Am I in danger?"

Noah was quiet—almost zoned out.

"Hey, you okay?" I asked, slightly worried. He looked like he had seen a ghost.

"You're not in danger. You're never in danger around me, Aria. You know that, right?" There was panic in his voice, and I couldn't understand why. "Do you really think I'm dangerous?"

"Noah, relax… I don't even think that about you."

He frowned, lifting his weight off me before sitting on the edge of the bed.

"I was just kidding, you know," I clarified, sitting up on my knees and hugging his shoulders from behind.

"I know, sweetie." He kissed my hands.

Vanessa's voice suddenly echoed from the hallway, breaking our magical intimacy. I wanted to keep him in my room and chat some more, but it was time to go.

ଝଔ

The festival was crowded with people when we arrived. A few streets had been closed for tents and attractions. The air was thick with the aroma of hot dogs, French fries, and cotton candy. The park was transformed into a wonderland of thrill rides and carnival games, flashing with colorful lights. When I was a kid, I used to go on every ride I could: bumper cars, drop towers, carousels, roller coasters, motion simulators, you name it. There was nothing I was afraid of—okay, maybe *some* stuff. Honestly, there were much worse things to fear in life… like an abusive stepdad who was a raging narc monster.

"Wow, it's more crowded than I'd expected," said Vanessa, stepping out of the car. "Vi, do you remember the last time we were at an amusement park?"

"Oh-my-gosh, yes! I had eaten so much ice cream before we went on that stupid ride." She paused. "What was it called? The Scrambler?"

"The *Twizzler.*"

"Yes! That ride kept pushing Nessa right into me… We were sandwiched together, and I felt so queasy."

"Her face was literally going green." Vanessa laughed.

"I barfed all over myself."

"Don't forget those designer jeans I was wearing! You barfed all over them too!"

They laughed while Noah and I glanced at each other with a smile.

I would be mortified if I hurled all over him on a ride. I made a mental note not to overdo it with food and beverages that evening.

Vanessa and Vienna walked ahead of us while I waited for Noah as he dropped some change in a parking meter. I was so happy to be there with him. I kept praying my stepmom would spend most of the night with her sister, so I could spend time with her sexy husband... who just happened to be my dad. It was always a shocking revelation to strangers.

"Are you ready to get your ass whooped?" Noah grinned.

"I'm a pro at carnival games."

"Well, prepare to have your ego deflated. I'm very competitive, and I never lose."

"We'll see about that." I playfully shoved my shoulder against him, and he shoved me back while we walked to the ticket booth. My heart skipped a beat when he grabbed my hand and held it. I started daydreaming about being on a date with him—a romantic one that would end in a perfect kiss.

Keep dreaming.

Noah bought some tickets for the rides and gave a bunch of them to Vanessa.

"Let's play the games first!" Vienna suggested.

"She just wants to win a big purple bear."

"All right, ladies—I hope you're not sore losers." Noah simpered.

∞

We played a variety of games that night. I did pretty well, considering the opponents I was up against and the tricky ways the games were rigged. I won nothing huge—just a glow-in-the-dark Slinky toy at a balloon dart game. The prize wasn't all that special. Noah ranked first out of all of us, and he also bought that purple bear for Vienna (after she begged him a hundred times). We played several water gun and Skee-Ball games, and a range of others that required skill or chance. I was having a lot of fun, even though Noah was claiming victory after victory.

"*Aaaaaaand* we have a winner!" shouted the carny man, chiming a big bronze bell.

"Hell yes!" Noah thrust a fist in the air. He wasn't humble about winning. "See, I told you… You just got owned!"

"Quit boasting." I rolled my eyes. "Bragging is not attractive."

"I think I've earned bragging rights," he proudly replied.

I shook my head and squirted him with the water gun.

"Hey!" Noah quickly grabbed one and returned the attack.

Screaming, I dodged the assault as our laughter filled the air. There wasn't much water left in the guns, so we weren't completely soaked.

"Okay, okay, you win!" I placed the weapon down and raised my hands in mock surrender.

"I'm glad you can admit defeat." He chuckled, airing out his shirt.

"Pick your prize, sir," said the man who was working the game stand. He was holding a long wooden staff that had a hook at the end.

"What do you want, baby?" Noah looked at me.

There were so many prizes to choose from, but I knew exactly what I wanted, pointing at a life size bunny, hanging above us. It was bigger than Vienna's bear.

"You got it."

Alice meets the white rabbit. In my case, blue *rabbit.*

I had won nothing that big before, and no one had ever won me the biggest prize at the game stands. Those big stuffed animals always seemed to be an impossible trophy to possess. My stepdad hated festivals and carnivals. When I was eight years old, we went to a fair, and I begged him to buy me this little plush bunny that was only five bucks. Rob had yelled at me, told me to shut up and quit my whining. He said he refused to pay for a "stupid stuffed animal that was a waste of his hard-earned money." The memory still stung a bit as I flashed back to it. Holding that ginormous rabbit now gave me a sense of justice. We'd always had financial problems in my family because of my parents' poor spending habits. Mom also had a chronic shopping addiction… especially at the dollar store. All Rob ever did was waste his "hard-earned cash" on booze, cigarettes, weed, and poker games. He was a cheap, hypocritical asshole, but Noah… I couldn't even compare them.

"Hey, you okay, sweetheart?" He noticed my sadness. "Do you want another prize? I can always just buy it."

The depressing memory disappeared when I wrapped my arms around him. "No, I love it. Thank you."

"How long have you two been dating?" asked the carny worker.

"Oh, we're not—" Noah let me go, laughing nervously. "She's my daughter."

My cheeks suddenly flushed bright red.

"Oops, sorry! Well, you folks have a nice night!"

"Thanks." Noah pleasantly smiled, hanging an arm around my shoulder. It happened so frequently, people confusing us as a couple. He just looked too young to be my dad.

We left the game stands and started walking toward the rides.

"Have you seen any of your friends here tonight?" Noah asked.

"No."

"It's fine if you want to ditch me—if you see them, I mean. I know I forced you to come with us, but you're young, and it's a Friday night. I want you to have fun."

"But I *am* having fun." I smiled.

Noah pulled me in closer and kissed the side of my head. "You're so sweet."

I wasn't. I was selfish, in more ways than one. He just didn't know that yet.

After a while, we met up with Vienna and my stepmom.

"Let's drop off our prizes at the car and go on the rides!" said Vi.

She sounded more excited than I was.

☙❧

We went on almost every thrill ride that night. Bumper cars were fun. I kept slamming into Vanessa's car on purpose. It would've been hilarious if her silicone breasts had busted open from the impact. Okay, it probably would have been painful, but it sounded amusing in my head. I got to sit next to Noah on most of the rides, except for the ones that were two-seaters. That's when my stepmom hogged him away because she was "too scared." It sucked, but he wasn't mine to possess.

Sitting next to Vienna was just as annoying because she screamed so damn loud—total rape of my eardrums. Plus, I couldn't help but feel this twinge of jealousy every time Vanessa held Noah's hand. I knew I had no right to be so possessive of him, but I wished so badly that it was only me and him at the festival together.

We went on a few roller coasters, surviving the rides with hurricane hair by the end.

"That was so much fun!" My stepmom laughed, hugging Noah's waist. "Honey, I wanna ride the Love Tunnel with you."

Gag. I hated how she was all over him, and I hated envying her even more.

"Do we have to?" he protested. "It seems like such a corny ride."

Refuse to go with her! I telepathically tried to influence him.

"Come on! Be a little romantic with your wife!" She pressed her lips against his cheek, kissing him repeatedly while my blood boiled. If I were a cartoon character, steam would've been blowing out of my ears. Yes, my jealousy was animated in my mind. Welcome to the strange world of Aria Hunter.

Vienna asked me if I wanted to ride the Death Drop with her again, but I couldn't answer fast enough—I was too busy monitoring interactions between Vanessa and Noah. My stepmom was whispering things in his ear and touching his chest, and I hadn't even realized that I had balled my fists, digging my nails into my skin to where it left half-moons upon release.

I imagined the sweet satisfaction of wrapping my hands around Vanessa's throat and throwing her down in a chokehold. WWE much?

"Aria? Hello? Earth to Aria…" Vienna waved her hand in my face, snapping me out of my violent dementia.

"Sorry, zoned out."

"I noticed."

I was about to respond when someone caught my eye in the distance.

"Ryan!"

The dream jock stopped and noticed me, smiling and waving back. He was with his usual entourage of varsity jackets.

"Come over here!" I called out.

He turned and said something to his friends before approaching. Vanessa was still making kissy faces at Noah—it was way past obnoxious. I bolted and jumped in Ryan's arms, hugging him tightly like long distance lovers. He wasn't my boyfriend, though. There was only one guy I wanted to go steady with, and he was sadly unavailable and biologically related to me.

"Wow, hey!" Ryan laughed. "Someone's glad to see me." He spun me around and placed me on my feet. I was never this affectionate with him. He probably thought I was on drugs, but I didn't care. I needed to cope with my jealousy somehow. Ryan was there at the most convenient time.

"Is this your boyfriend?" asked Vienna, smiling at him.

"I don't know, maybe," I coyly replied.

"Apparently, I'm still in the qualifying stages." He grinned, shaking Vienna's hand. Noah and Vanessa soon appeared as I formally acquainted them with one another.

"So, you're the guy my daughter can't stop talking about," said Noah, eyeing him like a hawk.

"She talks about me?" Ryan sounded surprised.

I blushed and gave Noah "the look," insisting that he stop.

"Indeed, she does. Are you here with your family as well?"

"No, sir, it's just me and my friends tonight. My folks are away for the weekend."

"Well, Ryan," Vanessa cut in, "we're looking forward to having you over for Aria's birthday dinner tomorrow. I can't wait to get to know you better!"

"Same here, Mrs. Hunter."

I slid my fingers between his and held his hand while looking at Noah. "Do you mind if I hang out with Ryan?"

"Don't go!" Vienna interrupted. "Please don't leave me as the third wheel with these two."

My stepmom laughed and grabbed her sister's arm. "I promise we'll lay off on the PDA and skip the corny rides."

"Thank God for that." Noah sighed in relief and glanced at me. "Sure, sweetie, you can go. But only for the hour. Make sure you keep your cellphone on and don't leave the park."

I nodded, eager to get away.

"Oh, and Ryan—you treat her right, or you'll have me to answer to."

"Don't worry, Mr. Hunter. She's in good hands."

I resisted an eye roll and walked off.

"Be good, kids!" hollered Vanessa.

"Sorry," I said to Ryan, "my dad's really protective of me."

"I don't blame him." He flashed a charming smile and kissed my hand.

ᏣᏐ

It was fun hanging out with the most popular guy at school. Ryan's friends were funny, and we had a blast going on all the thrill rides in large groups. He bought me a caramel candy apple, and we held hands as we walked past a few tents that had different events going on—burger-eating contests, circus acts, talent shows… there was so much happening everywhere we looked. After ordering some ice cream, the eight of us sat at a picnic table, enjoying the live music. An indie rock band was performing on stage.

Scanning my surroundings, I noticed Noah and Vanessa standing a few feet away from us. They were playing a game, the one where you have to slam this huge mallet down and see how high you can make the arrow reach on the meter. My stepmom kept kissing Noah's neck, and it was driving me nuts. I wasn't used to feeling this kind of jealousy. Standing up, I shifted over and sat astride Ryan's lap, taking him by surprise—but he didn't complain.

"Hey there." He grinned, holding my waist.

"Hi." I smiled flirtatiously, swaying my hips with the music. It looked like I was giving him a lap dance. "I *love* this song!" I shouted to catch Noah's attention.

And it worked. He turned his head and our eyes locked. I couldn't read his expression too well, but I think he wasn't happy with the show I was putting on in front of all the guys. Ryan's friends cheered me on while I tossed my hair back and dirty-danced on him. I kept switching glances from Ryan to Noah, and the more I stared at Noah, the hotter it made me. Vanessa was too distracted with the game to even notice what was going on. Closing my eyes, I imagined it was Noah I was dancing on. I could almost convince myself as Ryan's fingertips glided underneath my halter top, and—

"Aria!"

Noah's voice brought me back to reality. He was standing right next to me, and he didn't look too pleased.

"Your hour's up," he firmly stated.

Smiling, I relaxed in Ryan's lap; I think he was more uncomfortable than I was.

"Are you sure?" I said, rubbing Ryan's chest. "Gosh, time flies when you're having fun."

Noah seemed irritated.

Serves him right for making me watch all that PDA earlier, I thought. It was serious overkill.

"Aria, stop." Ryan chuckled. "Your dad's talking to you." He reluctantly pulled back. That's when I felt a firm hand grab hold of my arm and pull me off Ryan's lap.

"Which one of you gave her alcohol?" Noah demanded, sounding hostile.

"We didn't drink any liquor, sir." Ryan got up.

"God, Noah, stop!" I pulled my arm away and looked around. My stepmom and Vienna were nowhere in sight. They must have gone off on a ride before he came over.

"You'll have to forgive my daughter," Noah said. "She's usually not this *slutty*, ever. I'm not sure what's got into her."

My mouth hung wide open in shock.

"Um…" Ryan looked as awkward as I felt.

"Let's go, Aria. *Now,*" Noah commanded.

I glared at him while he stared me down. He would not back off. I had to accept defeat. Feeling embarrassed, I looked back at Ryan and mouthed an apology before following Noah.

"See you tomorrow night, Ryan!" Noah's enthusiasm couldn't have sounded more sarcastic.

"You have a good night, Mr. Hunter."

I'm sure he thought my dad was a total dick.

಄ೞ

"Slutty? *Really?* How could you humiliate me like that?" I cried out, scowling at my abductor.

"Excuse me?" Noah scoffed. "Did you expect me to just stand back and allow you to dance on him like a stripper while his buddies watched like a herd of horny voyeurs? His hands were all over you and under your top!"

"So? Vanessa was all over *you!* She was practically eye-fucking you all evening and kissing you every ten seconds! Do you really think I want to see that? No! Do I complain about it and embarrass you? No!"

"What the hell, Aria? She's my wife—and we weren't..." Noah lowered his voice, "... eye-sexing."

"Would it kill you to say it?" I crossed my arms over my chest.

"Say what?"

"*Fuck.*"

"Why do you love cussing around me so much?"

"It's a sign of intelligence. Every genius has a potty mouth."

With a dirty mind.

"Be grateful you contributed to my DNA," I quickly added.

"You're such a pain in my ass, you know that?"

"Good. Consider it retribution for seventeen years of being M.I.A."

"Ouch."

Okay... that was harsh.

"You're distracting me," said Noah. "I didn't like that display you were putting on."

"I don't care. It was tame compared to what Vanessa was doing with you… she had her hand down your pants!"

"So you were dancing all sexy on that boy to get back at me?"

He found it sexy? I was so mad I could have cried. I knew it was childish of me to react the way I did by using Ryan, but Noah made me crazy in the head. There was no better way of explaining it.

"Not everything I do is always about you," I denied. "I was dancing on him because I felt like it. You can't control my life twenty-four/seven."

"I'm your father, and technically you're not a legal adult yet, so yes, I *can* control your life, Aria." His blue eyes intensified and pierced through my toxic ego. Why did we have to fight so much?

"Enjoy your authority over me for another"—I glanced at my watch—"forty-five minutes! I'll be eighteen by midnight! And I've already thought of the perfect birthday present to give to myself."

"And what's that?" He flashed a patronizing grin.

"I'm dropping your last name and choosing my own. I'm not a Mitchell, I don't feel like a Miller, and I sure as hell don't want to be a Hunter!"

Noah studied me, folding his arms in his chest. "Well, good luck going through the legal process, because I sure as *fuck* won't be giving you any legal aid."

His F-bombs were such a turn on.

"Is that supposed to surprise me?" I shrewdly replied. "What do you think the internet is for these days? Changing my last name will be a piece of cake."

Noah pressed his thumb and index to his forehead, exhaling his frustration. "Are you PMS-ing or something? Why are you so up and down? What is your problem?"

"You! *You* are my problem!" I burst out in anger.

"I'm just trying to protect you. Don't you understand that? Those guys could've lured you somewhere and raped you."

"They're people I know from school!"

"So?" he shouted, startling me. "Do you think that takes the risk away?" He steadied my shoulders and said, "How can you trust a guy so easily? I didn't think you were that naïve, Aria." There was anger in his voice—I could hear it. I was fighting my tears again, averting my eyes.

His car was a few feet away from us in the parking lot as I kept my head down and tried to get away from him. Noah's footsteps followed behind me.

"Aria…" The crunching sound of gravel got louder until he caught up.

"I want to go home. You've officially ruined my night." I kept walking ahead, ignoring him.

"Hold on a minute, please." Noah grabbed my arm and forced me to turn around.

He towered over me, superior and intimidating, as I looked up at him. He made me feel so small. If this was a battle for dominance, he was winning.

"Can we please not let this disrupt our fun?" he begged. "Come on, baby, we were having such a great time."

Don't call me that. I'm not your baby.

I exhaled harshly and held my arms. Was it too late to salvage the evening?

"You embarrassed me and basically called me a slut in front of my friends. That hurt."

"I'm sorry, okay?" Noah sulked. "I was getting a little crazy and tried my best to control my temper. I didn't mean to insult you. I'll apologize to Ryan tomorrow if it'll make you feel better."

It wouldn't.

"I'm not perfect," said Noah. "I screw up. I make mistakes too." He looked at me with those ocean eyes.

How could I stay mad at him? I had a cat's temper around him… incredibly pissed and hissing in the heat of the moment, and then completely calm a few minutes later. At least, that's how Buffy's temperament was. I missed her. She was a British shorthair I had grown up with. Her death had hit me hard when she died four years ago. I hadn't had another pet since. Owning a fish was even hard. Death was a traumatizing ordeal for me.

"Can we hug and make up now?" he asked.

I preferred to *kiss* and make up but settled for a hug. Refusing to smile, I failed miserably when he wrapped his arms around me, hugging me close.

"You drive me nuts, you know that?"

"Good."

"Good?" Noah raised his brows.

I was about to respond but stopped when my stepmom and her sister showed up.

"There you are!" Vanessa said. "We've been looking all over for you. What are you doing in the parking lot?"

"Is the night already over?" asked Vi.

"Aria wanted to grab her hoodie," Noah replied.

"I left it at home. I forgot."

"Aw, well, you can wear my cardigan if you like," Vanessa offered.

Leopard print was *not* my style.

"No, it's okay. I'll survive."

Noah wrapped his arm around my waist. I was relieved he hadn't told her about our argument. It felt good to know that some things remained confidential between us. It made me trust him more.

"Nessa and I wanna go to the Haunted Fun House," said Vienna. "Do you wanna come?"

Noah gave my stepmom an uneasy look. "No, thanks."

"Aw, why not? You scared?" Vienna teased.

"Of clowns, yes."

"He suffers from a mild case of coulrophobia," Vanessa revealed.

My personal definition of that phobia was fear of red-nosed freaks.

"Seriously, a tough guy like *you* is afraid of funny little circus clowns?" Vienna laughed.

"*Little?* They're even scarier as midgets—no offense to little people." Noah shuddered.

"Why are you afraid of them?" I asked.

"Jeez, Vanessa," he exhaled. "You make it sound as if I cry like a girl when I see one, which is not the case. They just creep me out. I don't like to be in the same room as one."

"He gets terrible anxiety," she stated.

"Let's just say it wasn't a very pleasant experience when I got taken hostage by some convict circus clown at my sixth birthday party. The guy knew my family was wealthy. He attempted to kidnap me and keep me hostage for ransom. Fortunately, he didn't get very far. A gardener on our estate got suspicious and clocked the SOB in the head with a shovel when he heard me screaming. But I will forever remember Peepo the Clown as the scary man who repeatedly told me to 'shut the fuck up' while he carried me to his van."

Vienna's jaw dropped in disbelief.

Is he for real? That must have been so traumatic to experience as a child.

"Are you all right, sweetheart?" My stepmom rubbed Noah's back.

"I'm fine. You two go on ahead. Me and Aria still have a bunch of boring rides we haven't been on yet, so we'll meet you at the ticket stand in the front entrance in about… half an hour?"

"That's perfect—have fun, you two!" She leaned into his lips and gave him a quick kiss. I had to stop myself from rolling my eyes because I knew Vienna was watching me.

My stepmom and her sister disappeared in the other direction while Noah and I walked back toward the ticket booth. There was a beautiful Ferris wheel that was the highlight attraction at the festival, because of its monstrous height. Noah caught me staring up at it.

"Do you wanna ride the wheel with me?" he asked, slipping his hand into mine.

My frustration vanished as I smiled and said, "Let's go."

◌ℬ✤

Loud music echoed all around us while we stood in line. I wasn't familiar with the song, but it sounded awesome and gave me shivers, though I'm pretty sure it was the effect that Noah had on me. Moving ahead, he helped me into the passenger car before he sat beside me.

"What are the height measurements on this bad boy?" Noah asked the ride operator.

"It's approximately three hundred feet tall."

"Damn," I muttered.

We settled into our seat and waited for another employee to bring down the handlebar.

The wheel started floating upwards a couple of feet. I was getting anxious as we dangled in the air, going higher while other people got on the ride.

"You look nervous, Aria."

"Me? I'm good." I tried to sound convincing. "I've been on Ferris wheels, just never been on one this high before."

"It's always scarier when you reach the top. You have a moment where you just hold your breath for a few seconds. The trick is not to look down. Once the wheel rotates, you'll find it's not so bad."

"Most people wouldn't label the Ferris wheel a scary ride."

"It's scary if you're afraid of heights."

I shifted in my seat, feeling uneasy.

"Are you afraid of heights?" Noah asked.

"Nope."

That was a lie. My palms were sweaty. Sitting close to him made me nervous... and it only increased when he started rocking the car.

"Oh my God! Stop! We're gonna fall!"

"No, we're not." He chuckled, pulling me closer. "I guess someone *is* afraid of heights. Relax—we won't fall."

I was pressed against his body as he hung his arm around my shoulder. The car rocked back and forth until it eventually stopped moving. Closing my eyes, I tried to calm my nerves.

The wheel rotated backward, filling the other passenger cars with people. We were almost halfway up in the air now. Being with Noah felt like I was on a never-ending thrill ride—an emotional roller coaster, and there was no guarantee I'd make it off that ride in one piece. Anything manmade is flawed and can break down. Why is human nature so flawed and complicated as well? Our hearts can break, our minds can break, and our bodies can break just like a machine, yet life just keeps going. It doesn't stop. Is this the curse and blessing of time? I questioned, fading into a mist of thoughts.

"What are you thinking about?" Noah murmured in my ear.

"Just… how beautiful everything looks from up here."

"Yeah, it's amazing."

I relaxed against him, listening to the music. The lyrics were beautiful. Some artists have great lyricism, but if the instrumentals suck, it can really take away from the track. Art is subjective.

We were moving again, floating toward the starry sky. It was in that moment I knew I was ready to confess my feelings for him. The setting was perfect. We were on this amazing ride, and this incredible song was playing, like an epic soundtrack in a perfect romance movie. How could this all have been a coincidence? I desperately wanted to believe that someone or something out there truly wanted us to be together. Maybe it was my warped-out delusional mind fooling me, but I knew that fighting my feelings for Noah was impossible at this point. I wanted more. My body, my heart, and my soul desired every part of him. He needed to know that—even if it meant I'd lose him forever.

Nothing lasts forever.

A bond between a father and daughter does.

I replayed the conversation in my head, word for word. Whatever would happen, I had to believe he would never abandon me again. Maybe I was reading too much into the surrounding synchronicities, but I knew I needed to open up.

Aria, the hopeless romantic.

"Noah?" I looked at him, preparing for that crucial moment.

"Yes, baby?" He held my gaze, smiling.

What's the worst that can happen? It's not like he can run away from me. We're floating in the freaking air. I consoled myself, letting our fingers touch on the handlebar.

His electric energy flowed through my body, shocking my heart to life. I hated feeling so nervous. I couldn't even look at him.

"Are you all right? Don't worry, sweetheart, we're not gonna fall. I promise."

"I know. I just…"

You can do this. Say it. I shut my eyes, looking for courage.

"Aria?"

This was it. It was now or never.

"I…"

Quit stalling!

"I'm…"

"You're starting to worry me."

"Noah… I…"

"Are you feeling sick?"

"I'm in love with you!"

The words had been on the tip of my tongue for months, begging to be expressed. I couldn't take it back now.

Staring at him, he never blinked as our passenger car moved upwards again. My heart was beating so fast, I worried I'd pass out from the terror of confessing my feelings.

Don't freak out, I repeated in my head when we reached the top. We were smack in the center, three hundred feet in the sky.

"Please say something," I muttered.

He parted his mouth to speak, but no words came out.

God, I'm so stupid. How could I have blurted that out?

"Sweetie, I… I'm your father."

I imagined picking up a knife and stabbing myself in the chest. This was so humiliating. I wanted to die. Had I deluded myself into reading the signs wrong? I wanted to believe he could return my feelings.

"Don't you feel the same way?" I asked. "From the moment we met, I felt a connection between us. You can't deny that, Noah."

Bottling up my emotions was an epic fail. I could feel my tears forming, as the dam that held back all my feelings quickly broke. The river was running wild now, and I had no control anymore.

"Recently, I've sensed you've developed strong feelings for me," he finally said, "and I think it would be a good idea if we got counseling together."

"What?"

I wasn't expecting that.

"I know this amazing therapist who counseled me through my drug addiction. I went and saw him earlier this week."

"Are you trying to ship me off to a crazy hospital?" I felt so hurt and betrayed. How could he have kept this from me?

"Of course not, Aria!" His face contorted. "We'd both get counseling. There's a reason you feel this way about me, and it's normal—given our circumstances."

It sounded so rehearsed, like he had played this conversation over in his head. I hated it. How could he be so relaxed about all this while I was freaking out?

"I'm not getting any damn therapy!"

"Why are you so resistant?"

Because I don't trust people easily!

"Aria, I just want the best for you."

For me, or for you?

Noah was about to say something, but stopped.

Why isn't this damn ride moving? It was taking forever as we dangled in the air. Maybe something had happened to the gears, and they were doing a maintenance check. I secretly hoped the Ferris wheel would just burn to the ground, killing me along with it.

"These feelings won't go away, Noah. They never will, no matter how much therapy you think it'll take to cure me. What I feel for you is not curable!"

It's like he was asking me to change my sexuality, which was impossible.

"You don't feel the same about me," I said. "And as much as it hurts, I understand. I have no choice but to respect that. You can't force someone to love you."

"Aria—"

"But now you have to respect my decision." I brushed his arm off my shoulder. "I want to move back to New York. I can't be around you. It hurts too much."

"Please don't…"

There was panic in his eyes.

"Try to understand my feelings. I can't love you the way a normal daughter does. I want more."

"Don't do this. Let's give counseling a shot with an open mind. I just—"

"No! Don't you understand? Can't you see how it kills me, knowing I can never have you? You're constantly around me, in my space, and every time you're there, all I can think about is…" I wavered, not wanting to discuss my fantasies. "Wanting *more*," I finally expressed.

Tears streaked down my cheeks as I ignored them. I needed something to hold on to, something to keep me from slipping into a comatose state of delusions. The metal bar served its purpose as I grabbed on to it.

Why won't this fucking ride move? I screamed in my head.

My heart was broken. I'd never felt this vulnerable before. It seemed cruel that I had no route to escape. All this time, I'd been afraid he would run from me, but that's all I wanted at that moment… to run and never look back.

"I don't want to lose you again. Please don't move back to New York," he pleaded.

"I can't stay here while I feel this way about you. I know it's wrong, and you probably find me disgusting."

"Don't say that." He seemed hurt. "I don't think that way about you."

His compassion offered me no comfort. I felt broken and dejected, with my heart laying on the floor, bleeding out. It was tempting to lift that handlebar and plummet to my death. But he wasn't done as he raised his voice, startling me.

"I won't let you go back and live with that asshole!" Noah's eyes burned with fury.

"I'm not moving in with Mom and Rob."

"Then where will you go?"

Move! Please, just move this freaking ride! I felt like such a joke.

Tears kept flowing as I accepted my fate and made peace with the fact that we wouldn't reach the bottom soon.

"Tell me what I have to do to change your mind," said Noah. "Please, Aria, don't leave me like this, not after everything…"

I looked at him and lost myself. His calm ocean had turned into turbulent waters, reflecting pain and panic while I drowned in him.

Brushing my cheek, he wiped away my wet mascara. But his affection only caused more pain inside as I withdrew, rejecting his warmth.

Why did he even care so much? He should have been relieved I was choosing to move out. I felt like a force of nature, an F6 tornado that would run down a town and disappear, leaving nothing but death and destruction.

"Just talk to me," he whispered.

"You don't understand. You really don't." The walls I had reinforced around me crumbled to the ground, leaving me exposed once again. "Loving you this way hurts"—tears misted my vision—"feels like… a waterfall of pain pouring inside me."

"Aria," he breathed, reaching for my hand.

I pulled away, feeling hurt and angry at myself. I couldn't bear to face the devastation I had caused in his eyes.

"This attraction is like… demonic possession." I struggled to get the words out. "I feel nothing close to a father/daughter bond with you, Noah—it's the opposite."

"We can heal this. Just—"

"Let me finish. Please." I took a deep breath. "You're my greatest strength, and my biggest weakness. My mind keeps telling me I should hate you, but my heart just cries whenever my anger resurfaces. All it takes is one glance from you and I'm drowning in feelings I can't control. It makes me feel so powerless and… and…" I stammered as my chest got heavier.

The wounds I'd inflicted on him only made me feel a hundred times worse. He must have pitied me. It was written all over his face.

Noah's watch suddenly beeped twice when he tucked my hair behind my ear, which let me know it was officially midnight.

Happy Birthday to me. Not that I cared. I honestly wanted to die.

The song had approached its climactic bridge, and all I could do was shrink a little inside.

"I hate myself. I wish I was never born."

"Stop talking nonsense." Noah held my face. He slid his fingers through my hair, resting his thumbs against my jaw.

"My life's just been trauma after trauma. I'm sick of being here. I don't fit in anywhere. I'm lost and clearly fucked in the head."

"You're not." He wiped my tears, controlling the pain in his voice. "You have a purpose. I promise."

"Life fucked me up, Noah. Your demons are nothing compared to mine. I can't stay here with you while combatting this darkness. I'm sorry. I'm not as strong as you."

"You think you're the only one with demons?"

I stayed quiet, shedding tears.

"I won't lose you again, Aria." He searched my eyes. "Do you understand? I didn't go through hell and back to lose you again."

I didn't expect him to get so emotional, but the next thing he did completely caught me off guard. I. Was. *Not.* Prepared.

The force of his kiss rushed into me like a powerful wave, sweeping away all my pain. I felt resurrected and purified.

I wasn't on that ride anymore; I was free falling at a hundred miles per hour, surrendering to ecstasy. His kiss was all it took to make everything right in my inner kingdom. I had been at war with myself from the moment we met. It felt so good to just drop my sword and let him conquer me.

The ride was moving fast, whipping my hair around as Noah breathed against my lips. He parted them with a gentle tug before slipping his tongue inside… full collision. I moaned, unable to control the euphoria that rushed into my bloodstream. His inferno was consuming me as I poured all my passion into him, not caring about rules or the fact that we were related.

The Ferris wheel turned as we floated back up in the air, unable to pull away from each other. My spirit was soaring to places it had never traveled before. Noah's kiss was like astral travel. All I could focus on was sensation. He kissed me with a gentle intensity that only made me crave more. I wanted to hop on his lap and rip his shirt off.

Sweeping his lips over mine, he sucked on my bottom lip and tugged it back, watching as it bounced in place. I stole a moment to breathe and covered his hands with mine to steady his trembling fingers. Before the spell could break, I kissed him back with everything I had, like he was the only man I would ever kiss in this world.

A tidal wave of emotions washed over my being as our mouths crushed and glided in a perfect choreography. If this was forbidden, then why did it feel so right... so perfect? It seemed as if we were an ideal match with chemistry. It was undeniable. I couldn't break the kiss. I didn't want to. I was greedy for more.

Dominance seemed to come naturally to Noah as he took charge and tangled my hair in his fist, pulling me closer. The Ferris wheel went down fast in a third rotation, wildly whipping my hair. Our tongues teased each other in a dance of transgression, pushing boundaries and getting off on it. He explored my mouth with newfound confidence while my heart blazed with victory. My attraction was not one sided, and it was such a relief.

I didn't want to open my eyes, fearing I'd wake up and discover this entire experience was nothing but a dream. I didn't want this amazing moment to disappear like smoke and mirrors. If it wasn't for the risk of falling over, I would have shifted onto to his lap already, but the guard rail kept us from moving any closer. I *craved* so much more with him, and I didn't care how fucked up it was to desire that.

There was danger, of course: being seen every time we passed onlookers below. But we were so lost in each other that the risk of getting caught didn't matter anymore. This was so much better than I had imagined. A brilliant heat exploded from Noah's lips as I tapped into my dark goddess energy and nipped his lower lip. He groaned. It aroused me.

Loving Noah was like going on the scariest thrill ride at an amusement park. It was skydiving out of a plane, scared out of my mind, but taking comfort in knowing I was safely strapped to his harness. It was diving off a cliff, my hand in his, submerging under the deep water and resurfacing safely in his arms. Loving him was the most intense feeling I had ever felt in my life, and I never wanted it to stop. That's what made it so terrifying... the ending cycles of life.

Nothing lasts forever.

A bond between a father and daughter does.

It was hard to trust his words.

Our kissing intensified as our shallow breaths echoed around us, making me feel as if he had been dying to kiss me for months. My ex had never made me feel this way when we had kissed—and he was a good kisser, but this... it was on another level of attraction, burning me from the inside. What was our mutual goal? I wondered, feeling a delicious thrill every time he brushed his tongue over mine.

Oneness. Is that what we craved? Was that the destination of uncontrollable passion? The desperate need to merge energies? Spiritualists always teach that we're already "whole and complete." If that was true, then why do we walk this life feeling so *incomplete* and empty? Why do we feel "oneness" when we come into union with that special person? I didn't have the answers. All I knew was that my pain disappeared when Noah touched me.

Somehow, he had finally surrendered to my desires, as if they were his own, kissing me with uncontrollable intensity. Our breathing got harsh and uneven. We couldn't stop. I didn't want him to. Electrical pulses sizzled around my aura as the wheel kept turning, shielding us from the eyes of the world when we soared into the sky. But just as quickly, the wheel came down, reminding us of our sobering reality. We couldn't stay up there forever.

Maybe this Ferris wheel represented our mental turmoil: a wheel slowly turning like the mechanical gears in our minds. We had desperately fought to hold on to sanity, but that had failed the second Noah pressed his lips against mine. The wind, the electricity in the air, our kiss, and the music symbolized the wildness of our rebellion—love, lust, and passion, all fused into one.

The feeling of that rise and fall… nothing could compare to it. My senses were fully heightened and sensitive to his touch. My lips pleaded for constant contact as I unleashed my fire and melted his self-restraint. The feral sound of his sexy groans sent shivers down my body. Nothing and no one else mattered at that moment. It was just me, Noah, and the spellbinding magic that floated like stardust in the midnight air.

Our make-out session ended when the wheel slowed down. The spell seemed to break as Noah tore his lips away from mine. His eyes were wild with life and something more, staring at me breathlessly. We both seemed to struggle to recover from the heated seduction that still swirled around us, as if our energies had been infected by sinful lust; the same demon I had tried to fight off from the moment I met him.

I felt light-headed, but in a good way. We had ignited a dangerous fire that was bound to close in on us until we burned to ash. He knew it. I knew it, and there was no turning back. I just wanted to collapse in his arms and hide myself inside of him, hide our love from the world.

Our car swayed back and forth while we waited to get off the ride. My mind was in a state of incomprehensible chaos.

"Promise me you won't leave," Noah finally spoke. "Promise me you won't go back to New York." The fear in his eyes contradicted his calm voice.

How could I leave after that mind-blowing kiss? It was impossible to walk away. I had to make him mine, whatever it took.

"Aria—"

"I promise." I smiled softly.

Noah seemed relieved as he caressed my face, brushing away my runny mascara. His heated touch made my body respond in ways no one had ever achieved. I couldn't understand it. Our physical attraction made no sense; it defied all logic. We had waged war on morality the second he kissed me. But I had no regrets.

"I'd rather lose everything in my life than lose you," Noah whispered, making my heart shiver. I loved seeing this vulnerable side of him.

He gave me the world when he kissed me again, controlling his passion this time. I wanted to kiss him from the deepest depths of my soul, if only to bring us wholeness, but he pulled away when our passenger car reached the bottom.

Lifting the handlebar, Noah hopped out first and helped me off the ride. The way he held my hand felt different from previous times he had held it. Maybe it was because I knew he had feelings for me, the same way I had feelings for him. He gently squeezed my fingers and made me feel like I belonged to him.

"Hey, guys!" Vanessa called out. She left Vi for a moment and approached us. I watched as she threw her arms around Noah's neck and kissed his cheek.

I felt so awkward... and guilty.

"How was the ride?"

"Great." I plastered on a fake smile.

Noah seemed tense, as if he was uncomfortable with Vanessa's affection. I was pretty good at reading energy—but maybe I was wrong.

"Honey, let's go on a ride!"

"Actually, Aria's not feeling too well." He gave me a cryptic look.

"Yeah," I played along. "I think I'm coming down with a cold or something."

Vienna was now in my line of sight as she touched my forehead. I wasn't too comfortable with her motherly gesture.

"She feels feverish."

Yeah... but not for the reason you think, my shadow whispered.

"Aw, sweetie," Vanessa cooed, "hopefully it's just a forty-eight-hour bug—max. We should head home." She paused. "I don't know about the rest of you, but I had an amazing time tonight."

"The haunted funhouse was my favorite," said Vi. "It's too bad you two didn't come. Some guy with a chainsaw was supposed to jump out at us, but he tripped and fell flat on his face. I know my initial instinct should've been to ask if he was all right, but I couldn't stop my laugh attack."

"I guess that's better than a heart attack!" My stepmom giggled while I rolled my eyes at the lame joke.

We started back toward the car, with Vienna and Vanessa walking ahead. Noah and I followed behind them hand in hand. He kept caressing my thumb with his, like a secret reminder that we had something more going on between us, something we both were ready to explore, or so I hoped. That kiss was the best birthday gift. Nothing could top it… unless we went further. I was still worried he would push me away by saying he made a mistake, but I didn't want to think or worry about all the what ifs.

"I'm riding shotgun!"

"Duh, you're the wife," Vienna replied.

Unfortunately, I thought in dismay.

My stepmom irritated my demons. That's why I was so triggered. At least I was aware of it. Quietly grieving over my disappointment, Noah let go of my hand and opened the passenger door for Vanessa. It was time to go home, but at least I found comfort in knowing we would walk into that house as two different people. The dynamic of our relationship had got a hundred times more complicated than it already was. But it didn't matter to me. I didn't care about how wrong it was to want him. It felt right in my heart.

‼‽

The wind breezed through my hair as we sped down the freeway. Vanessa cranked up the music and started singing off-key to a Katy Perry tune, which didn't last long because Noah killed the radio and switched to his own playlist.

"Hey, I was listening to that!" my stepmom complained.

"Sorry, honey, but if I listened to another second of that song, I would've crashed the car."

"He meant your voice." Vienna laughed.

"You two are so mean!"

"Sorry, sis, the truth hurts. You're lucky Simon Cowell's not in the car with us."

"Oh, whatever! You're no idol either!"

"I never said I was!"

If Vanessa auditioned for *American Idol*, all of America's ears would bleed and suicide rates would spike uncontrollably. Exaggerating—again. (But she really did suck.)

Turning up the volume, Noah stepped on the gas, speeding past some cars. I loved the beats but didn't recognize the song. It was way better than the lamestream music that had been playing on the radio.

Are you thinking about that kiss? I wondered, catching him staring through the rearview mirror.

I couldn't get his sexy mouth off my mind as I tried to hide my smile and stole secret glances at him. It wasn't until he parked the car in the driveway that I realized I'd been dreading this moment.

 CB&ED

The hour hand was reaching close to one in the morning. Everybody was tired, which meant Noah and my stepmom would go to bed soon. The thought of Vanessa getting it on with him made me sick to my stomach. I silently prayed to whatever god existed to take pity on me and stop Noah from sleeping with her. Our situation was complicated, and I had underestimated just how much it would be. I didn't want to feel like the other woman, nor did I want to share him with her. Jealousy was not something I wanted to battle every day. I don't think it's healthy for a woman to compete for a man's attention; he either wants you and pursues you, or he doesn't—in which case you should move along and stop chasing. Grams often said that a woman should never chase a man. I think she was right.

"I'm off to bed," said Vienna. "I'll see you guys in the morning." She kissed Noah and Vanessa's cheek and then felt the need to pet me on the head like a child.

My stepmom was halfway down the hall when she turned and asked, "Noah, are you coming to bed, honey?"

"I've got some work to finish up. I'll join you later."

"Are you sure it can't wait until tomorrow?"

"No, it can't."

Wow, she really was desperate for sex. It infuriated me. My shadow imagined shooting arrows at her forehead like Katniss Everdeen in *The Hunger Games*. I would only need *one* arrow, because I wouldn't miss. The multiple attacks that would follow would strictly be for my amusement. I swear I wasn't a violent person… not in real life. However, in my make-believe world of shadow expression, just about anything was possible and permissible. Anyone who denied their shadow side was full of shit. You're supposed to acknowledge it and keep it in check so that you don't become a crummy human being. *Control* your shadow. Don't let it control *you.*

"Okay, sweetheart," said Vanessa, sliding her arms over Noah's shoulders. "I'll say goodnight to you now." She kissed him on the lips, making this obnoxiously nasal sounding giggle.

I didn't stick around to watch.

Part of me hoped Noah would've come after me, but as the minutes passed in my bedroom, I gave up hope. Maybe he thought it was too risky. Maybe he'd changed his mind about us, or maybe Vanessa had lured him to the bedroom. I hated feeling so powerless under Noah's roof. But it was better than living with my psycho stepdad.

Changing out of my clothes, I put on a white crop top and didn't bother with any shorts or pajama bottoms. Sleeping in black bikini panties seemed like the lazier option. My big blue bunny sat on my armchair, and I couldn't help but smile as I played back the entire evening in my head. I would remember this night forever.

Switching off the lights, I settled into bed and was about to pass out when I heard a faint knock.

Noah.

I could feel his energy penetrating the door as I got up and opened it. My heart fluttered when our eyes locked.

"Can I come in?" He sounded serious.

I nodded and stepped aside.

Part of me already knew how this conversation would go: *I made a mistake. We can't do this. It's wrong, Aria.* Something along those lines.

Shutting the door, my back was instantly slammed against the hard surface.

Noah crushed his lips against mine and kissed me hard, lifting my thighs and pressing his body into me. Everything happened so fast as I was hoisted up. His firm pectorals brushed up against my chest as we abandoned all self-control. I didn't care that I was drowning in sin. I was drowning in *him*, and that's all that mattered.

"I tried to stay away," he breathed between passionate kisses, "but you keep pulling me in."

"Don't stay away."

Like a man possessed, he kissed me with frustration and desire. Something hard throbbed against me when he groaned and gripped my thighs.

"Fuck… [*pants*]… why do you feel so good?"

"Because I'm yours."

My answer seemed to turn him on as he carried me to bed and dropped me on the mattress. His hooded eyes were drenched in lust, an unfamiliar gaze I hadn't seen before. I felt like a vulnerable deer that was about to meet its demise as the jungle's most dangerous predator closed in on its prey. I know it sounded sick and twisted, but my insides were pulling and contracting, causing my arousal to intensify and heighten with each passing second.

Pulling off his shirt, Noah tossed it over his head, allowing me to crawl over and touch every part of him I desperately needed to caress with my hands, lips, and tongue. This was sensory overload. This was Noah Mason Hunter, standing before me like the Greek god Adonis, who embodied beauty and desire. I wanted him to make love to me and transform me into his goddess Aphrodite. I admired every muscle, strikingly sculpted to perfection around his torso; his waist was a perfectly inverted triangle. I licked the dipping groove of his pelvis and watched him groan.

"Aria." He released a shallow sigh, tangling his fingers in my hair.

Kissing his abdominals, I grazed my lips against his warm, tanned skin. I hadn't even touched the throbbing bulge in his pants, and he already had his eyes closed, ready for me to unravel him.

Would he actually let me go that far? I wondered, feeling my dark goddess awaken.

"Holy fuck," he quietly groaned. "Your lips feel amazing."

I felt goosebumps prickling his skin as the satisfying sound of my moist lips trailed down his navel with kisses.

Noah threw his head back, lost in pleasure from my touch. I unfastened his trousers and was about to pull down the fly when he stopped me, placing his hand over mine. Staring up at him, I noticed his desire. Maybe he was contemplating things now, realizing how wrong this was. One of us had to stay sane and responsible. I didn't care about the consequences anymore.

"This is dangerous." His voice was hoarse, but it only turned me on more.

"Do you want me?"

"Isn't it obvious?"

We stared at one another, breathing through arousal.

He caressed the side of my face while I yearned for more. I wanted him over me, under me, in every way possible. His affection was warm and inviting, but his eyes betrayed something darker. Something fierce and feral.

Running my palm over his jeans, I outlined the length of his thick, long shaft.

"*Fuuuck,*" Noah growled, sucking in air. "Lie down."

This man was always composed as a perfect gentleman, but at that moment, the demon he had hidden away had come through… and I was madly in love with him. I craved his darkness. I wanted to be filled with it.

"Lie down, Aria."

It wasn't a request. It was a demand. Reclining on my sheets, I rested my head on a pillow and found his eyes.

"Spread your legs for me," Noah whispered.

I parted them slowly while my heart hammered in my chest, feeling his body heat when he slid between my legs. I was anxious and aroused at the same time. Something stiff pressed against my panties when he sank his weight into me, making me shudder with pleasure. I was ready for him to take me, even though it was wrong; it didn't stop our bodies from naturally molding together like a beautifully sculpted masterpiece. If Noah was the artist, I was his block of clay. All he had to do was believe in his ability to shape me to become whatever he wanted, and I would become exactly that.

Lost in the calm sea of his eyes, my arms took on a will of their own, winding around his neck and pulling him closer.

"You're so fucking beautiful, you know that?" he murmured against my lips. "Do you?" He kissed me slow and sensual.

"I want you," I breathed.

"I'm going to Hell for this."

"I'll be right there with you." I kissed him with a promise, pledging my undying love and loyalty as I placed my hand on his heart, where he had tattooed my name. If we were to burn, then we would burn together. His sins were my sins, and vice versa. My soul was prepared to carry the weight of that burden. Fuck the world. Fuck society. I wanted him.

My arousal was so intense, it was hurting. I craved penetration, as if it were the only way to feel complete. Noah's heart pounded against my palm as he bent his elbows to support his weight. Our kiss had amplified with passion, exploding with heat and desire. He was claiming every part of me in victorious conquest. I sucked on his bottom lip while he loosened it and dominated the kiss, making me moan in his mouth. Raising my hips, he pushed into me with a quiet groan, setting my insides on fire.

"We need to stop." Noah panted. "I can't control myself much longer."

"I don't want you to control yourself. Just let go." I kissed him hard and confidently, but he pulled away again, pressing his forehead against mine.

"Baby, listen to me… You're a virgin."

Was now a good time to confess?

"Is that why you don't want me, because I'm inexperienced?" I felt so crushed. "I can learn."

I should have told him the truth, but I didn't want to be slut shamed.

"Hey, look at me."

I wouldn't meet his eyes.

"Look at me, Aria," he said in that stern, sexy voice that made my stomach tighten. "Your first time shouldn't be with me."

"I disagree." I raised myself on my elbows, leaning into his ear and whispering, "Don't you wanna know what it's like to penetrate my tight, wet—"

"That's enough!"

Noah looked angry with a blazing ring of fire in his gaze; it hypnotized me. Mostly, I had tried to be prim and proper, but here I was seducing him, provoking his demon to come out from its cage. I knew there was a part of him that wasn't entirely human; I could see his inner beast. And there I was, a delicious little lamb, willing to sacrifice herself for the slaughter.

"Don't say those things to me." Noah frowned. He was armor-plated once again, hiding the monster within.

"And what if I don't stop? Then what? You gonna punish me?" I wrapped my legs around his torso. "Go on, Noah… what are you gonna do?"

I was testing his boundaries, but I got off on it.

"This is so fucked up," he huffed as I kissed his neck.

"Let's get fucked up together," I whispered, licking his jugular vein.

"You're not helping."

"You're not letting me." Reaching for his cock, it only seemed to make him panic as he rolled off my body and stood up.

"It's just a kiss, not cocaine," I foolishly blurted out.

"I'd argue you're worse than any party drug I've had in my life. And now I've fucked myself over because I tasted forbidden fruit."

"Are you saying you're addicted to me?"

He put his shirt back on and avoided my gaze. I'd gone too far. It was wrong of me to get so gutsy.

"Noah, I—I'm sorry. Please don't go."

The flaming phoenix had disappeared from his chest, covered by gray fabric.

"I don't know what I'm doing here, to be honest." He rubbed his neck. "I shouldn't be doing this with you."

Here it was: the guilt, confusion.

"I understand you're freaking out, but it doesn't have to be this way." I got off my bed and approached him.

"Aria, I can't have sex with you."

"You can kiss me, but you can't have sex with me? Do I repulse you that much?"

"Don't start—you know that's not true."

I noticed fading fragments of magma in his eyes.

"Please, don't push me away."

"I'm not."

"It feels like it." I wrapped my arms around his waist and hid myself in his chest.

"This is all moving way too fast. I need to process everything." Noah exhaled and lifted my chin. "I'm not pushing you away, I promise." His lips caressed mine.

A promise sealed with a kiss.

"I have to go, and you need to rest."

"Noah…"

He paused, looking back at me.

"I know you're married, but… Please don't—"

"I won't." He seemed to have read my mind. "Get some sleep."

The withdrawal symptoms were getting to me, and he still wasn't out the door yet. But my heart fluttered to life when he turned and took my face in his hands, kissing me long and deeply before he released me from his paradise.

"I love you, Aria," he whispered. And then his face got serious. "Never bring up my past addiction ever again. Understood?"

I nodded, feeling like shit as he pulled back and slipped away.

I shouldn't have made that comment.

Standing alone with regret, I desperately tried to recover from his kiss. I knew sleep wouldn't come any time soon.

My grandmother had lectured me once about "self-pleasure." She said it was "a horrible sin," and that "anyone who did it would go to Hell if they didn't repent." But what about me? Never mind the fact that my hormones were all haywire, or whenever I'd lie in bed, I'd touch myself in places that Noah couldn't… What kind of sinner was I? I never thought about some hunky actor when I'd pleasure myself. I would constantly fantasize about Noah. Could God ever forgive my wicked ways, even if I repented?

I kept replaying every intimate moment I shared with the man I was in love with. Sleeping on this bed would never be the same anymore. I had no choice but to bite down on my arm to mute my moans as I took myself over the edge. Drowning in erotic memories, they fell like invisible photographs from my ceiling, covering me from head to toe.

A contented sigh escaped my lips when I achieved sweet release. My hand went limp, and my muscles relaxed before I slowly drifted off to sleep. I dreamed of Noah making love to me, and it felt so real.

CHAPTER TWENTY-THREE
NOAH

My mind was reeling, my heart was racing, and I had the most painful case of morning wood. Sitting up, I was disoriented, letting my eyes adjust to the blinding light that had flooded my room. I'd been dreaming of her… again. After leaving Aria last night, I had locked myself in my study, crashing on the most uncomfortable leather sofa in our entire house— and yeah, it just so happened to be in my home office. Vanessa had purchased this atrocious piece of furniture, disregarding the comfort level I'd told her I needed. Women… always prioritizing aesthetics over comfort, like when they walk in a pair of six-inch heels for eight hours straight. The shoes will have murdered their feet by the end of the day, but apparently it's worth the pain. It was moments like this that I truly appreciated identifying as an average heterosexual male.

I felt weird today, like I was outside my body looking in or something. Everything that had happened the night before felt like a dream, but my reality begged to differ. Doctor Grey's advice had gone out the window the moment I'd gave in to Aria's affections. When she had told she was moving back to New York, I panicked. I think I kissed her out of desperation. It was impulsive and reckless. Nothing could have prepared me for the feelings that rushed over me when our lips collided. No matter how much therapy I might have received, I would've forgotten all of it once I inevitably kissed her. This was my conclusion.

Like a recovering addict, I had regretfully relapsed. Aria was the most dangerous drug I had ever experimented with, and I should have known better than to rekindle my love affair with drugs, because that's what it felt like to kiss her—as if her lips had injected this hallucinogenic substance into my bloodstream, triggering an instant rush of euphoria; a high that I didn't want to come down from. I felt so fucking guilty. I had kissed many women, and no one had ever made me feel the way she did. It fucking blew my mind.

What the hell did I get myself into?

Last night, I cheated on my wife. I broke the law. I committed an unforgivable sin, and I didn't even want to stop. My conscience shook its head at me as I argued my case in my head like I was on trial. Stopping things from escalating to the point of no return had been a sensible decision. We were never supposed to even get to that stage, but I blamed only myself. I was the adult—I should have stayed away. My plan had been to grab a glass of water and return to my study. But I ended up in front of Aria's bedroom door, and I couldn't turn around.

Maybe it wasn't too late to atone for my sins. I was sure Doctor Grey would have a few choice words for me when I visited him again. How did my life get so fucking complicated? Was this a karmic punishment for not being in my daughter's life when she was younger? I had sexually imprinted on her, and now I was suffering eternal torture because I couldn't stop these feelings or make my fantasies go away.

I hated seeing her cry on that Ferris wheel. But I admired her for being brave enough to be vulnerable; I struggled with that—always have. I couldn't handle breaking her heart; I had already broken too many since I could remember. No one, not even my wife, had power over my emotions the way Aria did. My intention was to stay rational and in control, but I couldn't live with the fact that I was shattering her to pieces. The fear of losing her was a reality I never wanted to experience, which was why I jeopardized my marriage, my morals, and my role as a father in her life.

I had told Grey in confidence that I would never touch Aria. Yet last night, I'd almost had sex with her. I was destroying her and myself. If we continued this, it was going to screw us up and hurt many people in the long run. There had to be a way to convince her to get counseling with me. I couldn't give up hope. How could I stick to my guns without losing her? She'd clarified that she couldn't love me the way a daughter does, and I had failed at rejecting her. What did that even mean?

Am I in love with her, too? Is it just attraction I'm feeling? I didn't want to think. I wanted to turn off the thoughts in my head, get high, and tune out the world. But I knew that wasn't an option. Maybe I should have taken up smoking again. I needed another addiction before I became addicted to her. This wasn't healthy. It was dangerous.

❧

The house was quiet as I made my way upstairs. It was a quarter after eight, and my wife was still sleeping when I entered our bedroom. I could go back to sleep or shower and head out to clear my head. I went with option number two.

It felt good to stand under hot water, surrounded by clouds of steam. My back was still sore from sleeping on that pathetic excuse for a sofa, but I'd live. Shutting my eyes, I listened to the sound of pouring water hitting the marble tiles beneath my feet. I was weighing out my options of how to spend my afternoon when I suddenly remembered the dinner party Vanessa was hosting for Aria's birthday... and Ryan was coming over. I didn't like the guy and wouldn't change my mind. There was something about him that rubbed me the wrong way. I didn't trust him for a second to be alone with my daughter. I didn't trust any guy being alone with her. I didn't even trust myself.

I'm going to hell for this, Aria.

I'll be right there with you...

Her voice echoed in my consciousness as a vivid image materialized before me: my body sinking into hers... our mouths colliding. I was disturbingly aroused just by thinking about her.

Great. How the hell am I going to function today? I knew I'd be more sexually frustrated if I didn't take care of the problem. Self-gratification was tempting, but I resisted and tried to erase any graphic image that jumped at me; Aria's lips, her body against mine… It was all so stimulating.

Don't you wanna know what it's like to penetrate my…

Her dirty talk looped in my head, enticing my demon. It sounded so wrong, but *fuck* was it hot when she said it. Aria was so goddamn beautiful. Her voice just did something to me. I'd heard nothing like it… the voice of a goddess. Her smile, her adorable laughter… she made my heart glow.

Facing the shower wall, I rested my palms on the tiles as water rained down on me. I fought the urge to relieve myself, but my "problem" refused to go down.

Freezing cold it is…

Twisting the shower knob, a fog of steam evaporated around me while my body temperature cooled down.

On second thought, she should probably start a blossoming relationship with that Ryan kid.

Maybe I was too overprotective of her and judging the guy too fast. I hadn't forgotten what it was like to be their age. Natalie had got pregnant at sixteen, and I was the one who knocked her up, so I couldn't claim saint status. I had a wife, and I'd promised Vanessa that we would work on our marriage. She wanted to have a baby soon. Being with my daughter was impossible. Last night felt like a crazy acid trip. I partly wished it had never happened.

My erection softened as I turned the heat back up.

Took long enough.

I was about to turn when a pair of arms hugged my waist.

"Mind if I join you?" Vanessa kissed my back, reaching for my cock.

Sure, it felt good to have her finish the task I was avoiding, but the fact that I wasn't thinking about my wife while she pleasured me was wrong. I felt so guilty.

"Nessa, you don't have to." I grabbed her wrist.

"But I want to," she whispered seductively in my ear. "Turn around," Vanessa demanded, twisting my body in her direction.

Determined to stop her, she left me powerless when she crouched on her knees and made me stand at full attention. Aria's gorgeous face flickered in front of me as I closed my eyes and tangled my fingers through Nessa's hair. Groaning in pleasure, my breathing was hard and uneven, the deeper she sucked me off. She took every inch down her throat, licking my shaft before engulfing me with her mouth again.

I remembered the sensation of Aria's sensuous lips pressing against mine. The smell of her strawberry vanilla shampoo, the heat between her thighs… It stimulated me more than Vanessa's mouth around my cock. Pulling her head down harder, I got aggressive with my thrusts while impaling her mouth. She started choking on my length, but it was too late to stop. I couldn't.

"Fuck! Open your mouth for me!"

She obeyed, waiting for me to release.

My twisted mind imagined Aria on her knees, devotedly sucking me off while looking up at me. Her stunning eyes kept flashing in my damaged psyche. Pleasure pulsed through my core as I released an animalistic growl and shot a whopping load.

"*Arrrghhh ffffuuuuuuck…*"

And then I uttered her name by accident.

"What did you just say?" Vanessa's panicked voice pulled me out of ecstasy.

Busted.

I opened my eyes as she rose to her feet. "I *said…*" My hand slid between her thighs. "Are ya ready?"

Nice save.

Nessa wrapped her arms around my shoulders and bit her bottom lip. "Always ready for you, Mister Hunter." She kissed me and guided my fingers inside of her.

I felt horrible. All I'd wanted was to shower alone, but I knew I had no right to get angry at my wife. She just wanted to make me feel good. Then how come I felt this overwhelming sense that I'd betrayed Aria?

What Aria doesn't know won't hurt her, another voice whispered.

My mind was a mess, but I hid that from my wife and focused on pleasuring her. It was the only way to end the shower play. If there was one thing I was confident about, it was taking a woman over the edge of ecstasy. After two minutes, I had her moaning. The wife was satisfied, and technically, I had kept my promise to Aria.

CHAPTER TWENTY-FOUR
ARIA

I woke up in the morning with a huge smile on my face. The night before had been a dream come true. I had butterflies in my stomach while I was showering and getting dressed. I didn't know everyone's plans for the day, but I knew Noah would be home. There was plenty of time to kill before Ryan would be over for dinner. Hopefully Vanessa wouldn't go all out.

My closet was thoroughly raided as I threw some outfits on my bed. I just didn't know what to wear. I wanted to look desirable. After several fittings, I decided on a white bikini top and ripped denim shorts. The weather was nice—best temperature for a swim in the pool.

Brushing on some gloss and mascara, I tied my hair in a high, messy bun and clasped on a necklace. The delicious aroma of pancakes wafted down the hallway as I made my way to the kitchen for breakfast. Vienna was already up. Unlike my stepmom, she looked frumpy, but didn't seem to care about her dressed-down appearance. I liked that about her: her no fucks given attitude.

"Good morning, Aria!"

"Morning." I smiled, walking past her to grab some fruit.

"Slept well?"

Pretty darn good.

"Yeah, what about you?"

"I don't know how I'll be able to sleep at three-star motels when I've experienced five-star accommodations here."

I chuckled dryly and sat on a stool by the island. Noah was right. Vienna was more down to earth than Vanessa. Manicures, pedicures, fake tans, and Botox weren't her thing at all. Slicing a juicy pomegranate, I felt my heart palpitate as soon as *he* walked in.

Mmmm... the scent of his cologne and body wash seemed to follow him everywhere he went, making me crazy with desire. I'd end up with a stupid smile on my face—it was all part of the Noah Hunter effect: you'd forget all rational thought and find yourself hypnotized by his alluring presence.

"Good morning, ladies."

"Hey, Noah." Vienna poked her head out from the fridge and handed him a jug of orange juice. "Hold that for me, will you?"

He flashed a dimpled smile at me, and I almost fainted. He just wasn't human. How could he be? Noah was too perfect to be categorized under the unfortunately flawed human race. Every woman swooned over him. I was certain he'd been a certified Casanova before he settled down with Botox Barbie. I was curious to know his "body count," but worried the truth would make me jealous. Some things were better left unknown.

"Are you raiding my fridge?" He laughed lightly.

"I'm looking for the mango juice." Vienna rummaged through the refrigerator while I stared at Noah.

My stepmom appeared out of nowhere and slid her arms around his waist. "Sorry, Vi. I drank the last carton yesterday."

"Thanks, Nessa," Vienna sarcastically replied. "So much for making the perfect breakfast!" She grabbed the jug of OJ from Noah and put it back in the fridge before shutting it with a sigh.

I watched my stepmom like a hawk as she hugged Noah's body and nipped his earlobe, murmuring things I couldn't hear because of all the ruckus Vienna was making with the pots and pans.

"That shower was fantastic!"

What?

"Wish we could start every morning like that."

I. Was. Fuming. She kissed his neck and groped his ass—which was an amazing ass, to be fair… but yeah, it triggered me. Grabbing my spoon, I gripped it so hard that my fingers went numb. Noah had promised he wouldn't sleep with her. Okay, technically he said he wouldn't last night… maybe he misinterpreted what I meant. I was crushed.

"Easy now." He unraveled himself from Vanessa's deadly spider web.

Yes, that's what Vanessa was like: a black widow spider that needed to be squashed! Sorry—shadow voice again. Her obnoxious giggling annoyed me as she wrapped her skinny spider legs around his waist and pulled him into a deadly widow's kiss. I stared down at my fruit salad and told my envious monster to calm the fuck down.

Tearing up, my cheeks felt hot, but somehow, I barricaded the door that Noah had passed through last night, and carried my bowl to the sink without even glancing at the blissfully married couple.

"Good morning, birthday girl!" said my stepmom, sounding cheerful as usual.

"Morning," I replied in a flat voice, feeling Noah's eyes on me.

"Are you feeling better today?" she asked.

I splashed on the fakest smile and soaked my voice in sarcasm. "I'm fine."

Knowing Vanessa, she was too clueless to even catch on to my condescending undertone.

"Glad to hear, hun!"

Totally called it. I met Noah's icy gaze for a second and looked away. Analyzing his facial expressions was not something I wanted to do that morning. We seemed to be good at telepathically communicating with each other, but I didn't want to let him in my head—not after discovering his little shower *sexcapade* with my stepmom.

"You hardly touched your breakfast." Vienna hovered next to me.

"Lost my appetite." I was about to walk out of the kitchen when Vanessa asked, "Is Ryan still coming over tonight?"

"Yeah, why?"

"I've invited a few more friends to dinner. You don't mind, do you? I can always cancel if you're not comfortable with it. I just thought having a little more company over for your birthday would be fun!"

I was anxious around strangers, but I appreciated her gesture.

"When exactly did you make this decision?" said Noah.

"I know it's last minute, but I called Teddy and Anna earlier, and also invited Amir and his family. I know you said that Aria doesn't want a party… I just thought it would be nice to have a casual dinner with some close friends. Is that okay, hon?"

He looked a little apprehensive, glancing at me. "If Aria's okay with it, so am I."

"It's fine. I don't mind."

There was no use in making a big deal out of it. Dipping out of their conversation, I marched into my room, grabbed some magazines, and headed for the patio. It was a perfect day to catch a cinnamon tan—but that was the last thing on my mind.

How can he sleep with her after what we shared last night? I fumed in silence.

Noah had never said that he was in love with me. Maybe all he felt was attraction and nothing more. Maybe my silicone stepmom had me beat in the love department. Depressing as it was, I promised myself I wouldn't allow him to get to me. I would only have to survive this night, and then I'd escape to New York with no one knowing. I'd get over him, somehow. If I could get over my breakup with Trevor, I'd get over this.

Reclining on a lounger, I opened an issue of *Seventeen* magazine and leafed through it. As the minutes passed, a tall shadow suddenly hovered above me. Someone sat down, and judging by the masculine feet, I knew who it was.

"Aria, we need to talk."

No. We don't.

"There's nothing to talk about." I avoided his gaze and put on my sunglasses, flipping another page.

"Listen to me, what you heard earlier is not—"

"I don't care. I honestly don't. She's your wife, right?" I looked up at him. "Let's put last night behind us, okay?" A lump in my throat started swelling, but I swore I wouldn't shed a single tear again. I was so tired of crying in front of him.

Noah parted his mouth to speak, but hesitated. Maybe this was what he wanted all along: to forget. Well, I sure as hell wouldn't tell him about my plans.

"Are you all right?"

"Why wouldn't I be?" I flashed a fake smile and focused on the magazine. It wasn't like I was actually reading it. None of the words were registering in my head, but he didn't know that. I just wanted to make it look as if I was completely uninterested in anything he had to say.

"Then why are you being so distant?" he asked.

"I'm not. I'm being realistic." Standing up, I shook off my shorts until they dropped to my feet. His eyes wandered down my body as I tossed my sunglasses on the lounger. "Last night was a mistake, correct?"

"Aria—"

Diving into the pool, I didn't let him respond. I started swimming laps, praying he'd be gone by the time I resurfaced. The mysterious demigod that had graced me with his unexpected visit had vanished by the time I came up for breath. A trace of Eternity was left in the air; the only evidence that proved our encounter had been real, and not in my head.

ೋღ

Avoiding Noah became a manageable assignment for the rest of the afternoon. In fact, I think we were both avoiding each other on purpose. I had called my mom and the twins on FaceTime, and they wished me a happy birthday. It was nice to see their faces; I missed them. Mom had sent me a heartfelt b-day card a few days ago, so I thanked her for that. She apologized for not being able to do more for me because of the financial problems she and Rob were having, but I'd told her I wasn't expecting anything, and that having her love was all I needed. Besides, Noah was rich as fuck… I didn't have to worry about finances.

Chatting with Jade and Ally brightened my day. I thanked them for the beautiful birthday video they had posted on Facebook. It was a video montage of all our favorite photos and memories together through the years. I'd spent about five minutes crying through the song they had used in the video: "Goodbye" by Spice Girls. We had performed that song during a talent show in eighth grade with another classmate. I was Sporty Spice, Jade was Scary Spice, and Ally was Baby Spice. My friends were amazing. No matter where we lived, we'd always be there for each other. I was sure of it.

That day, I spent most of my time out of the house, shopping with my girlfriends at the mall. Jessica took me out for a birthday lunch and a manicure like she had promised. By the time I returned home, it was almost five o'clock in the evening. Vanessa had gone overboard with the dinner preparations. She had hired a chef at the last minute to cook for us, and of course she would—the woman couldn't cook to save her life.

"Aria, is that you?"

"Yep! I'm home," I said, dragging my feet to the kitchen.

"Great. Did you get my text earlier? I wasn't sure if you had any semiformal dresses—you know, like a cute little cocktail dress? So, I went through your closet, and I've laid out some selections on your bed."

"Come again?"

I didn't like when people invaded my privacy. My mom used to snoop through my diary and show Rob my entries about my crushes before he'd get pissed off and humiliate me. I was thirteen when I'd confessed about wanting to kiss a boy. Not only did he slut shame me, but he fought about it with my mom and then embarrassed me further by sharing the incident with family members on the phone. Rob gossiped about me like it was amusing entertainment—all to induce crippling shame in me. Imagine how that feels for a child. It was hard to forgive the bastard when I still had so much pain inside. I was great at blocking out the ways my mom also traumatized me. I think it was scarier to vilify her. "Bloody Mary" was an urban legend that scared the crap out of me as a kid: the inverted expression of the feminine. If I could compare my mother's psychotic breaks and nervous breakdowns throughout the years… I'd say I lived with "Bloody Mary" herself, hidden behind my mother's "kind" social mask. Her persona outside was different from the unstable bitch she hid behind closed doors. I loved her regardless, but sometimes she made it really hard to endure her manipulative and passive aggressive style of abuse.

"I really think purple is your color," Vanessa added.

Purple was *not* my color.

"I thought this was supposed to be a casual shindig sort of thing," I said.

"Well, I just thought it would be fun if we dressed up a little! Don't you love getting dolled up? I'm sure you want to impress Ryan."

Nope, not him.

"Besides," she continued, "you only get to celebrate your eighteenth birthday one time, so you might as well look fabulous while you're doing it!" Vanessa winked.

"Fair enough." I smiled. "Thank you for everything. It really wasn't necessary."

"I love party planning! Make sure your friend knows about the dress code."

This was supposed to be a simple dinner, not line up in front of the Hunter residence and wait for Barbie bouncer Vanessa to enforce a dress code.

Feeling defeated, I sighed and sent Ryan a text.

ભ્ટ

After several dress changes, my stepmom finally approved of my evening attire: a short black cocktail dress that dipped low at the back in a V. My hair was styled in wavy curls around my shoulders, and I matched my ensemble with a pair of black peep-toe pumps. Vanessa looked amazing in her leopard-print mini dress, but it was so damn tight, I worried her boobs would pop out at any second. That would have been a mortifying wardrobe malfunction.

Ryan was the first to arrive, and everyone else rushed in shortly afterwards. Eight guests were over for dinner that evening (Vienna included). Anna and Teddy Deveraux were Vanessa's friends, and I had met Amir Crawford before, but I hadn't met his wife, Chelsea. They had a son and daughter who were my age, Max and Melanie. My stepmom had also invited her trainer, Tyrese. I think she was trying to play matchmaker for Vienna, since he was single and sexy.

Ryan looked great that night. Melanie flirted with him nonstop throughout the evening. I think she was crushing on him. I didn't mind, though. It wasn't Ryan I felt territorial over—it was Noah.

Dinner conversation wasn't all that interesting. Whoever that chef was, he had mad culinary skills. He served up these amazing Greek lamb skewers with parmesan-roasted potatoes and olives as the main course. It was *delicious*. I grew up making microwave dinners. Mom's cooking was great, but she typically cooked on the weekends because of her busy work schedule.

Everything was going smoothly at the party, but I couldn't help but notice how Noah kept giving Ryan the third degree, putting him on the spot more than once. I was thankful when Vanessa intervened, shifting everyone's focus to the other guests. Anna and Teddy had their firstborn on the way, and this sparked my stepmom's maternal instincts. She wouldn't shut up about how many times she and Noah had tried to get pregnant. The sheer thought of him impregnating her terrified me. I didn't want another brother or sister. Noah and I kept switching glances at one another throughout dinner. I wasn't sure what he was thinking, but he didn't look like he was enjoying himself.

After dessert, we split off into groups. Ryan, Max, Melanie, and I hung out by the pool and listened to some tunes, while everyone else sat on patio furniture in the glass solarium across from us. Drinking wine and eating fancy finger foods seemed to be the highlight of their evening.

Vanessa had placed paper lanterns around the edge of the pool. I liked the fairy lights that were coiled around the columns of the solarium, adding a romantic glow.

"So, are you two, like, dating?" Melanie asked. She was a cute redhead with freckles and deep blue eyes.

Ryan looked at me as I sat on his lap and fed him a strawberry off my plate.

"We're still trying to figure that out," he replied with a smile. "I just wish she would say yes and be my girlfriend already."

Melanie blushed. I think she was hoping he would take an interest in her. Her brother, Max, had this punk/goth style going on. His bottom lip and ears were pierced, and he had dyed his hair black and blue. It was cool. I dug his vibe.

"Do you guys wanna get outta here?" he asked. "I've got some weed on me. We could roll a J." He discreetly pulled out a freezer bag full of marijuana from his pocket.

"Tempting," said Ryan. "But I don't think we can sneak away while Aria's under her dad's radar."

So, I guess he *had* noticed Noah stealing glances at me.

"Put that stuff away." Melanie glared at her brother. "You're gonna get us in trouble. The last thing I need is to get grounded again because of your fuck-ups."

"Chill out, Mel."

"Sorry the party's so lame, guys," I said.

"It's not," Melanie replied. "Dinner was amazing. We're always forced to go to dinner parties with our parents. At least you two aren't obnoxious six-year-olds. Normally, I end up babysitting annoying toddlers for the whole evening while our parents 'party it up.' They should at least pay me!"

We all laughed with her as the convo moved on to music, movies, and our plans after graduation.

Ryan and I were getting cozy with each other. I enjoyed his company. He kept whispering sweet stuff in my ear and charming me, which seemed to piss off Noah. But whenever I looked at him, his eyes were glued expectantly on me.

"So... will you go out with me next Friday?" Ryan kissed my shoulder.

I smiled and was about to respond when Noah appeared. "Aria, can you come inside and give me a hand, please?"

Great.

"I'll be right back, guys." Standing up, I took my time walking to the house as my heels clicked behind me.

The music was louder inside. Noah had installed these state-of-the-art speakers all over the home. He loved his fancy gadgets. They had a wireless connection to a docking station mounted on the wall of the living room. Vanessa's taste in lounge music was good, much to my surprise.

Preparing for the worst, I was about to enter the kitchen when my wrist was grabbed from behind.

"Noah? What are you—"

The next thing I knew, I was forced into a dark room with the door slamming shut before Noah flicked on the light switch. We were in his library, and he looked… angry.

"Are you trying to make me jealous on purpose?" He glared at me, eyes fuming.

I paused a moment. "Jealous? What are you on about?"

"You know *exactly* what I mean. Don't play dumb. It's not cute."

Whoa. Okay… (1) the fact that he was jealous was insanely hot; (2) if this was an opportunity for some "friendly" verbal jousting, I was all in.

"I'm not playing dumb."

Pressing his palm against my stomach, he pushed me back, trapping me between his body and the door. His right hand slid against the wall above my shoulder. There was a dangerous calmness within the blue depths of his eyes. Here I was in the lion's den, unarmed and vulnerable. It exhilarated me and made me tremble at the same time.

"That boy's been all over you tonight."

"So?" I scowled at him. "Worry about yourself."

"You're *my* daughter. It's my job to worry about you."

"Well, you're wasting your energy, and I'm not a child."

I wanted to tell him I wasn't a virgin either, but it wasn't the time or place for that conversation.

"You don't own me, Noah."

"Yes, I fucking do."

"Look who's picked up a habit of cursing now." I smiled condescendingly.

"You're living under *my* roof…"

"You're such an alpha asshole."

"… *my* rules."

"I'm an adult! Quit being such a domineering prick to me whenever you're triggered, for fuck's sake!" I folded my arms in my chest. "Besides, you have no right to complain. I think you made your choice crystal clear when you fucked your wife this morning."

"Watch your fucking language, Aria."

All this cussing was turning me on. I wondered if it had the same effect on him.

"It's not what you think." He backed off and ran his fingers through his hair. "We didn't"—he lowered his voice—"fuck."

"No? Then what did you do? Because she looked pretty post-orgasmic when she walked into the kitchen and groped your ass in front of me and Vienna."

Exhaling in frustration, Noah fixed his piercing gaze on me. "I hadn't planned on showering with her—she just jumped in unexpectedly. What was I supposed to do? Tell her to get out? She's my wife."

"Exactly. Thank you *so much* for reiterating that fact. I really don't see the point in having this conversation. You've been hesitant about us being together, so you should be happy I'm moving on with Ryan."

"Is that what you're doing, moving on?" He sounded so patronizing. "I thought you were in love with me?" His eyes darkened with amusement.

Ugh! You asshole! I wouldn't let him win this battle. Time to go into bitch mode.

"Be careful, Noah. You almost sound like a jealous lover. And I say 'almost,' because technically, you're *not* my lover." I sarcastically smiled.

Searching my gaze, he stepped closer.

"So, you *were* trying to make me jealous." His voice was deceptively calm, like the stillness of a lake. But its undertone was hard and glacial, which only made the water freeze up and turn to ice in my mind.

Why did he have to be so damn attractive? He looked so sexy in black. I couldn't get the image of his half-naked body out of my head. It kept flickering every time I looked at him—Noah without his shirt on.

Mmmmmm.

"Answer me, Aria!" he growled, pulling me into his magnetic stare.

The energy in the room quickly shifted. I could feel it. He could feel it. We both felt it, or so I thought.

"I've done nothing wrong!" I blurted out.

"I don't like seeing him all over you. It's disrespectful."

"As I said"—I iced my tone—"You. *Don't.* Own me. Last night, I poured my heart out to you, and what do you do? You screw Vanessa the following morning like my feelings meant nothing! Like what we shared meant nothing!"

Oh God, here it was, those stupid tears. I dropped my arms and was about to leave when Noah stopped me.

"Not so fast." He twisted me around and slammed me against the door. Something raged in his eyes. It secretly aroused me. I think I enjoyed provoking him, even though he was clearly trying his hardest to control his temper.

"You keep pushing my boundaries."

"You like it when I do. I'd even argue that it turns you on—being an attorney and all." I grinned, ignoring my fluttering heartbeat.

"It pisses me off more than anything. You're seriously a pain in the ass."

I'd rather be a pain on your cock, I wanted to say, but kept that dirty comment to myself.

"You sure about that, Noah?"

He didn't blink. Not once. We seemed to challenge each other in our battle of will.

"You're gonna listen to what I have to say… and you're gonna listen well."

"I'm done with this useless conversation."

I tried to leave, but he pushed me back and said, "I'm not."

My cheeks were burning as I scowled at him. "You want me to listen? Then answer this: what did you do with her in the shower if you didn't fuck her?"

His piercing blue eyes always froze me in place.

"That's none of your business," Noah countered. "But since you're so curious to know…" Something in his tone had changed. Even the way he looked at me was different. I didn't feel like it was Noah staring back at me anymore. Had he removed his mask? Was this his true face? He sneered and leaned in, placing his palms against the wall. I was trapped now, with no way to escape.

"She gave me an *amazing* blow job… and I don't think I've ever come so hard in my life."

Um, who was this man? He was never this vulgar.

I suddenly regretted provoking him. Why did he have to say that to me? Why did he have to stomp all over my heart and wound my ego? I was about to defend my shattered pride when he pressed his index finger against my lips and silenced me.

"And I thought of *you* the entire time," Noah confessed. "I had to close my eyes. I couldn't even watch Vanessa, because the thought of you sucking me off turned me on in ways I never thought were possible. I'm a sick fuck for even admitting this, but you wanted the truth."

Un-be-lievable.

"I'm sure you returned the favor," I bitterly stated.

"I—*didn't*—fuck—her," he said through gritted teeth.

"I don't care if you fucked her. You can fuck her as much as you want! Fuck her until your dick falls off!"

"Watch your mouth, young lady!"

"Oh, so you can curse and be as lewd as you want, but I can't? Enough with the hypocrisy, Noah."

We both had a temper. I guess it was another thing we had in common.

"Damn it, Aria!" Noah raised his voice, though it had lost its intimidating effect. "Stop mind-fucking me!"

"At least I'm fucking *some* part of you, since you refuse to sleep with me!"

"I don't want you dating him." His face was serious.

"You can't stop me."

"I forbid you."

"You can't forbid me."

There was a loud bang as I jumped.

"Did you seriously just punch your fist through the wall?"

"Yes, I fucking did. It's *my* fist. I'll punch it where I want." He gripped his injured hand and flexed his fingers.

"Who's acting juvenile now?"

"Stop provoking me!"

"You betrayed me!"

"I betrayed my wife!" Noah's voice trembled with rage.

"You hurt me!"

"You've been hurting me all evening! Cutting my heart out and pouring salt all over it like you don't give a flying fuck!"

No way. Was he really that hurt over my flirtation with Ryan? I couldn't believe it, but the truth was right in front of me. Everything in his eyes expressed his emotional turmoil. He looked like a man haunted by a secret that so needed to come out. How was it possible that he was jealous of a high school boy? Noah was the alpha of the wolves, the highest in rank. Ryan was good-looking, but his attractiveness was nothing compared to the godlike beauty that Noah naturally possessed. He had to know this, didn't he?

Silence fell between us as we stared at each other.

"Now you know what heartache feels like," I murmured, regretting my spiteful comment.

"Don't you dare tell me what heartache is like, little girl." His voice was ice cold, contradicting the fire blazing in his eyes. "I suffered it for seventeen years without you."

God dammit. I teared up.

I felt like Little Red Riding Hood, trapped in a corner with the super villain. Was Noah the enemy? Was I just naïve thinking he was my hero?

"I have every right to say that to you!" I cried out. "Heartache has been my entire life in a fucking nutshell! Tell me, Noah, what have *you* gone through? You recovered just fine from your sad but inevitable breakup with your high school sweetheart—a.k.a., my mother. You moved on well without me. Your conscience never burdened you heavily enough to remind you I still existed and needed you.

"You were born into money, became a hotshot lawyer, got married, and created this perfect life for yourself. What heartache and hardship could you have possibly suffered along the way, huh? Not being there for me throughout my childhood? Don't bother labeling that as legitimate pain. I'm sure you regret the day you ever came back into my life. I hate you!"

What started out as egotistical warfare had transitioned to a heart-hunting game of slaughter. I had assassinated his character in under twenty seconds. I was ruthless and aware of it. I knew I had deeply wounded him. The look on his face crushed me inside. Immediately, I regretted what I'd said, especially my last three words because they weren't true.

How could I hurt him this way? Self-loathing sagged over my shoulders. I knew I was screwed. It was too late to take it back.

All the hurt in his eyes suddenly transformed into something else—the ocean tide was turning and gaining more height and strength, like a tsunami about to crash on the shore. I stood there alone, facing my fear, waiting for the violent wave to obliterate me.

"The line between love and hate is very thin, Aria." His face hardened as the monstrous tidal wave drew back and died down.

Noah had spared me. I didn't hate him. I loved him. I was *in love* with him. He made me feel so vulnerable, and I hated it. But I had to say something—I couldn't let this go.

"Is that your cliché attempt at admitting you're in love with me?"

He intensified his stare. "What if I am?"

"You either are or you aren't."

"I think you're trying to get a rise out of me on purpose. You're deliberately trying to hurt me and piss me off, so you can be justified in running away. Textbook self-sabotage tactic."

"You think you know me so well?"

"It's all I've done throughout these months… analyzed you—*very carefully*."

Oh, screw you.

"Do you really think I'd abuse you the way Rob did?" he said. "Throw you around and hit you?"

"You punched your fist through the wall!"

"And I'd rather break my knuckles a hundred fucking times over than to lay a finger on you!"

I had woken the sleeping dragon.

"You're hellbent on judging me as another abusive asshole that has been in your life, but I've got news for you—I'm not."

"I never made that judgment!"

"You don't know me well enough, Aria. You don't know who I am or what I'm capable of."

"Are you threatening me?"

"Did I not make myself clear? Are you deaf?" He searched my anxious gaze. "I told you I'd never be violent toward you."

"Well, you sure sound like a violent beast at the moment."

"I keep that beast tame around you. Show some fucking gratitude."

Seriously? I didn't like this Noah. There was no warmth in his eyes.

"So, emotionally abusing me is better?"

"If anyone's being emotionally abused here, it's *me*," he argued. "Is this a game to you? Manipulating my feelings and fucking with my head all evening—do you enjoy it? Does it get you off knowing you possess the power to completely mind-fuck me?"

My lips trembled as I struggled to speak up. "You're just too proud to admit that I get under your skin!"

"Oh, you've got *much deeper* than that. Trust me." He closed the gap between us, resting his hands against the wall as he leaned in and whispered, "You're in my veins, in my bloodstream… and I hate it."

He sounded resentful.

I couldn't move as I stood there, staring at him, trying to calm my racing heart. The dark mysticism in his ocean eyes transfixed me. Abandoning my stubborn pride was a struggle.

"If you hate me that much, I can easily solve your problem," I finally spoke and stepped forward, but Noah pushed me back again as I bumped into the door.

My mind was unraveling. I wasn't sure what he was going to do next. Even though our argument had got horribly heated, I couldn't deny the way he made me feel when he was standing so close, touching me.

"Tell me to kiss you, or get the fuck out," he said.

"I shouldn't have to tell you to ki—"

His sexy mouth crashed against mine, parting my lips and slipping his tongue inside. It happened so fast as all my defenses came down. There were no barriers between us now. The moment our lips came into contact, my instinct was to surrender and let go. It seemed like a lifetime had passed since we'd shared a passionate kiss. This was what I wanted: every part of him infecting me. I didn't care how wrong it was. Noah's kiss was ecstasy. His passion was heaven in my hell as he groaned, engulfing me in heat.

I wrapped my arms around his neck and pulled myself flush against him. I needed him all over me—his scent all over my body, claiming me. In my mind and heart, I only belonged to him. A strangled moan fled from my lips when he wrapped an arm around my waist, making me arch my back before he gripped my peach. I couldn't pull away from his kiss, nor did I want to.

Guiding my right leg to his waist, Noah supported my thigh with his free hand and kissed me harder. My skin was covered in land mines of pleasure, detonated by only his touch. He couldn't have been all human. He must have been a hybrid of some sort. Half man, half... fallen angel? I was free falling once more, but I knew he would catch me, shield me with his wings, and take me above the clouds to his hidden paradise, safe from prying eyes and persecution. I didn't care if those wings were black or stained in blood. In my mind, Noah embodied everything that was good and loving. In a perfect world, he and I were not related.

Soaking in the bliss of our lips gliding together, I felt all my chakras activate in my body. I could have kissed a hundred of the world's most attractive men, and not one of them would have been able to make me feel the way Noah did when he kissed me. He consumed me, body and soul. A soft whimper escaped me as my eyes rolled back when he bit my bottom lip. It felt heavenly.

"You're *mine*, Aria," Noah panted, grazing my jaw with kisses before licking my neck with a hunger that wouldn't be sated.

"I'm yours," I whispered breathlessly.

Tangling my fingers in his thick, brown hair, I pulled him down harder into my neck, secretly hoping he would give me a hickey, like a parting gift for our illicit encounter. I was insanely turned on, and it made no sense. I needed him to put out the fire he had ignited inside of me—badly.

Touching the nape of his neck, I brushed my hands over his sculpted shoulders and chest before I fumbled with the buttons on his shirt. I *needed* to touch his skin like I needed water to survive, and he didn't stop me. His passion for me was unrelenting. A feral groan vibrated from his chest when I placed my palm on the black phoenix that was inked on his heart space. It was my favorite part of his body because he had tattooed my name there.

Sexual tension had caused our argument. It was obvious now as he pressed his erection into me. I was scared out of my mind, afraid that my stepmom would barge in. I hated loving Noah in the shadows—it hurt. But right there in that moment, nothing else mattered: not my fears, insecurities, nor my desolating thoughts of the future.

"Fuck, baby," Noah growled against my lips and pulled back. "We have to stop." He panted. "I'm not thinking clearly. We have guests over."

This was *months'* worth of pent-up sexual tension. I peeled his shirt back over his shoulders and caressed his chest. "I don't want you to stop"—I licked his lips—"I want you all to myself."

"I could kiss you for hours."

His confession sent a thrill down my body, as an uncontrollable heat radiated between my thighs.

"Kiss me right now," I whispered.

His heated gaze shifted to my lips. "You're such a bad influence."

Our mouths collided once again in heat and desire, spiking my body temperature. Noah was always ridiculously warm, but I loved that about him. My hand wandered down from his chest to the throbbing bulge in his pants, and that seemed to trigger him as he broke the kiss.

"Do you want me?" I asked.

"So fucking bad." His eyes spoke the truth.

The hem of my dress had hiked up so tightly, I was afraid it would rip.

"I'm sorry for what I said earlier, Noah."

"I know you didn't mean it." He kissed me softly. "You don't know half of what I can handle from you… the strength of my love."

I wanted to cry, caressing the phoenix on his chest. That's when it hit me: *I* was that mythological bird. I was the only one who had the power to destroy him… the only one who could make him bleed. It explained why the phoenix had her talons in his heart. Noah was mine. I had burned and risen from my ashes, not as the daughter he had lost, but as the lover forbidden to him. The flaming phoenix was forged in fire, foreshadowing a prophecy that was so twistedly taboo, I don't think Noah had ever been aware of its metaphorical meaning… until seventeen years later, when that bird found its human host: me. I was a woman transformed.

We kissed as I made a wish to the other half of myself that was inked across his chest: an emblem of my spirit animal. I prayed for patience and compassion, so that I could take better care of his heart and not dig my claws any deeper than they already were.

"Noah, honey? Is everything okay in there?"

Vanessa's voice instantly broke our spell, putting us both on high alert.

Pulling away, Noah buttoned his shirt, while I tried to straighten my dress. We looked like guilty lovers on the verge of being exposed—guilty of committing unspeakable sins. We may have been safe from the eyes of others, but we weren't hidden from the eyes of God.

A look of worry flashed in Noah's eyes as I wiped my gloss off his lips before he composed himself and opened the door.

"Hey." He smiled casually. "Everything's fine. Aria just needed to talk."

"Oh, is she all right?"

"Yeah, she's fine."

My stepmom entered the room while Noah guarded the door, blocking the hole in the wall. Standing there, I felt nervous and territorial over him. I couldn't handle it if she kissed him in front of me again.

"Aria, you know you can talk to me whenever you need."

"I know." I tried to hide my guilt. "It was about my mom and Rob— needed Noah's advice."

"Oh, I understand." She turned and faced him. "We're kind of being poor hosts at the moment."

"I'll be right out."

I was relieved when she disappeared.

Holding out his hand, Noah smiled when I slipped my fingers through his and followed him back to the kitchen. His cologne was all over me, teasing my senses with the undeniable fact that we had been in proximity.

"There you are!" Ryan looked at us as I withdrew my hand from Noah's. "I thought you dropped a glass and had cut yourself."

"No, I just needed to talk to my dad about something."

Ugh, there was that dreaded D word again.

Ryan kissed my cheek and wrapped his arm around my waist. I'm sure Noah felt like a lone wolf had trotted over to his pack and was challenging him by pursuing his alpha female. Ryan wouldn't win. Noah's glaring aggression said it all.

"Do you need a hand, Mr. Hunter?" said Ryan.

"No, Aria can help me." There was an awkward pause before he added, "Thanks, though."

Ryan was my only friend to address Noah so formally. Usually, Noah insisted everyone call him by his first name, but I guess it didn't surprise me he didn't this time (given his extreme animosity toward the high school jock).

"I'll be right out, Ryan," I said.

He kissed my hand before he left. This must have infuriated Noah… I heard him curse under his breath once Ryan was out of earshot.

"Okay, I've got the margaritas prepared." Vanessa smiled. "Just carry out the other two trays I left on the counter." She gave us further instruction and left the kitchen.

Alone again, I thought, feeling happy inside.

Noah walked with an intimidating air of dominance, but I found it so sexy.

"You shouldn't lead him on like that, Aria," he said in a serious voice. "I want him in friend zone, ASAP."

Noah Hunter and his endless list of demands.

"I'll friend zone him just as soon as you friend zone Vanessa."

His arm brushed against mine as we stood side by side near the island, staring at each other. I'm sure he felt like I was pushing his boundaries again, but I didn't care.

"Fine."

What?

Wow… he caved. I'd been expecting him to reject my request and tell me that Vanessa was his wife, *blah, blah, blah…* but his response left me stunned.

Picking up my tray, I walked out of the kitchen with a gleeful grin. At least he would enjoy the view from behind. This was a battle I had won.

∞∞∞

Our guests started leaving a little after midnight. Ryan and Tyrese were still over. The trainer seemed to hit it off well with Vienna—they couldn't stop flirting with each other. They would have had the most beautiful babies if they ever got married.

"Sorry about the overcrowded evening," I said to Ryan. "It was unexpected." We were sitting on the patio, chatting away. The temperature was perfect. If there was one thing I loved about living in California, it was the climate.

"It's all good," said Ryan. "Made me feel more comfortable, actually. Your dad and stepmom are really nice."

"Yeah… Vanessa loves to take care of her guests. You don't want to see her on a bad day, though."

Once our laughter died down, he said, "Can I give you your birthday present now?"

"You didn't have to go through the trouble—I told you not to get me anything."

"It wasn't any trouble. I wanted to." Ryan reached into his pocket and pulled out two tickets. "So in case you didn't know, Tiesto's on tour and I have VIP tickets to his concert in July…"

"Oh, my gosh! No. Freakin. Way!"

I loved Tiesto. Some of the world's best DJs were from the Netherlands; Armin van Buuren, Sander van Doorn, Hardwell…

"I know it's only three months from now, but he won't be in LA sooner and—"

"You're amazing!" I squeezed him in my arms. "Thank you so much! I've always wanted to see Tiesto live!"

The upbeat lounge music faded to something slower as Ryan took my hand and smiled. "Dance with me."

"Oh, no… I'll step all over your toes," I lied.

"No, you won't. Come on." He pulled me to my feet and led me away from the pool before he wrapped his arms around my waist and murmured, "Last dance before the night is over." His body felt warm and welcoming, but it didn't have the same effect on me whenever I hugged Noah.

"I love this song," I said, resting my head on his shoulder. "It's by Sting, right?"

"'Every Breath You Take' was originally sung by The Police—Sting used to be in the band."

"Weren't they an English rock band?"

"Yeah. I recognize this cover, though. My sister's obsessed with YouTube cover artists, especially this guy."

"Who covered it?" I asked.

"Pretty sure it's Aaron Krause."

A female vocalist was singing with him. The acoustic duet sounded beautiful—perfect for prom.

Vienna and Tyrese soon appeared next to us, swaying to the music. "It's been forever since I danced with someone," she confessed.

"We wanna join the party, too!" Vanessa hollered, dragging Noah with her. She took his drink out of his hand and set it on a table, forcing herself into his arms.

I looked over Ryan's shoulder and locked eyes with the one man who truly had my heart. Noah didn't look too happy. I'm sure he thought I was having a good time, but I wished I was dancing with him instead of Ryan.

The song ended and transitioned to a medley of cellos that sounded beautiful and seductive. Sean Ryan's soul riveting voice echoed around us. One of my favorite trance artists, ATB, had produced the track. Sean's voice gave me goose bumps as the lyrics touched me to the core. I felt sad because I wanted Noah's hands on my body—just the two of us, alone, dancing under the stars. Everyone and everything had faded away as we stared at each other. I hated wanting him.

CHAPTER TWENTY-FIVE
DISCOVERY

The night had finally come to a close. What Aria had expected to be a dull and uneventful evening had subverted her expectations. Standing in the foyer with Noah, she said goodbye to Ryan while Vanessa cleaned up in the kitchen. Unbeknownst to them, Vienna was keeping a watchful eye on her. She noticed Aria's flirtatious ways with Noah; how she intertwined her fingers in his before he pulled her into his arms… and kissed her on the lips, slow and sensually. Vienna's heart dropped in horror and disgust as she clasped a hand over her mouth and raced into the kitchen.

"Vanessa, there's something I need to tell you."

"What's up?"

"Stop what you're doing and come with me."

"I'm still loading the dishwasher, though and—"

"Leave it! You *need* to hear this."

"Vi, what's got into you?"

She grabbed her sister's hand and led her out of the kitchen.

ೞೞ

The guest bedroom door swung open as Vienna stepped inside with Vanessa and braced herself for the moment of truth. Reluctantly, she met her sister's eyes and tried to remain calm.

"Are you okay?" Vanessa asked. "You look like you've seen a ghost."

"No, I'm not okay. I'm actually sort of freaking out."

"What's wrong, Vienna? Why are you pacing?"

Rubbing her temples, Vienna exhaled. "It's about your husband."

"What about him?"

How do I break this news to her? She questioned apprehensively.

All she knew was that the truth had to come out.

"I was heading toward my room when I noticed Noah and Aria standing in the foyer. They were talking with Ryan."

"Were you eavesdropping on their conversation?" Vanessa quirked an eyebrow.

"This is the part where you're gonna get mad, but please believe me when I say I was justified to eavesdrop. Hear me out."

Vanessa heaved and made an encouraging gesture with her hand. "Fine, go on."

"There is no other way to say this, so I'm gonna come right out and say it." Vienna paused, preparing herself for the ugly truth. "I saw Noah and Aria… kissing, right after Ryan left."

An awkward silence fell upon the sisters. Neither of them moved until Vanessa spoke.

"I've seen Aria give her dad a quick peck on the lips before." She laughed. "Many times, in fact. I'm sure you're misjudging what you saw, which I don't blame you for at all, given your past."

"Vanessa, I *know* what I saw! Your husband wrapped his arms around your stepdaughter's waist, pulled her in close, and kissed her on the mouth like the French do in France!"

Has she lost her mind? Vanessa thought.

She did not want to blow up at her sister, but there was so much anger and resentment that still lingered inside of her. The two of them shared an unpleasant history of jealousy, competitiveness with boys, and turbulent teenage years.

"Are you saying," she began, "that Noah is having an incestuous affair with his daughter behind my back?"

"That's exactly what I'm saying. You took the words right out of my mouth—thank you."

"Stop this right now, Vi. I don't think you understand the damage this can cause my marriage if I confront Noah with these absurd accusations."

"Why don't you believe me?"

Vanessa exhaled and placed a hand on her sister's shoulder. "I know Cousin Tom really messed you up, but this isn't the same situation. For one, my husband is not an adulterer, and second, he's not an immoral scumbag preying on his teenage daughter."

"What happened with Tom is irrelevant to this situation. I know what I saw! And I'm telling you that you need to confront Noah!"

"I will do no such thing. Clearly, you're still sick in the head and haven't got over what happened all those years ago."

"How can you even say that to me?" Vienna jerked her shoulder back. She was never good at expressing herself. Masking her sensitivity with anger always seemed like the safest and easiest option. "I'm trying to help you out here!" she snapped.

"How are you helping? Just because you had an incestuous love affair with our cousin doesn't mean everyone else is! You're constantly projecting!"

"Vanessa, I'm not!"

"You *are!*"

The sisters shared a dark family secret, a secret Vienna had burdened them with many years ago. She had fallen in love with her cousin when she was sixteen, and Tom was much older than her—six years her senior. Her parents had disapproved of the relationship and were horrified when they eventually found out she was trying to get pregnant.

"Let me set the record straight for you… I wasn't having an affair! I was in love with Tom! I was young and stupid. He took advantage of me, and I needed years of therapy to recover. You know how it all went down, Nessa."

He had done more than take advantage of her. Tom had convinced Vienna that incest was acceptable and should be practiced in every family—fathers and daughters, mothers and sons, brothers and sisters.

Vanessa had discovered her sister's disturbed mental state when she read her diary one night. Vienna wanted to have a child with Tom, so that he could engage in a sexual relationship with his own offspring once they reached the age of consent. Vanessa suspected he was a closet pedophile and told her parents. They had no reservations about intervening. Vanessa had begged her mother not to tell Vienna that she had read her diary, so her mother shouldered the blame. All hell broke loose, relationships were broken, and the Carlisle family unit was destroyed for a long time.

"You believed there was nothing wrong with incest and that everyone could do it."

"That's because of Tom's brainwashing!" Vienna defensively answered. "I was in love with him. The sad part is that he just used me for sex and had this sick obsession with incest! Why can't you understand? I was young and easily influenced. Do you even know how badly that ordeal emotionally scarred me? I've been in and out of therapy ever since. Mom and Dad still won't treat me the same because they feel ashamed of me. I humiliated the family."

"I understand you were young and weren't aware of the consequences, but Noah and Aria are naturally affectionate with one another. I've seen her kiss him on the cheek countless times, even quick pecks on the lips. It's all very innocent. We used to give Daddy little kisses on the lips. That's not so weird in my eyes."

"We were toddlers, Nessa! Aria's an adult!"

"My husband would never be unfaithful to me." Vanessa adamantly shook her head, refusing to listen. "He's an honorable, high-minded man. He's *not* Cousin Tom."

"Are you not hearing me properly? I know what I saw! It was full-on tonsil hockey!"

"Stop it!" Vanessa huffed in frustration. "This is Christmas of '03 all over again."

"No, it's not."

"This isn't the first time you've accused other family members of having incestuous relationships. Remember what happened that year when you came home for the holidays?"

They had checked Vienna into a psychiatric hospital for six months after finding out about her and Tom. Her parents had forbidden her from ever seeing him again, and she had got so depressed that she had attempted to take her life. Sending her away to receive proper psychiatric care had seemed like the only solution to restore her mental health.

"You accused Uncle Lenny and our Cousin Jenna of having an affair."

"They were always way too close and affectionate," Vienna replied. "It wasn't normal in my eyes, okay? Therapy made me extremely sensitive to the whole 'good touch, bad touch rule.'"

"They hugged a lot, and you obsessed over it just because she was fond of him. I know they were only three years apart, but you always justified their alleged affair in sick ways! And then, of course, the entire family eventually found out that Uncle Lenny is gay, and the only person who knew that was Jenna. They were like best friends, and you accused them of being incestuous lovers. You were wrong then, and you are wrong now."

"Stop treating me like a mental patient!" Vienna cried out. "I know I was messed in the head for a while, but I was young and victimized by our sicko cousin. Thank God he's in jail now. I knew that bastard was bound to fuck up and get caught."

These secrets were too ugly and humiliating for Vanessa to have shared with Noah. Her family had conveniently dusted everything under the rug and had not pressed charges against Tom because of the shame it would have brought upon the family. Instead, they had moved away and placed Vienna in the hands of psychiatrists to deal with the problem.

Unlike her sister, Vanessa had deceived herself and everyone close to her, making them believe she had the best childhood. She had painted a picture-perfect family, when in reality, behind that portrait was a rotting canvas covered in maggots.

"Please, listen to me," Vienna insisted. "It wasn't a quick peck on the lips. They were kissing like…" She dug her fingers through her hair. "Like lovers! Nessa, you need to confront him about this."

"I'm not gonna confront my husband with these ridiculous accusations!"

"Fine, if you won't, then *I* will!"

"Like hell you will! I can't believe you're trying to sabotage yet another relationship of mine. You just can't stand to see me happy, can you? You resent me deep down inside because I was always Mom and Dad's favorite, and you were labeled the disgrace. Vienna, you need to get over those years! We're not rivaling teenagers anymore! Stop fucking up my life because of your uncontrollable jealousy!"

"How the hell can you say that to me?" Vienna could hardly believe her ears.

"You're envious of my lifestyle. Look around you"—Vanessa held out her arms—"and compare it to your ordinary life. What the hell have you achieved in comparison?"

"You think I envy your lifestyle?" Vienna laughed out loud. "You're miserable! Your spending habits are out of control… you fill your closet with handbags and clothes you don't need because you're so fucking empty inside! At least I have the freedom to travel, and I'm not locked down by a mortgage. I care more about experiences and relationships than collecting shit I don't need! Don't even get me started on your addiction to plastic surgery."

"Oh, no"—Vanessa shook her head—"you are *not* gonna go there with me. My body is none of your fucking business!"

"Truth hurts, Nessa."

"Don't think for a second that I haven't noticed the way you've been eyeing Noah throughout your visit with us."

"I've been watching him and Aria, you bitch! I'm not a home wrecker!" Vienna could no longer hold back her explosive temper. "Open your damn eyes and watch the way they interact with each other. All the signs are there. You are so blind! I'm not jealous! Why should I be jealous of you? You've totally fucked up your face and body. At least everything on me is *real*!" she blasted, hoping that Noah would barge in.

"I'd rather have a fake ass, tits, face—fake *everything* than a fake heart—so shut the fuck up with your criticism!"

The sisters had both crossed a line as they argued back and forth until Vanessa sadly said, "We can never get along, can we?"

Leaning against the wall, Vienna hugged her arms and frowned.

"I want you to let this go," Vanessa continued. "Let go of this sick obsession you have with playing undercover detective, and act normal, please! Don't embarrass me or yourself by getting in a fight with Noah about this. It will not go down well. If you can't respect my wishes, then I think it would be best if you stayed at a hotel tonight."

"I never expected you to have this sort of reaction, Nessa. I've got over our issues in the past, but it seems you haven't. I felt you had a right to know because I don't want you to spend the rest of your life with a man who's not all he says he is."

"You are unquestionably ill!" Vanessa exclaimed in disgust. Breathing out her anger, she lowered her voice and said, "I shouldn't even be mad at you. It's not your fault. Tom really did a number on you."

Vienna's dynamite temper was instantly triggered. "Shut up!" she yelled. "Please, just shut your mouth before I rip your extensions out of your scalp!"

"Keep your voice down! Enough with your threats!"

"I doubt your husband can hear us, anyway—and I'm not the one who's ill, *you* are! I'll gladly leave. I don't want to stay under the same roof as any of you for another second. You're all damn crazy!"

Marching toward the closet, Vienna dragged her suitcase across the hardwood floor, lifting it onto the bed. She then strode to the dresser in the corner of the room and opened the drawers one by one, grabbing her clothing.

"It hurts me you think I'm deliberately trying to ruin your marriage." She cried.

In that moment, Vanessa had a miraculous moment of empathy. She realized she did not wish to burn a bridge with her only sister.

"Wait, don't go," she pleaded. "I'm sorry for what I said. I got angry and lost it. We both did."

Still fuming, Vienna wanted nothing more than to leave, but a part of her wanted to prove her sister wrong. She needed her to see that she wasn't crazy, and that she was right about what she had witnessed. In the middle of packing, she stopped, took a deep breath, and faced Vanessa. Losing her temper with fighting words was not the best approach. She knew she had to handle things like a two-faced politician if she was ever going to collect enough evidence as a double agent. Vienna was good at that when her temper was under control. The only way to make her sister believe her was through concrete evidence—on camera. She didn't want to leave California on bad terms. She couldn't let this go.

"I love you, Vanessa. You're my sister, and I want nothing but the best for you. Maybe you're right. Maybe I'm still messed up because of what happened with Tom."

"I love you too, and I don't want to kick you out of my house. I just want you to understand that Noah's my husband, and I know him better than anyone. My marriage is rocky enough as it is. I don't want things to get worse."

But she was already risking her marriage in other ways. Vanessa had a dirty little secret of her own. For the last year, she had been having an on and off affair with Noah's best friend, Amir Crawford. He reminded her of her first love, a man her father had forced her to break up with in college because her family rejected interracial partnerships.

"Please," Vanessa began, "just trust me when I say you're making a big mistake."

I'm not, but you'll find out the hard way, Vienna thought.

"You're right," she answered in mock defeat. "I'm sorry for the hurtful things I said. I didn't mean them. Forgive me?"

"Of course—we're family, and you're my only sister." They hugged. "I'm sincerely sorry you went through all that in our younger years."

"It's okay, it wasn't your fault. Besides, it's all in the past now." Vienna pulled back. "Let's make these next couple of days memorable before I go MIA for the next six months."

"I'll book us an appointment at the spa first thing in the morning. I think we could both use a day of pampering."

Disappointed that her sister did not believe her, Vienna was confident she would catch Noah and Aria fooling around. She would spy on them until she had the proof she needed. She would be the wolf in sheep's clothing.

CHAPTER TWENTY-SIX
ARIA

Was I an awful person for feeling a little bummed that Noah didn't get me a birthday present? I know I had said I wanted nothing for my birthday (and I meant it), but I guess I was just expecting... I don't know.

The kiss, I told myself, getting ready for bed. Being trapped in a room with Noah was the best b-day gift ever.

It was almost 1:30 a.m., and I had enjoyed the evening, despite my reservations at first. Vanessa had given me hundreds of dollars' worth of gift cards to shop at her favorite boutiques. The Tiesto tickets from Ryan were an awesome surprise. I was happy my stepmom respected my wishes and didn't turn the dinner party into a birthday party. I didn't want a cake, didn't want to blow out any candles, and did not want to open gifts from a bunch of folks that I didn't even know. It would have been awkward, and I don't mean that rudely—they were all pleasant people. I was just glad the night had not played out like it did on my sixteenth birthday.

Changing into a pair of black shorts, I put on a white crop top before I brushed my teeth and headed to the kitchen. Smooth jazz softly played in the background as I walked down the hall. The pot lights in the kitchen ceiling were dimly lit. Noah was sitting by the island, drinking a glass of white wine, all by himself.

"You're still up?" I asked, feeling my heart palpitate when he looked at me.

"I was putting some food away. Vanessa and Vi were tired, so they headed to bed." His eyes followed me as I moved past him. "You thirsty?"

"Yeah." I opened the refrigerator and helped myself to a bottle of water.

"Did you enjoy the evening?"

"Which part?" I smirked, sitting on a stool across from him.

Noah let out a quiet chuckle, shaking his head while drinking his wine. "Are you happy I refrained from throwing you what could have been the most amazing birthday party ever?"

"Totally content."

"You sure?" He raised a sexy eyebrow.

"I hate birthdays, and I hate birthday parties. They're so overrated. Call me a birthday Grinch. I'm not changing my mind."

"I should be the one to feel that way."

"Why?"

"Because I'm not getting any younger."

"Please," I scoffed. "You don't even look thirty."

Noah glanced at his watch. "Well, since your birthday is officially over"—he stood up—"you can't get mad at me for giving you this." He opened the fridge and pulled out what looked like a blue pastry box.

Gulping down my water, I set it down and asked, "What is that?"

Noah lifted the box cover and took out a big chocolate cupcake that had blue icing on it, covered in silver edible glitter. He opened a drawer and stuck a small white birthday candle in the middle of it.

"It's not a traditional birthday cake."

"Then what kind of cake is this, exactly?"

"Isn't it obvious?" He flashed a sly grin. "A cupcake."

I rolled my eyes. "I knew that."

"Chocolate coconut swirled. Think of it as… *I-love-you-so-I-bought-you-a-cupcake* kind of cake."

Hmm. I like that. Folding my arms on the counter, I gazed at the deliciousness in front of me. "What about the candle? That seems pretty birthday traditional to me."

"I'm trying very hard to break tradition here. You see, this candle I'm about to light is not a birthday candle."

"No?" I giggled.

"Nope."

"Then what is it?"

"Just a simple candle… wouldn't hurt if you made a wish, though."

Right, and we're just mysteriously in a modern-day fairy-tale reality where magic is real, and wishes come true!

"The rules are simple," said Noah. "Think of me as… your genie."

He'd be a hot genie.

"Make a wish out loud, blow out the candle, and your wish is my command."

Oh, I liked this. I *really* liked this.

"Where's your magic lamp?"

He lit the candle and blew out the flame on the matchstick. "I don't have a magic lamp, Aria. I have a magic wallet."

Of course. I smiled.

"So, can I make any wish?"

"Any wish that money can buy."

Damn it. Well, there goes wishing he would sex me.

"Come on, what do you want the most?" said Noah.

Isn't it obvious? I'm looking right at you!

"I… I don't know. I want nothing."

"Come on, baby. Now is the perfect time to take advantage of my money."

Giggling, I thought for as long as I could.

"This candle has an expiry date," he warned. "We don't have all…"

I shut my eyes and blew out the flickering flame.

"You just broke the rules." Noah furrowed his brows.

"I enjoy breaking rules if you haven't noticed already."

"What did you wish for?"

"If I tell you, it won't come true."

He chuckled.

"What's so funny?"

"I tricked you into making a birthday wish."

"Technically, it's no longer my birthday, so it wasn't a birthday wish—and you didn't trick me."

"I was, and I'm still serious about getting you whatever you want, but I knew you wouldn't make any demands."

He was right. It felt odd to ask him to buy me expensive things. I'd learned at a very young age that if I made such requests, I'd get punished—by Rob.

"I wish you would let me spoil you," Noah sighed. "If it was up to me, I would."

"I don't need extravagant gifts to be happy."

He gave me an inquisitive stare and said, "Hold that thought. I'll be right back."

Assuming he took a bathroom break, he quickly returned and sat across from me again.

"What are you hiding behind your back?" I asked.

Noah smiled and revealed… a toy model… of a car. It was candy red with a black phoenix painted on the hood. He set it on the counter and rolled it toward me.

"I knew you'd get mad if I bought you something super expensive, so I decided on a more sensible gift." He pointed at the toy. "That's a '69 Pontiac Firebird Trans Am."

Inspecting the toy, I rolled it on its wheels, back and forth. It was approximately ten inches in length. "… Thanks," I finally said.

My tomboy phase had long passed. I was sure the twelve-year-old me would have appreciated the present.

"Your name is on the license plate," said Noah.

I looked at the back, and sure enough, there it was.

"I used to have a car like this back in college." He stood up and sat on a stool next to me. "It was the love of my life at the time."

At the time?

Did that mean that Vanessa was the love of his life now? Where did I stand in his estimation? I wondered how many women he had made love to in that convertible. Did he still have it? A muscle car like that was a chick magnet. For a moment, I imagined a younger Noah in his early twenties, driving the vintage vehicle on a bright sunny day, shades on, looking Hollywood-cool.

"Do you still have the car?" Curiosity got the best of me.

"No."

"What happened to it?"

"I almost considered selling it to pay off some—ah—debts I owed a few dealers. I didn't want to go to my father for help."

It was still hard for me to grasp that he used to have a drug addiction. I just could not imagine Noah being anyone else other than the man he was at present.

"But…" He exhaled. "Things worked out, and I didn't have to sell it. I kept it in storage for a while after college, and then I eventually gave it away to someone who needed it much more than I did."

A charitable donation? How could he ever part with a car like that? Evidently, he was not a materialistic man.

"Do you miss the car?" I asked.

"You've seen all the cars in my garage. Clearly, I've overcompensated the loss." He grinned. "I don't miss things, Aria. I could lose all my wealth tomorrow and I'd be able to survive. However"—he took my hand in his—"if I lost *you*… that would kill me."

Noah wouldn't lose me. Never again.

"It still scares me knowing you could walk out on me," he added, looking distressed.

"Why would I even consider doing such a thing at this point?"

"Because I feel like I've descended to Hell and taken you there with me. You're blind and can't see the surrounding flames."

The only fire I saw was the flickering flames of passion in his eyes every time he looked at me.

"I guess that explains why I feel so feverish around you." I raked my teeth over my bottom lip.

"Be serious. Stop seducing me."

"You call *this* seduction?"

"It doesn't take much from you—and I shouldn't be telling you this."

I was smiling from ear to ear.

"I don't believe we're in some allegorical Hell, Noah. How could I possibly be in Hell when an angel has rescued me from exactly that?"

"The Devil was an angel—fallen."

"Are you suggesting you're the biggest villain of the world? I don't see horns and glowing red eyes."

"I don't need horns or a pitchfork." He snickered.

That was true. Lucifer was deemed to be the most beautiful angel in Heaven.

"Anyone can embody devil energy should they lose their life to their vices."

"You're not a Biblical character allied with darkness," I reasoned.

"Since when did you become a religious philosopher?"

"I'm nothing of the sort." I wrapped my arms around his neck. "I'm just reminding you that you're an exceptional human being. You're out of this world, but you're nothing remotely close to evil."

Holding my gaze, he let my words sink in before saying, "I should not have done what I did with you earlier tonight." Noah looked remorseful.

It killed me because I had not regretted it. Not one bit.

"You didn't force me." I frowned, sliding my hands down his muscled chest.

"I shouldn't have encouraged you. I keep crossing lines, and I promised myself I wouldn't." He touched my face. "I'm disappointed in myself." His eyes radiated warmth and affection.

"I'm not a little girl, Noah," I murmured, desperate to remind him I was, in fact, a legal adult who was accountable for all my decisions. Was there even a right and wrong in loving someone? Who made the rules of love, anyway? God?

"Eat your cupcake." Noah tried to smile.

I guess he didn't want to debate about the limitations of our forbidden relationship.

"It looks so pretty. I almost don't want—"

"Oh, you're *definitely* gonna want to eat it."

The sweet scent of coconut made my stomach growl. Holding the cupcake, I slowly took a bite, savoring the delicious taste of chocolate and cake mix.

"*Mmmmm…*" My eyes rolled back while my taste buds exploded in pleasure. "This… is *legit,* the *best* cupcake I've ever had in my life!"

"You've got some on your…" He smiled, pointing at the corner of his mouth.

"Oh!" I tried to wipe the icing away with my tongue, making Noah laugh as he helped me out.

"There we go," he said.

I blushed, watching him suck the blue icing off his thumb.

"Delicious." He beamed. "I hope you like your *un-birthday* gift." He kissed my cheek.

My heart let out a lovesick sigh. I wasn't sure what I was going to do with a toy car. It's not like I had a collection, but his gesture was sweet. If the whole point was to break the birthday tradition, then he had succeeded.

"You should go to bed, sweetie. It's late."

I didn't want to sleep. I wanted to stay with him and steal another kiss while we still had the chance, but Noah stood up and carried his wineglass to the sink. Following him, I wrapped my arms around his neck just as he turned around. He hesitated for a second, as if he hadn't been expecting my embrace, but his arms seemed to recognize where they belonged as they lovingly enveloped me. I had to shut my eyes every time he held me, like it was the only way I could enjoy the contact. We were like two puzzle pieces that fit together just right.

"Can I tell you what I wished for?" I murmured in his ear.

"Tell me."

"I wished we weren't…" I stopped, unable to finish my sentence because I didn't want to say it. "That we weren't…"

"Aria." He said my name with sympathetic eyes. "It's okay. You don't have to say it."

Maybe he didn't want to hear it out loud because the truth was so disgustingly shameful.

I kept hoping he would kiss me passionately, like he had earlier, but all I got was a tender kiss on the forehead. There was nothing he could say or do. Our problem was something that could not be fixed with money.

"Get some sleep, beautiful." Noah caressed my face, looking just as torn as I was.

"Goodnight."

⁝⁞

Sitting in bed, I stared at the toy car that was parked on my lap. It would have been awesome to drive an actual car like this. It wasn't a showy modern vehicle—it had character. I was about to set it on my nightstand when my thumb accidentally pressed on something that popped the trunk open. There had been a button at the back I hadn't noticed.

Car keys... what?

It took me a couple seconds to figure it out, but when I did, I immediately strode out my bedroom door and headed for the garage.

No... he didn't...

A life-size replica of that Pontiac Firebird was parked right next to Noah's Audi, and my name was on the license plate. It was a pearlescent red convertible with sparkling chrome rims and custom black leather upholstery. I was speechless as my eyes filled with tears.

"I was wondering when you'd find the keys."

Noah's voice echoed behind me as I turned and faced him. Leaning against the doorframe, he flashed a dimpled smile.

"I... I can't believe you did this..." I was at a loss for words. It was the most stunning car I had ever laid eyes on. It was *his* car; the same one he used to drive in his college days.

"I know you wanted nothing huge for your birthday, but that was yesterday, so..."

I leaped into his arms and hugged the life out of him. "Thank you! You didn't have to do this."

"You're eighteen now, Aria. You needed a car much sooner than this." Stroking my cheek, he brushed a tear away.

"This is the best surprise ever!"

"Take it out for a spin tomorrow. It's a full-blown Z-28 and has a five speed Hurst shifter. Can you drive a clutch?"

"Yes."

That was the only useful thing my stepdad had ever taught me.

Stepping around the vehicle, I was in awe that it was actually mine. Rob would never have done something like this for me—even if he had the funds. I would have been happy with an old, beat-up car, as long as it got me from point A to B.

A black phoenix was airbrushed on the hood of the Firebird, just like on the toy version, and the design was even more beautiful. It reminded me of Noah's tattoo. His smitten smile remained as I walked over to him.

"I'm speechless."

"I told you I wanted to improve your life. I meant it."

Noah was the kind of father every girl dreamed of having. He was loving, nurturing, and so supportive. He was the type of dad I wanted Rob to be. He possessed every amazing quality I had wanted in a father, and as the realization settled in my mind, I felt an overwhelming sense of despair because I knew I was jeopardizing our bond. I wanted things from him he could never give, things he wasn't supposed to. It was unnatural. Why couldn't I love him the way a daughter loves her doting dad? Why couldn't I eliminate lust from the equation? Would that have helped? Was that even possible through cognitive efforts?

"I'd do anything to see you smile like this every day." Noah reached for my hand and kissed it.

"I don't deserve this." I sniffled, wiping my tears. "I don't deserve any of this."

"You deserve so much more, Aria." He cupped my face. "So much more."

"But this is your car. It's a classic!"

"And I want *you* to have it. California is your home now, and you need a nice convertible to match your lifestyle. I thought about buying you something newer, but this car is so special to me. I restored it for you."

My heart trembled. "I'm sorry."

"For what?"

"For complicating us."

"It's not your fault."

Then whose fault was it? I think he realized we had been careless during the dinner party, or maybe he was sober now that we weren't tangled in each other… *sinning.*

"It's late, beautiful."

It was.

"Kiss me goodnight, Noah."

His gaze was contemplative as he leaned in and left the softest kiss near the corner of my mouth.

"Goodnight, Aria."

I craved his touch. Fate had been so unkind to me, to us. I would have traded in this beautiful car to live a beautiful lie with Noah if it were possible—and by "lie" I mean living in denial of our blood ties. I would have given up everything if it meant that I could have my own happy ending in this fucked up fairy tale.

CHAPTER TWENTY-SEVEN
ARIA

The wind danced through my hair as I stood on a big white yacht, sailing into the sunset—but I wasn't alone… he was nearby… I could feel him. His arms slowly snaked around my waist from behind as he kissed my neck and shoulder. I felt the wind in my hair and the sun bathing my skin with warmth. He untied my white bikini top, brushing his fingertips down my naked shoulders until they found their way to my breasts. Cupping them gently, he teased my hardened peaks, whispering naughty things in my ear. I shivered and arched my back against his firm chest, resting my head in the crook of his neck. He wasn't wearing a shirt, which only made my heart pound faster. Flesh against flesh, Noah's scent all over me.

"I told you I'd give you the world, Aria. But you don't want the world, do you? You want *me.*"

His whispering seductions echoed in my ears as I felt a pleasurable pull inside. Something hard pressed into me. I was beyond aroused and ready to surrender to him. The thought of experiencing the most taboo sex positions with Noah didn't feel like such a physical violation. It turned me on.

Disappointment was hard to digest when I woke up, abducted from my blissful place of paradise.

Sigh. I knew it was too good to be real.

I could still feel his breath against my neck as I sat up in bed. My shoulder tingled when I touched it, smiling at the dream hazed memory.

Time to shower.

Pulling off the duvet, I swung my legs over and stretched. It was tempting to go back to sleep and conjure an X-rated Noah dream, but I had to get up and start my day.

ೞ

My morning was monotonous. Vienna was acting strange. I could feel her eyes on me all throughout breakfast. I wanted to ask her what her problem was, but every time I looked up, she'd just smile. It was very awkward.

Noah and I kept sneaking glances at one another every chance we got. I badly wanted to be alone with him and was so thankful when my stepmom told us she and Vi were going to the spa after breakfast.

"Would you like to come along with us, Aria?" she asked.

Vienna's reaction rubbed me the wrong way as she gave my stepmom an unsettling yet serious stare. I don't think it was registering with Vanessa. I was just as confused.

Does she not want me to come? I didn't want to go anyway, I decided.

"Aria?"

"No, that's okay. I've got an essay to write that I've been procrastinating on all weekend." That was a bit of a lie. "Thanks for inviting me, though."

"All right, honey. I'll bring you back some amazing body lotions."

Did I feel guilty at all for seducing her husband? Yes. But there was a blood contract between me and Noah. Vanessa could never compete against that. No one could understand it.

"When will you two be back?" he asked.

"I'd like to spend the day with my sister, since she'll be leaving tomorrow evening. We'll probably go shopping afterwards and do lunch and then shop some more. I think we'll eat out for dinner too. I feel like sushi today. You good with that, Vi?"

"Yeah, I love sushi!"

"Have fun, ladies."

My stepmom abandoned the coffee machine and sat on Noah's lap. "What are you gonna do today, sweetheart?"

"Gym and work."

"You're such a workaholic." Vanessa sighed, sliding her arms around his neck. "I'm not letting you fall asleep again in your office." She kissed him on the lips, triggering black snakes to float out from under my hair. They hissed around me as I envisioned turning my stepmom into stone with Medusa's death glare.

I appeased my wounded, mythological goddess by visualizing alternate ways to ruin Vanessa's morning, but my higher self knew better. Envy. Must. Be. Conquered.

Vienna's dark gaze snapped me out of a homicidal daydream.

What is her deal?

"Sorry for stealing your wife away for the afternoon," she said to Noah, "but I'm sure you'll survive."

Why is she glaring at me?

"With that said," she continued, "please avoid texting each other unless it's an emergency." She pulled Vanessa off Noah's lap.

"I have no problem with that." He chuckled.

It annoyed me how my stepmom always threw herself at him… but it was only because I was jealous. I didn't want to be in love with a married man. I didn't want to be in love with my father.

I had no idea what Noah and I were going to do once Nessa and Vi were gone, but I hoped it involved a serious make-out session—and possibly more. Maybe we'd go for a drive in that sexy Firebird.

Heading down the hall, I was about to phone my mother when the doorbell rang.

Strange. We weren't expecting any visitors.

"Aria, could you get that, please?" Vanessa hollered.

Changing direction, I leisurely entered the foyer and unlocked the front door, only to freeze like a like a deer in headlights. The stranger standing across from me had the same expression on his face. He was tall (about Noah's height), with a head full of thick dark hair, which was cut short and styled. His eyes were beautiful, a deep mahogany with flecks of caramel, complimenting his skin color, which reminded me of desert sand. He looked like he was in his late twenties. There was a faint hint of stubble around his chin, creating a shadowed goatee. I noticed an attractive set of dimples when he smiled. This stranger was ruggedly handsome… and ripped.

Holy muscles. Who are you? I pondered.

"Bloody hell… Noah's one lucky bastard."

Oh. My. God.

Sexy avatar: check

Sexy deep voice: check

Sexy British accent: check

"I know he's a good-looking bloke, but how the hell did he get a ring on that finger?"

Was that a compliment? I couldn't think as I stared down at my hand.

"Let me guess, you're getting that missing solitaire resized, huh?"

There was something about this stranger's voice that made my heart shiver. I couldn't understand it. I did *not* expect it. His voice was deep like Noah's, but there was a charismatic warmth in his tone.

"Um…"

Words! Use them! A voice berated me in my mind.

"Now I *really* regret not showing up for the family reunion." He stepped forward while I awkwardly stood there.

"What's that supposed to mean?" I asked, resting a hand on the door frame.

Seriously? Why can't you just ask him who he is like a normal person? I had no explanation for that. This mysterious stranger was just… I was surprised by the attraction I felt.

"It means"—he reached for my hand and raised it to his lips—"if you had cast those gorgeous eyes on me three years ago, you wouldn't be married to my brother."

My face flushed in heat when he left a soft kiss between my knuckles.

"You… you're Noah's brother?"

Whoa. Rewind please.

"It's probably a good thing I wasn't invited to your wedding, love. I would have put a stop to it." He showed off another amazing smile before releasing my hand.

Sexy canines. I loved his teeth, which explained his million-dollar smile.

"Maybe that's why my invitation got lost in the mail."

I listened as he cleared his throat and altered the sound of his voice.

"*Should anyone here present know of any reason that this couple should not be joined in holy matrimony, speak now or forever hold your peace.*" He laughed, and I loved the way it sounded. "I wouldn't have been able to hold my peace."

Mom always warned me to stay away from charismatic men...

"Are you gonna invite me in, love? I'm not the Big Bad Wolf—that's my brother." He looked up and stared at the monstrosity that was Noah's mansion. "It's not like I can huff and puff and blow *this* house down." His magical eyes found mine again. "And I certainly won't bite." He paused. "*Hard.*"

I shivered.

"What the hell are you doing here?" Noah's hostile voice blasted behind me. He appeared at the door and pulled me closer to him, which was ridiculous because it wasn't like I was at risk of getting kidnapped.

"That's no way to greet your little brother." The handsome stranger smiled.

Little? I specifically remembered a conversation I'd had with Noah about his siblings... Noah was the youngest, at least that's what he'd told me.

"I like your wife. She hasn't said much, but she doesn't need to when she's an absolute stunner." The attractive Englishman winked at me.

"What the—she's not my wife!"

"No? Oh, thank God." He sighed in relief and handed me his cellphone. "Drop your digits, sweetheart. I'd love to take you out."

I wanted to tell him I was his niece, but Noah beat me to it with another raging outburst.

"Stop hitting on my daughter! What the hell is wrong with you?"

His charismatic smile disappeared when he looked back at me, wide eyed. I stood there as this strange man switched his gaze from my face to Noah's several times. I assume he was comparing our physical features.

"Wait, she's…"

My uncle looked at me long and hard, narrowing his eyes in disbelief.

"*You're* Aria?"

I nodded with a shy smile.

Is he Uncle Isaac?

"Wow… she doesn't look like you… at all," he said to Noah. "That's a good thing, though."

Noah placed his hands on my shoulders and lowered his voice to a stern tone. "Sweetie, I want you to go inside."

"No."

I didn't want to be shooed away.

"At least allow me to introduce myself," said my uncle, "since I probably creeped her out."

"No, I want you gone. How the hell did you even get past the gate?"

That was a good question, but he ignored Noah and extended his hand. "Hello, Aria. It's a pleasure to finally meet you. I'm your Uncle Evan."

His smile was amazing. I got lost in his eyes when I shook his hand.

Wait—Uncle Evan? Noah had never mentioned having another brother apart from Isaac. This I was a hundred percent sure of, and I planned to interrogate him later.

"How did you know my name?" I asked.

"You were always a hot topic of discussion in my family."

I wasn't sure if that made me happy or upset.

"I want you to leave, Evan." Noah moved me aside and went head-to-head with his brother.

"Honey," Vanessa interjected. "Who's at the door?"

I peered at my handsome uncle without getting noticed.

"This must be the Missus then, huh? I'm Evan." He offered his hand. "Good to meet you… at long last."

My stepmom seemed reluctant to shake his hand. Did she not know about him, either? I wondered.

"I'm the brother-in-law you never met," Evan added.

"Funny… my husband never mentioned you." She glared at Noah. "Not once."

Funny indeed. Apparently, Noah hasn't mentioned a lot of things!

"Nessa, look—there's bad blood between me and Evan. I'll explain later, but right now, I want him off our property."

"Nonsense, he's family!"

"No, he's not. Not part of *my* family, anyway," he said with contempt.

"It's rude to let him stand out here, and even worse to send him away. What's wrong with you?"

"Who's the new house guest?" Vienna asked, shuffling beside me. I swear I could see the floating hearts in her eyes as soon as she looked at my uncle.

"No one," Noah bitterly replied. "He was just leaving."

"Don't be ridiculous." Vanessa scowled. "Come on in, Evan! I'm curious to know why your existence was kept a secret."

"That's because I was adopted."

A look of rage flashed in Noah's eyes. "Your adoption has nothing to do with why I've cut you out of my life, you fucking prick."

Okay… so they weren't related. The eyes were a dead giveaway, but he had the same masculine frame as Noah, so I'd assumed he was my biological uncle.

"Stop being a jerk and let him in," Vienna said, squeezing between Noah and my stepmom. She formally introduced herself and dragged Evan inside. She probably just wanted to flirt with him and punch her number into his cellphone, and why wouldn't she? My uncle was so easy on the eyes.

We were about to gather in the living room when Noah pulled Evan aside and told us they would return shortly.

Why didn't he ever tell me about Evan? And why is he so hostile toward him? The questions were killing me.

CHAPTER TWENTY-EIGHT
NOAH

Great. This was the last thing I needed… this asshole showing up at my doorstep. Pacing my study, I glared at my brother and did everything in my power to not get violent. The last time I'd seen him, he was nineteen. Now the guy was almost twenty-eight.

"What do you want, Evan? Why are you here?"

"What a wonderful way to be greeted after all these years apart."

"Cut the shit and get to the point."

He relaxed in his armchair and flashed a condescending smile, which only aggravated me.

"You need to relax, Noah. Married life has made you crankier than I remember."

"You were flirting with my daughter, for fuck's sake!"

"I didn't know she was Aria. I thought she was your wife."

"That's just as bad! What kind of man are you to put the moves on another man's wife?"

"Take it easy." He chuckled. "It was just some friendly banter. Show some class."

"*Class?*" I folded my arms in my chest. "Is that what you tell yourself?"

"Your bird's not much of a head turner, anyway. Who's her plastic surgeon? You should sue them."

His insult made me snap as I grabbed him by the collar and yanked him out of his chair before I slammed him against the wall.

"I'm not gonna allow you to come in here like some punk and disrespect my family to my face!"

"The truth always does more harm than good, yet it must be spoken… regardless."

"Shut the fuck up!" I was furious. Nothing had changed about him.

"Calm down, Brother."

"Do *not* call me that. I am *not* your brother." I stared him down threateningly before releasing him. Giving Evan a shiner was far too tempting, so I kept a safe distance and resisted the urge to swing my fist.

"When are you ever going to forgive me?" he asked.

"We're not going there."

"It was an accident, Noah. I wish I could take it back. Every day of my life I live in regret over the tragedy."

"It wasn't an accident. You had every motive to kill our father. Do you even remember that weekend? Or have drugs and alcohol permanently screwed up your brain?"

"I experimented when I was sixteen. I'm not the addict in the family."

Indirect low blows. Now I really wanted to knock his teeth out.

"It makes little sense to me," I started, "but since you're so curious why I doubt you, let's go through the tragic chain of events, shall we?" I paced around him like a district attorney. "Dad sits us down one evening and reveals his will. Dad drops a bomb on us, declaring you his rightful successor when he dies. Dad dies four weeks later."

Was I accusing him of murder? Yes.

"You were gonna take over the company. Isaac and I fought him on his decision because—let's be honest—you were never gonna buckle down and get serious about life. To this day, I can't understand why he had so much faith in you to even consider you first. It's mind-boggling. You were flunking school, getting yourself in trouble almost every weekend, and partied as a full-time job instead of establishing a career for yourself."

"Honestly, Noah, you make it sound like you've forgotten what it's like to be eighteen and in college."

"That's not the point. My point is, you murdered Dad at the cabin because you were afraid he would change his will since Isaac kept badgering him to come to his senses. You never got along with our father. He loved you enough to believe in your ability to run his company one day. And what did you do? You shot him. You murdered our father for money."

"How can you even accuse me of that? You weren't there, Noah! I had driven up to the lake house because I wanted to be on my own to think things through regarding Dad's will. I didn't want to run his company! I'd made that clear to you, Dad, and Isaac. What's wrong with your memory?"

"To reflect on the will or get high with your friends?"

"Dad was never supposed to be there."

"He was worried about you and your 'suicidal tendencies'—which we both know was always attention seeking behavior. You're an absolute sociopath, Evan."

"I wasn't suicidal!"

"He shows up at the cabin, and you shoot him point blank."

"I was high out of my mind on a cocktail of drugs, and paranoid! I thought an intruder had broken in! There were lady friends staying with me."

"Ah, yes. Your whores. You killed our father to protect those drugged up bitches. How noble of you."

I could see the anger in his eyes. He wanted to knock me out.

Do it. I dare you.

"Is that why you put on that huge drama with Dad, to make him worry so that he'd follow you? It was premeditated murder, wasn't it?"

"Noah—"

"And don't give me a bullshit excuse for you being inexperienced with a gun. You may have skipped out on the hunting trips, but you were obsessed with the shooting range. Dad had a collection of firearms, and you always took a keen interest. You knew exactly how to use that gun."

"Would you please listen to yourself? Why are you still accusing me when you know it was an accident? Why do you hate me so much? Because I had the balls to live for myself, while you bent over backwards trying to please everyone in the family? You even abandoned your own daughter to please 'Mummy dearest.'"

"You son of a bitch!" My fist was inches away from his face. I had stopped myself just in time. "Keep my daughter's name out of your filthy mouth!"

There was a long pause before Evan said, "You know what's sad, Brother? We both struggled with drug addiction. The difference between you and me is that I'm not pointing fingers at others and blaming them. I take accountability for all my fuckups in life. I can own it. Can you?"

"You always hated our dad because of how strict he was."

"I loved our father. I shot him by accident out of panic. I didn't know it was him."

"You saw an opportunity to stick it to the old man and take over everything he dedicated his life to. What you didn't know was that Dad had already changed his will, replacing your name with mine. Your DUI arrest was a blessing in disguise because it made our father see what a colossal fuck up you are! So thank you for that!"

"I'm getting bloody tired of repeating myself: I never wanted to run the company! Our crazy bitch mother never questioned my innocence. Everyone knows it was an accident, except you."

That's when it hit me like lightning. My God… my mother. I stopped pacing and rubbed my forehead.

"You know what?" I looked at Evan. "Maybe you're right. Maybe you are innocent in all this. You always were Mother's lapdog. She probably couldn't wait to get her greedy hands on Dad's money. You were just the perfect scapegoat."

"What the fuck are you talking about?"

"Mom told you to kill him, didn't she?"

"Are you accusing our mother of being my accomplice now?"

"I'd heard her conversations with you to sell the company once Dad was dead and buried in the ground."

"She was a shareholder in the company, Noah. She was only giving me advice when the time came."

"What the hell does Mom know about the business world?"

"I trusted her wisdom more than anyone else's. When Dad said he was giving the company to me, I was overwhelmed. Mum had lectured me about all the responsibilities that would follow—responsibilities I didn't want. Don't jump to conclusions based on two minutes of conversation you overheard between me and our mother."

I was silent, desperately trying to rationalize the chaos of that tragedy.

"I know you're angry," Evan sighed, "but you need to stop looking for someone to blame. I miss him, too. He was the only one who understood my issues."

Ignoring my brother, I focused on facts and motives. It all made sense now. Dad had been planning on divorcing Mom because he wasn't happy with her anymore. Our mother had always been cold and emotionally withdrawn throughout their marriage. I didn't blame him for wanting out. He'd spoken to me about it one day after a tennis match. I was always closest to Dad. Before he and Mom got married, he told me they signed a prenuptial agreement. With divorce, Mom would walk away with only a million, and this would secure my father's right to hold all other assets. She didn't take it so well when he eventually told her they were headed for splitsville. But my father was known for being a generous man. He owned Hunter Oil Corporation. Dad had expanded the company, bringing in billions of dollars in profit. I was certain my mother had got greedy, because she kept insisting that I step down as CEO and relinquish all control to her so she could "take over" for Dad. I knew she just wanted to sell the company and sit on top of the family fortune, gaining complete control over Dad's assets. The best decision my father ever made was entrusting me with all he had.

"Dad's death was an accident," Evan reiterated. "It wasn't premeditated murder. You don't know how many times I've wished I could turn back the clock and never have gone on that trip. I was tired of being the prodigal son. I didn't know that Dad had changed his will. But even if I'd known, it would have been a relief.

"You think you're the black sheep in the family for your love affair with cocaine once upon a time? You're dead wrong, Noah. Dead wrong." His cold eyes pierced through mine. "I could never compete with you or Isaac! I could never measure up. How could I? I'm not part of the *famous family tree*—not by blood. Only by name."

"Do you want to know what really does my head in?" I shouted. "How could you get all fucked up on drugs that weekend if you wanted to make him proud?"

"I'm disappointed that you'd even ask me that, considering you were an addict yourself."

"Are we comparing drug addictions now?"

"I used to be so depressed. I was getting high on Oxy, LSD, and a shit ton of other drugs almost every day that year. You don't know the trauma I've been dealing with."

"You don't talk about it!"

"Because it's in the past! I took a trip up to the cottage to sort myself out. It was my last *hoorah* before relinquishing my freedom and becoming a corporate slave. I had originally planned on discarding my drugs and turning a new leaf, but that didn't happen—not after I overheard you and Isaac talking about me earlier that afternoon before I left for the lake house. Do you remember that conversation, or would you like me to refresh your memory?"

I said nothing because I truly didn't remember that discussion. It was so long ago.

"'Evan's the new CEO? What the fuck is Dad thinking?' 'Little brother's gonna burn the company down to the ground.' 'That kid is dumb as a donkey.' 'Yeah, a kid. That's what he is.' 'He's always screwing up. He's making us all look bad—wish Mom and Pops never adopted the little hellraiser.'"

Oh. *That* conversation. Later in the evening, Dad had told me he had changed his will and had made me CEO. I told him it was best if Isaac took over, but he insisted I was his first choice all along, and that he had only chosen Evan because he'd hoped it would give him an incentive to change his life around.

"Do you remember now? Need I say more?"

I stared at my brother.

"You all thought less of me because I wasn't really part of the family. I was always the outsider, the bad seed. Eventually, I gave up and lived up to everyone's expectation of me."

"Stop playing the victim, Evan. Why can't you come to terms with your adoption? You were just up to no good—and no matter how much we tried to help, you never listened. My animosity toward you has nothing to do with the fact that you were adopted. You've had a history of behavioral problems. I think you were the one who had difficulty accepting yourself—you still do."

"I always felt like a failure compared to you and Isaac. You knocked your girlfriend up at sixteen and you still never fell from grace. You were always the golden boy, while I was the pitiful, undeserving, lowlife."

Christ, look at all that pent-up rage.

Evan and I were so alike in our temperament. Maybe that's why we never got along—we were constantly clashing. As a child, I was used to being the youngest, spoiled with attention. When Evan joined our family, he was six, and I was twelve. I resented my brother at first, but that slowly went away as I grew up. I think he looked up to me in my teen years, but I was too busy with other things to hang out with him. By that time, Isaac and Breanne were out on their own, building their futures. Maybe that was what screwed him up so much: the family pressure, expectations, and loneliness. There was always chaos and discord at the Hunter mansion.

Evan had messed up so much throughout the years—it was hard to forgive and forget. I had taken Dad's death badly because of how suddenly he died. The aftermath of his passing burned a bridge between me and my brother. Isaac was never close to Evan. As for Breanne, I had no clue what her relationship with him was like. Our mother was the only one who always had a soft spot for him, despite his continuous dickish behavior. I'd had to beg her not to talk about him when I brought Vanessa home to meet my family for the first time. We were all estranged from Evan ever since he left for college. Mom stayed in contact with her favorite son regularly and wanted to invite him to the wedding. I was afraid he would show up at the reception hall and set fire to the place—no joke. Evan had been a pyromaniac ever since I could remember. We had some things in common: being reckless and irresponsible. The difference was that I had got my act together, and he hadn't.

"Let's skip going down memory lane, shall we?" I stated. "It clearly brings out the worst in both of us."

Sighing, Evan ran his fingers through his hair.

"I'm gonna ask you again… what are you doing here, and what do you want from me?"

"I've been living in LA for a couple months now," he said, "because of my job. I've got some renovation projects going on in a few houses. Breanne and I have kept in touch. I asked her about you yesterday. She told me you were living here, so I thought I'd drop in and see how you were doing. It's been too long since we last saw each other. I was kind of hoping my years of karmic bad luck would be over and done with."

Leave it to our sister to feel sorry for him and go against my wishes.

"You're an architect now?" I asked.

"No… not exactly." He rubbed his neck. "After I flunked out of school, I got into a trade—got myself an apprenticeship, and now I'm a skilled carpenter. I can build you just about anything. I spent a year in Haiti building houses and a school in one of the village communities."

Well, I'll be damned.

"Impressive," I said.

"Not really, just doing what I love."

And here I'd thought he was squandering his inheritance away in Europe.

"By the way," he added, "your daughter's fucking gorgeous."

"Stay away from her—I mean it." My daddy instincts immediately kicked in.

"I've only just met her."

"And you're not gonna get to know her any better."

"Why won't you give me a chance? Why does everyone in our family have to paint me as the fucked-up spawn of Satan?"

"We never painted you that way. You did a great job of fucking up your own reputation all by yourself."

"I'm human as much as you are—we all make mistakes."

"And we learn from them. I know your pattern. You're all talk, Evan. You're unreliable, untrustworthy, and there's no way I'm gonna allow Aria to be around you. You're nothing but a bad influence."

"Is this about me flirting with her earlier?" He crossed his arms and sighed. "Look, I honestly didn't know she was your daughter. We haven't been on speaking terms in years, Noah. How was I to know you had got in touch with her again? I thought she was your wife—and I was only takin' the piss by flirting with her."

Right.

"You only bring bad news everywhere you go," I said. "Pains me to say it, but it's true. There's no reason for us to reconcile, and I refuse to let you into my daughter's life."

I had to protect her. That was my responsibility as her father. She had been hurt enough in life. I had to shield her from the toxic people in my family. Evan was one of them. My mother was number two. Just because she had brought me into this world didn't mean she had the authority to control my life. Her fears and projections were her own to reconcile. I learned this lesson the hard way, but I would never forget it. That was the silver lining.

You didn't protect Aria from yourself last night. My guilt hit me like a ton of bricks.

"Noah, please be reasonable. It wasn't easy for me to park my pride and show up at your place unannounced. I just—"

Aria suddenly stormed into the room, yelling at me. "I just found out today I have another uncle, and you're already pushing him out of my life? How can you disregard my feelings? I'm an adult, Noah! What gives?"

Was she listening this entire time?

"You don't know him like I do," I defended myself, trying not to snap.

"Then let me get to know him better. Can't you understand how lonely I feel? I have all this family I know absolutely nothing about. You never go into detail or even talk about my aunt and uncle. You refuse to tell me about my grandmother, and now that your brother's shown up at our front door, you turn him away and decide based on what *you* feel is best for me. You never even told me about Uncle Evan! Seriously, Noah, do you have any other siblings I should know about? Or are they just dead to you? Is that what you do when people no longer serve a purpose in your life? You discard them?"

If she only knew. I hated arguing with her.

"Aria, listen to me. Evan is reckless and dangerous!"

"That's not who I am anymore!" he shouted.

"What is going on in here?" My wife appeared behind Aria.

"Nothing. Evan was just leaving." I glared at him. "*Now.*"

"Breanne was right," he scoffed, shaking his head. "I never should've come here. I just thought I knew my brother better than anyone else. I was wrong."

"Noah, what is the meaning of this?" Vanessa looked upset.

I couldn't stand the idea of him getting close to my daughter. I was protective of her. I would die for her, and kill for her, but I would have to be blind, deaf, and paralyzed to let those two spend time together. And no, it wasn't because of jealousy, or that Aria kept blushing around Evan. I just wanted to protect her from his destructive ways.

"Why is everyone yelling?" Vienna cut in.

"No one's yelling," I said, feeling ganged up on. She didn't know my brother. I'd learned a long time ago that Evan could never be trusted.

"You see what you do?" I looked at him. "Are you happy now? I let you in my home for ten fucking minutes, and—"

"Stop shouting!" Aria came to his defense. "You're the only one who's been hostile from the second you saw him."

"You don't know the history between me and my brother."

"I eavesdropped on enough." She raised an objecting hand. "How can you blame him?"

"Wait"—Nessa looked confused—"Blame him for what?"

Great.

This was perfect. This was exactly how I wanted to spend my Sunday.

"Can we all just go back to the living room," Vienna said, "and clear up this confusion?"

"That won't be necessary," Evan replied. "My brother doesn't want me here, and that's fine. I'm not the type to impose my presence on anyone, especially when I'm unwelcome."

Clenching my jaw, I gripped the edge of my desk when he walked past Aria.

That bastard better not be undressing her in his mind.

"Wait!" she called after him. "You can't leave, I… I just met you. You're my uncle. Don't you want to know me?"

My heart sank when she reached for his arm.

Why, Aria? Why do you need him in your life? Am I not enough? Why can't you trust me when I say he's bad news?

Alarms were going off in my head. It took every ounce of strength to not lift her over my shoulder and carry her out of there so I could lock her up in her room.

You really believe he's as sick in the head as you are? There was that sinister voice again, mocking me.

You're the last person to cast a stone, pal.

Evan handed an ivory-colored business card to Aria and smiled. "My cell number's on there if you ever need to talk. Call me anytime, love."

I hated how women instantly fell for Evan's British charm. Our mother wanted to make sure his accent didn't fade, so she'd hired private teachers from the same area he had grown up in throughout his studies, being home schooled. His accent never left. Did I envy him? No.

Liar, liar…

"I mean it," said Evan, locking eyes on my daughter. "Anytime."

Wanting to punch that smile off his face, I yanked the card out of Aria's hand.

"Hey! Noah, what the hell?"

I ignored her and fixed my threatening gaze on Evan. "I said, I don't want you talking to my daughter! Now do us all a favor and get the fuck out!"

My inner peace slipped away from me as I surrendered to rage. I was furious and I couldn't hide it. My wife looked appalled by my behavior, and so did Vienna, shaking her head at my reactive outburst.

"Come on, Evan," said Vi. "I'll show you out. I don't know what's wrong with Noah today."

They soon disappeared, and Vanessa followed. Aria was about to leave when I grabbed her arm and pulled her back.

"Oh, no you don't, young lady."

"Let go of me!" She scowled, trying to free herself from my clutches. "How could you be so rude and mean?"

"Because I'm trying to protect you—that requires wearing 'the asshole' mask sometimes."

"He's your brother!"

"You have no idea who he is. *I* grew up with him. You need to listen to me."

"No, I don't." She withdrew, folding her arms in her chest.

"I'm your father, and yes, you do."

"I'm not a child!"

"You're *my* child."

Arguing like this was only going to lead to a dead end.

"Is that what you're always gonna do now?" she said. "Play the 'dad' card whenever it's convenient for you?"

"I'm not playing anything. I'm your father. It's who I am, and you need to obey me because I know what's best for you."

"My father? Or a patriarchal asshole? Which is it, Noah?"

"Both." I grinned.

"You're such a dick."

"When I need to be. You'll appreciate it one day."

"No, I won't. I just find it so hypocritical how you say you 'know what's best for me,'" she scoffed. "Did you feel that way last night too when we were lip-locked… *Daddy?*"

She was pushing my buttons. It was working.

"Be serious, Aria."

"I *am* serious. Give me back his card."

"Why do you want it?"

"That's such a stupid question."

I don't know why I felt so hurt when she said this to me, but my reaction didn't make things any better. Impulsively, I shredded Evan's card and tossed it in the trash. I thought it would give me satisfaction, but it didn't. The look in my daughter's eyes made me feel like crap.

Nice work. You took that too far.

"Why are you trying to isolate me and stop me from meeting your family—*my* family? Are you ashamed of me? Are you afraid I'll tell, or they'll know? Because if that's the case, nobody knows and nobody ever will!"

I felt like a scumbag. Violating my morals had already resulted in long, sleepless nights with a tormented conscience. I wanted to argue my case, but she fled from my study in a flash.

"Aria!" I ran after her and got as far as her bedroom, only to get the door slammed shut in my face.

She locked it before I could even reach for the doorknob. I hated walls between us. With my daughter, I just couldn't handle it. It was like a chronic case of anxiety. She made me crazy.

Opting for a gentle approach, I rested my hand on the door and lowered my voice to a soothing tone.

"Baby, come on. Please let me in."

Not only was I the concerned father, but the rejected *almost*-lover, desperate for forgiveness. I was panicking inside because I was losing control of my feelings for her. My emotions were running wild like river rapids. This was how I constantly felt around her, and she had no clue because I hid it well.

Losing hope, I turned and found Vanessa and Vienna glaring at me, expecting explanations. We headed for the living room, where I briefly summarized why Evan and I didn't get along. You'd think they would finally side with me once I uncovered his poor track record. But no, after wasting my breath for twenty minutes, the only thing Vienna could say was "People change." And my wife backed her up with: "Brothers never abandon each other. They get over their differences and bury the hatchet. Give him a chance."

We ended the discussion with those last words before they both went off on their scheduled spa day. I avoided Aria because I knew I'd only lose my temper again, so there was no point in apologizing. I had to cool down.

☥☦

Raising a child—that was something I'd been deprived of. The sad part was that I couldn't blame anyone but myself. I was responsible for all the choices I'd made in life. My mother always interfered in my personal affairs, but I had the power to stop her—I just gave up. Inviting Aria to come and live with me and Nessa had turned out to be a double-edged sword. Never in a million years had I expected something like this to happen. I wasn't even thinking about the possibility that this could happen when I saw her for the first time. Did I feel attracted to her then? Was I just ignoring it? Every time I thought about her in any sort of romantic way, I either felt infuriated with myself or despairingly hopeless. This wasn't something I could change overnight. I never should have crossed the line, but I had, and it was too late to take it all back. I felt like my only choice now was to keep my distance from her… as in thousands of miles. That would have been the safest solution, but I couldn't even do that. Why? Because I had already abandoned her once before. I couldn't do that again. It would have been selfish of me. The only way to go about repairing our relationship was through counseling. Lust did not dominate my feelings for my daughter. In the short time that we had reconnected, I'd instantly felt a fatherly instinct toward her. That desire to protect her from all harm had been there from the moment I laid eyes on her. I wanted to shield her from the dangers of life and the wickedness of the world. The messed-up part was that every day I was around her, I felt like the danger, the wicked-minded bastard. I had to get over the attraction and take control. If I let her steer, we would both get hurt.

Throughout the afternoon, I kept myself busy with work. I stayed productive and distracted, but there was only so much researching I could do. Feeling fed up, I finally left my study and changed into my gym gear to work off my frustration with weight training. Nothing was worse than stagnant energy.

My thoughts were chaotic as I ran on the treadmill: *Aria… Doctor Grey… Vanessa… failing marriage… work… Evan… Aria… Aria… Aria.* Cranking the volume on my iPhone, I increased the speed on the machine. Sprinting until I cramped in pain seemed like the only way to get her out of my head.

Drenched in sweat, I killed a good forty-five minutes of cardio. Assaulting a punching bag only fed my underlying rage toward my brother. I couldn't stop. *Left hook, right hook*—I was throwing jabs harder and faster, feeling the painful impact on my gloved knuckles. I embraced the pain. I needed it.

Evan threatens you. You want to keep Aria all to yourself.

I threw one last punch, growling through my anger as I panted. There was always quiet competition between me and Evan. My mother was to blame. She's a textbook narcissist.

Using my teeth, I ripped off the Velcro straps around my wrists and removed the gloves.

What the fuck am I doing? I questioned.

I was cheating on my wife with my daughter. You can't get any sicker than that.

You're not in love with Blondie anymore.

I was the world's most fucked-up human being.

I suggest you let me out before you lose her. I'm getting restless in here, Noah. Let me out to play, just for the evening.

I negotiated with my darker half while I tried to rationalize and stay in control. But that didn't last long. Pulling off my shirt, I grabbed my water bottle and squirted cold water on my head.

Come on, you know you want to.

I breathed out until I was at a normal resting heart rate.

Decisions, decisions…

"Fuck it."

CHAPTER TWENTY-NINE
ARIA

Growing up, all I ever wanted was a father who truly loved me enough to protect me. Rob had failed in that respect, and now that Noah was trying to shelter me from "harm," I just wanted him to back off. Be careful what you wish for, right? Maybe I had overreacted. Noah had a point—I didn't know who Evan was. The only information I had discovered about my uncle was that he had a troubled youth. His back story wasn't all that great. But when I met him, his eyes betrayed a warm and gentle nature that contradicted his notorious reputation. He didn't have the same intimidating intensity as Noah's eyes—then again, maybe Noah was just subtle about his badass qualities, whereas Evan was more out there and in your face. I knew Noah wasn't a saint, but he was on his best behavior around me. I think he was trying to set a good example.

Arguments were never fun, but it seemed like me and Noah couldn't avoid a confrontation. I genuinely wanted to know my uncle better. I was sure there was lots he could tell me about my father, since Noah wasn't willing to share himself. It sucked. Living with Mom and Rob had been so turbulent. No one on Rob's side of the family was interesting or nice. Evan was sweet to me. I guess I just wanted more family involved in my life. His adoption didn't matter. I could only imagine how ostracized he felt growing up. I could relate.

Charging my phone, I was about to switch on a playlist when a loud knock startled me.

"Let me in, Aria."

It was him.

"That sounds like an order," I said, standing up from my bed.

"It is. Now stop being a smart-ass and open the damn door."

Was it wrong of me to feel suddenly aroused? I swear it was like he gave off sex pheromones through the wall or something. Stepping closer, I pressed my palms against the door and listened.

"Aria, don't make me wait," he said exhaustedly.

For a moment, I shut my eyes and tried to imagine Noah standing on the other end: I could see him leaning his weight against the door frame. He had just showered, and I could smell him—his cologne, shower gel…

"What the hell are you doing in there?"

"Why don't you ask me nicely?"

I wasn't sure why I was giving him such a hard time.

Because you enjoy pushing his buttons, my subconscious answered.

"I was hoping you wouldn't force me to do this," Noah sighed.

Twisting the doorknob, he broke the lock with brute strength as the door slowly creaked open, and in walked one very pissed-off hottie.

"You… broke my lock." I looked up at him, stunned.

"I can fix it." He intensified his stare. "But I won't replace it. It's hard enough getting inside your titanium fortress. I don't like barriers between us."

My heart trembled as he edged closer, inches away from my face. Even when Noah was pissed off, he still looked like sex.

Quit thinking about how sexy he is and stay focused!

"I'm mad at you," I mumbled.

"I know." He gazed at me intently and reached for my waist, pressing me against his body.

"What are you doing?"

"What does it look like? Defusing your anger." His expression remained unchanged—eternally brooding.

I wanted to pull away, but my arms coiled around his neck as I yielded to a much-needed hug.

"You didn't have to react the way you did," I firmly stated.

"I don't regret the way I reacted or how I spoke."

Smug bastard.

Noah's fingers slid under my shirt, slowly rubbing the dimples in my lower back.

"You shouldn't hate your brother and blame him for what happened with your dad. He was Evan's father, too."

"You shouldn't assume Evan's 'your friendly neighbor Mr. Rogers.'"

I stifled a laugh. That was a good one. Sarcastic Noah—totally in his element.

"You should give him a chance."

"You should listen to your father."

It irritated me every time he said that. But what annoyed me more was how he had this amazing ability to dominate my body and make it surrender without physically forcing me to submit.

"I have the right to let him into my life," I argued.

"I have the right to prevent that from happening."

"No, you don't."

"Yes. I *do.*"

"I want to see my uncle!"

"I want you to shut up and save your breath."

"Make me."

"Are you sure about that, Aria?" His heated stare pierced through me.

Fuck. Noah was on another level of hotness. I should have been infuriated with him, but I got off on our back-and-forth fencing with words.

"And what exactly should I *save my breath* for?"

"For this—"

He crushed his mouth against mine and kissed me passionately, moving his hands down my back before he traced my peach and squeezed it. Coaxing my lips to open, he brushed his minty tongue over mine, filling me with liquid desire. I didn't know if I was drowning in him or burning in the firestorm that blazed around us. All I knew was that every time I felt his lips, it sent me to another world. Everything and everyone would fade, and it would just be me, Noah, and the incredible sensations that overpowered me whenever we touched.

Gaining confidence, I locked my arms around his neck and pulled myself in more. My love for this man overwhelmed me to the brink of tears. How was it possible to feel so happy just by being in the same room as him? Was there something unique about his energy? It couldn't have been all in my head. No one could ever make me feel the way Noah did. It just wasn't possible.

Our breathing grew labored as our lips melted into each other, moving in perfect synchronization. It was worthy of being captured on camera in slow motion—like a cinematic kiss sequence, where the camera slowly pans around the couple, overlapping different angles to create a more romantic, magical moment. Every moment with Noah felt surreal. I kissed him for as long as my lungs could last before I pulled back, equally breathless. The lustful heat in his eyes turned me on.

"Get changed," he said. "We're going out."

"Where?"

"It's a surprise." Flashing a crooked smile, he leaned into my ear. "You'll just have to trust me."

Sigh. His voice. I had hearts in my eyes.

"Wear something nice," he added.

"Um… you're gonna have to be a little more specific."

"Short, tight, and black. How's that for detail?"

Was this even Noah at the moment? I didn't know who it was, but I loved this sexy, dominant side of him—mega turn-on.

"Are you feeling all right?" I questioned.

"Less talking, more undressing."

Something must have snapped in his head. He'd done a total 180. Normally, I was the one who attempted to bring out the naughty.

"But—"

My body suddenly jolted forward as I lost balance.

Let's rewind in slow motion, shall we? Keep going… keep going… now pause. Freeze frame, play. The following occurred in under five seconds:

1. Noah unbuttoned my shorts so aggressively that the fly came undone.
2. He clutched my open waistline and yanked me forward, pressing me against him.
3. I was sandwiched between his body and an invisible wall.
4. I steadied myself and held on to his shoulders for support.
5. My breasts were crushed against his hard pectorals.

"I said," he lowered his voice, "stop talking."

My breathing was so shallow that I couldn't focus on anything but our intense physical attraction.

"Technically, you said… less talking."

"I'll just have to shut you up myself." He stared at me, switching glances from my eyes to my lips.

Oh God, I couldn't focus. Not when his hands were so close to my panties.

"How?" I breathed, feeling his lips graze against mine. He still hadn't released his grip on my shorts.

"I can think of many ways." Noah controlled the momentum of that barely there kiss.

I felt him smile near the corner of my mouth. Was he acting on instinct? How much time did I have to spend with this untamed part of him before the human would take over and cage the beast within?

Releasing his grip on my shorts, Noah rested his hands on my hips. I was up on my toes, leaning on his body for balance. My heart pounded in my chest as he bit my bottom lip, groaning softly. Was he really crossing over to R-rated territory with me?

"Be a good girl and obey me."

"You're such a tease. Why are you torturing me?"

"You consider this torture?" He smirked. "It's a good thing you haven't slept with me."

"*Yet*," I blushed when he grinned.

Noah was so much more experienced; it made me insecure.

"I want you ready in ten," he said.

"What? I take ten minutes just to heat my curling iron!" Exaggerating—I know.

"Fine," he sighed. "You have an hour, which will be enough time for me to finish up my work. Meet me in the garage when you're ready."

Whatever he had in store for us was going to be amazing… I hoped.

⸙

Music was blasting from the garage as I walked down a narrow hallway. I was dressed in a strapless, black mini dress that had a see-through mesh at the back. I had styled my hair straight, matching my outfit with a pair of black Gucci pumps. I considered going commando, but changed into a black thong instead. I was nervous. Noah always gave me butterflies, and that feeling only intensified when I walked through the garage door.

Hovering over the car engine, his black sleeves were rolled up to his elbows. I couldn't help but check him out while he was still distracted. He didn't hear me enter, since the car stereo was playing on max volume. I was unfamiliar with the song, but it had an electro dance beat.

Walking down the steps, I smiled when he nodded his head in time with the music. I had no idea what he was doing, but if I had to guess, he was inspecting the oil. My stepdad was a mechanic, and I remembered taking an interest in his line of work when I was twelve. He had been fixing Granddad's car in the garage one evening when we went to visit, and I was desperate for praise from him, so I offered my help by handing him tools. But that jerk just yelled at me most of the time and told me I was an annoying distraction. Feeling hurt, I ended up running away that night, hiding out in a tree, until my mom tracked me down. Yeah… bad memories.

The recollection quickly evaporated when I heard Noah mumbling the lyrics of the song. It was the first time I'd ever heard him sing. I was about to surprise him with a hug when he shut the hood and turned around.

"Oh, hey!" Noah smiled charismatically, grabbing a rag from the table.

"Hi," I replied shyly.

He leaned over the drivers-side door and turned down the volume. "How long have you been standing there?"

"Just stepped in, actually."

His eyes slowly cascaded down my body, making me blush. Someone was pleasantly surprised to see me. Noah looked so sexy, like he always did, clad in a fitted black shirt, with a couple buttons undone, exposing a bit of chest. His outfit really came together with his dark blue denim trousers. A black leather belt was looped around his trim waist, and I especially liked the steel AX buckle in the front. You could never go wrong shopping at Armani Exchange. I loved his footwear: black leather army boots. How was he a lawyer? He could've easily been a model at Milan Fashion Week. Clothing didn't make Noah look attractive—*he* made clothing look attractive.

"You look…"

Sexy, hot, drop dead gorgeous?

I was hoping it was all the above.

"Breathtaking," he finally said, sending chills down my body with his deep voice.

I stopped breathing when he slid his arms around my waist and kissed my neck sensually.

Is this actually happening?

"Nice whip," I said.

"Ferrari California, 2013 model." Noah glanced at the car. "It's a seven-speed, dual-clutch transmission. Sexy ride, huh?"

His winning smile and nonchalant attitude were way sexier. Honestly, I would have ridden in anything, as long as Noah was beside me. But the car was definitely hot—a black on black convertible. I couldn't wait to get inside.

"Noah, can I ask you something?"

"Of course."

"How much money did you exactly inherit?"

He paused. "Enough to afford all this—and then some."

I guess that meant millions… hundreds of millions… billions?

"Buckle up, beautiful." He opened my passenger door.

"Thanks." I strapped on my seat belt, feeling nervous when he sat next to me.

The engine fired up, and the stereo came to life. Noah put the Ferrari in reverse and backed out of the garage.

"So, where are you taking me?" I asked, feeling the wind in my hair.

"You'll find out soon enough." He looked over at me and flashed a killer smile.

Swoon.

CHAPTER THIRTY
ARIA

Shopping was so much fun. Noah took me down Rodeo Drive and spoiled me. It was sheer royal treatment. Dinner was even better. We went to this amazing Italian restaurant called Scarpetta. The food was to die for. It was hard to avoid my dirty thoughts throughout the evening. Even the way he chewed his food was hot—taking his time to enjoy every flavor and texture. My favorite moment was when we shared a delicious cannoli, an Italian dessert. It was like biting into a piece of Heaven and staring into the eyes of God at the same time. My love for Noah had no boundaries. I was a pagan, proudly idolizing him.

Driving in the car with him was a rush. It gave me nostalgic feelings, similar to how I'd felt when we were on the Ferris wheel at the festival. I cranked up the volume so high that the subwoofers in the trunk vibrated. I remembered the first time I tried to adjust the volume on my stepdad's stereo. Rihanna's "Umbrella" had just been released. Not only did he smack my hand away and curse, but he changed the radio station too (total ass). Noah was different, though. He was laid back, and that quality only attracted me more. He had introduced me to a whole different genre of tunes. I loved it. I wasn't familiar with most of the songs he listened to, but his deep house tracks were eargasmic. The most amazing thing about electronic music was that it had so many transitions, constantly building up to an unbelievable drop that would send chills through your body. I couldn't live without music; it had saved my life.

I wanted to run away with Noah. Almost every song I listened to made me daydream about him. Fading into fantasies, he brought me back to earth when he reached for my hand and placed it on the stick shift. I felt his warmth as he gently loosened my fingers and helped me switch gears. It wasn't like I was touching him down there, but still... just entertaining that fantasy while gripping that stick shift was a scandalous turn-on. I admired his ability to hide his emotions so well—something I was envious of.

We soon pulled onto the freeway, and I felt a surge of happiness every time he tightened his grip over my hand, shifting into fifth gear. The revving engine sounded sexy as I closed my eyes and imagined him guiding my hand up and down on *something else*, showing me exactly how he wanted me to please him. My triple-X fantasy would not disappear. I had to get my hand off that stick shift. But I didn't want to—not really.

For a moment, I imagined Noah putting the car in cruise control, resting his arm along the edge of his window, allowing me to unzip his fly... pulling out his raging hard-on. I'd wrap my slender fingers around him, squeezing gently.

Like this, baby...

He'd show me how to stroke every inch of him, enjoying the pleasure while we'd race down the freeway.

The louder the engine got, the faster we went as I held on to my fantasy. I was right at the part where I was close to making him come when suddenly, my hand moved as we shifted into sixth gear.

My eyes fluttered open, forcing me to abandon my illicit fantasy. Noah fixated on the traffic ahead while I stared at him, catching a hint of a smile as the corner of his mouth swept upwards. He must have known I was mesmerized. His fearlessness was something I admired. My body leaned left and right as he swerved in and out of lanes like Paul Walker's character in the *Fast & Furious* films. Passing a few cars, Noah pulled out of the fast lane and guided my hand back to the stick shift. The Ferrari slowed down until we were at the legal speed limit.

"Switch to seventh!" I shouted over the music.

He let go of my hand and lowered the volume. "That's dangerous," said Noah. "It's bad enough I started speeding. I'm not putting your life in danger."

Fortunately for us, there were no patrol troopers on the road. I think he was an adrenaline junkie, and much to my surprise, so was I. Speeding was against the law. It was hazardous, but it was so badass. Life on the edge of danger is something else… it's… exciting, I thought as we sped away.

It was almost ten o'clock when Noah killed the engine. We were parked on a cliff, surrounded by darkness with no vehicles around us. The lights below us glowed and glittered, brilliantly illuminating the city. It was such a scenic view. This spot was an ideal make out location with a hot date. I wondered if that's why he had brought me up there.

"This view is something else…" I said, unfastening my seat belt.

"It's too bad we can't see the stars so well. We need to leave the city if you want to stargaze." Noah turned the key halfway in the ignition, keeping the battery on so the music could play.

"I love the stars," I confessed, staring at the sky. "When I was a kid, I often prayed, asking God to take me away from my bed for one night and turn me into a star so that I could find you… wherever you were in the world. I was convinced it was the only way I could ever see you."

There was a moment of silence between us.

Damn it, why did I tell him that? I couldn't meet his eyes.

Relaxing in my seat, I stared straight ahead.

Did I make things awkward with that confession? I anxiously wondered.

"You never needed God to turn you into a star, Aria. In my eyes, that's what you already are."

"I stopped believing in Him a long time ago."

Noah leaned toward me and gently touched my cheek. He traced the curve down to my chin and coaxed my head in his direction. "I know how you feel."

At least I wasn't alone with my wavering faith.

"I've always had a fascination with celestial objects," he said. "Shooting stars in particular. The few times I had been lucky enough to see one, it always reminded me of you." Noah brushed back my hair, hiding a bittersweet smile. The haunting sadness in his eyes made me want to reach out and hold him.

Hoping he would kiss me, I was disappointed when he withdrew and reclined in his seat.

"Lean your seat back."

It was an order. Slipping off my heels, I turned on my side, and hugged my knees to my chest. Noah was resting on his back, staring up at the sky with his hands folded behind his head. I couldn't take my eyes off him. He was just too handsome. I enjoyed admiring him. What girl would complain about free eye candy?

Lost in thought, we listened to music, and enjoyed the romantic ambiance around us. I blushed when he turned his head and looked at me. Obviously, he'd felt my eyes on him.

"Looking for flaws?" he said.

"All I see is perfection."

"Are you that obsessed with my profile?"

"We've already established the fact that you have a very attractive profile. But to be honest, I think I'm obsessed with many things about you, even the undiscovered parts."

His laughter made me smile as I imagined the sound waves traveling up into the universe, pleasing whatever celestial goddesses that lived within the stars. Maybe they would gather their energies in prayer and ask God to clear the clouds, just to give them the viewing pleasure of watching over this angel—this heartthrob who was sitting next to me. If I were a star, and if God truly existed, then that's what I would want: to watch Noah every night.

"What am I gonna do with you, Aria?"

"Anything you want."

"You shouldn't encourage me." His heated gaze met mine.

"It's not my fault you bring out the naughty in me."

"Do you always have a ready answer prepared in that pretty little head?"

"No, but… should I prepare myself for a brooding Noah moment soon?"

"I'm always brooding." He leaned forward and shuffled through some tracks on the stereo. There was a drastic change in the musical genre we were listening to: It went from chillstep to hip hop—a mix of various artists.

"Wow, since when do you listen to J. Cole, and Drake?"

"You already know I have an eclectic taste in music." He smirked.

"Evidently."

"Biggie, Tupac, DMX, Kanye, 50 Cent… the list goes on."

I watched him relax into his seat, folding his hands behind his head once more.

"I know what you're thinking," he said. "I guarantee I'm really not that much of a mystery."

I so want to solve you.

The song played on, and I was shocked that he listened to such explicit lyrics. "Please tell me you know what he's rapping about."

Raising himself on an elbow, he looked at me. "I'm thirty-three, Aria, not sixty-three. Trust me, I know exactly what he's saying. I can rap you the entire song if you want." His smile was confident.

"Do it!"

Noah nodded his head in rhythm with the beat. Once Drake began to spit the second verse, he started rapping along to "Worst Behavior."

"Oh—my—God!" I laughed. "You're amazing!" I was stunned. "You killed those bars." His flow was flawless.

"Is that so?" Noah chuckled.

"I was *not* expecting a rap star!"

"I think I'd be the next Vanilla Ice, if not Eminem." He laughed.

"JB's the new Vanilla Ice, only in resemblance to his newest hair style."

"Please tell me you're not a die-hard fan."

"I think he's kind of cute. His music has improved, and he's undeniably talented, but I've never gone to a concert. I think it's safe to say that I'm not a *Belieber*."

"Are you a One-Directioner?"

"I'm not really into boy bands."

I was just into *him*.

"Not to discredit those guys, but I don't listen to pop music. Vanessa, though…"

We both laughed.

"Hey, can you open the glove compartment?" he asked. "I've got some breath mints in there—aspartame free."

"Yeah, sure."

Was this a sign? What does the average person normally do before they engage in a passionate make-out session?

Freshen their breath.

I held the tiny container over his mouth and tapped it lightly.

"Thanks."

"No problem." I took a few mints myself.

This probably wasn't the best time to bring up the next subject, but he was quiet, and I couldn't think of anything else to talk about.

"Noah…"

"Mhm?" He sounded so relaxed.

"Can you please tell me why you won't let me see Uncle Evan?"

"I told you…" He clenched his jaw. "My brother's dangerous. I don't trust him."

"Why is he dangerous, though?"

Noah let out an exasperated sigh and looked at me. "Evan's got a history of driving under the influence and doing drugs. He's also set fire to objects and property before. The list goes on. I don't want him around you."

"But that was all in his past, right?"

He stayed silent and then gave a reluctant nod.

"What if you let me have supervised visits with him?"

"You mean you want me tagging along? No way." He shook his head adamantly. "I can't stand him. My relationship with Evan will not be repaired. I'm sorry I never mentioned him, but I had my reasons."

"How would you feel if I refused to let you in my life when you came looking for me? It would have killed you if I told you I hated you and passed judgment because you were never there for me as a child."

"That's not the same—please don't compare the situations."

"It *is* the same, Noah. My point is, if I judged you, we wouldn't have got this close."

"Sometimes I wish you told me to go to hell and shut me out instead."

"What do you mean?" I panicked. "Do you regret knowing me?" My heart sank. How could he say that?

"No, Aria." He frowned. "I just mean that if I'd never come looking for you, your life would have progressed properly. You would have gone to college, got yourself a nice boyfriend, and…" Noah collected his thoughts. "You wouldn't be in this predicament with me. I feel responsible."

"Is that what you label us as, 'a predicament?'" I couldn't help but take offense.

"No," he replied, growing frustrated. "What we have isn't normal. It doesn't happen to everyone. Fathers and daughters aren't supposed to feel this way about each other."

"We're not like other fathers and daughters. What we have is rare and special." I touched his face. "I didn't want to fall in love with you, Noah. I knew it was wrong, and I tried so hard to get over these feelings. I really did, but it only intensified. After you kissed me, I knew for sure that you felt what I felt, too."

There was a stillness between us.

"Maybe we shouldn't analyze all this tonight." He gently took my hand and lowered it.

Please let me touch you.

Noah was so hot and cold. I guess I had overwhelmed him.

"I'm not trying to analyze us," I said. "I was talking about Evan."

"Look, if I tell you I'll think about it, will you give the subject a rest for a while?"

How long was "a while" exactly? Not wanting to anger him, I nodded and was agreeable.

"Great." Noah sighed. "Thanks."

I took a deep breath and settled in my seat, rubbing my arms. The weather had got a little windier.

"Are you cold?" Noah asked.

"I'm fine."

"Come here." He adjusted his seat back a bit.

"Um, where?" I stared at him.

"On my lap."

Did I hear that right? Hesitating, I eventually shifted over. My heart was working harder than usual as I sat astride his lap, facing him.

His fingertips found their way up my arms, gently brushing my cool skin. The heat from his hands instantly warmed me up. We were shrouded in darkness, but I was convinced that Noah had night vision. Yes, I was still holding on to my delusional fantasy about him being a semi-supernatural being—perhaps a wolf or a vampire. I knew it was impossible. I swear I wasn't a "Twihard," but the vampires and lycans from *Underworld* were awesome.

The song ended, and the stereo switched tracks to something more chill-casual with a sexy beat. Even though the music was on low, the bass was high. I could feel Noah's blazing eyes on me. I couldn't hold his gaze. Sitting so intimately in his lap caused nothing but desire in the pit of my stomach. I started fidgeting with the edge of his shirt while he affectionately rubbed my arms.

"What are you thinking?" he asked.

"Nothing." I tried to smile. "Just enjoying my time with you."

"I know you, Aria. Tell me what's on your mind, I'm curious." He let go of my arms and held my hips, which made me straighten my posture when I felt the goosebumps.

"Are you really that cold?"

"No, I'm…" Well, this was embarrassing. "You just make me shiver when you…" I fumbled with my words.

"When I what?" Noah gripped my waist, seemingly amused.

"When… you…" I met his eyes. "When you tease me like that."

He was deliberately trying to get me all hot and bothered.

"Hmm, I'm not, though." He traced my hips. "You consider this teasing?"

"I'm sure it's too PG for you."

"I don't think you're ready for R-rated territory."

"Please," I scoffed.

"Sometimes I forget you're still a virgin." He chuckled and stopped moving his hands.

"Wow, Noah—should I be offended?" I honestly didn't know what to make of that comment.

He mimed my expression and rolled his eyes. "You're always quick to get defensive. Relax. I just meant you have sexual prowess. It's there every time you walk into a room. I see it when you look at me, even when I watch how you interact with other guys. I'm basically saying that you're seductive by nature, which is why I have to remind myself…" He exhaled. "… that no one has touched you."

Okay, time to be brave. You need to come clean. Don't blow it.

"Noah, I'm not a virgin."

There was a moment of silence as he looked at me. "What?"

"I couldn't tell you the truth when we talked about sex back in New York because I was afraid you'd judge me." I paused and collected myself. "I gave my V-card away to my ex years ago. He broke my heart when he left for college and dumped me for another chick. I've been coping with the loss by convincing myself that my romantic history with him is null and void. He was my only intimate partner. I really thought we would get married—it's all he talked about… wanting to move out of NYC together and settle down." I did my best to erase Trevor's face. It still hurt to recall our last conversation… how cold he was toward me.

"Aria, I'm sorry I made you feel you couldn't open up." Noah rubbed my arm. "I wouldn't have judged you. I don't think any less of you. Sexual energy is sacred; I just wanted you to understand its importance. I'm sorry I wasn't there when he broke your heart. Try not to hold a grudge. He has yet to grow up and truly step into adulthood. He's on that path… just like I was years ago. I made a lot of mistakes along the way, broke my fair share of hearts. It's okay to have regrets. But it's best to arrive at a place of acceptance and avoid looping in shame spirals. You have nothing to be ashamed of, Aria. You loved him."

I felt relieved. Crazy how our fears hold more power in our mind, and that's only because of us—our self-limiting beliefs, what we devote our attention to, etc.

"You don't think I'm a 'slut' just because I had pre-marital sex?"

Noah laughed. "Of course not. Who am I to judge? Have you forgotten how you were conceived?"

He had a point.

"Thank you for trusting me enough to confide in me." He stroked my cheek. "You're perfect. You can talk to me about the breakup if you need."

"No. I'm over it."

I just wanted to forget. I couldn't turn back the clock, nor did I want to. Trevor belonged in my past, not my present.

"You can touch me," I bravely stated, guiding his hands to my breasts.

Expecting rejection, I was shocked when he looked at me and said, "I know."

He sounded like he knew what he wanted. His eyes seemed to glow in the darkness as he moistened his lips. I covered his hands with my own, encouraging him to feel, if not taste, forbidden fruit.

We stared at each other for the longest time as the music echoed around us. My hands landed on his chest, reaching for his collar to steady my balance.

Please don't let this be a dream…

"Open your eyes, Aria. I want you to look at me."

How could I? Looking at him would only magnify my feelings.

"Don't deprive me." His voice took on a darker tone.

Obeying his request, I allowed him to put me under a deep hypnosis.

"That's much better. I like to watch your eyes." He smirked, staring through me.

"Why?" I whispered.

"Because they're so expressive. They tell me things you're too afraid to say."

"What are they telling you now?"

"Everything I can't communicate with words."

He could have hosted his own international conference on how to sweet talk a woman. I'm sure thousands of guys could have borrowed a page or two from his handbook.

"Why do you always pull me in like a magnet?" I didn't mean to say that out loud.

"Is that what I'm doing?" His voice sounded rougher.

"Definitely."

Noah grabbed my thighs and yanked me forward.

Hyperventilation mode: enabled. Arousal level: maximum degree. Warning! System at risk of overheating! Overclocking the operating system. SYSTEM SHUT DOWN!

I couldn't think anymore. But to be honest, I loved the idea of being manhandled by Noah.

"Now, *this* is what I consider pulling you in." His sexy smile never disappeared from his face as I reddened and tried to control my impulses. We were siting much closer than before. All he had to do was lean forward and kill me with a kiss.

"And I'm not the magnet," Noah added. "*You* are. I can't stay away from you, even though I should." His mouth was inches from mine.

"You shouldn't," I whispered, wrapping my arms around his neck.

Teasing my lips, he licked them softly. He seemed to enjoy the way I teased him back, playfully biting his bottom lip.

"You make me crazy," he confessed between a kiss, sliding his fingers through my hair.

The stereo auto-switched to a seductive house track, awakening my sleeping sex goddess before I transformed into a stripper as I gave Noah a lap dance, swaying my hips, slow and hypnotic like a serpent. This wasn't just foreplay happening between us; it was deeper than that; it was a ritual. Noah had taken me to his sacred altar, and was initiating me to become his earthbound deity.

To trap me, or liberate me? I wondered, losing myself in imagination.

His body language showed his desire for me. His touch possessed magical properties, as if he were writing a prophesied destiny on my skin that the naked eye couldn't see. I could see it, though, when I closed my eyes. Foreign symbols glowed all over me, activated by every stroke of his fingertips, gliding down my shoulders, arms, and thighs. A divine foretelling was about to unfold. A psychic had once told me I possessed clairsentience, clairaudience, and clairvoyance. I didn't believe him, but now I questioned reality… including my lens of existence. If I was psychically gifted, would I even want to nurture that? What if it was more of a burden than anything?

My breathing became more labored when I felt Noah's lips on my neck. He teased me, placing soft kisses along my jugular. I moaned when he swirled his tongue over my exposed flesh, gently sinking his teeth into my skin before kissing the bruised area. Hanging my head back, I gave him easier access to my throat, panting in pleasure. Every sensation was intense. I had read an article a while back about "the battery effect" when yin and yang energies unified. It was supposed to activate spiritual ascension, releasing emotional blockages and trauma. Noah's magical touch healed me in ways I couldn't describe. I was addicted to every part of him.

"You don't want to do this with me, Aria."

"I do."

"This will permanently fuck us up."

"We're already fucked up."

I traced his chest to his shoulders while he left a trail of kisses to my collarbones. We both seemed possessed by a passionate flame that would not burn out. The veins in Noah's neck were pulsing as I leaned in and pressed my lips against his, surrendering to instant euphoria.

Pulling on the back of my dress, he wrinkled the fabric into his fist and groaned in pleasure. I wanted to taste his lust, and I finally found satisfaction when he kissed me hard, persuading my lips to open for him so he could finish tattooing me with his invisible scripture. I willingly surrendered to this fallen angel who was preparing me for the most crucial moment, when I would magnificently transform for him.

Panting between kisses, Noah slowly hiked up my skirt, sending chills through my body. He was untamed, and I loved it. Pulling back for breath, he wove my hair around his fist and tugged it firmly, forcing my head to tilt backward.

"You can't handle me," he said in a husky voice.

"What makes you think I can't?" I breathed, touching his pectorals.

"I have... dark impulses."

"So do I."

My stomach stiffened when he traced my jawline to my neck. I couldn't move. He still had his fist tangled in my hair. His lips must have been laced with some sort of psychedelic drug, because everything in the sky was moving at sonic speed. I watched the clouds clear away, unveiling a mass of sparkling stars while the earth spun like a cosmic globe. It was a trippy hallucination—a side effect of his kiss.

"I can make your darkness look like sunlight compared to mine." Noah slid his hand around the nape of my neck and coaxed my head forward. We were at eye level again. The sexual tension was killing me.

"I love the way you touch me," I said, caressing his heart chamber.

"Where do you want me to touch you?"

The intensity of his stare was turning me on in ways I never thought were possible.

"Here..." I guided his hand between my thighs, to the source of the heat.

"Aria, I won't be able to stop. I'm dead serious." The hunger in his eyes was palpable.

"I know." I leaned in, desperate for stimulation as waves of pleasure consumed me.

"Fuck..." Noah's breathing got heavier, rubbing my sweet spot.

Without warning, my body fell forward when he reclined his seat all the way. I steadied myself against his chest, disappointed that his hand was no longer between my thighs. He held my hips and looked up at me.

"You want me," I whispered in his ear, sensually kissing his jaw.

"Is it that obvious?" He throbbed beneath me.

"I can help you out with that." I reached for his belt buckle.

"I should stop you."

"You don't want to."

"Tell me to."

"No."

"Please?"

"Never."

Staring into his lust drenched eyes, I started unbuttoning his shirt while his shallow breaths got heavier. A force field of sexual energy circled around us like a cyclone—love mixed with lust, heat, sex, and sin.

"I don't like what you do to me," said Noah, caressing my thighs while I reached his last button.

"How come?" I pulled his shirt open, revealing his amazing abdominals. His body was unreal. I touched every undulating muscle with greedy hands.

"Because… Aria." His eyes pleaded for me to stop. But his voice betrayed him; he wanted me to continue.

"We can't fight the inevitable."

Our powerful connection seemed to strengthen the longer we stared at each other. Reaching for his fly, I was about to unzip it when he grabbed my wrist and yanked me forward.

"I love your aggressive side." I giggled, biting my lip.

"It's the quiet ones that are absolute psychos behind closed doors… don't forget that."

"Is that a threat?"

"Why do you perceive it that way?"

"Um… maybe because I view the world as a hostile place."

"Am I being hostile to you right now?" Noah caressed my arm, never taking his eyes off me.

"No…"

"Stay present. Your power is in the present moment, Aria. Always." He stroked my chin with his thumb. "It was a sexual innuendo—albeit, inappropriate."

"I like it when you're 'inappropriate.'"

"Is that right?"

I couldn't help but smile.

"You're such a bad influence on me." Noah sighed.

"I like being a—"

"Stop." He laughed. "How the fuck are we in this situation right now?"

"I don't know, but I don't mind your F-bombs. I think you should use them more often."

"*Tsk.*"

"No witty response?" I gasped. "I think I won this round!"

"I'm gonna tell you something, princess of hearts, so listen carefully." He raised himself on his elbows and stroked my face. "Every time you think you've won in a power struggle with me… it's just an illusion, because I've let you win."

"Is this your twisted way of reaffirming your power in this—whatever the fuck we are?"

"Perhaps."

"Well, allow me to show off my intellect and respond with: if you *let me* win… then who has true power over who? You became powerless the second you let me into your heart."

"I guess that explains all my karmic suffering through the years."

"You can either let me empower you at present… or you can choose to disempower yourself by pushing me away."

"And why would I do that?"

"Because I'm hell spawn."

"If you're 'hell spawn,' then what am I?" Noah asked.

"My maker."

"Don't remind me."

"Come on… it's kind of hot."

"No, it isn't. It's fucked up and wrong."

"And yet, here we are…" I caressed his chest, admiring his handsome features.

"It doesn't help that you look so damn kissable all the fucking time." He leaned in and let our lips collide, kissing me like a man on fire. The only way to douse the flames was through my lips. But the relief was just an illusion. I had only ignited the inferno.

Groaning in pleasure, Noah growled when I rocked into him. He gripped my peach and took control, grinding me against him. An uncontainable moan fled from my lips when he pulled me down harder, intensifying my primal need for penetration. The lace fabric of my thong was soaked. I couldn't concentrate on anything anymore. The only thing I was aware of was that I was kissing Noah. All he had to do was pull down his boxer briefs, shove my thong to the side, and it would be skin on skin.

"I'm a horrible father." He panted, breaking our kiss.

Guilty conscience. Right on time. Sigh.

I much preferred the dominant, uninhibited Noah who didn't give a fuck about rules or anyone else but me.

"You don't feel like my father," I said, rubbing his chest. "I can't stop fantasizing about sex with you. I've tried—but I can't. I don't understand it. I don't think any rules should apply to us." I raised his hand to my lips and slowly sucked on his index finger.

"Fuck… you need to stop that." He pulled his hand away, throbbing beneath me. "There are always rules to abide by, otherwise, there'd be chaos… anarchy."

"Maybe I enjoy being an anarchist. We've already broken some rules—why not break the rest?"

How could he reject me when I was willingly inviting him into my body? I knew exactly what I wanted. It would have been such a rush if we actually banged in his car, up there on that cliff. I knew I wasn't considering the aftermath. Thinking with logic was almost impossible; I was too lost in my emotions.

Mrs. Jennings's voice suddenly echoed in my head. She had been my eleventh-grade health teacher, and I remembered her mentioning how it was a good idea to carry condoms in the glove compartment of your car (just in case you would need them for later). I wondered if Noah had any.

"What are you doing?" he asked.

"Looking for something." I rummaged through the glove box until I felt a foil wrapper. "Nice to know you came prepared!" I simpered, flashing the Trojan. But my victory was short-lived when Noah grabbed my wrist and pulled me in. He stared me down with those fierce blue eyes.

"If we're gonna do this, then I won't be using *these*. Ever."

Ho-ly. Shit. My ovaries exploded as I opened my hand and let the condom fall.

"Good girl," he said with a wicked smile. "Don't move."

Gripping my waist, he thrust his hips into me, teasing me before he reclined in his seat.

"Hands on my chest."

I obeyed him.

"Closer."

Our lips were now inches apart.

"Stay still," he murmured.

Stroking my cheek, he stared through me with a penetrating gaze before he kissed me passionately. I shut my eyes, feeling his lips graze over mine, igniting a fire within me. Our mouths were wet and slick, fusing together in a flawless choreography. Nothing else mattered at that moment, just energy and sensation. Noah's tongue slid and smoothed over mine in a perfect rhythm. I trembled when he brushed his hand over the small of my back. Our passions intensified as a breathy moan fled from my lips. I could tell he wanted me, but was still holding back.

"You're so fucking beautiful." His kiss became needier.

I didn't want to stop. I only wanted more. It took every bit of strength to not abandon my self-control. The scent of his cologne was overpowering my senses as I breathed him in.

"I'm getting addicted to you," he confessed, pressing his hot lips against mine.

Passion poured from his kiss and swept through my entire body. A firestorm of lust blazed around us, engulfing us in flames, while the scorching heat of our sinful desires consumed us. Hoping that I'd break him, he impressively showed self-restraint.

"I want you."

"Aria…"

"You want me, too."

"I don't think I have a convincing argument to prove otherwise."

He pulsed beneath me, sending a tantalizing thrill through my core.

"Then take what you want." I kissed him hard, loving the way he growled.

Sliding his hands up my thighs, Noah reached for the edge of my thong and hooked his finger around it.

Oh God, this was it…

He must have tapped into superhuman strength, because our steamy scenario suddenly ended. The sex spell between us seemed to have broken when the music died.

Facing each other, we panted in the darkness. The only sounds that could be heard were the wind in the trees and the natural vibrations of wildlife around us.

"Not here, baby. Not like this." He readjusted his seat in the upright position.

I calmed my breathing and hugged his neck, whispering, "But you want me, right?"

"You already know the answer to that question." Noah hugged my waist, kissing my neck and shoulder.

"That feels amazing…"

"What, this?... [*kiss*]."

"Mhmm…"

"Maybe I should stop… [*kiss*]."

Don't you dare! I *loved* having my shoulders kissed by him; it made me feel warm and fuzzy inside.

Slipping into a lustful coma, I was disappointed when he pulled back. At least his seductive eyes were on me. Drawing in a breath, he held it for a few seconds and exhaled.

"We need to cool down." Noah leaned forward and turned on the stereo again, switching tracks to something mellower—not as sexually suggestive as the previous lineup of tunes. He turned down the volume before he cast his eyes on me and smiled.

Mood music and Noah: best combination.

Reaching down, he pulled on a lever and reclined on his back again. I smiled when he beamed at me.

"Let me hold you," he said.

The music was moving. I just felt things so deeply. It was more a curse than a blessing.

"Aria, what's wrong? Did I do something?" He searched my gaze.

This moment wouldn't last forever. It made me sad.

His feelings will change, just like Trevor's did.

My abandonment wound was something I still hadn't healed from. Tears filled my eyes as I looked away, not wanting Noah to see my face. A painful memory had resurfaced against my will: The last time I'd made out with a boy in a car was in a dumpy old parking lot in New York. He was a senior, and he almost forced me into putting out. Yet here I was, practically throwing myself at Noah, and he was man enough to control himself. Secretly, I was hoping he would make love to me once we were finally on our romantic getaway in Italy.

"You've done nothing wrong," I finally said. "You're amazing."

"Then why do you look like you're about to cry?" He sat up on his elbows and reached for my face.

"I'm not. It's just… everything feels intense with you, Noah. I can't seem to control my feelings around you."

He was quiet as he searched my eyes in the darkness.

"Come here."

Collapsing on his chest, I molded myself into him. A contented sigh left my lips when he wrapped his arms around my waist.

"You're an angel," Noah whispered. "Behold, your demon."

"You're not a demon." I listened to his heartbeat, enjoying the way he played with my hair.

"I've corrupted you… us. I thought I had changed. But I haven't. I guess I'm still that same asshole I was back in law school—no conscience."

"Don't say that." I frowned.

"You don't know what I was like, and I'm too ashamed to tell you."

Does Vanessa know? I wondered.

"I'm not a good man. I'm a demon, and a demon is not worthy of touching an angel."

"Aren't they basically the same thing?"

"You've got the good guys and the bad guys, and, well, I think it's obvious where I stand now."

"Is that what you really compare yourself to?"

"What if I am, Aria? What if I'm Lucifer's son, corrupting the world?"

No way. I was not living some fucked up sequel of *The Omen.*

"Well…" I arched an eyebrow. "If you are, then clearly Lucifer's been misunderstood."

"Why do you say that?" He chuckled.

"Because if the Devil is evil incarnate, how could his son possess the ability to love?" Leaning back, I placed his hand on my heart. "How could he care more about me than himself? Why would he tattoo my name on his chest?"

"He's cheating on his wife and lusting after his daughter. He's committing sin after sin. He's not as noble and chivalrous as his angel believes."

"He showed self-control when his angel couldn't."

"Maybe that's all part of his plan, to get his angel vulnerable enough so he can drag her to Hell with him."

"Maybe she's his salvation," I suggested, feeling my heart flutter when he gazed into my eyes. He looked so beautiful. Noah always looked strikingly handsome, even in the darkness. I wished I could peer into his mind and hear his thoughts.

"My chest feels lonely." He caressed my face.

Shifting my weight, I lay sideways and curled up in Noah's lap, resting my head in the crook of his neck. I felt the slow, drumming rhythm of his heart beating through my palm.

So perfect.

I did not want to move. I felt relaxed and safe. We cuddled like this for the longest while, caressing each other and enjoying the music.

ೞ

Fall out of the Heavens, and dive into a dream. For all is not as it may seem...

The sound of my voice echoed in my ears as I opened my eyes and looked at the time. It was a quarter to midnight, and only an hour had gone by. I had dreamed I was falling from a dark, thundering sky in slow motion. My arms had been reaching up toward an entity I could not see, but I wasn't afraid. I knew I must have had this dream because of all the talk of angels and demons. Being in Noah's arms made me feel safe. I didn't want the night to end. Wondering if he had passed out, I tilted my head and looked at him.

"Looking for stars?" I asked.

"I can see some, actually."

"Really?" I twisted my body, resting on his chest with my head cushioned against his shoulder.

Squeezing me tightly, he kissed my right temple. We were both staring up at the sky now with our fingers intertwined.

Tonight feels magical. Maybe those celestial goddesses had their prayers answered after all, I thought, mesmerized by the stars.

"We have to get home soon." Noah broke the silence.

"A few more minutes, please? I don't have school tomorrow."

"Oh, yeah. I forgot. I might take the day off then so we can hang out."

I hoped he would. I couldn't get enough of him.

We were quiet for a while, and then I said, "I love stargazing."

Brushing his lips along my earlobe, he whispered, "I love stargazing with *you.*"

I felt like I was one with his body. Everything was so perfect: the music, the secluded environment, and the mysterious diamonds that sparkled above us. It only added to the dreamy atmosphere of the night. A sense of calmness overcame me as soothing melodies carried me off to sleep like a lullaby.

CHAPTER THIRTY-ONE
THE WAITING GAME

Vanessa couldn't sleep. She had stayed up, worried about her husband's whereabouts. Her sister had kept her company while the minutes turned to hours.

"Vanessa, it's three in the morning!" Vienna paced the kitchen. "Where do you think they are?"

"I'm sure there's a reasonable explanation. Maybe his phone died."

"Aria's too?"

Vanessa had no answer.

"Honestly, who the hell stays out this late with their kid?"

"Stop it, Vi. Maybe something happened to them. I should call the cops."

They probably rented a motel room and did the nasty, thought Vienna. She poured herself a glass of milk and drank it down.

"I can't deal with this." Vanessa's patience expired as she dialed 911.

"You're actually calling the police? Look, if they were in an accident, the cops would have shown up at the door already."

Vanessa ignored her sister and started speaking to an emergency operator.

ဆပ

A handsome man in a dark suit walked into an impressive hotel in Venice, Italy. The first thing he did was check in at the front desk. He noticed some young women sitting on a cream sofa in the lobby. They eyed the good-looking gentleman and started gossiping in Italian about how attractive he was. Hearing their conversation, he smiled. Although he was not a native of the country, he understood the language.

"Here is your room key, sir. Do not hesitate to call the front desk if you should need for anything."

"Thank you…" Leaning forward, he read the concierge's name tag. "Vincenzo."

"Not a problem, Mr. Montague."

He was about to leave when he doubled back. "Has anyone else checked into my suite yet?"

"Forgive me for not mentioning this earlier. Ms. Capulet arrived about an hour ago. I believe she is waiting for you, sir. Allow me to summon a bellhop to assist with your luggage."

"That won't be necessary. Thank you." He smiled politely and headed for the elevators.

On the top floor, he walked down a luxurious hallway with marble floors. Music echoed in the distance. The recognizable melody made him smile; he knew it was coming from his suite. Lana Del Rey's beautiful voice got louder as he made his way to room 366.

Sliding his keycard into the security lock, he waited for the click and opened the door.

"Baby?" He shouted over the music. "I made it! I'm sorry I'm late—there was a delay in my flight!" Settling his luggage against the wall, he walked through the massive suite.

"Where are you, beautiful? I've got a surprise for you!" He thought about lowering the volume on the stereo but didn't want to waste any more seconds. All he wanted was to feel her in his arms and breathe her in.

"Are you playing hide and seek?" He chuckled, opening the bedroom door.

No… NO!

Frozen in shock, the chilling discovery made him paralyzed with fear.

"Aria… what have you done? Oh, my God!" Noah pulled her lifeless body into his arms while his brand-new suit got soaked in blood. Immediately, he tried to find her pulse, but it only heightened his panic.

"You can't be dead… you can't be! Don't leave me, Aria!"

Rocking her back and forth, he choked on tears, knowing his prayers would never be answered. His angel was dead. Someone had killed her.

⋘⋙

Gasping for breath, Noah opened his eyes and was so shaken up that he almost woke his daughter. She purred in his arms and snuggled up to him. Feeling thankful to find himself back in his car, he wiped the sweat off his forehead and tried to calm down. That nightmare had nearly given him a heart attack. It had felt so real, he thought. "Gods & Monsters" was playing on the stereo. He quickly shut it off. Lana's beautiful voice was now tainted; it had become a horrific trigger for him.

Glancing at the time on his phone, he cursed under his breath when he saw all the missed calls from his wife. He had to wake Aria and head home. This was going to be hard to explain to Vanessa, but he wasn't too worried about that. He was relieved his daughter was still alive and in his arms. That nightmare was the worst he had ever had. He prayed to God that it wasn't foreshadowing a tragic prophecy.

"I love you, Aria," Noah murmured in her ear. "I love you more than anything in this world." He softly kissed her head and lifted her off his lap. The Ferrari's engine roared to life before he put the car in reverse and headed home.

CHAPTER THIRTY-TWO
NOAH

Throughout my drive, my thoughts were consumed with the past and present. Nothing in life ever prepared me for this moment—not my mother's harsh discipline or my father's spiritual teachings on right and wrong. Before Aria, I was certain I knew who I was; my identity was never in question. My college years were tough, but after I kicked my drug habit, I knew I had found myself. Everything post-Aria was like organized chaos in my head. I knew what I was doing with my daughter was wrong on so many levels—actually, on every level possible—yet everything felt oddly natural. It wasn't thought out or planned. She was like a force of nature. Imagine the following scenario:

You're walking down a street on a bright sunny day, and suddenly a freak storm approaches out of nowhere. Thunder splits the sky as it pours. A powerful gust of wind pushes you in the opposite direction of your intended destination. Instinctively, you try to fight it and maintain your balance, so you grab on to something, anything. But there's nothing there for you to grab. You're in the middle of a hurricane, and you have no control anymore. There's no choice but to surrender, because when you've got winds coming at you at 115 mph, your fate is sealed. Everything had changed since Hurricane Aria had coasted into my life.

The black iron gates slowly creaked open before I pulled into the driveway and parked the Ferrari. I knew I'd have to drive it into the garage later, but right then, my only concern was getting my sleeping beauty into bed, safe and sound. Dawn was breaking as I got out of the car and headed to the house to unlock the front door.

Aria stirred in my arms when I carefully carried her out of her seat. Her hair smelled like strawberries. The sweet scent of her perfume had rubbed off on my shirt. I had texted Vanessa before driving home, but she had never responded, and I hadn't exactly come up with a good excuse as to why I was out so late with Aria. I was hoping I'd have enough time to think, and that Vanessa was fast asleep and not waiting up for me.

Quietly, I carried Aria through the foyer and walked down the long corridor.

"Where the hell have you been?"

I froze.

That voice was familiar, but it wasn't my wife's. Reluctantly, I turned around and faced my sister-in-law.

"We've been worried sick!" Vanessa appeared by Vienna's side. "Where have you been all night, Noah? I called the freaking cops, thinking you were both lying dead in a ditch somewhere!"

It was worse than I'd thought: they were tag-teaming against me. Aria's eyes flickered open.

Great.

I didn't want to wake her.

"Close your eyes," I whispered before I looked at my wife. "Let me get her into bed first."

I could hear the two of them muttering things behind my back, which was irritating the fuck out of me, but I controlled my flaring temper and made it to Aria's bedroom.

"Noah… where…" She woke up half disoriented. "Where are—"

"Go to sleep, beautiful. We're home now. You're in your bedroom." I took off her heels and set them down on the floor. "Rest."

"Don't go." She reached for my arm.

"I have to, Aria. I'll check on you later." I didn't want to leave her, but I had no choice. Kissing her forehead, I walked out and made my way back to the living room, where two pissed-off sisters were waiting for me. This would not be fun.

"Well?" Vienna glared at me, as if I had committed a crime. It was a little unnerving. "Are you gonna explain yourself?" She folded her arms in her chest and tapped her slipper on the floor.

"We fell asleep." I sighed in frustration.

"Fell asleep?"

"Yes." I regarded my wife. "I took Aria out for dinner in the evening, and then we got some donuts and parked the car by the beach to talk. She was feeling down and had a lot on her chest. I was trying to comfort her all evening."

I hated lying. Hated it.

"She had a big cry," I continued, "and fell asleep because it tired her out—by that time it was almost midnight. I wanted to take a quick power nap before driving home… woke up a few hours later, realizing that I'd lost track of time. My phone was on silent because I didn't want to be disturbed while she was opening up to me. I sent you a text as soon as I got up, but you didn't text me back, so I figured you were sleeping."

"I called the police, Noah. I thought something terrible had happened!" Vanessa walked over to me and hugged my waist. "I'm so relieved you're okay."

"I'm sorry I worried you."

Vienna's scowl refused to disappear.

"*Both* of you," I added, though it still didn't turn her frown upside down.

"You better let Officer Raymond know they're back," said Vi.

"I will." Nessa grabbed the cordless phone.

"You should get some sleep, Vienna." I tried to smile. "Today's your last day with us—let's make the best of it."

"Yeah, I bet you're happy I'm leaving soon."

"Uh… what is that supposed to mean?"

What the fuck? Where is all this hostility coming from? I wondered. *Maybe she's ticked off about Evan.*

"Relax, I'm kidding—and yeah, I need to sleep." She yawned and turned to leave.

I was about to head into the kitchen and make some coffee when my wife finished her phone call and stepped in front of me.

"Okay, it's all taken care of. Let's head upstairs and sleep, honey."

"Actually, I'm not tired anymore. I was thinking I'd shower and get some work done before noon."

"Noah, take the day off. You're always working. Give it a rest, please, at least for today."

Stall, stall, stall—it was all I could do at the moment.

"Give me an hour and then I'll join you."

"No." She shook her head and pulled my arm. "Those cases can wait. You need to sleep."

I tried to object, but before I knew it, Vanessa dragged me into our bedroom and was slowly undressing me.

"I can disrobe myself," I stated.

"I know." She smirked, unbuckling my belt.

I stopped her before she tried to do anything more. "Get in bed. I'll be right with you."

"As you wish." She stripped down to her panties and slid under the covers.

I left my boxers on and got in next to her. I was about to close my eyes and sleep when I felt her hand move down my stomach. "Vanessa, I'm tired." Grabbing her wrist, I slipped it away from my cock.

"Oh, all right." She sighed and kissed my cheek. "You'll probably have more energy when you wake up."

Feeling guilty for rejecting her, I had promised Aria that I wouldn't sleep with Vanessa, and I didn't want to let her down.

What do you think this means, Noah? She's your wife, yet your loyalty lies with your daughter. Think about this long and hard. What... do... you... think... this... means?

Christ, not again. I grabbed a pillow and placed it over my ear as I turned and tried to fall asleep.

CHAPTER THIRTY-THREE
ARIA

Waking up alone was disappointing. I'd had a deep sleep, and although I didn't dream of Noah, last night definitely felt like a dream. For a second, I thought I was late for school, but then I remembered I had no classes. This Monday morning didn't have to suck, and I welcomed it with a big smile. Last night's memories filled my mind. Everything had been so perfect and romantic. It still didn't bother me knowing I was engaging in a risky relationship with Noah. How could I explain these feelings to my friends? No one would understand. Imagine how that conversation would go if I told my mom about him and me. I was sure she would collapse from shock or call the cops right away. The sheer thought made me shudder in fear. I never wanted to get him in trouble with the law. I was an adult now, free to make my own decisions. I was in love with him, and there was no way I would let him take the fall if we ever got caught. This was something *I* wanted. The world didn't have to understand. All that mattered was that we understood each other. From the moment we met, Noah got me in ways no one else could. He could read my emotions without me even breathing a word. He gave me all the affection and love I needed. But the more he gave, the greedier I got. Fatherly affection wasn't enough anymore.

Forcing myself out of bed, I headed for the bathroom and took a quick shower before I blow-dried my hair and dressed myself. It was ten in the morning when I walked into the kitchen. No one else seemed to be awake.

Maybe Noah's in his study. I smiled at the thought and skipped downstairs to wake him up with a sexy surprise… but he wasn't there. He had probably gone to work, even though he'd mentioned taking the day off. Stepping into the garage, I checked to see if his cars were parked.

Oh God, please don't tell me he's sleeping next to her.

I didn't want to believe it, but somehow my feet took me upstairs, straight to their bedroom.

He's at work. He's at work, I repeated in my head, approaching the white double doors.

Reaching for the doorknob, I took a deep breath before I slowly opened it and peered inside.

This can't be real… Why did I come up here?

Crystal tears misted my vision and fell down my face. I wasn't prepared for this discovery. Vanessa was spooning with Noah. They were under the covers, and I was certain they were sleeping in the nude because all their clothing was on the floor.

He slept with her. How can he do this to me?

I felt like I had woken up from a beautiful dream, only to realize that I was stuck in a sick, nightmarish reality. I couldn't stomach watching any longer. That heart-shattering image was already burned into my brain.

Rushing down the stairs, I tried not to make too much noise, but I feared my stifled cries were louder than my feet hitting the floor.

Why does Vanessa always have to ruin every amazing memory I create with Noah? Does she know about us? Maybe I was just losing my mind… yeah… definitely.

Collapsing in bed, I buried my face in a pillow. I wanted to give Noah the benefit of the doubt, but my jealousy was interfering with my logic. I was hurt and angry. Separating my emotions from certain situations had always been difficult for me. With a heavy heart, I cried in silence, feeling so betrayed. He'd promised me to keep her in the friend zone. Was he so sexually frustrated that he'd needed an easy lay? As if that was supposed to make my wounded ego feel better… it didn't. Even if Noah was using

Vanessa for sex, he hurt me deeply. I didn't want him to share any part of himself with her—or any other woman. I was possessive of him, and I hated it.

Finding him in bed with my stepmom crushed me. He'd been so unbelievably sweet the previous night. What we had shared with one another wasn't just "fooling around"—it was so much more. We had connected on a physical and emotional level. At no time had I felt guilty or dirty. Making out with Noah made me feel pure and loved. I knew he was still freaked out by everything that was going on between us. It had all happened so fast. But that was expected since we ignored our attraction for six months; it was bound to avalanche over us. All those feelings had hit me with an unbelievable impact.

Sitting up, I wiped my tears away, refusing to let him screw me up like this. Noah was the only man who could hurt me so much. I would not imprison myself in my room all day and cry my eyes out. No, I was going to get *even.*

Hoping that Vienna was still asleep, I tiptoed into her room. Her iPhone was on the nightstand next to her bed. All I had to do was reach over and grab it. At least she didn't sleep in the nude—although if she'd been sleeping next to Noah, I doubt she would have kept her clothes on either. I knew I wouldn't.

Careful not to wake her, I stealthily grabbed the cellphone and scrolled down her contact list. Evan Alderson, Evan Gallagher… Jeez, how many Evans did she know?

Found him! I memorized his number and placed her phone back in its original position. It helped to have photographic memory.

Vienna suddenly shifted on her side, and I freaked out because I thought I had woken her. This was my cue to get the hell out of there. Leaving her bedroom, I pulled out my cell and saved Evan's number before I'd forget.

Guess who's texting u? ;)

I had no idea why I was nervous. Half a minute later, my cellphone vibrated:

Britney?

I stared at the name and texted:

Nope.

Ten seconds later:

Jill?

It had never occurred to me he was popular with the ladies. My uncle was good-looking—that shouldn't have surprised me.

Try again.

I waited and received another incoming message.

Um… Kiki?

Not even close.

It took him a little while to text me back this time.

Look sweetheart, if ur the chick I banged last night, the sex is all I can remember. In which case, I strongly urge u to tell me ur name, and preferably ur location if ur looking to get some more of what I gave u last night ;) Or we could just meet up @ that strip club again…

Well, this had got awkward.

It's Aria :/

Seconds turned to minutes before a sudden dread took over me. I had probably embarrassed him. Stepping into my bedroom, my cellphone finally vibrated.

Shit, I'm sorry. Plz delete the last few texts from ur phone… and ur brain.

No problemo.

Although it wouldn't be as simple to press "Delete" on everything I'd just read in his previous text. But I did what he asked and cleared my SMS inbox.

Done :)

Another text came through:

I was afraid I wouldn't hear from u. I'm glad u texted :)

He hadn't seen how Noah had ripped up his number right in front of me.

Can we hang out today?

Is Noah cool with that?

I had two choices: lie or tell him the truth. And since I was just getting to know my uncle, I figured our friendship wouldn't start off on the right foot if it was built on lies, so I texted:

Technically, no…

Please respond, please respond…

Even better :) Want me to pick u up?

I'd been expecting him to be reluctant, but it didn't seem to bother him at all.

Can we meet @ the food court inside Westfield Century City Mall @ 12:30pm?

He responded much faster this time.

Sure can. see u there :)

I noticed he had a habit of texting the same way I did—shortening the words with abbreviations and adding emojis. I was about to get dressed when my phone rang.

"Hey, Jess, what's up?" I said. "Oh, crap… I totally forgot… No, it's fine… It's just that I made plans with my uncle… Yeah, he's in LA… No, we can still go shopping… Sure… Okay, I'll see you then." I hung up and tossed my phone on my bed.

I had forgotten that I'd made plans to go shopping with Jessica. But it was fine. It wasn't like I was spending the whole day with Evan.

∞

Skipping breakfast, I hung out in my room for the next hour, waiting for Jess to pick me up. I could have driven to the mall myself, but I didn't want to drive that Firebird. It belonged to Noah. Even though he had relinquished ownership to me, I couldn't bring myself to get in the driver's seat while upset at him.

I remembered how Jade, Ally, and I used to take the subway everywhere. Living in a huge house with a big pool and expensive luxury vehicles was not something I was used to.

I was in the middle of reapplying my makeup when someone rapped on my door.

"Come in, I'm decent."

The door opened, and in walked his royal highness himself. Noah was all smiles, but I ignored him and devoted my attention to my mascara.

"Hey, beautiful."

"Hi," I replied in a flat tone.

"You're looking extra pretty today." He walked over to me and placed his hands on my shoulders. "What's the occasion?"

"I'm going to the mall with Jess. She's picking me up soon."

"Oh." He looked disappointed.

Don't look at him! Eyes on the makeup! I dipped my mascara brush back inside the waterproof liquid and applied it to my other lashes when something caught my attention: Noah had thrown down a shiny black credit card next to me.

"Take that with you—buy whatever you want."

"I don't need it."

He would not bribe my love.

"Aren't you girls going on a shopping spree?"

"No, we're just hanging out at the mall and meeting up with some friends for lunch."

"Is Ryan gonna be there?" He said his name with contempt.

"Not that I know of... he might show up."

Does that make you paranoid, Noah?

"What time should I expect you home?"

I wanted to scream, *never* but controlled myself.

"Probably around four, the latest."

"Are you all right?" he asked.

Placing down my mascara, I looked at him through the mirror. "I'm fine."

"Are you sure? Because normally when a woman says 'she's fine,' that's code for 'No, I am *not* fine, and you definitely *should* worry about it.'"

Damn you and all your thirty-three years of wisdom.

"I have no reason not to be fine." I shrugged, forging a smile.

"Please, Aria, I can tell when you're getting passive aggressive on me. Your mother was the same."

"I'm not my mother," I bitterly replied.

It wasn't like I hated my mom. We were just two different people, and I wanted him to acknowledge my individuality. I didn't like to be compared; Rob had done enough of that throughout my childhood.

Gathering my hair, I tied it in a high ponytail so that Noah would stop playing with it.

"Did I upset you last night?"

"No." I pulled my chair back and stood up. I was wearing a red flower-printed sundress, with the hem resting above my knees. The featherweight fabric hugged my body around the waist.

"Why are you being so…" He paused when I met his eyes.

"So… what?"

"Distant."

"I'm not."

"You're hardly making eye contact with me."

Yeah, there's a reason for that.

My cellphone suddenly rang.

"It's Jessica." I picked up the call and grabbed my handbag. "Hey, Jess, I'll be right out."

"Aria, wait…"

I moved the phone away from my mouth and looked at Noah. "I won't be home late."

Pivoting on a swift heel, I left my bedroom and headed out the door.

"Pick up your phone when I call you!" he yelled out, but I ignored him and got into Jessica's pink BMW.

"Everything all right?" she asked, chewing on gum.

"Yes, just drive."

"Okay, babes." She turned up an Avicii track on the stereo and sped down the driveway.

CRO

We strolled into the mall around a quarter to one. I was ten minutes late and not happy about it.

"I hope he's still here," I said, fidgeting with the bracelet Noah had given me. I hadn't taken it off, despite my anger, which contradicted the way I stubbornly refused to drive the Firebird.

You're just a walking contradiction, I said to myself.

During the drive, I'd told Jess about my uncle, and how Noah didn't want me seeing him. At least she understood I needed more family in my life.

"Aria, you're not that late. Chill out. Are you sure you don't want me to stay with you?"

"Yes, I can handle this. We're just gonna have lunch and talk. I don't need you to hold my hand, Jess."

"Sheesh, you're edgy today, aren't you?"

"Sorry, I didn't get enough sleep last night."

She had no idea.

"Were you out with *Ryyyyan?*"

"No." I quickly sent Evan a text and scanned the food court, hoping I'd find him sooner than later.

"Well, that's too bad. You two should start dating already. I mean, come on, Aria. Please tell me you're at least considering him as your prom date."

"Yeah… Can we please have this conversation another time?"

She sighed. "Okay, fine. I'm gonna meet Steph and Chrissie upstairs at the H&M store—"

"Found him!" I beamed, ignoring everything else she shared with me. "Where?"

"See the brown-haired guy sitting by that table near Subway? He's wearing a gray T-shirt."

Turning her line of sight, Jessica's jaw dropped. "Whoa—it's official. Good looks *definitely* run on your dad's side of the family. I have to ask again, are you sure you don't want me to stay?"

"I'll text you and come find you girls when I'm done having lunch with Evan." I hadn't told her he was adopted. Not yet.

"Okay, good luck!" She gave me a quick hug and headed toward an escalator.

I appreciated her coming with me. Jess was a great friend. Ally and Jade would love her, I thought as I calmed my nerves and approached my handsome uncle.

"Hey, Evan!" I smiled shyly, tucking my hair behind my ear.

"Aria!" His face lit up. "I was thinking you had changed your mind." He got to his feet and gave me a big bear hug. This took me by surprise, but I hugged him back. Evan didn't wear the same cologne as Noah, but he still smelled good. I think it's safe to say I had a fetish for men's hygiene products.

"Sorry for the holdup. My friend drove me here."

"No worries, love." His smile never left his face. "What would you like to eat?"

I wasn't very hungry. I couldn't eat when I was feeling so nervous. "I'll have a Greek salad."

"Are you trying to watch your figure?"

"No." I laughed anxiously.

"Good, because you don't need to."

He made me blush.

"I had a heavy breakfast," I explained, "so I'm not hungry at the moment."

"Okay, sit tight and I'll order our food. What would you like to drink?"

"Bottled water, please."

"Look at you, Miss Health Freak."

My cheeks went from pink to scarlet.

"I'm just teasing you, Aria."

Crap, he noticed. I laughed it off and watched him stand in line to order our food.

What was it about him that intrigued me so much? I couldn't figure it out. I loved his voice and British accent. He made me shy. I didn't know what I would ask him once we'd sit down to talk. Maybe this was a bad idea. I'd probably end up embarrassing myself. My motive behind this excursion was strictly to piss off Noah. Childish, I know.

Evan shortly returned, holding a tray full of food, and sat across from me. The food court was crowded, but not so much in our area. The sushi bar and burger joint had more hungry customers occupying the seats near the restaurant counters.

"What did you get?" I asked.

"A turkey sub on whole wheat with lettuce, tomatoes, green peppers, cucumbers, Swiss cheese, and honey mustard—oh, and it's toasted."

"That's exactly what I order whenever I eat at Subway!"

"I know." He chuckled.

"Are you psychic?"

Evan shook his head. "I just meant I know this is the *best* damn sub ever—doesn't surprise me you order the same thing." He took a bite of his food and chewed, while I stabbed my salad with a fork.

"You sure you don't want some?" he asked.

"No, I'm good." I smiled. Thankfully, my salad didn't have any black olives. The server must have forgotten to add them in when they were prepping my order. I wasn't complaining.

"Tell me something, Aria." Evan took a sip of his Coke and gave me his undivided attention. "What made you decide to go against Daddy's wishes and secretly organize a rendezvous with me?" The way he said *rendezvous* made our meeting sound so scandalous.

I had never seen a pair of brown eyes that looked so attractive before. It only added to his sex appeal.

"I feel like…" I struggled to find the words. "I have a right to decide whether I want to know you."

"That's very bold of you." Evan smirked. "I like that."

I looked down at my leafy greens and took another bite.

"So, let me guess," he said. "You lied and told Noah you were going shopping with your mates for the afternoon, right?"

"Are you trying to make me feel guilty?" I laughed.

"Is that what you feel?"

Leaning closer, his mouth curved up into a lazy smile.

"No." I paused and thought about it some more. "Well, maybe a little."

Evan drank his soda and stared at me, amused by my indecisiveness.

"All right, yes—" I said. "But I have my reasons."

"I'm sure you do." He chuckled lightly. "We all do."

"I'm eighteen now. I can make my own choices."

"It doesn't matter how old you get, you're always gonna be his baby, and he's always gonna be protective of you."

Fair enough.

"Noah's a control freak," he said. "He loves to control people. I feel sorry for you."

"He's not so bad." I felt compelled to defend him, despite how betrayed I felt inside. "How old are you again?" I asked.

"I'll be turning twenty-eight in November, so let's do the math. That makes me…"

"Twenty-seven." I giggled.

"And you recently had your birthday. April sixth, to be exact."

"Yeah—wait, how did you know that?"

"Noah used to talk about you a lot."

"He did?"

"Yes." Evan nodded. "Why does that surprise you?"

"I don't know." I wasn't sure if now was a good time to explain my daddy issues.

"You felt abandoned," he said. "I don't blame you. Grandma Hunter's a crazy bitch."

That was certainly very forward of him.

"Your dad and I used to be close at one point," he added.

"What happened between you two?"

"Everything went downhill after the accident at the lake house." There was an intense sadness in his eyes. Instinctively, I reached out and touched his hand.

"That's exactly what it was, though," I said, "an accident. I think Noah didn't have the chance to grieve properly, so it was probably more convenient to blame it all on you."

Evan stayed quiet and studied me, making me feel self-conscious. I kept thinking he was looking for flaws in my face—though it was probably just my inner critic projecting and jumping to conclusions.

"I never thought about it that way," he said after a while. "You're wise beyond your years, which I'm sure you hear a lot."

I nodded with a smile, retrieving my hand.

"I want to share a secret with you," said Evan.

"Tell me."

He wiped his mouth with a napkin and placed it on his tray. "I have a God-given gift."

"Oh? What's that?" I was genuinely curious.

"I have this ability to read people—and not just read their personalities. I can tap in so deep into their minds that I'm able to connect a chain of events that actually occurred in their lives."

"I knew it." I laughed. "You're psychic."

"Not at all." He shook his head and took another sip of Coke through his straw. "The eyes can say and betray so much. You just have to read them. They have a language of their own. A person could walk into a room with the biggest smile on their face, fake all the happiness in the world, and still fool everybody around them. But they wouldn't be able to fool me, because I know the truth. It's all in the eyes, Aria."

"Then try it on me." Losing interest in my salad, I shoved it aside and folded my arms over the table. Evan stared at me, and I started giggling. I couldn't keep a straight face.

"You don't need to widen them like that, love." He laughed. "Relax your expression and stare at me."

It was hard to stay serious, but I took a deep breath and stared back at him. I wasn't sure if he was trying to hypnotize me or if that was naturally occurring while gazing into those dark pools of mystery.

"All your life," Evan began, "you grew up feeling misunderstood and alone, like it was you against the world. You have two grandparents who were there for you and practically raised you in your infancy, since your mum was still trying to get her shit together." He paused for a moment and navigated through me.

"Your mother got married, and your stepdad hasn't exactly been a good role model for you. You wanted him to be the type of father who would come to all your plays and dance recitals. Instead, he spent his free time getting drunk in front of the telly with a beer in his hand."

Okay, the first part he could've already known. Maybe he'd overheard that tidbit of information during family discussions regarding me. The part he mentioned about my stepdad, however… how could he possibly have known that?

"He would beat you and your mum after a drinking binge, too, huh?"

This wasn't fun anymore.

"All you ever wanted was to be loved, accepted, and respected. But you never really felt that from anyone. You love your half-siblings, yet you're not very close. You resent them because you feel they are more valuable than you. That bastard kept impregnating your mum while she popped them out, one after another, and dumped the responsibilities on you. Why? Because she had to work full-time to make ends meet. You missed out on some crucial stages in your childhood."

I was almost on the verge of tears. Evan didn't know about the twins. Mom went through only one pregnancy with Rob.

"And then Noah suddenly comes to the rescue, and you hate him. You hold a grudge against him for abandoning you. I bet you wanted nothing to do with him, but he won custody in court and forced you to come here."

"That's where you're wrong," I said. "I didn't hate Noah when I first met him. I didn't even hate him when I was a kid. It just hurt not having him there. I came to California of my own free will. He never forced me."

"I see." Evan smiled and finished the rest of his sandwich.

"I think you're just good at psychology."

"And yet I never got straight A's in school."

We both laughed and made lighter conversation. He told me about his charity housing projects and what it was like to give back to communities in Haiti. He planned on building his own house one day, but he wasn't sure of the location yet. I asked him if he had anyone special in his life, and he openly talked about his relationship with his ex-girlfriend—how she'd emotionally crippled him. This Ashley woman basically screwed him over. She was the reason he had such a hard time trusting women. My heart went out to him. I knew what it was like to feel dead inside and afraid to trust. I couldn't understand why Noah hated him. Yes, Evan had made his fair share of mistakes (which he briefly discussed), but he didn't deserve to be burned at the stake.

"I hope you don't mind me asking you this, but Noah mentioned you were, um"—I hesitated—"a bit of a pyromaniac."

"Did he now?" Evan laughed out loud, shaking his head. "I had a fascination with fire when I was eight years old. I used to light matches constantly and toss them anywhere and everywhere. One time, I accidentally set the east wing of our house on fire because I wanted to see if the match would burn the drapes. Obviously, it did. Fortunately for me, no one got hurt. Dad had to renovate that entire side of the property."

"Wow…" I was at a loss for words.

"Yeah, I was a naughty one. But it wasn't like I was evil by nature or trying to be bad on purpose. I was just naturally curious. Unlike the cat, my curiosity did *not* kill me."

"Yeah, seriously," I replied in disbelief. "I'm glad you're still here, though. You seem nice."

Nice? Really, Aria? You're basically a walking thesaurus, and of all the words to describe him, you choose "nice"? My ego was giving me a beating. It was probably my karma for lying to Noah.

"I'm parched." Evan reached for my bottled water. It was half full, but he drank it all down in three big gulps.

"Apologies, love. I always get thirsty after I eat. I'll buy you another."

"It's okay. I was done with it, and I can't eat any more of this."

"You know, in most impoverished countries, people never let food go to waste." He grabbed my bowl of salad and slid it in front of him. "We shouldn't take the most basic things that are crucial to our survival for granted."

"Now you're making me feel bad." I sighed.

"Trust me, if you saw what I saw down there, you'd think twice before dumping a plate of food away." His compassion for humanity touched me.

"I'll keep that in mind next time."

"Good girl." He smirked and devoured my salad.

₧)(₧

We wound up talking much longer than I'd expected. Two hours flew right by without us even realizing it. I covered a lot of details about my life, and Evan shared more about his travels abroad. He made me feel like he was someone I could trust. It only dawned on me to check the time when his cellphone rang.

"Hey, Gary… Are you sure…? Well, put Anderson up to the job… He quit? Are you serious?... bloody hell… Look, I'll be there soon—twenty minutes tops." Evan hung up and looked at me. "I love being my own boss, but I have to get back to work, love."

"Is everything all right?"

"It's more an inconvenience than anything. One of my guys just quit."

"Oh, that sucks. I'm sorry."

"Sorry?" He furrowed his brows. "Why should you be sorry? Never apologize for something that's not your fault. Promise me that, Aria." His eyes were serious as he reached out and held my wrist.

"I promise." I watched his expression relax.

"I'll hold you to it." Evan winked at me, encouraging another smile to touch my lips.

Grabbing our trays, he stood up and threw out the empty contents in the trash. I followed him and we exited the food court together.

"So," he said, "are you gonna hang out with your mates for the rest of the day?"

"Well, that was the plan, but I want to get home. I have a project I need to work on. Can you give me a lift?"

"Of course, sweetheart. But uh, if your dad sees me, I'm sure he'll ground you for at least six months."

"That's quite a harsh punishment."

"I don't think you want to spend your summer under house arrest."

"He won't put me under house arrest—he won't even ground me because he can't."

There was no way in hell I would let him do that.

"You sound so sure."

"Well, it's not without reason."

"I'll take your word for it." Evan chuckled.

I quickly texted Jessica and told her that my uncle would drive me home.

"Before we go, could you do me a huge favor?" he asked.

"Sure."

"I want a picture of you on my phone. Do you mind?"

I hated posing for photos, but I pushed through the discomfort and said, "No, not at all."

"Give me a big smile." Evan held up his phone, angling it just right.

I tried to smile as naturally as possible—and then came the blinding flash.

"I think I blinked."

"No, it turned out perfect." He stared at my photo. "You're very photogenic."

I blushed. "Can I take one of you?"

"On one condition."

"Which is?"

"We take a picture together."

He made me smile again as he wrapped his arm around my waist and pulled me closer to his buff body.

"Wait—hold it," he said.

I lowered my phone and looked at him.

"I just remembered something. We have this great-aunt in the family, Aunt Joanie. You can't help but laugh when you see her pictures in the family photo album because all her facial expressions are the same. She never smiles or laughs. I was taking a photo with her one afternoon, during my thirteenth birthday party, and Mum kept taking picture after picture, wasting my time because Aunt Joanie wouldn't smile. It was like she was physically incapable of smiling. Finally, I got frustrated, stood up, and told her that a dog's arse had more facial expressions than her."

I burst out laughing—and that's when Evan started taking a bunch of pictures of me.

"Oh my gosh, no!" I said. "I look horrible!"

"Not even close. I told you that story on purpose to get you to laugh up a storm. Would you like to hear the conclusion?"

"Yes." I giggled some more.

"Well, ironically, after I said that to her, the old bag laughed her arse off."

"No way!"

"I kid you not. But my mum was pissed at me for being so rude. I was just being honest. Anyway, get your camera ready." He hung his arm over my shoulder, and we took turns taking pictures on our phones.

"Thanks for that," I said, dropping my cell in my handbag.

"Don't mention it."

"We better go. I don't want you to be late for work."

"I don't care if that house burns down—you're worth it."

ଓଓ୭୦

Luckily, we didn't hit any traffic on the drive back to my place. Evan didn't drive a luxury vehicle like Noah did. His whip was a black '67 Impala that direly needed a carwash. He stopped the car in front of my driveway and looked at me.

"Will I see you again?" I asked, unbuckling my seat belt.

"If you like." He flashed a charming smile. "Text or call—I'm usually free after seven, depending on my work hours." Leaning forward, he peered through my window. "You better get inside before *you know who* sees us."

The only reason I had asked Evan to drive me home was so that Noah would see me with him. I guess the rebel within wanted to piss him off after what I'd seen that morning.

"Hey, Aria," Evan called out. "Thanks for contacting me. I know you don't know me too well, but I hope that in time you'll see that I'm someone you can count on."

"You're sweet." I smiled.

"Just being honest, love." He matched my expression.

I was about to leave when Noah's angry voice echoed in the distance. He had burst through the front door, staring right at us.

"Aria!"

Mission accomplished.

"I'll text you later." I kissed Evan on the cheek before stepping out. "You better go before he tries to fight you."

"He wouldn't win. Tell my brother I said hi." He smirked, cranking the volume on his stereo before he floored it out of the driveway.

I watched him leave the gates and turned around, colliding with Noah.

"What the hell were you doing in his car?"

Noah's furious eyes pierced through me.

"Um… hello to you too…"

"Answer me, Aria!"

"Calm the fuck down!"

"Watch your mouth!"

"As if a cuss word even hurts your feelings." I rolled my eyes.

"Quit being a brat and answer my question!"

I folded my arms in my chest and sighed. "We ran into each other at the mall. He offered to drive me home, so I let him." I brushed past Noah and entered the house. He followed and slammed the door shut, making me jump.

"Don't lie to me." His tone was threatening.

"I'm not." I tried to meet his eyes, but I just couldn't. Ignoring his interrogation, I headed straight to my room.

"Noah, honey, what's going on?"

The last thing I needed was my stepmom sticking her nose in my business.

"Nothing you need to worry about," he calmly answered and came after me. "Aria!"

I closed my bedroom door, which was essentially pointless since my lock was broken. Noah stormed through the door and slammed it so hard that it thrust me into a flashback: my arguments with Rob.

"Since when do you lie to me?"

"Stop shouting! Have you gone completely psycho!?"

"You haven't seen psycho, but I'm sure Evan will show you if you keep sneaking off with him."

"The only person who is acting psychotic right now is *you*!"

"Really? Why? Because I'm pissed off?"

"I don't like to be yelled at! My parents did enough of that in my household."

My bottom lip quivered as I hugged myself and stepped back. I did not want to cry.

Noah exhaled and tried to compose himself. Disappointment and outrage—it was all on his face.

"Why did you lie to me, Aria?"

"Because you lied to *me*!" I seethed.

"What the hell are you talking about?" He frowned, resting his hands on his hips.

"You know exactly what I'm talking about."

"Are we gonna do the same song and dance every time we argue? Act like an adult, please."

"Trust me, Noah. You don't wanna do this with me right now." I lowered my voice. "Not when your wife's at home."

"Is that a threat?" He slit his eyes.

"I don't know. Is it?"

"Will you please just tell me what the fuck is going on?"

I looked away from his compelling eyes and tried to soothe my nervous system.

"Why were you riding in a car with my brother?" he snapped.

A shuffling sound caught our attention as we looked at my door.

Are they eavesdropping? I can easily solve this, I thought, turning on my music at full blast.

CHAPTER THIRTY-FOUR
SECRETS AND LIES

"Vi, what are you doing?"

"*Shhh!* I can't hear them when you're talking," she confessed. "Is that Chevelle she's blasting in there? That was my favorite band back in the day."

"Aria's a rebellious teenager. They live for that die-hard rock music. What more do you expect?" Vanessa grabbed her sister's arm and pulled her away from the door. "Noah's trying to discipline her. Stop eavesdropping."

"Well, he's doing a pretty poor job. I would have broken that iPod by now. Don't you think you should be in there with him? She's your daughter now, too."

"If Noah needs me, I'm more than happy to help." She paused. "Are you all packed? You have a flight to catch tonight."

"Yeah."

"Come on, give me a hand in the kitchen. I want to bake some brownies."

"Oh, please, we both know you can't bake a cupcake to save your life." Vienna laughed as they walked down the hall. She was disappointed that she hadn't gathered enough evidence to incriminate Noah. Determined as she was to expose him, she couldn't pause her personal life to save her sister's.

Vanessa was about to wash her hands in the sink when her cellphone vibrated:

Down for a quickie tonight? I miss that sweet ass ;)

Amir had texted her.

"Who's giving you the giggles over there?" Vienna asked, opening the refrigerator.

"Oh, just one of my friends from work—Hannah. She sends me these funny tweets now and then." Vanessa forced a short laugh and quickly responded to Amir's text:

Not tonight, sex machine. How about tomorrow during lunch, same place? xx

Waiting for a reply, her phone chimed again.

I'll be there. Bring those furry handcuffs and your vibrator ;) :P

The man never held back with the graphic emojis (not that Vanessa minded), laughing at the row of eggplants. Deleting his texts, she finished her task and gave her sister a hand. The last time she'd slept with Amir was two weeks ago.

I really need to get laid, she said to herself. Vanessa had an itch that desperately needed to be scratched.

CHAPTER THIRTY-FIVE
ARIA

Our arguing hadn't stopped. It was only getting worse as Noah and I battled through a shouting match.

"You broke your promise to me!" I cried. "I thought you were sleeping in your study when I went looking for you this morning. You weren't there. I thought you'd gone to work, but the cars were in the garage… went upstairs and found you both in bed… naked!"

"Aria, listen." Noah softened his eyes and came toward me. He parted his lips to speak, but stopped and rubbed his temples. "This music's driving me nuts!"

"Don't turn it off! They'll hear us arguing."

Pete Loeffler was halfway through singing "Send the Pain Below" when his voice suddenly cut off.

"We're gonna talk about this calmly."

My heart started racing as Noah walked toward me.

"No raising our voices. Do you understand?"

Sigh.

"Answer me when I'm speaking to you."

Facing defeat, I gave a brief nod.

"Good." He closed the space between us and cupped my face. "I didn't have sex with her, and I wasn't entirely nude, either. I wanted to sleep in my study, but she dragged me upstairs, and I had no choice but to get in bed and sleep next to her."

"I'm done." I didn't want to hear his explanations. It was all excuses. He'd been right all along: this was a dangerous game we were playing. And frankly, I didn't want to play by his rules anymore. It was so unfair. Why did I have to be the other woman? He had to make a choice.

"*Done?* What do you mean by that?"

"I can't be with you like this. You need to choose." I slipped out of his arms. "Me or her." It was an ultimatum.

"Aria, be reasonable. You realize that it's only been three days since our entire relationship changed drastically."

"I told you how I feel about you." I wanted to scream it, but I had no choice but to keep my voice down.

"Baby, things aren't always so black and white." He grabbed hold of my hips and pulled me in close. The next thing I knew, he was caressing the side of my face, wiping away a fallen tear with his thumb. "I still want you to consider getting counseling with me. I'm visiting my therapist this Thursday."

"Seriously? You're gonna lecture me about that again? *Now?* When will you give it a rest? Why are you playing with my feelings, Noah?"

"I'm not." His eyes pleaded for understanding. "Please don't think that way."

"You can't just kiss me the way you do, make out with me for *hours* in your car, and then act like there's a way we can undo all that!"

"We didn't make out for hours. It was one lengthy kiss, and I should have stopped it."

How could he regret that amazing moment between us?

"I can't believe you're downplaying everything," I said. "You have no idea how much you're hurting me right now!"

I tried to whisper my frustrations. But honestly, I just wanted to yell at him. All this pent-up rage was unhealthy for me. I had to purge it. Tearing myself from his arms, I sat on the edge of my bed, feeling sorry for myself.

"I'm not trying to hurt you," said Noah.

"Just leave me alone." I sniffled, angrily wiping my tears away.

There was a brief pause before he sat next to me.

"I'm not gonna leave you alone when I know I've caused you pain."

"It doesn't matter."

"It does to me. Aria, I'm your father. I know we may have crossed a few boundaries with each other, but I'm still your dad," he said sternly, keeping his eyes serious as ever.

I didn't know why his words hurt me so much. He was only being honest and realistic. I guess I just didn't want to live in reality anymore. I much preferred to live in my dream bubble, a place where Noah and I were not related and were free to love each other and be together forever. I was content with imagining us prancing around as Teletubbies if it meant we would be together in some warped dimension other than here. Noah would be the Dipsy to my Laa-Laa...

Okay, scratch that. I did *not* just say that.

"You still haven't told me what you were doing with Evan—are you listening to me? Anyone alive in there?" He waved his hand in front of my eyes, and that's when I came crashing down to Planet Earth.

"I don't want you to be my dad!" I yelled loud enough for my stepmom to hear. "I don't need a father! All these years I did just fine without one. Rob doesn't exactly qualify. You want to know why I was riding in a car with your brother? I stole his number from Vienna's phone this morning, after you made my heart bleed! I contacted him and we met up at the mall."

All the life suddenly faded from Noah's vibrant eyes.

Standing on my feet, I distanced myself from him. But it was pointless because he got up as well.

"We were talking over lunch for hours and guess what I found out? He's an even better person than I had imagined! He's not bossy and controlling like you! He cares about my feelings! And he's funny!" I just had to throw that in there.

"Are you saying I lack a sense of humor? You really believe I'm controlling?" Noah frowned, towering over me once again. Maybe he did this on purpose to make me feel inferior to him. I hated it.

Raising my hands in defeat, I backed away from him and said, "I need to get out of this house."

"Where are you going?"

"Anywhere but here!" I took off my sundress and stood in a red bra and panties. He didn't look away, which sort of gave me a gratifying sense of pleasure.

"Aria, stop this."

"Stop what? The undressing part, or the leaving part?"

"Both."

I padded toward my dresser and pulled on a pair of black denim shorts. Without the slightest care, I unfastened my bra and tossed it onto the bed.

"Oh, for fuck's sake!" Noah looked away, obviously embarrassed by my lack of modesty.

"You felt these up for hours last night—"

"I did not!"

"Now you won't even look at them? Unbelievable." Marching into my closet, I put on a peach-colored tube top, and walked out again.

"Just stay." Noah stepped in front of me. "Calm down a bit, please."

"No! *Move!* I want to leave!" I stared him down with scathing eyes, but he refused to surrender. "You can't keep me locked up in my bedroom!"

"I can and I *will!* I told you how I felt about Evan, and you went behind my back, conspiring to meet him!"

There was an eerie silence between us, like the calm before the storm.

"I hate you," I said, icing my tone with spite. "You'll never understand me."

Attempting to step around him, he obstructed my escape.

"You're driving me nuts!" I said. "Let me go already!"

"No!"

"I said, *move!*"

Frustrated, I pushed him back, but it was like trying to move a boulder. He hardly even budged.

Well, that was a failed effort. Comical, in fact.

Noah grabbed my shoulders and stared at me with a vicious fury in his gaze. I wasn't sure if it was rage or desire. Maybe it was both. Our emotions were out of control, and we both needed a time-out.

I was prepared to scream at him when my stepmom knocked twice and opened the door. "Is everything all right in here?"

So much for knocking.

"Yes, honey, we're fine." Noah released me and turned around.

"More than fine!" I smiled condescendingly, grabbing my handbag and walking out on them.

"Aria!" Noah shouted after me. "Come back here!"

I was halfway down the hall when I heard Vienna say, "You okay, kiddo?"

Bad timing, Vi.

Stopping in my tracks, I turned around, eyes blazing. "For the hundredth fucking-time… do *not*—call me—kiddo!"

She seemed shocked by my hostility, but I let it fuel my anger as I got in her face and said, "I don't know why you hate me suddenly, but don't think that I haven't noticed the way you've been giving me dirty looks every chance you get. And to be honest, I really don't like you. So, that being said, have a safe flight, and just know that your next visit here is most unwelcome!"

Was this self-sabotage? I think it was. I was burning bridges— attempting to, at least.

"Aria!" Noah yelled again, but I was already out the door, headed for the garage.

Glancing at the Firebird, I shut my eyes and took a deep breath.

Desperate times call for desperate measures.

That American engine was like music to my ears as it came to life when I turned the ignition.

Pulling out of the driveway, I raced onto the street. Where was I headed? I had no fucking clue.

CHAPTER THIRTY-SIX
NOAH

I was about to chase after my daughter when my wife grabbed me by the arm.

"Give her some space, Noah. She probably just needs to cool off."

"She didn't even tell me where she was going! I'm responsible for her, Nessa!" I opened the door and stepped outside.

"Jess lives in the area—most likely, Aria's gone to her place." She was trying to comfort me, but I couldn't calm down. I felt so fucked up.

"Why is she so mad at you?"

"She's mad because I forbade her from seeing my brother. The bastard dropped her off in front of the house earlier." I sighed in frustration.

"Look, give her a couple of hours to herself. It's not even dinnertime yet. She'll come back. Maybe she's homesick and acting out."

My wife did not know what was going on between me and Aria. I felt like the world's biggest asshole because I was technically cheating on Vanessa and engaging in a wrongful affair with my daughter. Who the hell was I anymore? I didn't know.

"Come on, sweetie, let's head inside. Vienna and I are making brownies. I'm sure that'll cheer her up when she returns."

Her sweet nature only worsened my guilt.

"Teenage girls are always starving themselves," Vanessa continued, "striving to look like supermodels. It takes a physical and psychological toll on them. She just needs some sugar in her system, and then she'll be good as new!"

Vanessa had a long battle with eating disorders, but this certainly wasn't the case with my daughter. Sugar would not fix our problems. Eventually, I gave up and took my wife's advice, following her back into the house. I knew I'd have to talk with Aria later, preferably with more privacy.

And hopefully no arguing.

My mind was suddenly flooded with hot images of her standing half naked in front of me. I'd been so tempted to stare when she took off her bra. Looking away didn't help, because I could still see her breasts in my peripheral vision. I should have just turned around.

Fuck my life. I'm cursed.

"I'll fix you a drink. It'll mellow you out." Vanessa kissed me, yet I couldn't reciprocate her affection. It didn't seem to bother her, though. I guess she assumed my aloofness was because of my mood swing.

"Nessa, wait!" I called out as she walked away. "Can you get me Evan's number? Vienna's got it. I need to call him."

"Sure, sweetie." She left me in the living room and returned shortly after with a yellow Post-it note in her hand. "Here you go."

"Thanks."

"I'll be right back with your drink."

Sitting on the sofa, I took out my cell and dialed his number. That bastard was going to get an earful, because I had a lot to say to him.

"Hey, you've reached Evan. If you're listening to this, I'm not available…"

I rolled my eyes when he laughed.

"But if you leave your name and number, I'll call you back… hopefully—unless I accidentally delete your message, which has happened a couple times! Anyway, you know what to do."

The guy probably thought he sounded so slick. I couldn't help but shake my head in ridicule. After the beep went off, I unleashed my wrath.

"Listen up, you little punk. Stay away from my daughter! Do you understand me? If you don't, I promise I'll make you regret it. I'll make your life hell! Don't you fucking test me, Evan. I'm dead serious. If Aria contacts you again, ignore her. Just pretend she doesn't exist, because she *shouldn't* exist in your life! You don't belong in my family! So do me a favor and stay the fuck away!" I was shouting so loud into the phone that I didn't even notice Vanessa and Vienna standing by the doorway, watching me in shock, until I hung up.

"You need to take a chill pill," Vienna remarked.

I apologized and stood up.

"Give him a break." My wife regarded her sister and handed me a homemade Kamikaze. "Drink up, babe."

I gulped down the vodka drink like a relapsing alcoholic and left the room.

"Where are you going?" asked Vanessa.

"Stepping out in the yard to get some air."

"They just had an argument," Vienna said to her. "It's not like someone died."

"Shut up, Vienna!"

I heard their last bit of exchanges before I opened the patio doors and tried to turn off my thoughts.

೮೦೮೩

It wasn't long before the ladies appeared in the yard dressed in bikinis, holding a tray full of refreshments. I guess it didn't occur to them I wanted to be alone.

"You need some more liquor in your system," said Vanessa. She sat on my lap and handed me another Kamikaze. "Come into the pool with us. The weather's perfect!"

"I think I'm gonna work on that Corvette I've been meaning to fix." I shifted her off and got to my feet.

"Oh," she said with disappointment. "Okay, hon. We'll be out here if you need us. I love you."

"Love you, too." I tried to smile and downed the alcohol as quickly as possible. Hiding away in my garage was probably the best option. They wouldn't follow me there.

◌◈◌

Dropping by my study, I grabbed my lighter and ten deck of smokes from my desk drawer. I knew I had made a commitment to my wife (and to myself) to never smoke again, but just feeling that pack of Marlboros in my jean pocket gave me a sense of comfort. I couldn't explain it. Only smokers would understand.

A 1968 Corvette coupe had been sitting in my garage for well over a year. I had purchased it at an auction, and it needed a tune-up, but work kept me so busy that I continually procrastinated giving it a proper fix. It was a classic American muscle car, painted in silver. My dad had been obsessed with vintage vehicles, and I was sure I had this passion because of him. We used to hang out in the garage on weekends, and I'd help him polish his collection of cars. His father had been a mechanic, so my old man taught me everything I needed to know about car transmissions, fuel injections, replacing plugs, points, adjusting the carburetor, and so on.

Pulling back the dusted car cover, I popped open the hood of the Corvette, and glanced at my watch. It was a quarter to five. If Aria wasn't back by seven, then I'd hunt her down. I didn't understand why she was giving me ultimatums like this. Didn't she realize how difficult this situation was for me? It wasn't like I was an expert. These feelings were just as new to me as they were to her. But I had responsibilities. I was not a free agent. I was a married man, and I never thought I'd cheat on my wife. I never thought I'd be the type of father who would lust after his daughter. This was another huge problem for me. The further we explored each other physically, the more I wanted to abandon all the rules.

The most fragmented part of me kept whispering sinful temptation in my ear. Like the night before, I'd failed miserably to control myself, even though I tried my best to ignore it. I had no idea how I could stop just in time. I wasn't so sure about next time. Aria was so willing to give herself away to me on a silver platter. I'd be lying if I said I didn't want to accept. My desire for her was so fucking strong; it only grew more each day. I had never felt this kind of attraction toward any other woman in my life, ever. I felt so mind-fucked. What if I didn't know she was my daughter? Would I have still felt this way about her?

Yes, a familiar voice answered.

Seeing her with Evan had sparked my rage. He was lucky he made it out of my driveway in time. Otherwise, I would have pulled him out of his car and beaten him up. Was I being too possessive? Why did she make me transform into a territorial alpha male?

Jealousy.

No. I wasn't jealous of my kid brother. I was protective of Aria, but in a healthy way. Fuck, who was I kidding? There was nothing healthy about our relationship. I really needed a cigarette.

Light one up, my demon encouraged. *It's just a cigarette. Not like you're snorting cocaine here...*

I stopped what I was doing and leaned my weight into my palms, resting on the edge of the hood. I could do this. I could fight temptation. I didn't need to smoke.

That's why the legendary ten deck is in your pocket. That sly voice taunted me.

Stepping toward my workbench, I switched on the radio.

"This next track is by A Perfect Circle, 'Weak and Powerless.' I'll be taking requests within the next hour, so call in! You're listening to Stevie B, live on 906.3 Rock Radio!"

I tried to distract myself while changing the transmission fluid, but I still couldn't drown out the endless rambling in my mind. I hated overthinking; it only increased my stress.

Washing my hands, I dried off and grabbed the polish wheel to give the Corvette a nice new shine. I usually enjoyed this part, but not that day. Normally it relaxed me, but my head was one huge clusterfuck, and I couldn't focus on anything except Aria.

Fuck this," I muttered, switching off the polishing wheel before I pulled out my ten deck. Opening the box, I reread the little inscription I had written inside. I was contemplating a crucial decision with potentially detrimental consequences. The last time I'd been dangerously tempted to smoke was in New York with Aria six months ago. We were at that hotel I was staying in, and I had gotten into a terrible argument with Nat and her dirtbag husband on the phone. If Aria hadn't stepped out onto the balcony that night, I was certain I would have broken my promise.

Well, here I was, alone in my garage, and my daughter wasn't around to stop me this time. Aria wouldn't be here to save me from myself.

She shouldn't have to. That's not her job. My conscience intervened.

The thought kind of depressed me as I took out a cigarette and smelled the nicotine. I missed smoking so badly. It was a great stress relief for me. I wasn't sure if I was trying to punish myself, destroy myself, or keep myself from having a full-fledged psychotic break. Maybe it was all the above. I didn't give a fuck anymore.

Lighting a cigarette, I inhaled a deep puff into my lungs, feeling pleasurably satisfied. A year and a half of being smoke-free had gone out the window. So much for effort. To celebrate my failure, I took another drag, tapping the excess ashes in a plastic cup on the table. I'd have to expunge the evidence later.

So… how do you feel now?

Just as fucked as before.

It'll pass. Smoke away your sorrows, pal.

I felt crazy for having this conversation in my head, but I finished my smoke and made a silent pact with myself to lay off on the remaining cigarettes. I would have to buy another deck to replace the missing one so that Vanessa wouldn't ever know the difference (if she checked). It would be as if I never smoked it.

Except you did. You know it, and I know it. Yep, we both know it.

Clenching my fist, I kicked the rear tire of my Corvette in a fit of frustration before I put out my cigarette and lighted another.

Fuck this life. Fuck everyone. Fuck it all.

CHAPTER THIRTY-SEVEN
AT LONG LAST

It was almost eight o'clock when Evan Hunter finally arrived home. He was greeted by a furry full-bred Russian Blue.

"Hey, Baxter! Come here, buddy." Crouching, he untied his boots. "Did you miss me?" Evan gave the purring feline a pet on the head.

"I bet you're hungry. Let's get you fed!"

Strolling into the kitchen, he filled Baxter's bowl with cat food before heading to the bathroom to shower and freshen up.

It had been another exhausting workday, and he was glad it was over with. Evan lived in a modern, three-bedroom loft downtown. He had purchased the property when he moved to LA. It looked like an abandoned old warehouse, but in a quick renovation, he had transformed the place into a stylish bachelor pad. It had an open-concept design, with high ceilings and tall, wide windows. Some walls were red and brown brick, with a collection of contemporary abstract paintings mounted on one side in the living room. His leather sofa set was a dark espresso, and all his furniture was custom made, manufactured out of industrial products.

He had thrown down a beautiful red Persian rug, right underneath the coffee table. Long oval-shaped lamps were stationed in every corner of the room, adding a warm glow to the space at night.

His kitchen was just as impressive—all stainless-steel appliances and a large marble-topped island in the middle. The only thing his place lacked was a woman's touch. It was clear in the way he had designed his home that he had masculine taste. His loft was every bachelor's dream.

After showering, Evan dressed himself in a pair of black CK boxer briefs and acid-washed jeans that hung low at his waist. He decided not to wear a shirt as he got ready, not until the last minute, before heading out on his nightly hunt for loose women. He was an attractive man with a muscular frame, broad shoulders, and a mesmerizing smile you wouldn't forget. Evan took care of his body. If Noah were to stand next to him, one would easily assume they were brothers, since they appeared so similar in stature.

Evan had the looks, the charm, and the winning personality that made most women fall in love with him. Unfortunately, he had broken many hearts during his dating years. These days, he kept it simple: one-night stands. No strings attached, no expectations, and no emotional involvement. That was the way he preferred it. His lady friends tried their hardest to change his ways and make him commit, but they were always fighting a losing battle. Friendships ended as a result on bad terms. Evan never felt bad, though, because he always warned them from the get-go. He was emotionally unavailable, and that hadn't happened without a reason.

Baxter scurried over and brushed past his leg, watching his human companion enter the kitchen to fix a turkey sandwich. Opening a jar of mayo, Evan started thinking about the conversation he had had with Aria at the mall. She was so smart for her age, and incredibly beautiful. He was extremely fond of her and thought she looked more like her mother than like Noah.

Biting into his sandwich, he placed it back on the plate, and walked to the window to watch the sunset in the horizon. Darkness would soon blanket the sky, welcoming the midnight hour when promiscuous men and women of LA would come out to play. It was all about the thrill of the hunt. Evan thoroughly enjoyed the chase and was good at it. He took his time eating, carrying his empty plate to the sink.

"You want a beer, Baxter?" Opening the fridge, he grabbed a cold Corona. "You're underage."

A subtle smile spread across the corner of his mouth when he remembered something. Ambling toward his home theater system, Evan turned on some music and shuffled through the tracks. He stopped when he found the tune he was looking for: Azari & III – Hungry For The Power (Franky Wah Edit). The song held a special meaning to him; he listened to it before every nightly outing. Setting it on repeat, he cranked up the volume until the sound waves were vibrating through the walls, just how he liked it.

The music started out with a rhythmic synthesized bass line, followed by a hypnotic drumbeat. There was a dark undertone in the song, as if the Devil was in the music. A vocalist started singing his evocative lyrics about power and desire.

Baxter let out a quiet meow and crouched down on his hind legs, hiding underneath the dining table. Swigging his beer, Evan wandered into his bedroom. The space was modernly furnished and had a monochromatic color scheme. There was a king-sized bed in the middle. What stood out the most was a collection of erotic photography that hung on the wall, right above his black leather headboard. They were printed on canvases and were the main focal point upon entry. The pictures were black and white, mostly of a man taking a woman from behind, in the missionary position, lotus position, and various erotic poses. Other pictures displayed female models tied up and lying naked in bed. The only similarity among these enticing women was that they all had long, dark, flowing hair that reached past their breasts. All of them had blue eyes, because of the way they were Photoshopped. The intensity of their eye colors varied, and some of them had penetrating stares, while others looked demure and soft. The male models' faces were not visible, but a hard-built body seemed to be a crucial component of the photographs' eroticism.

One of Evan's favorites was a picture of a nude model bent on all fours on a bed. White sheets were tangled beneath her as she tilted her head back, parting her full, sensuous mouth. This gave the viewer the impression that she was releasing a pleasurable moan from her lips. A naked male model had positioned himself behind her, visible only from the neck down. He had pulled her hair back and had slid his other hand up the curve of her spine. The location of entry of their consummated coupling was undetermined, left up to the imagination of the observer. The young woman looked provocatively sexy, wearing nothing but a string of diamonds around her neck, accentuating her attractive collarbones. She had a heart-shaped bottom and was the only model wearing jewelry in the pictures. That photo was the only picture above his headboard that was blown up on the largest canvas.

The songstress continued her enchanting melodies as Evan sat at his desk and connected his cellphone to his laptop. He needed to upload some pictures from the construction site and get them printed. Waiting on the photos, he let them upload and clicked the Print command. His printer came to life and did its job while he walked toward a black bookshelf near the corner of his room. Sipping his beer, he carefully removed three books from the middle shelf, revealing a security keypad. He took another gulp of his beer and punched in a six-digit code: 040695. There was a little click, and then the bookshelf slowly opened like a door that led to a secret room. Stepping through the threshold, he stood in the darkness.

Music echoed in the distance as he reached up and pulled on a string, illuminating the room with faint yellow light. He walked around and yanked on four other strings. Hanging light bulbs swayed from the ceiling as Evan stepped back and smiled at the wall. There were no windows in this room. It was empty except for a shabby red leather armchair right in the center of the floor.

Retracting his steps, he stepped back into his bedroom and approached his laptop. All the pictures had successfully printed. After shuffling through the photos, he found the ones he wanted, grabbed some double-sided tape, and returned to his secret room.

"Fuck me… so beautiful."

One by one, he taped the pictures to the wall until there were no more photographs in his hands. Stepping back, he stared at the colorful collage he had created throughout the last few months, feeling proud and pleased with himself. His project was not as complete as his previous one in his last place of residence, but it was a work in progress. When he had moved in, he had to reprint some older photos to replicate the other masterpiece. Although it was not identical, it satisfied him.

Each photo displayed a beautiful young woman who had dark brown hair, blue eyes, a gorgeous smile, and a stunning, slender body. Every shot of her was taken from a safe distance—as if someone had been spying on her.

Aria Hunter's face was plastered all over the walls of that room like a holy deity being worshiped in a shrine. The front wall was covered in pictures of her walking to school, hanging out with her friends at the mall, laughing, smiling, crying, dancing, and being her usual self. Her every emotion and expression was captured on camera. Each picture appeared to tell a story, depending on her appearance and location. Evan's obsession seemed to start on the left, spreading across the center and adjoining wall. There were pictures of seventeen-year-old Aria having dinner with her family at a restaurant in New York, photographs of Aria walking alone through Central Park, photos of her feeding the ducks and eating ice cream, Aria wearing a short blue sundress, Aria wearing a fall jacket, Aria wearing a winter coat, Aria blowing on a dandelion in a park, Aria at Laguna Beach, Aria in a bikini, Aria trying on clothing at the mall… Aria everywhere.

Hundreds of photos were taped on the walls like a mosaic. Evan smiled as he gently stroked his fingers across her face. The recent additions were the ones he'd taken from his niece at the mall. Edging closer to one photo, he closed his eyes and placed a tender kiss on her lips.

"I waited so long to meet you, Aria." He gazed into her eyes as if she were standing there, looking back at him. "Now you know I exist."

A section in the center of the wall was empty; Evan had reserved that spot for more "special" pictures. He had always wanted to have snapshots of her staring into the camera and smiling, and he had finally achieved that, after months of photographing his niece in the shadows.

"You smiled for me," he said aloud, feeling as though he had accomplished a tough challenge.

An overwhelming sense of pride washed over him. Aria looked so free-spirited and blindingly beautiful when she laughed. He felt lucky to have caught it on camera, up close and in person. In Evan's obsessive mind, he truly believed he was talking to the blue-eyed beauty in real time. He had even deluded himself into believing that she could really hear him.

Kissing her photo again, he backed away and sat in the armchair. It had a little wear and tear on the sides, but it was comfortable. Placing his beer on the floor, he relaxed his body and closed his eyes. Aria's face and attractive figure appeared before him as he listened to the music and fantasized.

Something instantly stiffened in his pants. Breathing out, he remembered the way her supple breasts had pressed together, showing off the sexiest cleavage in the plunging neckline of her floral print dress. Evan had nearly slipped up during their lunch meeting. There were no black olives in Aria's salad because he already knew she hated them, so he had asked the server to leave them out. He had ordered the same sandwich because he knew it was her favorite. That was no coincidence. And he had stolen her bottled water to drink out of it because it was the closest thing to tasting her lips. He couldn't help himself. Evan was obsessed with her. He was her stalker, and she did not know.

Touching his chest, he imagined Aria's hand caressing him. His fingers lightly brushed his tanned skin all the way down his chiseled abs before stopping at his trousers. Unzipping his fly, he pulled out his throbbing shaft and squeezed it in his fist. Thinking about Aria always got him hard and ready. He was aching to be stroked.

Opening his eyes, Evan fixated on Aria's pictures, which only stimulated him more. He rested his elbows on the armchair, feeling his base lubricate, drizzling down his shaft. He didn't even need to stroke himself. As his breathing grew harsh and labored, his eyelids got heavy, drooping shut. He tried to remember every detail—the way Aria smelled when she sat next to him, the way she crossed one leg over the other, exposing her naked thigh. The delicious smell of her strawberry vanilla-scented hair drove him wild as he violently throbbed down below.

Aria's pleasant laughter filled his ears, which only stimulated his desire even more. He wanted to dominate her body, tie her up, and take complete control of her day and night. He needed to be inside of her, penetrating her until she was flooded with him. And he wouldn't stop there. No, he wanted so much more than that. Evan wanted to claim her and violate her mouth until she would gag and choke from his forceful thrusting. It was all he could think about ever since he saw her for the first time.

"*Fu-fff-fuck...* Aria!" He breathed out, feeling his body convulse as he opened his eyes and stared at her beguiling beauty.

Edging toward release, Evan groaned in pleasure and surrendered to the music that was amplifying his sexual fantasy. It carried him away to a place that only existed in his mind. Digging his fingers into the armchair, his muscles tightened as he refused to touch himself. He was determined to explode in pleasure, hands free.

"Oh, I can't *wait* to tie you up… [*pants*]… I'll have you gushing…"

He always imagined Aria as his own personal sex doll. He would make it a routine to come into the bedroom, spread her legs, and violate her whenever he wanted. And then he would leave when he was done, only to return and repeat. By the time he would let her stand, all his juices would drip down her thighs.

"You're gonna be my sex project…"

He wanted her addicted to him; and he believed he could achieve this. This was his fantasy. This was his sickness.

"Fuck! *Fuuuuuuuuuuuuuuuck!*"

The sexual images were just what he needed to send him over the edge as he climaxed, spraying sticky fluid all over his chest and abdomen. White lava flowed out in waves while he breathlessly groaned in pleasure and relaxed his elbows over the arms of the chair.

Recovering from a mind-blowing climax, Evan reached for his beer and gulped what was left, sighing in relief. He knew he would have to get up soon, but he just wanted to enjoy that moment a little longer. Closing his eyes, he let his mind roam.

Evan was infatuated with Aria. He didn't know how he had remained so calm in her presence. She was the only girl who could make him feel nervous. Undeniably, he was obsessed with her and had been stalking her for the past two years. His sick obsession was consuming his life. Every woman he bedded resembled the blue-eyed goddess who was his niece, not by blood, but by law. He knew that all these women could never compare to the real thing; they were substitutes. Yet he had promised himself that he would wait until her eighteenth birthday, and then she would be all his for the taking. Only then would he commit himself and stop chasing skirts forever… once she was his.

Evan had not expected Aria to come to California. He had originally relocated from Boston to New York to be closer to her. Her sudden move had messed up his plans, but he had moved, carefully strategizing, before entering her life out of the blue. He had to remain patient and wait. Good things come to those who wait, he reminded himself.

For the longest time, Evan had stalked Aria on and off, and as the years progressively passed, he felt like he knew who she truly was. He enjoyed learning everything there was to know about her. Aria had been no stranger to him when he introduced himself at his brother's place. Their first-time acquaintance was entirely an act, and his flirtations were deliberate. He believed himself to be her dark prince, who was going to take her away from the arms of his enemy and make her his sex-hungry princess. What had started out as an evil plot for revenge against Noah had turned into a sick, psychotic game of obsession. Evan had originally planned on toying with Aria's feelings. He wanted to make her fall in love with him so that he could sleep with her. Once that was achieved, he would vanish out of her life the next day, leaving nothing but an unpleasant note behind for her to read.

His hatred of his family was real and ran deep, especially toward Noah. But he decided not to carry out his cruel vendetta when the private investigator he had hired showed him the pictures he had taken of Aria. This had been two years ago, while he was still in Boston. He had lied about traveling to Haiti. Prior to seeing those photos, he did not know what she looked like. But as soon as he cast his eyes on her, Evan was awestruck by her innocence and allure. As much as he hated his brother, it was hard for him to hate his niece so blindly when she appeared so pure and captivating. He wanted to corrupt that innocence in his own way. Aria had stolen his heart without him even realizing it. He had no explanation for why or how she could do that. All he knew was that he needed to be with her.

Moving to New York, Evan followed her every chance he got, observing her behavior and activities from afar. When he was at work or playing the field, his PI kept tabs on Aria until she moved to California. His licentious nature defined him as a man with a hungry appetite for sex that never seemed to be satisfied. He had never had a particular type regarding women. As long as they had a banging body and all their teeth, he didn't care. But ever since he had seen Aria, his preference had changed. Every woman he slept with had to resemble his niece. She was the first person he thought about when he woke up, and his last thought before he went to sleep. He knew he was technically her uncle, but that minor detail didn't seem to deter him from pursuing her. He had never been the type of guy to abide by the rules—he always broke them.

Despite his religious upbringing, Evan had known he was an atheist from the early age of twelve. He believed that religion was a social construct, "a crock of shit" created by some clever men who wanted to instill the fear of God in people just so they could assume power over the population, thus turning the masses into puppets. Aria gave him something to believe in, and he worshiped her like the idol she was. He didn't care if it was wrong, perverse, or sacrilegious.

Burdened by the weight of his hatred and tortured by his darkest secrets, all he wanted was to feel a sense of justice. Aria had become the key to everything he desired and hoped to achieve. His vengeance motivated and imprisoned him within the four walls of his obsession. Evan vowed to never give up until he had her. He didn't care about who had to get hurt along the way... or die.

Grinning in the dark, he left his secret shrine to clean up. Phase one of his evening was complete. Now he had to put phase two in action and head over to the Star Lounge. Noah had been right to warn his daughter about his brother. There was a new predator in the jungle, and he was just as fast and vicious as Noah. But Evan had an advantage. Aria wasn't safe.

THE STORY CONTINUES!

Don't miss out on the second volume of the series:

I Shouldn't Love This Way

COMING SOON

For updates, please follow me on Twitter @MinaAlexia

NOVEL SOUNDTRACK

- Monaldin - Save Me
- The Raveonettes – Curse The Night
- Mr. FijiWiji – Submerged (ft. Coma)
- Coldcut – Autumn Leaves
- Frank Sinatra – Fly Me To The Moon
- Dash Berlin feat. Chris Madin – Fool For Life
- Edward Maya & Vika Jigulina – Stereo Love (Motella Remix)
- Radiohead – Nude (Holy Fuck Remix)
- Lyves x Synkro – Body Close
- Chase & Status – Flashing Lights
- Robbie Rivera – Girlfriend
- Volor Flex -You In Me
- Plant Plants – Embrace The Real
- Micha Moor – Love is Chemical (Original Mix)
- Mads Langer – You're Not alone (Sako Isyoyan Remix)
- Plan B – Love Goes Down
- Blind Benny – No Honor (Different Sleep Remix)
- Vario Volinski – Falling In Love (Original Mix)
- The XX – Do You Mind (Derek Walin Remix)
- Jhené Aiko - Mirrors (J£ZUS MILLION Edit)
- Cosmic Gate feat. Eric Lumiere – Run Away
- Volor Flex – Fake Love
- Volor Flex – You In Me
- J. Cole feat. Miguel – Power Trip
- Sunlounger feat. Zara – Crawling (Anymood Remix)
- AL034 - Mathame - For Every Forever
- Stoto – My Love (2nd edit)
- Duke Dumont – The Giver
- Burial Archangel (Uppermost Remix)
- Mike Snow – Silvia (Hook N Sling Goodwill Remix)

- Above & Beyond – Stealing Time
- Cavid Askerov – Rhythm Of The Night
- Cavid Askerov - Insensible (Original Mix)
- Autre Ne Veut – Ego Free Sex Free
- David Hopperman – Feel (Original Mix)
- DNDM – Lips Like Roses (Original Mix)
- Tiesto – Somewhere Inside Me (Alexander Gorshkov – Chillout Remix)
- Lana Del Rey – Gods & Monsters
- AL018- Mathame (with Lyke) - Nothing Around Us
- CamelPhat, ARTBAT - For A Feeling ft. RHODES (Extended Mix)
- Drake – Worst Behavior
- Azari & III – Hungry For The Power (Franky Wah Edit)
- ATB feat. Sean Ryan – All I Need is You (unplugged)
- ATB feat. Flanders – Behind (Club Mix)
- AVAION, MAGNUS - Where Did You Go
- Aurora Night- Aero
- Aurora Night – Everlasting
- Aurora Night – Our Love
- Aurora Night – Stay
- Aurora Night – To Me
- Ben Böhmer & Panama - Weightless (jamesjamesjames Remix)
- Horisone - Feel So High
- Stoto - Another Day

ACKNOWLEDGEMENTS

Where do I start? There are so many wonderful people who encouraged me to publish this series. Without my amazing readers, Noah and Aria's journey never would have made it this far. This story began as a social experiment online, I never thought it would touch the hearts of my readers and become one of the most complicated love stories ever. I want to personally thank my biggest supporter, lifelong friend, and guardian angel, Chuck. I love you. You've been my rock through this crazy publishing roller coaster.

To my talented fellow authors and friends, Patti and Brian: thank you for reading and reviewing. You're AMAZING! Sammi, Bella, Tarra, thank you for all the love and support throughout my writing journey.

I am in deep gratitude to my wonderful publisher Reagan Rothe and the Black Rose Writing team for helping me with the publishing process of my series. Thank you for believing in me and my potential.

My heart is full of gratitude, and I am deeply thankful to all the angels who worked behind the scenes to help me with my writing journey. You know who you are, and I love you all.

ABOUT THE AUTHOR

Mina Alexia was born in Tehran, Iran. She moved to Canada with her family at the age of three and was raised in a small town in Ontario. She graduated from Wilfrid Laurier University with a bachelor's degree of Arts, Honors English.

Having faced many adversities in life, she decided to use her artistic gifts to heal through the medium of creative writing. Mina uses her social media presence to spread awareness on trauma recovery and mental health. Her novels include trauma-informed themes that are rich with emotion. She believes "we need to feel to heal."

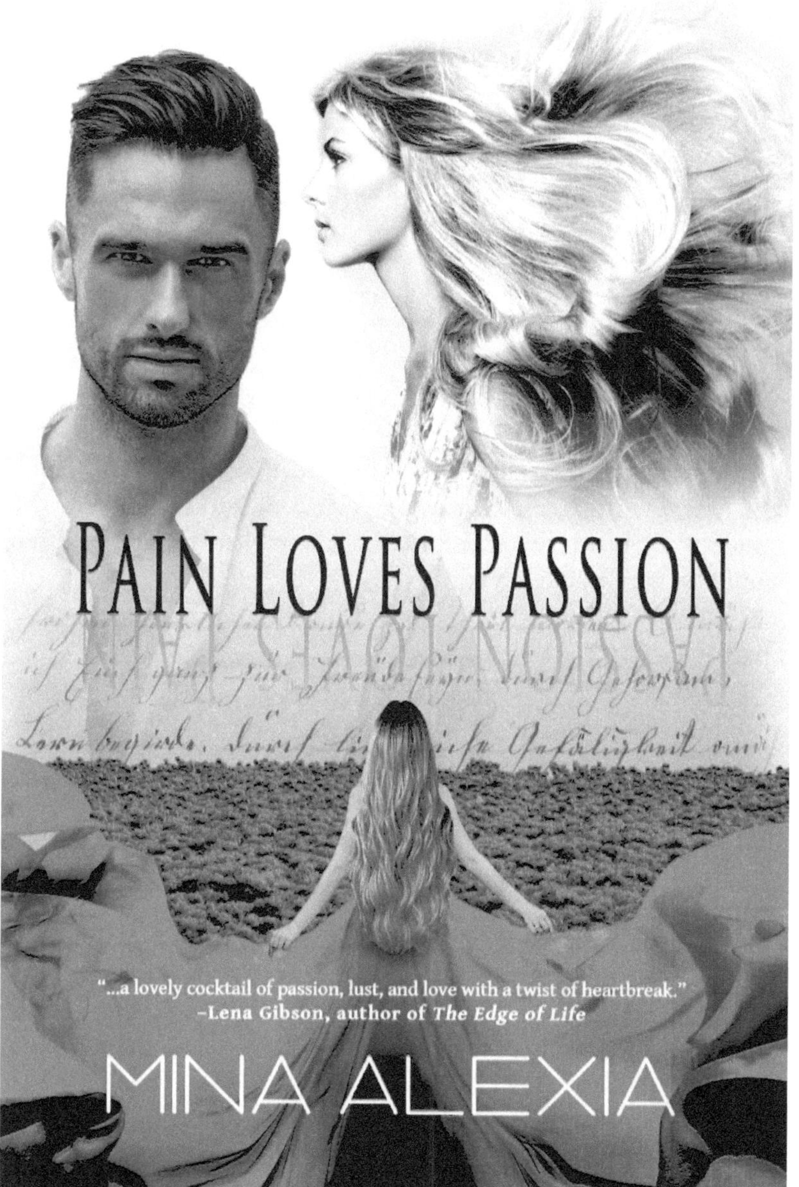
Pain Loves Passion
"...a lovely cocktail of passion, lust, and love with a twist of heartbreak."
-Lena Gibson, author of The Edge of Life
MINA ALEXIA

NOTE FROM MINA ALEXIA

Word-of-mouth is crucial for any author to succeed. If you enjoyed *I Shouldn't Feel This Way*, please leave a review online—anywhere you are able. Even if it's just a sentence or two. It would make all the difference and would be very much appreciated.

Thanks!
Mina Alexia

We hope you enjoyed reading this title from:

www.blackrosewriting.com

Subscribe to our mailing list – *The Rosevine* – and receive **FREE** books, daily deals, and stay current with news about upcoming releases and our hottest authors.
Scan the QR code below to sign up.

Already a subscriber? Please accept a sincere thank you for being a fan of Black Rose Writing authors.

View other Black Rose Writing titles at www.blackrosewriting.com/books and use promo code **PRINT** to receive a **20% discount** when purchasing.